W9-BOL-803

PRAISE FOR RALPH PETERS

"A thrilling multilayered masterpiece of mayhem. While most writers use only their imagination to tell tales of the worst war imaginable, Ralph Peters also taps his background as a top intel officer to spin a terrific tale. His insight into the world of secret operations—and the what-if horrors our military must consider daily—makes this page-turner a must-read."   —W. E. B. Griffin,
New York Times bestselling author of The Corps,
on *The War After Armageddon*

"Mr. Peters [has] proved himself a master storyteller."
—*The Washington Times*

"Peters's battle scenes are masterpieces of perspective. . . . It is hard to imagine a better portrayal of modern war. Going Tom Clancy one better."
—*Newsweek*

"The military counterpart of Orwell's *Nineteen Eighty-four*."   —*The New York Times Book Review*
on *The War in 2020*

THE WAR AFTER ARMAGEDDON

RALPH PETERS

FORGE®

A TOM DOHERTY ASSOCIATES BOOK
NEW YORK

THE WAR AFTER ARMAGEDDON

Copyright © 2009 by Ralph Peters

All rights reserved.

Map by Jackie Aher

A Forge Book
Published by Tom Doherty Associates, LLC
175 Fifth Avenue
New York, NY 10010

www.tor-forge.com

Forge® is a registered trademark of Tom Doherty Associates, LLC.

ISBN 978-0-7653-6340-4

First Edition: September 2009
First Mass Market Edition: September 2010

Printed in the United States of America

0 9 8 7 6 5 4 3 2 1

To those who solemnly swear
to support and defend
the Constitution of the United States
against all enemies, foreign and domestic.

The fury of zealots, intestine bitterness and division were the greatest occasion of the last fatal destruction of Jerusalem.

—ATTRIBUTED TO KING CHARLES I
BY DR. JOHNSON

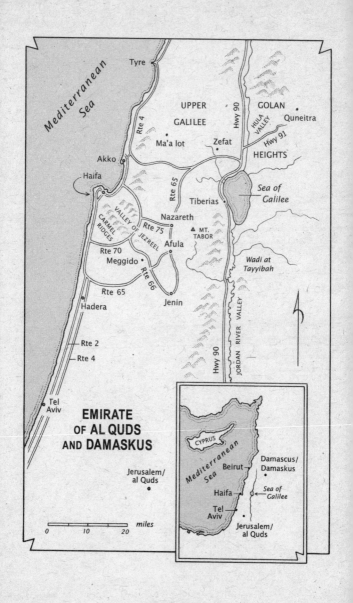

Tyre

Mediterranean Sea

UPPER GALILEE

GOLAN

Rte 4

Hwy 90

HULA VALLEY

Quneitra

Ma'a lot

Zefat

Hwy 91

HEIGHTS

Akko

Haifa

Rte 65

Tiberias

Sea of Galilee

VALLEY OF JEZREEL

CARMEL RIDGES

Nazareth

Rte 75

▲ MT. TABOR

Afula

Rte 70

Wadi at Tayyibah

Meggido

Rte 66

Rte 65

Jenin

Hadera

JORDAN RIVER VALLEY

Hwy 90

Rte 2

Rte 4

Tel Aviv

EMIRATE
OF AL QUDS
AND DAMASKUS

Jerusalem/ al Quds

miles

0   10   20

CYPRUS

Mediterranean Sea

Damascus/ Damaskus

Beirut

Haifa

Sea of Galilee

Tel Aviv

Jerusalem/ al Quds

THE WAR AFTER
ARMAGEDDON

PROLOGUE

I could be jailed for writing this. But I am old and must set down the truth. I do not fear for myself. I shall soon pass, and the Lord will dispose of my soul as He deems just. But were the Elders to find these pages during a Helpful Visit, my family would suffer. Unto my children's children.

I am a fool for doing this, I know. But I have been a greater fool before. I see that now. And some sins belong to this world. Telling this tale is my penance.

"And a child shall lead them." I long had sparred with thoughts about our errors but kept things to myself, as wise men do. My brethren in these United Godfearing States of America might disagree, but silence, too, can be a dreadful sin.

My grandson held up my sin and made me see it.

He is a lovely boy, much like his mother. One autumn day as sweet as the Lord's caress, he came home full of lies. Or, if I would be honest, filled with more lies than usual.

"Grandfather?" he asked. "Were you *really* in the Holy War?"

I nodded. His innocence made me wary.

"Did you kill lots of Mussies?"

"Don't say 'Mussies.' The word is 'Muslims,' Noah."

"But *did* you kill any?"

"No, I didn't."

"Not even *one*?"

"Not one."

His face displayed a child's unshielded grief. I had been severe. Worse, I was disappointing.

"I helped, though," I told him. Shamelessly and shamefully. "I helped kill a great many of them."

The cloud passed, and his features shone with pride. "That's what I told Gabriel. That you were in the war. I told him you took Jerusalem."

I had not been at Jerusalem. Thanks be to God. But I let his bragging pass. I had been close enough to the Holy City. Close enough to smell the blood and corpses.

"Is that what you were taught today? About the Holy War?"

"Yes, sir." His eyes burned pyres of imaginary corpses, the enemy's dead, atop which he imposed himself in triumph. Isn't it strange how sweet war smells to boys? At times I fear we are born of the Book of Joshua, not of the Gospels.

I wondered, briefly, if I should tell the truth. But the young want heroes, not old men's remorse.

"I'm glad there are no more Muslims," he said. Then he added, "General Harris was a traitor. I hope he burns in Hell!"

"Noah!"

I caught myself. In time. He had unlocked the darkness in my heart. The nagging sorrow.

"A good Christian boy would pray for the soul of General Harris," I told him. My words rose from an empty barrel hammered with a stone. "It's our duty to pray for all sinners."

My grandson took on a devilish look. No doubt, he sensed my falsity. The pure of heart do that.

"That's not what Blessed Teacher says," he told me. And he ran off, the victor of the argument. In the good order of our system, no family member contradicts a Blessed Teacher. Faltering Christians have been jailed for less.

When the boy disappeared, I slumped. I felt as if Noah had struck me. As if the world had knocked me to the ground. As if the past had hit me from behind.

Lieutenant General Gary "Flintlock" Harris was no traitor. That is a lie. There. I have written it. In black ink. And I will say more: He was not only a magnificent soldier, but a better Christian than those who brought him down.

Of course, not all of us could see it then. Even fewer see it now, since the Cleansing of the Books.

I do not recall the past the Scribes approve. But I remember other things. I still see Flintlock Harris on a deck, a dozen miles offshore, with Mt. Carmel ablaze in the land of Israel.

His fate was a tragedy. For all of us.

That is heresy. And my task is to chronicle, not judge. Should any reader ever see these pages, the privilege of judgment shall be his.

ONE

· · · · ■ · · · · · · ■ · · · · · · ■ · · · ·

He stood on the deck in the darkness, stealing a moment to discipline his thoughts. A few blind missiles streaked across the sky, desperate shots that fell between the waiting ships. A killer drone exploded in orange fireworks, stopped short by antiaircraft guns. Ashore, on the horizon, artillery fire lifted the night's skirt. The Marines were pushing inland, beyond the crest of Mt. Carmel. But Lieutenant General Gary "Flintlock" Harris remained intrigued by the war he couldn't see.

He had warned of the danger. Still, he had been appalled by how badly his generation had judged the coming wars. The overreliance on technology had troubled him for years, while his peers had dismissed him as an eccentric, hopelessly conservative, backward. His insistence on training his troops to fight on without their advanced systems had earned him the mocking nickname "Flintlock."

Now the military he served was fighting a longer-range version of World War II, scorched by the few technologies that still worked.

Science had undone itself. Harris tried to visualize the wild electronic war playing out in the darkness, with each side canceling the other's capabilities with hyperjammers, signal leeches, and computer plagues. Only a handful of his country's satellites remained aloft, and the devastating effects of electromagnetic-pulse simulators destroyed every electronic system with the least gap in its shielding. Harris recalled the easy days when, as a company commander in Iraq, he could e-mail his wife on the other side of the world. Back then, generals could talk to anyone, anywhere, anytime they wished. Later, as a battalion exec, he had cursed the BlackBerry that kept him on an electronic leash. Now he longed for such a tool, but had none he could trust.

The sky pretended to be empty. But a mad duel raged on wavelengths no human eye could see. Harris turned back to the battle of metal on metal, of flesh and blood. He was waiting for the signal from Monk Morris and his Marines to send the 1st Infantry Division ashore. The 1st Cav would follow. Given the shortage of appropriate landing craft, the operation was bound to be a mess. This time, the Army had to rely on the Marines for support. Their new "get-ashore" boats were the operation's lifeline, given that every port facility that hadn't been destroyed remained hot from nuclear ground bursts and bombs with dirty triggers.

The Jihadis had expected his corps to land to the south, where the terrain was more inviting and Jerusalem waited. Instead, only the MOBIC corps obliged the Muslim high command, plunging ashore through the patches of radioactive debris just north of the ruins of Tel Aviv. Harris's chosen landing zone, the Mt. Carmel sector, had been lightly defended. Relatively speaking. Monk Morris's Devil Dogs faced rugged terrain, ambushes, and suicidal fanatics. But Monk thrived on that kind of fighting. The last message received before comms went down again had been a sitrep describing the slaughter of Druze civilians by the retreating Jihadis. According to Monk, the atrocities were the worst he'd ever seen.

And Monk had seen a great deal, from Anbar a generation before through the Saudi intervention—where they'd first served together—and on to Nigeria. More recently, he'd brought his Marines up from Pendleton for the recovery operations after the nuclear terror attack on Los Angeles. Monk joked that he'd never need a night-light, since he glowed in the dark himself.

A volley of rockets scrawled arcs in the sky. Again, they were as ineffective as holiday fireworks. But it would take only one to hit the wrong ship. Then the pyrotechnics would be a great deal more dramatic.

It was hard to resist ordering the lead brigade of the Big Red One ashore immediately, to get things moving, to push deep and hard and fast. But the narrow beachhead, with the cliffs and steep slopes shooting up behind it, would be on the verge of chaos as it was. Harris didn't envy the beachmaster. And he could trust Monk, who knew how much time mattered. The Army, with its heavy gear, couldn't go ashore until the roads winding into the hills had been secured.

Harris heard footsteps descending a metal ladder. A moment later, his aide, the newly promoted Major John Willing, stumbled from a hatch.

"Sir?"

"Word from General Morris?" Harris asked.

A head shook in the darkness. "No, sir. Nothing yet. But the Deuce has an update. One of the overheads got clean imagery."

"Tell him I'll be down in a few minutes. And tell the Three I need to know the status of the MOBIC landings down south. Even if he has to swim down there to find out."

"Yes, sir. Got it."

Harris liked and trusted his G-2. But the man was a little too eager to brief when there wasn't anything vital to add to the picture. Loyal, but too demonstrative about it, he needed to learn to listen to things he didn't want to hear. The G-3 was his opposite: taciturn, with the quiet sort of loyalty that would sacrifice life and limb but might explode if disappointed—the kind of man you didn't dare let down.

Flintlock Harris granted himself a few last minutes of quiet. Watching the manmade lightning on the horizon, he remembered.

BREMERHAVEN, GERMANY

The northern sky threatened rain. The Germans had torn the roofs from the dockside warehouses out of spite, and the vast herd of refugees waiting to board a ship to safety had no protection against a downpour beyond what they wore on their backs. The tentage the U.S. Army had brought to Bremerhaven barely met the requirement for sick wards. Half of the kids in the dockyards had diarrhea, the shitters were too few for one-tenth the number of refugees who staggered from the trains, and Doc Brodsky worried about cholera. The doc wanted the Navy to give priority to bringing in saline solution. But his claim for aircraft space was just one among many. There weren't enough rations aboard the advance vessels to feed the refugees. A shortage of potable water meant that the throng on the wharves was dehydrating. They already smelled of death.

Harris heard gunfire. Inland. Less than a kilometer, he judged. Inside the fence. Near the railhead.

His greatest worry had been a shoot-out with the German border police, who were behaving a little too much like the worst of their ancestors. Given all that had occurred, he understood the Germans' anger. He just couldn't fathom their cruelty. In his more cynical moments, he wondered if it was in their DNA.

The simultaneous detonation of dirty bombs in Berlin, Hamburg, and Frankfurt, as well as in Paris, Brussels, Amsterdam, Barcelona, Milan, Rome, London, and Manchester, had been the signal for the Great Jihad. Muslim radicals told their kind that Europe had lost its will, that it needed only a push to topple and leave a new caliphate standing.

It had been all madness. The Islamists hadn't had the numbers. The majority of their fellow Muslims in Europe wanted no part of the violence. But enough rose up to seal the fate of the rest. The Muslim rioting had been severe, with atrocities committed in the streets against any ethnic European on whom the radicals laid hands.

In less than a week, the equation shifted decisively. The anti-Muslim pogroms that followed did not distinguish between those who had committed crimes and those who had only tried to wait out the chaos. In every country, the authorities either tolerated or abetted the revenge killings.

Within a month, the counterattacks on Europe's Muslims spread so widely and grew so brutal that the United States led the world in demanding that Europe's governments end it. But the governments answered to the people, and the people wanted blood. Mobs ruled, even in parliaments. It was as if the rebellion had broken a dam behind which decades of fury had been rising.

NATO dissolved amid the threats aimed at ending the butchery. Infected by the continental hysteria, the European Union—whose Islamic delegates had gone into hiding—voted overwhelmingly to expel Muslims from the continent. The United States demanded a monitoring role to ensure that the refugees were treated humanely. Of course, that was more than a year before the nuclear destruction of Israel and the terror attacks on Los Angeles and Las Vegas.

The Great Evacuation had come first. Bringing the U.S. military back to Europe for the last, brief time. From Bremerhaven to Brindisi.

With his first star on his uniform and the clouds brooding overhead, Harris turned to his forward staff and snapped, "Find out who's shooting. Now. And get the Rapid Reaction Force out where everybody can see it." Wind slapped canvas down along the wharf.

"Already moving, sir."

"Hold them at the warehouse line. I just want them visible. I'll call if I need them."

"Sir? It's Cavanaugh. He's at the railhead."

Harris drew on his headset. "This is Trailmaster Six. What've you got?"

The voice that answered sought to be steady and failed. "Rodeo Six Alpha. No ketchup. We had to shoot in the air to get their attention. But you've got to see this. The bastards."

"Get yourself under control, Six Alpha. *Now.* I'll be there in one-zero mikes. And I don't want to hear any more shots unless you mean it." Harris looked around at the what-the-hell? faces. "Let's go."

"Want the RRF to make a hole, sir?" That was the Three.

Harris looked out over the mass of refugees and shook his head. "They've already had enough of men with guns." But he reset the holster on his thigh, a reflex action. There were radicals seeded among the refugees, those who hadn't quite been up to suicide attacks but who were dangerous enough—and bitter that the United States, the Great Satan, had come to the aid of Muslims, queering their schemes. In Marseilles, a Marine colonel had been stabbed as he reached to lift a child, and there had been a riot on the wharves at Rotterdam, with a Navy SP beaten to death. Here, on the Bremerhaven docks, where the U.S. armed forces long had shipped out the autos of its members returning from Germany, Harris's biggest problem had been preventing the radicals from further terrorizing their fellow Muslims.

Followed by his forward staff, Harris jounced down to the dock and pushed beyond the cordon of soldiers and sailors that kept the command ship from being stormed by desperate human beings. He walked fast, with his face set hard to warn off anyone with a complaint or petition. He had no time now for the dead-eyed women picking the lice from their children's hair, or for the shattered fathers struggling to put together a few words of beggar's English. Most were ethnic Turks, their pride broken, as recognizable by their somber looks as by the olive tinge to their pale complexions.

The wind filled his nostrils with a smell that made him think of concentration camps.

A few hands reached toward him, some voices called. But these were people who had learned fear and learned it suddenly. Only those who had lost their last grip on reality cried out for his attention.

Even aboard the ships putting in—most of them contracted freighters—there wouldn't be enough of anything. The makeshift showers wouldn't suffice, nor would the medical care. The entire effort had been cobbled together so swiftly that even the rules of engagement remained in dispute, with the EU reps venomously obstructionist.

Europe, the continent of peace.

Harris saw a thin girl in a headscarf standing up amid the thousands huddled on the gravel. She wore jeans, an orange sweater, and a red plaid cape, and she watched him as if he were an alien being. He figured her for a rape victim. Given the Muslim obsession with chastity, rape had been a common sport in the retaliatory pogroms.

He refused to think too much. There would be time for thinking later on. He had to keep his head and make things happen.

His pace quickened to a range-walk. Flipping his

headset to "talk" he said, "Rodeo Six Alpha, Trail-master Six. We okay?"

The voice did not respond so quickly as he would've liked. Then the captain, who had struck Harris as solid since the day they docked, repeated, "You've got to see this . . ."

"Your location in five."

The sea of refugees parted as he advanced.

He turned a warehouse corner and passed a plot used as an open-air latrine, as foul as anything he had ever smelled. Before him, at the railhead, a half-dozen *Bundesgrenzschuetzen* sat on the ground by a line of boxcars. The German border police no longer had their weapons, and they looked extremely un-happy. U.S. Army Infantrymen stood over them with their rifles ready.

Harris ordered himself to maintain his self-control, not to judge before he had the facts. But young Cap-tain Cavanaugh would need a damned good explana-tion for this one.

Wiping his face, the captain trotted toward him. Harris realized the man had been crying.

"What going on, captain?"

"Sir . . . You've got to see this."

"You told me that. Twice. What do I have to see?"

"You've just got to see it." The captain turned back toward the rust-colored boxcars with the white letters "DB" on their sides.

"Sergeant Z," the captain called. "Help me."

The sergeant shouldered his rifle, reluctantly, and moved toward the first boxcar.

They opened the door. And the stench hit every-one like a fist. Even the Germans winced.

The corpses rose almost to the middle of the car's interior. Men. Women. Children. Stiff. Wide-eyed. Mouths agape. Even a day or two into death, they retained their Turkish pallor. Hands had literally clawed themselves to the bone in their last, desperate moments.

As Harris watched, a woman's corpse broke from the mass and began to slide, accelerating as it dropped to the ground. Dead bones broke.

One cold raindrop struck Harris on the lips.

"They thought it was funny," the captain said. His voice had broken to a child's tone. "Somebody closed all the air vents. They suffocated. And the Krauts thought it was funny."

Harris allowed himself a long look. He needed time to master himself.

When he felt ready, he strode over to the Germans. Half of them looked worried. The rest smirked.

"Who did this?" Harris asked an *Oberleutnant*, the highest ranking figure he could see among them.

"I don't speak pig English," the officer said. With quite a good accent. He made a spitting sound. *"Ihr sind doch alle Rassenverraeter."*

A *Feldwebel* spoke up. "We have nothing to do with this. They are dead a long time. Days. We only make the *Sicherheitsdienst* here. Nothing with the trains. *Da ist die Bahnpolizei verantwortlich."*

"They knew," Cavanaugh said. "They knew. They were laughing about it."

The German officer decided to speak English, after all. He snickered and said, "Maybe Osama bin Laden is in there. *Was meinst du, Herr Brigadegeneral? Nach dreissig Jahren!* Maybe you should look. If you Americans love these *Dreck-Muslimen* so much. But you have no right to take away our weapons. It is against the agreement. I will make a protest."

Harris looked at him. For a moment, he considered shutting the Germans inside the boxcar with the corpses and locking it shut. He would've loved to do it. And he wasn't worried about protests. He would've faced a court-martial without blinking. But he realized that anything further done to the German guards would simply be taken out on other Muslims before the next train entered the compound.

"Give them back their weapons," he told the captain. "Unless you have evidence of their direct involvement."

"But, sir, we—"

"Just execute the order, Captain." He turned to the German first lieutenant. "You have the formal apology of the United States Government for this misunderstanding. Now get out of here before I have you shot."

The lieutenant kept up his smirk as he met Harris's eyes.

"Three," Harris said, turning back to business, "I want them put in body bags and taken out for burial at sea. They will not be buried on German soil."

"I'll have to get the doc to sign off. They might be infectious and—"

"*They will not be buried on German soil.* Work it out, Three. Cavanaugh?"

"Yes, sir."

"Walk with me."

"Yes, sir."

Harris led him back toward the docks. Just far

enough for privacy. And shy of the open-air latrine. "Look. I understand. I understand what you're feeling. But an officer focuses on his mission. And our mission is to evacuate the living." Harris gestured toward the sea of discarded humanity as the sky began to spit rain. "Focus on *them*. There's nothing we can do for the dead. Got it?"

"Yes, sir."

He didn't get it, of course. Not completely. But he'd be all right. Harris had been through his own moments years before, as a company commander in Diyala. Plenty to make a man sick, to make him angry. But a good soldier just kept marching and did his duty.

It seemed to him the world was going mad. His intel officer had just briefed a report that concluded that the top Islamist extremists in Europe had never expected their uprising to succeed. The whole purpose had been provocation, to deepen the split between Islam and the West, to make coexistence intolerable. They *wanted* all this to come to pass. Even Iraq and all that had come after had not prepared him for the irradiation of cities, the rabid slaughter of the innocent, and Europe's reverting to the continent's age-old habits—such as the German tendency to stuff unwanted minorities into boxcars. Of course, the French were behaving worse, according to the daily updates. And of all people, the Italians had gone maddest. Maybe it was the destruction of the Sistine Chapel, but the *dolce vita* Italians had turned out to be militant Catholics, after all. They put down their espressos and killed with gusto.

When Harris had been a young officer, pundits

had warned of "Eurabia," of a Muslim demographic takeover of Europe. Looking out over the terrified thousands for whom he was responsible, those warnings seemed a wicked, sickening joke. Strangers were never welcome, in the end. All men wanted was an excuse to kill.

Even before the attacks on his own country began, Harris sensed that this wasn't an end, but a beginning.

Without waiting for his staff to catch up with him, Harris plunged back into the mass of refugees. That night, typhus broke out.

■

So much had happened in the five years since he looked into that boxcar that the world in which he now led troops to war seemed unrecognizable. Dreamers had changed the world, but their dreams were grim. The great American effort to evacuate Europe's Muslims had turned into a debacle. None of the states from which their ancestors had come would accept the refugees. Islamist firebrands declared that all that had transpired in Europe had been an American plot to oppress Muslims. Overcrowded ships lay at anchor in the Mediterranean or in the smack-down heat of the Persian Gulf. Arab governments took their cue to blame Washington for the suffering, unwilling to welcome Muslims who had lived in Europe amid liberal ideas. American counterarguments were mocked. The global media accused the United States of making pawns of the refugees. When a riot aboard a converted cruise ship turned deadly, the European pogroms were forgotten as if they had been an embarrassing soccer match. All agreed that Washington was the true enemy of Islam.

When the refugees were landed by force in Alexandria and Beirut, in Saudi Arabia and the Gulf sheikhdoms, the local governments let them perish on the docks until, with tens of thousands dead and headlines blazing, they belatedly opened their arms to their fellow Muslims "to save them from America."

But the Islamists had gone too far at last. Obsessed with their dream of reestablishing the caliphate, they provoked the rise of a wildfire reaction among Christians. The Reverend Dr. Jeff B. Gui, an evangelist from Arkansas, mesmerized millions with sermons bewailing "the captivity of the ancient Christian heartlands." While Muslims raged and demanded the restoration of their medieval empire of the sword, ever more Christians remembered that almost all of the cities that had cradled Christianity were now in Muslim hands: Alexandria, the great school of the faith, as well as Antioch, Damascus, Ephesus, Tyre, Tarsus, Philadelphia, Smyrna, Nicea, Constantinople . . . these daughters of the church cried out to be redeemed from the ravishes of the Antichrist. According to the Reverend Dr. Gui, it was time for a crusade.

The movement spread with a rapidity that left secular critics agape, from Nashville to Nairobi, from Little Rock to Warsaw. When *The New Yorker* ran an article mocking the Reverend Dr. Gui's message and his credentials, the managing editor was shot down in the street, and the gunman was acclaimed as a Christian soldier by millions of Americans.

Muslim extremists had conjured demons they could not put down.

At that fateful moment, Iran launched a barrage of nuclear missiles at Israel, killing two million people. On the same day, nuclear devices exploded in downtown Los Angeles and on the Vegas Strip. Islamists proudly claimed responsibility.

That was the beginning of the Holy War. With elections looming, American politicians from both parties rediscovered their religious roots. Even Princeton recollected its Presbyterian heritage. Clinging adamantly to his peace policy, the president refused to respond to the attacks. He lost his reelection bid by the greatest landslide in American history. The Reverend Dr. Gui took his oath of office as vice president.

At the new administration's behest, Congress authorized funding for a religion-based reorganization of the National Guard as the Military Order of the Brothers in Christ. Regiments of young men and women lined up outside the church halls used as MOBIC recruiting centers. When a call went out for officers and NCOs from the active-duty military to staff the new corps and divisions, devout Christians and opportunists volunteered by thousands. Six months later, the Army and Marine Corps were ordered to sign over their latest weapons systems to the now-activated MOBIC units and to rearm themselves from reserve stocks.

"We must give the best weapons to those who yearn to take the fight to the Antichrist," Vice President Gui announced.

With bewildering speed, the Military Order of the Brothers in Christ and their supporters had gotten their crusade against Islam, an invasion to retake the Biblical heartlands from the infidel. And as the favored MOBIC forces battled toward Jerusalem, Lieutenant General Flintlock Harris had the mission of taking Damascus with what remained of the Army and Marines.

TWO

·····■·······■······■·····

MT. CARMEL RIDGES, EMIRATE
OF AL-QUDS AND DAMASKUS

Tracers streaked down the alley, but the shooting inside the house stopped. Sergeant Ricky Garcia heard the snap of a magazine going home.

"Ground floor clear." Freytag's voice. Hoarse.

"Coming in," Garcia shouted.

"Going up."

Garcia had lost his night-eyes several streets back, and the interior of the house was a filthy mist. Cordite and smoke cut his sinuses.

Footsteps pounded up the stairs. Freytag and Corporal Kovack. Just stay out of their way. Raise the lieutenant. Find out who's on first.

Garcia thumbed the crud off his mike and pushed the black bead to his mouth. Huddling near the doorway. Covering the street. Guns up. All the time.

"Clear one," Freytag yelled. Boots thumped overhead. "Go, go, *go*."

"Cease fire!" Kovack yelled. As if deafened and unable to hear himself. "There's women—"

The blast upstairs blew Garcia back through the front door. His rifle let off a round as he landed, bucking, with the muzzle inches from his eyes. Stunned, he lay on the ground like a tossed sea bag. For second after second. Many seconds. No idea how many. Then the fear buzzed him, and he patted himself down.

No wetness. Vital parts accounted for. Everything seemed to work. Tracers wasped overhead, the Jihadis shooting wildly. No fire discipline. The fucks deserved to die.

When he tried to get up and crawl back through the doorway, he was unsteady, even on all fours. Like the end of the worst drunk of his life. More tracers chased each other down the alley. He remembered, suddenly, that there should be noise to go with those lights. All he could hear was head-under-water emptiness.

Garcia flattened himself, weapon close, and counted to ten. Then he tried to make it through the door again. Arms and legs back in formation. Small miracle. The fog of dust inside was so thick he could only breathe in gasps.

"Corporal Kovack? Freytag?"

He shouted the words but couldn't hear himself. An echo, though. Strange. More underwater follies.

"Yo? Anybody?"

He knew. No way any Marine was walking down those stairs alive. Then he realized there were no stairs anymore. Not above the first three or four. A new hole in the roof sucked in the starlight. Right through the swirls of plaster dust.

Garcia kicked something soft. Didn't want to, but

he reached down. A torso. Weight-lifter muscles. Nothing else. Just a rib cage and guts in bloody uniform cloth. Fresh meat from the butcher's counter.

Somewhere in the mess, a kid began to wail. The buggers could live through anything. Hadn't *he*? As a kid?

"Get your own fucking daddy," Garcia told his fellow survivor. And he slipped back outside, almost in control of his balance now. Another concussion. He didn't need a corpsman to tell him. Christ. How many could you take? End up punchy like the old guys at the gym. San Sebastian.

One more time, he scraped the minimike with his thumbnail. Like that was going to make it work. Right.

Movement. Not Jihadis. Marines.

He realized he could hear gunfire again.

One of the Marines raised his rifle.

"Belleau," Garcia called. Hoping the other guy's ears were in better shape than his own.

"Wood." Gotcha, Devil Dog.

One Marine rushed across the street, keeping low, while the other covered him. Just like in training. Okay. The sprinter turned out to be Corporal Banks.

"Sergeant Garcia? Where you been, man?"

"Where's the platoon commander?"

"Dead."

"You know that?"

"I saw him. Headshot."

"Shit."

In nomini Patri . . . The lieutenant had been all right. But they could all feel bad about him later. Just now, there was more immediate stuff going down.

"That Barrett with you?"

"Nervous in the service. First Squad's one street over. Hunkered down. After Staff Sergeant Twilley got hit—"

"Where's the lieutenant?"

"I told you, he's—"

"Where's the fucking body?"

"Back a couple streets."

"Can you find him?"

"Yeah. Sure. Sergeant Garcia, you're the last—"

"Get his headset. And don't forget to come back. I'll be with First Squad."

"Where's Freytag and—"

"Just move out, Corporal."

The platoon had walked in on a suicide company. Rear guard for the Jihadis pulling off the high ground. Bad *hombres*. The first thing that hit Garcia's squad was a volley of flash grenades, blinding them through their night-sights. The headache from Hell. The new platoon sergeant went down trying to get things unscrewed, along with Sergeant diMeola. Now the lieutenant was dead. Fucking lot of good college did him. And Sergeant Twilley before him. One ambush after another. They'd caught it good. Tired as shit. And higher pushing them to keep moving.

Now what was left of the platoon was his. Until company sent down somebody with a higher rating.

He wasn't ready for this.

Garcia followed Corporal Banks back across the alley. Machine-gun fire chased them. The Jihadi on the trigger didn't know how to lead a target.

"Barrett." He slapped the lance corporal's shoulder as he passed him. "Come on. Let's go."

"Where we—"

"Move. Follow me."

He didn't want this. Not now, not yet. Goddamned Jihadis. Maybe the MOBIC pukes were right. Only good Muslim . . ."

"*Belleau.*"

"*Wood.*"

"Coming in."

"Hold for covering fire!" Corporal Gallotti. Head screwed on right. In a moment, several guns were up and nailing the darkness to the night.

"*Go!*" Garcia told Barrett. He followed. Splashing through muck that smelled like every sewer pipe in the country had broken at once.

The squad was too bunched up. Waiting for somebody to give an order. Gallotti was the natural leader but didn't have the rank. Everything going to hell.

"Listen up," Garcia said. Loud enough to be heard. But not too loud. Anyway, the Jihadis were making a noise like Cinco de Mayo in the Plaza de Armas. "We're going to get our asses unfucked. Right now. Corporal Gallotti's in charge of this squad. Because I said so. Corporal, get the roofs covered. Both sides."

"Pullman's topside, Sergeant." He pointed across the street. "With Jamal."

"I said *both* sides. This is it. We're not moving back one goddamned inch from here. We're fucking Marines. We're going fucking forward, if we go any-place."

"Yo, Sergeant Garcia? Anybody ever tell you that you got a limited vocabulary."

Laughter. That was okay. If they could laugh, they could fight.

"Buy me a dictionary. Now, check your ammo."

Banks scrambled up along the wall.

"Corporal Gallotti," Garcia continued, "get your squad set up with proper fields of fire. No more monkey-fucking. Banks, give me that."

Banks handed over the platoon commander's headset and drop transmitter. Garcia wrapped it around his skull, feeling the plastic scrape the bristles at the nape of his neck.

Before he could transmit, figures ran up behind them. The right helmet silhouettes and body-armor shoulders. Marines.

It was Captain Cunningham.

"Third Platoon?"

"Yes, sir," Garcia said.

"Who's in charge?"

"I am, sir. Lieutenant Delaney's—"

"Well, *take* charge. You've got a squad and a couple of strays a block back playing with their dicks. We've got to clean this shithole out *now*. So the Army can go for a Sunday drive." The captain paused for a moment. Looking at Garcia in the flickering light. "You're the last E-5 in this platoon?" As if he doubted what he'd been told. Or doubted the man in front of him.

"I'm it, sir."

The captain nodded, but hesitated. As if something in his head wouldn't come clear. "Well, you know the mission," he said at last.

"That a question, sir?"

After another flash-to-bang delay, Garcia realized

that the captain wasn't really thinking about him at all. He was thinking about his losses. One of his platoons shot to shit. Maybe thinking about the mission, maybe about his own future. It was a revelation Garcia would have preferred to postpone, but he saw to his bewilderment that officers had no special magic, after all. The captain was as shaky as he was. And struggling just as hard to hide it.

"No," the captain said. His voice was firmer now. "It wasn't a question. You've got the platoon. And the mission."

A mortar round shrieked in. Everybody flattened. It struck in a courtyard behind high walls, close enough to give the earth a shiver. Another screamed toward them, falling short and biting into the street. Shrapnel stung the air.

"They're bracketing us," Garcia yelled. "Get out of here, sir. I got it. Just get us some mortars on that line of buildings up on the crest, if you can."

"Fires on the way in five. Semper Fi."

"Semper Fi, sir."

Gallotti looked at him. The corporal's eyes caught the glow off a fire down-range. "You still want us to—"

"No. Round 'em up and move out. *Forward.* Bring some heat on those sonsofbitches. No Navy Crosses, just keep 'em busy."

Where did plans come from? The Virgin of Guadalupe? He knew exactly what he was going to do and how he was going to do it. So the Army could go for its Sunday drive.

Buy me a candy-apple-red, extended-cab pickup when I get back . . .

He told Corporal Banks and Barrett to stay with Gallotti and then hustled back to round up the rest of his platoon. *His* platoon. Wasn't the way it was supposed to happen, but life was tough in the big city.

I can do this, he thought. Fuck, yeah. *Go, Marine.*

OFFSHORE

"Okay, Deuce," Lieutenant General Harris said as he dropped into his chair, "talk to me."

The G-2, Colonel Val Danczuk, stood up and made his way through the packed wardroom until he reached the screen.

"Sir," he addressed Harris, "we had a solid imagery feed for almost a half hour. The Third Jihadi Corps has definitely been pulling back and—"

"Plan, or panic?"

"I'd say 'panic.' The deception worked. They were locked and cocked to defend south of the ridges. Thought we'd come ashore between Netanya and Caesarea, right on the flank of the MOBIC assault. Now they've abandoned Hadera, and it looks like they'll tie in a new forward line of defense on the Megiddo-Qiryat Ti'von line."

"Main line of defense?"

"Afula-Nazareth-Shefar'am."

Harris nodded. "You sure they didn't stop jamming the overhead link on purpose? To show us what they wanted us to see?"

The G-2 took a quick chaw on his lip. Tall and blessed with the sort of good looks that gray hair only improved, Colonel Danczuk looked like a general from the casting office. It amused Harris, who was five-eight and as plain as a church supper, to think that, if you took off their rank and put the entire staff in a line-up, any right-thinking civilian would pick out the Deuce, not him, as the corps commander.

"No, sir," Danczuk said. "I wouldn't ever want to underestimate an enemy, but I don't think this was on purpose. The highways feeding back into the Jezreel Valley looked like a giant clusterfuck."

Harris turned to the senior Air Force officer in the room. "And you boys still aren't flying? We used to call that a target-rich environment, back in the days of the horse cavalry."

The brigadier general reddened. "Sir . . . We'd like to be flying . . . We *will* fly . . . You'll get your support . . . But right now, the jamming . . ."

Harris's entire corps had just a few more artillery tubes than a division would have fielded a generation earlier. The Air Force was supposed to be the Army's flying artillery, delivering precision munitions on any enemy foolish enough to fight. Except that now, the smart bombs didn't work, and the airplanes couldn't fly.

Harris mastered his temper. Maybe the zoomies would deliver down the road. And the blue-suiter looked sufficiently beaten up. "Yeah, I know. Wipes out your computers. Gonna take up a collection and buy you boys a squadron of old Phantoms from the Paraguayans—Deuce, the Paraguayans still have Phantoms?"

Danczuk took the question seriously. "Sir, I don't think they ever . . . I mean, maybe some old F-16s. I can check . . ."

"Forget it, Deuce." He turned back to the Air Force officer. "I still love you, Hank. We *all* love you. But I'd like to put some hot metal on those bad boys before doomsday. Which reminds me," he shifted his attention back to the G-2, "tell me if I'm coughing up fur balls, but Meggido's Armageddon, correct?"

"Roger, sir. The tel's one of the most important archaeological sites in the—"

"And our Muslim friends are digging in *there*? It's just about high enough for an Egyptian spear-carrier outfit to control a chariot crossing." Harris got it, but he wanted the others to see the logic on their own, if they could. "*Why* do you think they're digging in at Megiddo, Deuce?" He scanned the crowded, steaming hot room. "Anybody? Any ideas?"

A Navy captain sitting in for the admiral raised his hand. "It's a protected site. They figure we'll be reluctant to attack an archaelogical treasure and—"

"Bingo!" Harris said, pointing a gun made of fingers at the captain. The general turned to his senior Artilleryman. "Chris, I want everybody in this room to hear me giving you this order: If the Jihadis use Meggido Hill as part of their defenses, I want you to hit it so hard that there's nothing left but a smoking hole. Got that?"

"General," the pol-mil rep from State jumped in, "we can't do that, that's one of the most important sites in the entire Middle East . . . in the world, really . . ." He looked as if he were fighting seasickness. And probably was.

"Cultural Understanding 101," Harris said. "On my first tour in Iraq, as a lieutenant, we were under orders never to enter a mosque. Know what that accomplished? It guaranteed that mosques were going to be used as insurgent bases and safe houses and to hide arms caches. Because we failed to take down one mosque at the outset, we turned a thousand of them into sanctuaries." He snorted. "As for Meggido . . . two things: First, if they're really there—you get me confirmation, Deuce—they're not going to be there long. Our Jihadi friends are going to get an education in what happens when a commander picks a lousy defensive position just because he thinks we'll be too limp-dicked to hit it. After that, I suspect we'll see fewer historical sites occupied in the future. Second," he looked around, wondering, as he always had to now, which of the officers present were reporting to the MOBIC's internal intelligence unit, "I want everyone to be absolutely clear on one thing: I will not sacrifice one American soldier or Marine to save a single pile of sacred rocks between here and the Pacific Ocean." He shook his head. "We're going to *win* this campaign. And there'll be plenty of history left over. Okay, Deuce, one more question. Same one as always: Any sign of nukes?"

Danczuk shook his head. "Sir, as I've briefed—"

"I don't want 'as you briefed.' I want right now. Listen, Val, you're doing great." He swept the room with the commander's gaze he'd mastered over the years. "You're *all* doing great." He turned back to the G-2. "But I want you to watch for any sign of nukes. Any least hint. Maybe they're just an urban legend . . . but I want you to watch for them."

"Sir, the DIA and the CIA are both convinced that the Jihadis have no nuclear weapons. The last Iranian weapons were expended in the exchange with Israel, and the made-in-Pakistan arms were all detonated during the war with India and in the subsequent terror attacks on the United States. We've never seen any indicators of more nukes, sir. None."

"Yet, the rumors continue." Harris nodded to himself. "Two, maybe three. Held in deep reserve. Watch it for me, Val."

"Sir, they would've used them on the MOBIC landings down south. *If* they had them."

Harris wiped a hand across his jaw. "Maybe. Speaking of MOBIC, what's the latest you got, Three?"

Colonel Mike Andretti, the G-3 operations officer, swapped places with the G-2. "Two divisions already over the beach, sir. Sounds like a bloody mess, but they're pushing ahead. The latest situation report—the last one that came through from MOBIC—has their forward elements fifteen clicks up the Jerusalem highway." The colonel shook his head. "It's all just hey-diddle-diddle, straight up the middle."

Harris did what he could to suppress his disgust. Regulars or MOBIC troops, he didn't believe in wasting American lives.

"Casualties? Any numbers?"

His aide, Major Willing, rushed in. "Sir? General Morris is on the horn."

Harris jumped up. "Secure or nonsecure?"

"We have him secure, sir. He wants to talk to you ASAP."

Harris scanned the room. Quickly. "Excuse me, gentlemen. Just hold in place."

The general hurried to the commo cell next door,

footsteps slapping metal. A staff sergeant held out a headset. Harris motioned for everyone to clear the room.

"Monk?"

"Green light. Road's open as far as Isfiya. Not one hundred percent secure, but I'd call it close enough. We're pushing down toward Daliyat. First Battalion, Fifth Marines have been tangling with stay-behinds all night. Suicide commandos mostly. One company got hit hard up in a ville. But the Jihadis pulled back their heavy metal. Whatever isn't broken down by the side of the road."

"Good work. Great work. Remind me to buy a Marine a beer when this is over. How's the beach?"

"What beach? Christ, we just put a Marine division-minus over a shingle the width of a sidewalk."

"When do you think you can get down to Route 70?"

"Recon's knocking on the back door right now. The Jihadis didn't expect this one. Even after they figured out that it wasn't a feint, they didn't seem to want to risk their armor up here."

"Their gear's in even worse shape than ours. Maintenance a *lot* worse."

"Well, thank God for lazy mechanics. Listen . . . sir . . . from one fancy-pants Marine to one dogface grunt . . . I had my doubts about this. I wasn't really sure we could pull it off."

"We haven't pulled it off. Not yet. But thanks."

"We caught them with their pants down."

"So to speak. Okay, Monk. Good work."

"Tell it to the Marines."

He clicked off. Immediately, Harris returned to

the wardroom. "Three. Green light. Get the Big Red One on the beach. Scotty still colocated with his Fourth Brigade?"

"Yes, sir."

"Good. You tell him I want Quarter Cav headed uphill by BMNT to coordinate the forward passage of lines. We need to keep punching while the Jihadis are still reeling."

"Yes, sir."

The G-3 headed for the hatch, followed by his deputies.

"The rest of you can clear out," Harris said. "Sorry I kept you waiting. Go do what you've got to do, then get a couple hours' sleep. Let your subordinates earn their pay. Four, you hang back. We need to have a pow-wow."

The staff members cleared the room, moving through air so humid the next stage would've been swimming.

"Okay, Real-Deal. Talk to me. How you going to make this work?"

The colonel responsible for logistics, Sean "Real-Deal" McCoy, threw up his hands in the polar-bear salute. He had worked for Harris at battalion, brigade, and division, and he still played the staff-clown role that Harris had tacitly agreed to tolerate a decade before.

"Work? We've got less than a quarter of the force ashore, and I'm already holding things together with chewing gum and baling wire."

"POL?"

"Over-the-beach will keep the tanks full for three, maybe four days. Then we're up against it. Basic physics. Once we're down in the Jezreel, we're not going to be able to move enough fuel over those ridges without asking the engineers to spend a year or two building pumping stations." He waved his arms, as if the world were ending. "Eighty-four percent of the big boys and about seventy percent of the infantry tracks have been refitted with the miniaturized engines. But 'miniaturized' is still relative."

"Got it."

"Sir, I need your permission on something."

"Talk to me."

"The SeaBees want to play. They're good guys."

"And?"

"They want to suit up and go ashore at Haifa, check out the condition of whatever's left, see if we can run any of the old pipelines . . ."

"You've seen the radiation charts. Most of Haifa's a dead zone. It was hit even harder than Tel Aviv."

"They'd just be in and out. Suited up. The radiation's patchy. Or so Tolliver tells me. Once we've taken a bite out of the Jezreel, we might be able to run a line and keep it going with robotics." He waved one arm, then the other, a scarecrow on a caffeine jag. "Beats trying to pump enough POL over those ridges to get us to Damascus."

"I just want to get this corps ashore, at the moment." Harris sighed, something he did only when he was too weary to catch himself. "All right. If the 'High Lord of the Admiralty' has no objections, the SeaBees can go in. And God bless 'em. But Sean . . ."

The Four perked up. Harris used his given name, rather than "Real-Deal," only when things were deadly serious.

". . . I don't want you going ashore at Haifa. Not now. I need you."

"Doesn't sound like my kind of town, anyway, sir."

"And ask me, before you decide to go in the future. No surprises. You hear me?"

"Yes, sir."

"I could piss on my boots for saying this, but you're the indispensible man on this one, Sean. We can fight blind, if we have to, and we even can fight without a plan, if it comes to that. But those soldiers and Marines can't fight without bullets, water, POL, chow, and Band-Aids."

"And T-and-A mags? Ah, for the good, old days of the Internet . . ."

"I'm serious, Sean. You know my priorities on this one: ammo, potable water, POL, then chow. As long as they've got something to shoot and something to drink, we'll at least survive."

"Loggie Basic for the Middle East, sir: warm water, cold rations, rounds in the chamber, and fuel in the tank."

"Don't carry this load yourself. Come to me if you need supporting fires."

The G-4 looked at the man he had served for half of his career. "You're not carrying a few short tons yourself?"

Harris smiled. "That's what I do for a living, Real-Deal. Beats working. Try to get some sleep yourself, all right? I don't want to see a thousand-mile stare at tomorrow night's briefing."

"Which will be where, exactly?"

Harris smiled. "In the Land of the Bible, as our MOBIC brothers put it. Now, march, soldier."

Flintlock Harris signed nine papers, then dismissed his aide and walked two bulkheads down to his stateroom—which reminded him of a room in a motel bypassed by the Interstate in the last century. The moment he shut the hatch, he let his shoulders sag. And he closed his eyes where he stood, touching them lightly, as if probing for damage.

After washing his face and brushing his teeth, Harris took off his uniform blouse to sleep. He kept his trousers on, though. In case he had to move fast. But before he dropped onto the bunk, he got to his knees, just as he had done since his childhood.

His prayers were never long, but always earnest. This night, he was as brief as he had ever been and didn't even pray for his wife and two daughters. He just said:

"Dear Lord, give me the strength to see what's right and the strength to do what's right. Help me be a just man. Amen."

MT. CARMEL RIDGES

A male form emerged from the burning house and ran toward the Marines.

"Peace! Peace!" he cried. "America good!"

"Halt!" Sergeant Garcia yelled. *"Stop!"*

The man kept running through the darkness, shifting his course to head straight for Garcia and repeating, "America good!"

"Halt!"

Garcia pulled the trigger at the same instant the suicide bomber detonated himself. He felt the shock wave, but the bomber had not gotten close enough to do any damage. Garcia hoped.

"Everybody okay? Check your buddy."

No casualties. This time.

"Drink some water. Everybody. *Now.* If you're out of water, piss in your hand and drink it."

Bad enough to lose good Marines to the Jihadis. Garcia wasn't going to lose them to dehydration. But the fact, which he did not broadcast, was that his own camelback was empty. He figured most of his men were in the same boat.

Drink it, if you got it.

They had flanked the Jihadi positions on the ridge as mortar rounds, then serious artillery fire, thumped down on the houses the Mussies had turned into rent-a-forts. In the flame-scorched night, twisted re-bar scratched the air, and the block-shaped buildings looked like the faces of junkies with their teeth knocked out.

The street bums back home. So far gone on one drug or another that even their families didn't want any part of them. Could've joined that outfit, too. One more road Garcia had never gone down. No gang tattoos, either. Just the Virgin of Guadalupe. And she'd done okay by him so far. Patron saint of the Marine Corps. From the Halls of Montezuma. The brass just hadn't figured that one out.

"Larsen, Cropsey. Take the flank. Move out!" Garcia pointed toward the backside of the ridge.

The Marines worked forward, maintaining good combat intervals. No one fired at them. But Garcia had his street sense turned on. There were still bad guys up in that mess, behind the remaining walls.

Armed and dangerous. The human body was *loco*. You could trip on the sidewalk and die, or live through an artillery barrage dumped on your head.

"Sitrep?" he heard through his headset. The captain. Solid again. Mr. Annapolis.

"Rounds on target. Moving in now."

"Resistance?"

"There's gonna be. It smells like it smells."

"Keep moving. Battalion needs that ridge cleared."

And I need an ice-cold Bud, Garcia told himself.

"Roger. Moving now."

He waved at the remainder of the two squads he'd rounded up and brought this far. Several streets away, Corporal Gallotti's squad was still laying down look-at-me fire. Less of it, though. Which was righteous. No need to waste ammo. Anybody left alive in those buildings was going to play dead until he had somebody in his sights point-blank. Unless his nerves got him. Then he'd fire too soon.

Yeah, triggerman, Garcia thought. We're coming. Just give me a sign. Squeeze one off early. Just one.

The Marines worked their way forward, with Larsen and Cropsey acting as flankers where the ridge dropped off toward Indian country, the two of them disappearing into the shadows. Twice, Garcia held back when he wanted to bitch at the way his Marines were moving. Perfection wasn't in the cards. They were all five-o'clock-Sunday-morning tired, running on pure nerves.

He was getting jumpy, thinking too much, he told himself. When it was down to the bone like this, you didn't get through by thinking. The streets had taught him that much. You had to trust what you *felt*.

Cold Bud really would do the trick, though. Or a rat-piss Corona, for that matter.

They were good for another thirty meters, Garcia figured. Working their way up the rutted chute that pretended to be a street. Then it was going to go nuts. It was just too quiet. Every back-on-the-block nerve in his body said that the Jihadis left alive were just waiting for them. Watching them. There wasn't even any crying from their wounded—which would've been a sign that the Jihadis had lost their grip on the situation. The battalion Two had briefed that the suicide commandos cut the throats of their own casualties to keep them quiet. So the quiet meant that the bad *hombres* were still in control.

Garcia wondered if he could do that. To one of his Marines. Cut his throat, if the mission required it. Truth was, you never knew. Until the moment came.

Plenty of shooting farther down the ridge. In another battalion's sector, maybe another regiment's. His thighs and back ached from humping all the way up from the beach, a march that, physically, had been worse than the fight. Clambering up those slopes gave you the *burn*.

Pay attention! he told himself. Jolting himself back from the mind-drift.

Gunshot. No. Lance Corporal Polanski kicking a brick. Lamest Marine in the platoon. But the noise charged Garcia's battery.

"*Everybody down. Now!*" he called. Loud. So anyone whose headset was busted would still hear him. "*Guns up!*"

The Marines scrambled for cover. As they did, a

machine gun opened up. From a second-floor window. Or the hole where a window had been.

Too much return fire. Weren't going to get him that way, unless it was pure luck.

"Aimed fire only!" he said into the mike. "Tell your buddy. Don't piss away your ammo. Larsen, Cropsey. You read me?" he said into the mike.

No answer.

"Larsen? Cropsey?"

"Yeah, Sergeant." Cropsey. A kid like a coiled snake. Attitude problem.

"Larsen with you?"

"Roger."

"You see that machine-gun position?"

"Just the tracers."

"Hold where you are. I'm coming around behind you. Everybody else, stay alert. Let that asshole on the machine gun get nervous. And no firing to the left flank, unless you've got a one-hundred-percent positive ID. Don't want no blue-on-blue."

A few murmurs, plenty of static. Half the headsets were broke-dick. He just had to hope that the rest of them would figure it out. Hate to take a nail from another Marine.

Garcia slipped back into the darkness, then worked around behind a compound wall. At the rear of somebody's private world, the sloped dropped off sharply. He felt the steepness even more than he saw it in the murk. Working his way carefully, back to the masonry, he ground his heels into the earth as he sidestepped along. Like a duck in a shooting gallery at some rat-bite fair down in Durango, at his grandmother's. Anybody firing at him now was going to win the prize at the fiesta.

He paused for a stolen moment to kiss the sleeve covering his left forearm. Under the cloth, the Virgin of Guadalupe prayed for him.

"I'll do the prayers right later," he told her. "I promise. But you know what I need right now."

He got around the far corner of the wall. To reasonably level ground.

"Cropsey? Where are you, man?"

"By the twisted-up tree."

"That's an olive tree."

"Whatever."

"Coming in. On your six."

The firing to the right, back down in the street, came in short bursts followed by nervous quiet. Each side daring the other to really open up.

"Cropsey?" he whispered to the form ahead of him.

"I'm Larsen, Sergeant. Cropsey's over there."

"Listen up. Either of you got grenades left?

"One."

"Same here."

Shit. He'd used all of his own in the street fighting. Two grenades wasn't much to clear that house. And whatever else was waiting for them.

"Give them to me. You're going to keep everybody off me while I'm laying these eggs. You can't see it, but the gunner's in the second building up there. We're almost behind him here. And we're going to try to come in *right* behind him. But we're going in there figuring he's not feeling lonesome." Garcia fit the grenades to his armored vest. "Larsen, you're on point until we get to the back wall. Then you're tail-gunner on the outside. Cropsey, you're first in. But don't open up unless you're damned sure there's something to open up on. No yelling, no grab-ass. I want to *smell* that motherfucker before I throw any of these. You'll have the first deck. I'll take the stairs. Now move out."

Larsen was a good shot, just short of sniper level, but this wasn't a rifle range. It was going to be all close quarters. And Larsen was clumsy as an Anglo on the dance floor. He could watch their backs when they went in. Cropsey was a mean little bastard, though, born for a razor fight in a closet. Almost crazy mean. But not stupid. The kind of Marine who spoiled your Saturday night when the duty officer took a call from the San Diego cops. But good when the killing started.

Garcia gave his sleeve another furtive kiss. He'd taken a lot of grief about the tattoo. But he was still alive. Half the punks he went to high school with were dead. *Before* the Day of the Dead came early.

He tapped the bottom of his magazine, making sure he had a tight lock. Nervous habit. Everybody had one. Trick was not to let people see it.

They moved up between black trees, trip-me stumps, and small boulders. Everything in this world seemed disordered, messed up. Crazy people. Who started all this. For what? The nuclear blast hadn't reached his hood in East L.A. But the radiation did. He'd been on Okinawa. His family had been home.

Now the Jihadis were going to get their shit handed to them.

The machine gun sent another burst into the night. Exploring. Limited field of vision from where he was hunkered down, Garcia figured. Dude was probably shit-scared. No matter what he believed in, he had to be scared in a hole like that. The hunted, not the hunter. Death comes knocking.

We're coming, *amigo*, he told his invisible enemy. Your old pal Ricky Garcia is coming to the party. Just for you.

Larsen reached the rear wall of the building, with Cropsey just behind him.

Garcia whispered into his mike, still worried about friendly fire. He told the Marines down in the street, "We're up his ass. Just hold his attention."

Larsen edged along the rear wall of the line of ruined houses. Garcia wondered how many more Jihadis might be inside, just waiting for a Marine to walk up and wave.

Only hand signals now. Time to stay real quiet.

Lit by starlight, Larsen leapt past the rear door. Then he crouched, ready to fire at anyone who appeared from the far side.

Garcia waved Cropsey forward. The lance corporal crunched down like a boxer who liked to hit below the belt. Weapon jutting out at crotch level.

The machine gun fired. Different sound from behind. Like being the safety NCO on the range. Better than being in front of it.

Cropsey looked back for the go-ahead to enter. Garcia put a finger to his lips, then signaled "Go!"

One piece of luck: They didn't have to break down any doors. The rear entrance gaped, blown out by the mortars and artillery.

Cropsey was good. Garcia had never known an Anglo kid who could move like that. He was already inside, quiet as the confessional on Saturday night.

Garcia checked the grenades, then moved forward.

Inside the masonry house—what was left of it—a burst from the machine gun rang impossibly loud. Still no sign of any back-up protection for the gunner.

Garcia signalled Cropsey to clear to the bottom of the stairs. The kid had it figured out. Without being told, he hugged the right wall. In case any friendly fire came in the front.

Nice and quiet. Nice and easy. Cat-foot the rubble. Take it nice and slow.

Garcia wasn't sure if he hated what he was doing, loved it like sin, or both. But he wasn't tired anymore. Zooming on body chemicals. Aware of every breath sucked down in the world.

Then he heard it. A voice speaking Arabic. Whispering. Not the way a man talked to himself or cursed, but the way he spoke to someone else nearby.

Shit. But better to know it now.

Cropsey was looking at him. Kid had it figured out, too. But he needed to be looking everywhere else.

Garcia motioned for him to be ready. Then Garcia put his rifle on burst, switched it to his left hand, and gripped the first grenade.

Carefully, he thumbed out the pin, keeping the lever clasped death-grip tight to the curve of the metal. And he started up the stairs. Back to the wall. Ready. But already dead, if any fuck was watching from a back room up there.

Again, he heard a whisper in Arabic, followed by a rip from the machine gun.

One last split second prayer to the Virgin. And Garcia stepped up high enough to peer over the lip of the second floor.

His head struck something, and he froze. Unsure if the noise amplifed inside the helmet was equally loud to anyone else.

Silence.

Were they onto him?

The hand that held the grenade was sweating. Bad shit. Didn't want it slippery when he threw it.

Artillery fire had torn loose an iron railing, leaving it dangling over the staircase. A twist of its metal had scratched his helmet.

Don't let this goddamn-it-to-death grenade cook off. *Please*.

He heard more Arabic whispering. Too loud for them to be worried about anyone hearing.

He saw the pattern now: Whisper, then shoot. When the machine gun kicked out the next burst, he used the noise and its echo to scoot under the railing.

A wedge of exterior light shone through a doorway, leading his eye to the blown-out window frame where the machine gun perched. But he couldn't make out the gunner or his companion, who were out of his line of sight and and wrapped in darkness.

As Garcia placed his foot on the next step, it creaked.

He threw the grenade over the railing, hoping it would go through the door and not bounce back at him. Then he fired toward the front room, double bursts, as he plunged for cover.

The blast was doomsday loud. The wall that shielded him shook. But Garcia was going full throttle now. He leapt back to his feet, charged forward, and hurled the second grenade into the room an instant before diving behind another wall.

He hit his elbow hard. Bitch hard.

The explosion seemed powerful enough to tear the house apart. But that was just the confined-space effect.

"Shit, shit, shit, shit, *shit*," he barked. Cradling his elbow.

"Sergeant?"

"Shut the fuck up. Stay there."

He flipped magazines and edged back toward the room where the machine gun and at least two Jihadis had been at work. He wasn't going to mess it up now. No hot-dogging. Human being could live through a lot. Even two grenades.

At least one of them was cooked to serve. The second blast had blown the Jihadi halfway through the door. Dead meat.

That left at least one more.

Garcia heard a moan. Sounded real. But the bastard could be faking it.

He put a short burst into the room, then ducked back.

Fucker groaned again. Like he was trying to take a last shit before dying.

Garcia went in, ready to lay down another burst. By starlight and fireglow, he saw a figure gleaming with blood, propped against a wall in the settling dust. The man was alone, and his eyes were ablaze with the struggle for life. He was dying, but he wasn't quitting.

Garcia knew what he was supposed to feel. Pity. Compassion. All that shit. But he *didn't* feel it. Instead, he saw his mother dying of radiation sickness, her skull bald and raw, her body bent like a witch's in a cartoon and her skin loose over Popsicle-stick bones.

He walked over to the Jihadi, got his attention, then put a bullet into his forehead.

"That's for the City of Angels," Garcia told him.

THREE

...... ■ ..... ■ ...... ■ ....

"DAYTONA BEACH," EMIRATE OF AL-QUDS AND DAMASKUS

Lieutenant Colonel Patrick Cavanaugh just wanted to get off the beach. With all of his men and all of their gear. But the gentlest word that came to mind to describe the scene before him was "clusterfuck."

"Nothing's ever easy in the Big Red One," the battalion command sergeant major said.

It was a popular saying among the junior enlisted troops. Typical soldier talk. But it was jarring to hear Sergeant Major Bratty even whisper anything that might be construed as critical of the Army he seemed to have joined at birth.

The sergeant major spat on a rock. "Brigade-forward's somewhere up the road, sir. And the buggers down at the division forward CP wouldn't even talk to me. 'No time now, Sergeant Major.' Like I was six years old."

Cavanaugh smiled. Ruefully. "Well, nobody at the beachmaster's set-up has time for a lowly lieutenant colonel. They haven't done this in a while."

"Neither have we, sir."

"Neither have we."

"But *we're* not belly up."

"No, we're not." But Cavanaugh wasn't so sure they wouldn't be belly up soon, if things didn't start moving again.

"Think I'll stroll on down and see if Sergeant MacKinley's ever going to get Charlie 14 off that beach." But the sergeant major didn't stroll. He marched double-quick into the confusion roiling below, heading for the broken-down track.

Cavanaugh remained by the side of the road. The surface was already breaking up under the armored traffic. He glanced up along the line of Charlie Company's Bradleys, vehicles more than twice the age of their drivers. Three times older, in some cases. Idling wasn't good for them. The battalion had already had two go down before they left the beach. And spare parts were as rare as thoroughbred unicorns.

Captain Walker came up to him. Again.

"Any word about what's holding us up, sir?"

"Jake, nothing's changed since you asked me that ten mikes ago. You're on the battalion and brigade nets. I don't know anything you don't."

Have to watch Walker for nerves. But Cavanaugh understood. The desire to get up into the hills, to get into the fight, to go anywhere, just to move. Instead of sitting here, vehicles nose-to-butt because the one road that wound off the beach was backed up with traffic that had come to a dead stop and nobody knew why.

The maps, engineer briefings, and old sat photos showed a steep two-lane blacktop that could be blown out at dozens of points. One big boy broken down on a hairpin curve would be enough to stop the entire brigade.

Add to that the screw-up in the landing and march tables, with the brigade put on hold after 1/4 Cav went ashore so that two artillery battalions and an attack-drone squadron could be rushed forward. Followed by a jerk-the-leash resumption of the brigade's landing operation.

And the Jihadis had a lock on them now. Waiting offshore in a made-to-sink "get-ashore boat," one of the infamous GABs designed badly and built in haste, Cavanaugh had watched successive waves of drones pop up over the ridges and bluffs. He'd caught himself hoping only that none would hit the GABs carrying his battalion, as if wishing the fate on comrades outside of 1-18 Infantry.

Well, at least the Marines had fought to build the boats, as shoddy as they were. Cavanaugh gave the Corps, the Army's eternal rival, credit for figuring out fast that the old days of exploiting existing port facilities had ended when Israel's coastal cities vanished under a dozen mushroom clouds.

Two GABs bearing old Marine M-1 tanks had taken on water and sunk when the pumps failed. Without any help from the attack drones or blind missiles. But without the landing craft, crappy as they were, the entire operation would've been impossible.

Thus far, all of 1-18's allotted GABs had stayed on top of the water, where they belonged. With only Delta Company and the ash-and-trash from HHC still waiting to come ashore.

At the moment, there was no place to put them.

Out in the haze, the closest Navy ships were distant smudges, but the near waters roiled with GABs, fast boats, picket boats, beachmaster craft, and oceangoing tugs dragging barges loaded with God-knew-what or towing floats to be rigged as temporary docks. Buoys ringed the spots where GABs had gone down under drone attack, and enough debris bobbed on the mild waves to start a cargo cult.

But the real pandemonium had broken loose on the narrow shingle between the water's edge and the elevated road where Cavanaugh stood. With even local comms heavily jammed and erratic, petty officers, Marine loggies, and Army engineers trotted about with megaphones, snarling tinny commands. Vehicles splashed ashore through shallow water, churning the pebbled seabed into mud that sucked at their tracks until one vehicle in every four or five had to be winched onto the beach. Stevedores worked mobile cranes or manhandled supplies into little mountains waiting to be hauled forward. As Cavanaugh watched, a burdened forklift listed in the sand and toppled onto its side. Then there were the burned-out vehicles not yet cleared away and, near the beachmaster's op center, four long rows of dead Marines in body bags, laid out reverently at perfect intervals. More and more casualties were coming down from the hills, evacuated along firebreaks by all-terrain vehicles.

Thousands of people were doing their best, he knew that. But Cavanaugh still wanted to punch something. A commander had to appear stoic, to control his emotions, to set the example. At times, that seemed the hardest part of his job.

Why wasn't anything moving? The beach was getting as crowded as a stadium lot on homecoming weekend. Soon even the blind missiles wouldn't be able to miss.

He'd sent his XO forward, on foot, to find out what had blocked the road. But for all they knew, the stoppage might be a dozen clicks up the line, on the high ground. The XO could be walking for a while.

And then what? Cavanaugh could talk intermittently to his companies lined up ducks-in-a-row and to those still afloat, but brigade forward had disappeared into the hills and the electromagnetic spectrum.

Old Flintlock Harris had trained them for this, for the day the make-it-easy technologies would fail them. But no amount of training could lessen the sheer frustration. You grew up in a force accustomed to talking secure to anyone, anytime, and now, the inability to reach over a ridge for information made you want to break things.

Well, they'd get to breaking things soon enough.

He wished he'd marched up the road himself, instead of sending the XO. Just to have the illusion of accomplishing something. But Cavanaugh knew his place in the great scheme of things: The commander had to remain where he could exercise maximum control over his unit.

To the extent he controlled anything.

His earpiece crackled and made him jump.

"Bayonet Six, this is Five." The XO.

"Whatcha got?"

"Tank retriever lost its brakes. Not one of ours. Went over the side dragging an M-1. Then a drone hit the goat-rope on the road. Big ammo fry. They're clearing it now."

"Estimated time to movement?"

"Christ if I know. It's a mess up here. I'd guess at least thirty mikes."

"Roger. Stay there and hitch a ride with Bravo as they pass. Break, break. Bravo, you copy?"

"Good copy. We'll watch for him."

"All right. Break. Net call, net call, this is Bayonet Six. When we get this unscrewed, I want march discipline back in force. Keep your distance from your buddies, no snuggling up, no matter how slow you're moving. If the drones come again, I don't want any sympathy detonations. Out."

Cavanaugh saw two GABs that had been holding a thousand meters out begin to head toward the beach. Others appeared to be jockeying for a place in line behind them.

The beachmaster had to be crazy. There was no room for the rest of his battalion until the road opened. He wasn't going to have them lined up hub to hub on the beach as if it were inspection day in the motor pool.

Cavanaugh strode down from the roadway and across the rutted dirt strip that led to the beach. It struck him out of the blue that he had not had anything to eat since the middle of the night. Without slowing his pace, he fished a ration fruit bar from his pocket, tore it open, and chomped on it as if biting into a living thing he meant to kill.

The GABs were coming in, all right. God*damn* it.

Somebody with a stopwatch trying to keep to a schedule that no longer made any sense.

On most days, he loved being in command. On others—not least, today—he felt like an impostor. Pat Cavanaugh realized full well that he would not have gotten his early promotion to lieutenant colonel or a prompt command billet had it not been for the migration of so many field-grade officers to the MOBIC side.

He'd never considered such a move himself. Cavanaugh was all Army. As for religion, he went to Mass on most Sundays and checked that block. He believed that he believed in God, he had doubts about the Vatican, and he had meant his marriage vows to a wife who dumped him for one of his Leavenworth classmates who switched to the MOBIC side early on and got a double jump, from major to colonel. He hoped Mary Margaret was happy. And eating ground glass.

She'd blindsided him utterly. And Pat Cavanaugh was determined that no one would ever do that to him again.

His kids. With that shit-faced ass-kisser. And *his* wife.

Whenever he came up against the MOBIC types, they made him uneasy, as if he were being sold a thing it made no sense to buy. He had no patience with "car-lot religion," as his sergeant major put it. Maybe he wasn't a real believer, after all. He certainly wasn't one by MOBIC standards.

He'd thought seriously about killing the man who stole his wife.

What was left to believe in? Not "reclaiming the

Holy Land." He was here because he believed in the U.S. Army, which had never let him down. And he believed in Flintlock Harris. Who should have booted him out of the Army as a captain in Bremerhaven, back before it all went nuts. Instead, he'd gotten a glowing efficiency report and a private, undocumented counseling session that left him with invisible third-degree burns.

Cavanaugh's front boot reached the pebble-and-sand mix that passed for a beach. Just as he came alongside a burned-out Marine track, the alarm sounded.

Drone attack. He hadn't seen a single manned aircraft from either side, except for a couple of friendly helicopters risking low-level flights from ship to shore and back. But the drones ruled the skies.

He ran back toward his lined-up vehicles, unable to do one damned thing to help them except be with them. He watched machine guns swivel up, despite the risk that they'd draw kamikaze drones down on top of themselves. Then he saw the wave of drones break over the ridge, chased by angry surface fire and a few hapless ground-to-air missles.

Even as he ran, he could pick out the various shapes and sizes against the hard blue of the sky. All Chinese-built, bought in large quantities before that country slipped into turmoil. Less sophisticated, but sturdier and more dependable than anything his own military fielded, the unmanned aircraft were deadly. The informal motto he'd adopted for his battalion applied: "Fuck Finesse."

The escort drones came in high, with the hunter-killer drones behind and below, accompanied by a swarm of "expendables" programmed to detect ground fire and dive into it.

The Navy's robotic interceptors had been up much of the morning, covering the landing. But they were nowhere to be seen at the moment. And the Army's air-defense drones still didn't seem to be operational.

Soldiers who weren't manning weapons or buttoned up in armored vehicles ran for any cover they could find: ditches, overhangs, blasted buildings by the roadside. Cavanaugh heard the first explosions but kept on sprinting, weapon clutched in both hands, body armor lightened by the adrenaline rush.

Couldn't even let a man eat a fruit bar in peace.

The gunfire aimed skyward sounded like a full-scale battle. Which it was. Cavanaugh worried about the rounds falling back to earth. Multiple deployments to the Middle East had taught him the danger of that. The locals shot automatic weapons into the air as a substitute for getting laid. People died at random.

Whatever programs the Jihadi drones were running, they were shielded well enough to punch through all the jamming and erasure signals his own side was putting up. Manned aircraft had become as delicate as teacups, but hardened, mission-programmed drones had become the terror of the battlefield for both sides. The situation was especially tough on the Army, since its air defenses had been neglected for decades as the Air Force assured Congress it could sweep the skies.

We could use a little sweeping now, Cavanaugh thought, as the blasts at his back chased him.

"Spread out! Spread out, goddamn it!" The soldiers in the ditch didn't even look up at him. His men? He hoped not. Probably loggie strays.

The noise and shock wave from the next explosion clapped his ears and thumped his back. He turned to look. Couldn't help himself.

A drone had struck a Marine ammo load down the beach. A No. 4 GAB struggled desperately to reverse its engines as secondary explosions at the water line sent metal flying in every direction. There were only two kinds of human beings left alive on the beach: those who had already slapped themselves face-down on the earth, and those who were running as fast as they could go.

Overhead, dozens of drones swooped and curled in dogfights: The Navy interceptors were up again. A flaming drone fell seaward, exploding halfway to the surface. Cavanaugh wasn't sure which side it belonged to.

Nothing he could do about the duel in the sky. But the continuing explosions on the beach made him feel the weight of his gear again and the burden of too little sleep. He trotted on toward the line of his battalion's vehicles and saw Jake Walker and the sergeant major waving their arms, berserk with urgency, as they guided the ancient Bradleys off the road into a herringbone formation.

I should've done that, Cavanaugh thought. An hour ago. Jesus Christ. I am screwing this up worse than a lockjaw epidemic at a cocksucker's convention.

He banged on the side of the nearest Bradley, then smacked the driver's helmet to get his attention. Behind his goggles, the specialist's eyes looked paralyzed by shock.

First time under fire.

"Go! Go! *Go!*" Cavanaugh pointed to the left, into the bit of open space by the roadside.

After a five-second eternity, the driver jerked the big vehicle into motion. The engine was one of the new "miniaturized" power-packs, but the adjective exaggerated. The Bradley still snorted and belched like an angry bull.

The driver oversteered, and Cavanaugh had to leap out of the way. He moved on to the next track, but realized, on time-delay, that he had not heard any further explosions and that the ground fire had dwindled to intermittent bursts.

The attack was over. Cavanaugh looked back down along the beach. The ammo fire was still cooking, but the noise had fallen to popcorn level. Offshore, a GAB burned, flames toasting the sky. Small figures ran madly across the deck.

It wasn't one of his GABs. His battalion was still intact. Some other commander would report the loss and figure out how to reorganize his unit. Cavanaugh knew he shouldn't feel good on that count, since they were all in this together. But he *did* feel good. In a crummy sort of way he doubted he'd ever explain to another human being. Now that Mary Margaret had become the colonel's lady, instead of Rosie O'Grady.

The loss, the shock of betrayal, still had the power to twist his stomach after more than two years.

Betrayal. The most shit-rotten word in the English language.

He took off his helmet and ran a palm over the stubble that passed for hair. Combat trim. Like a worn-down toothbrush. Overhead, the sky was clean and clear and impossibly blue. Under other circumstances, he thought wryly, it might've been a nice day at the beach.

As he looked up the road that led onto Mt. Carmel, Cavanaugh saw vehicles inching forward.

All *right*, he thought. Let's move 'em out.

He turned back to the labor of command.

MT. CARMEL

Harris marched along the shaded path that traced the military crest. He still felt queasy from the helicopter's outlaw maneuvers on the flight up. To avoid any prowling drones, the pilot had taken them on a tree-clipping ride through a succession of ravines, popping over intervening ridges and dropping again until it seemed they'd smash into the boulders that flanked the seasonal streams. They had swooped over a site where a vehicle accident and the debris of an attack had blocked the road at a hairpin turn, holding up one of his brigades. There had been no spot level enough to set down the light helicopter, and Harris was glad of it now. He would only have been in the way. But it was hard not to go hands-on when you saw your war machines backed up all the way to the beachhead, burning fuel and serving as perfect targets.

One of his 155mm batteries fired from a meadow behind and below the path, close enough to send shock waves through the air. Sending the guns forward had been the right thing to do, even though it played hell with the landing schedule. But the First Infantry Division's entire chain of command would be cursing him for the foreseeable future.

He caught himself. There was no "foreseeable future." This was war.

When the firing paused, Harris turned to his companion and said, "All right, Monk. Good. But I'll feel a whole lot better when you tell me we've got an actual highway open. At the moment, I'm more worried about opening up additional MSRs than I am about the fighting. Get a reconaissance-in-force down toward Jenin as soon as it makes sense, and send a patrol down Highway 6. Your call on the size. See if they've really pulled back down there. If it's clear, set up a coordination point at Tulkarm. Tie in our flank with the MOBIC corps. In case we need to shift forces."

"I'm more worried about mines than Jihadis along 6. My intel shop puts their new defensive line halfway back to Nablus."

"Better ground. They're doing the smart thing. At this point."

The howitzers barked again, joined this time by other batteries scattered in the clearings amid the groves behind the ridge. It was a good sound, as were the distant thuds that followed fifteen to twenty seconds later. They were going after deep targets. Which meant that no local counterattacks had materialized.

"I never would've given up this ground so easily," Harris told the Marine two-star. They walked up through scents of pine and cedar, their security detachments prowling ahead and following behind, giving the two generals space for a private conversation.

"Well," Monk Morris said, with a tinge of irritation, "they didn't just hand it over. But I take your point. Not the sort of blunder I would've expected from al-Mahdi. Based on his track record. 'Conqueror of Jerusalem' and all that."

"That's the point," Harris said. "It's all about Jerusalem, al-Quds, at the moment. We're dinosaurs, the two of us. Thinking like old-fashioned military commanders. This is the age of the believers. Suleiman al-Mahdi may be smarter than Saladin when all other factors are equal. But they're *not* equal right now. He wants to hold onto Jerusalem, the third holy city of Islam. After all, this is the Emirate of al-Quds and Damaskus, not the Emirate of Haifa. He sees us as the secondary enemy, the new Lesser Satan. He knows he has to beat Sim Montfort and the MOBIC corps. That one's a zero-sum game. He figures he can take care of us later."

"So what does he do? Now? Up here?" Morris asked.

"You tell me, Monk." Harris shifted his body armor and felt the sweat-grease on his back. "If you were Sully al-Mahdi pulling out all the stops to hang onto Jerusalem and you didn't have the numbers you'd like to have . . . What would you do?"

"I've been wrestling with that since they started

pulling off the heights last night," the Marine said. "If I were al-Mahdi and running an economy-of-force operation up here, I'd concentrate on retaining control of the key interior roads. I'd tell al-Ghazi, the sector commander, to dig in deep and hard from Afula up through Nazareth, with a swinging-gate defense to the north, from Shefar'am back to Golani Junction."

"Bingo. He knows he's going to lose Megiddo Junction. He already has, for all intents and purposes, since he can't hold it. It's just a delaying action down there. Testing us." Harris pushed a low branch out of the way. "I agree with you, Monk. So does history. The junctions in the Jezreel have been strategically vital since the battles in the Old Testament."

"Probably longer."

Harris smiled. "Don't let Sim Monfort hear you say that."

The artillery let loose again. Which meant that the forward observers were calling in hard targets. If the fates were in a good mood, it might even mean that his recon drones were flying and linking back targets.

The growl of the heavy vehicles climbing the road below them deepened as the breeze shifted.

"I'm told you were at VMI with Montfort," Morris said. "All those secret handshakes. Any insights?"

"The noble and pious MOBIC corps commander . . ." A fly the size of a bomber brushed Harris's nose. He waved it away. Behind the scent of the evergreens, the odor of death teased. "Fact is, Sim's an extremely talented officer. Truly gifted. Always was. And he just may be the most ruthless human being I've ever met."

"I'd have to measure him against an old girlfriend or two," Morris, a lifelong bachelor, said.

"Well, Marines do have peculiar tastes. But don't ever sell Sim Montfort short. Behind all the Bible verses and the Crusader rhetoric, he's smarter than a billionaire televangelist cross-bred with an entire faculty of Jesuits. Write him off as a nut, and you'll get blindsided. And you won't get back up on your feet again."

"But *is* he nuts? I've known my share of men who were brilliant and utterly crazy at the same time. Not least, in this neck of the woods."

"I'd call him 'obsessive'."

"To the point of being nuts?"

"Monk, did anybody ever tell you that you even *look* like a bulldog? You make Chesty Puller look like a beauty queen. No, Montfort's not nuts. He can project a quality of madness. But you never know how much of it's calculated."

"Doesn't sound like much of a drinking buddy."

"He was a model cadet, Sim was. Monk, I realize you think *I'm* nuts for dragging you up here like this. When we've both got plenty to do. But our staffs can handle things for an hour. Commanders need to step back. Talk a bit. Catch their breath." He grunted. "If I wouldn't be setting a poor example, I'd take off this goddamned body armor."

The path steepened just as Harris finished speaking.

"Hell of a way to catch your breath," Monk said.

Then he grinned. "You did *not* just hear a Marine complain. It was your imagination. Anything else? On Montfort?"

Harris thought about the absent figure for a few steps. He didn't want to put devils in Monk's head. But he owed Monk honesty. As much as the moment would bear.

"Sim was one class behind me at VMI. By his second year, upperclassmen had learned to fear him, and even the faculty handled him carefully. Which didn't stop him from being elected to every office he wanted. Or from being the faculty's darling." Harris smiled, not fondly, at the memory. "Sim had one big advantage over the rest of us. We were teenagers, with all that goes with the package, barracks discipline or not. But Sim was born with the mind of a forty-year-old. From day one, he knew what he wanted and concentrated on getting it." Harris snorted. "It's probably an exaggeration to say he *never* let anything distract him from his goals. He was an infuriatingly handsome man. Women chased him from one end of the Shenandoah Valley to the other, then followed him back home at Christmas. We were all jealous as hell."

"That mean he took your girl?"

Harris laughed. "No woman on Earth could've been attracted to both Sim and me. That may have been the *only* thing that wasn't a point of contention."

The smell of death strengthened. Harris glimpsed a break in the trees. He could feel the high ground waiting.

"So . . . You'd categorize him as pure ambition?"

Harris smiled. "No ambition's pure, Monk. It's always muddled up with something."

"And that should tell me?"

"There's a kind of ambition . . . a form of ambition that needs something to believe in. It's incomplete, unfulfilled, without a cause." The corner of Harris's mouth twisted into his cheek. "I don't mean that Sim Montfort can't be cynical, when cynicism works. Just that he found his cause, and his cause found him. One feeds off the other, empowering the other. Men like Sim *need* a great cause to allow their ambition to unfold, to bloom. Their ambition has to have a rationale greater than themselves. And that doesn't mean that they don't truly believe in the cause they take up. The human capacity for belief is a very adaptable thing."

"Sounds almost like you respect him. Despite all his preaching and screeching."

Harris stopped and flashed a look of utter frankness. "No, Monk. I don't respect him. I fear him."

They walked on in silence, approaching the wall of light beyond the trees. The bodyguards on point fanned out more widely. You could feel their hyperalertness notch up yet another degree.

Monk Morris changed the subject. "Your G-2 sent my intel shop some interesting reports this morning. Haven't seen 'em. Just got a verbal. But I'd like to know what you make of it."

"About the refugees? The lack of them, I mean?"

"No sign of any heading out of Afula or Nazareth. Or leaving any other Arab towns."

"The local commanders are probably under orders not to let them leave. Civilians as hostages. The Jihadis have been doing that since you and I were kids playing Army."

"I played 'Marines'."

"Well, at least neither of us played Air Force. They're probably just trying to complicate our operations. Figuring we're still jumpy about dead civilians."

"*Those* days are gone. Good morning, L.A., good night, Las Vegas."

"It's like that defensive position at Megiddo. They're testing us. Seeing how far we'll go."

"I can understand that. But what about the reports of civilians being bussed *into* Nazareth? Seems like a lot of trouble to go to, when you've got military convoys to move over those roads."

"The reports might be wrong. Val Danczuk's relying on one special operator we've got in place up there. In Nazareth. The overheads don't necessarily corroborate his messages about bussing in civilians. Those buses could've been full of troops. But we're watching it." He smiled. Wryly. "Val's the most forward-leaning Two I've ever known. Problem is restraining him when he starts painting scenarios with invisible colors."

"Sir?"

"Monk, can't you call me 'Gary'? When we're not onstage?"

"Marine habit. And, to tell you the truth, you never struck me as a 'Gary'."

"It's the only name I've got."

"Except 'Flintlock'."

Harris shook his head. "Never cared for that one,

myself. Always sounded like a cartoon character to me."

They marched through the last stretch of shade, and Monk Morris changed the subject: "You didn't really mean that, did you? About being afraid of Sim Montfort?"

Harris stopped and looked into the other man's eyes. As deeply as he could.

"I meant it."

▪

The two generals stepped out of the trees into glaring light. Beyond an empty parking lot, a ruin crowned the mountaintop. Beside the ruin lay a pile of corpses. The bodies were naked. The stench announced that the dead had been rotting for days.

"Welcome to Mukhraka," Harris said.

Someone had taped out a perimeter around the ruins. Harris's lead bodyguard was deep in an argument with two men in Army uniforms.

Then Harris spotted the black crosses sewn onto the left breasts of the officers who were giving his point man a hard time.

"What the hell?" Harris said. He looked at Monk Morris.

"I have no idea," the Marine said. "We didn't have any MOBIC troops with us. Just the two liaisons at headquarters."

In the background, other soldiers wearing the MOBIC black cross puttered in the ruins.

Harris strode up to the scene of the argument. A MOBIC major, supported by a captain, waved a finger in the face of the Special Forces sergeant first class who was second-in-command of the general's personal security detachment.

"What's going on here?" Harris demanded.

Before his NCO could speak, the major turned on the general. "This is a Christian heritage site. It's been reclaimed. No one can enter without authorization."

"Do you know who I am?" Harris asked. In the quiet voice he used when truly angry.

"Yes, sir. You're Lieutenant General Harris."

"And who are *you*, Major?"

"Major Josiah Makepeace Brown, commander of Christian Heritage Advance Rescue Team 55."

"There are no CHARTs authorized in this corps sector at present."

"We have authorization orders from General Montfort."

"Lieutenant General Montfort does not command this corps. I believe you'll find him a couple of hours south of here."

To Harris's bewilderment, the major wasn't the least bit intimidated, but seemed to be talking down to him.

"You'll have to take this up with General Montfort, sir. We have our orders."

Harris was tempted to arrest the lot of them. He was angry enough. The team's presence was a violation of painstaking agreements and published orders. But you had to pick your battles. And Harris didn't believe for an instant that Montfort had slipped CHARTs into his area of operations just to preserve Biblical heritage. The atmosphere was paranoid enough to make him wonder if his old classmate were trying to draw him into an act that could later be used against him.

"Major," Harris said, trying a different approach, "we all have our missions. My mission is to defeat the Jihadi corps facing us. I'm sure you'll agree that the Jihadis are our mutual enemies. We've come up here to have a quick look at the terrain because we have to refine the next phase of our operation. Now, if you don't mind, we're going to spend about ten minutes up on that pile of bricks where the church used to be."

"This is the site," the major announced, "where God used the Prophet Elijah as his instrument to shame the priests of Ba'al and slay them."

"And we're trying to slay the Third Jihadi Corps. May we pass, Major?"

The major eyed them as if he were a drill sergeant examining two suspect recruits. "Are you both Christians?"

Again, Harris restrained himself. "Yes, Major. We're both Christians."

"Your bodyguards will have to remain outside the perimeter."

The SF sergeant jerked his head around. Harris made a sign for him to keep quiet.

"That's fine. Whose bodies are those?"

"The monks. They were living up here secretly, even after the forces of the Antichrist conquered this dwelling place of the Lord. The local infidels protected them. Probably for mammon. But a Judas betrayed them. We found them."

"Piled up like that?"

"No. Crucified."

■

Morris said, "I would've liked to knock that little prig's teeth down his throat."

"Not worth it, Monk. Pick your battles. That CHART's bait. Although I'm not quite sure what Sim Montfort's fishing for. But look at this."

They had picked their way past the toppled statue of Elijah and climbed as high as they could on the remains of a staircase hugging a scorched wall. Harris truly didn't intend to stay long. The Jihadis would have observers watching the site from across the valley—they would've been crazy not to keep an eye on such a vantage point. And Harris didn't intend to become anyone's free target.

But he had needed to see this. And he wanted Monk Morris to see it, too. The splendor of the Jezreel Valley.

"Well, fuck me," the Marine said, with a short, sharp whistle. "Nuclear war, rampage, and neglect," Monk said, "and it is *still* one beautiful place."

"Always has been," Harris said. "God knows, it shouldn't be. So much blood has been spilled down there for so many centuries that the whole place ought to sink under the weight of all the death."

"Well," the Marine said, "we'll see how much more weight we can add."

And yet, the scene before them was strangely un-warlike. Despite the thousands of military vehicles dug in or creeping about and the distant eruptions of smoke, a stillness wrapped the mountaintop, a sense of standing briefly apart from time. The artillery fire and the complaints of hundreds of gear boxes shifting on mountain roads might have been echoes from a parallel world.

"You know, Monk, I've never believed that God cared about dirt, that He valued one patch of soil more than another. Years back, when I was a lieutenant, I read an article that said America was blessed because God didn't lay claim to any real estate in our country. I always thought that was true, that we were lucky to be free of the need to tie God down to some patch of dust like Gulliver." He looked away from the splendor before him, lowering his eyes to the rubble. "Now here we are."

"People are always going to find something to fight over, sir. That's why we've both got jobs. If it isn't about the name you give God, it's about what you called their sister."

"But 'Holy War,' Monk? I can't think of a greater contradiction in terms." He raised his eyes again and saw the glory of the sun upon the valley. The earth gleamed in the April light, and the puffs of smoke where artillery struck in the distance seemed no more than small, low clouds. He hated the thought that his country had sent him and his soldiers to fight here.

The seductive landscape spread before him was nothing but one mass grave.

"All right," Harris said, turning to business. He stretched out his right hand to orient his companion. "The glimmer at the end of the valley's Afula. The sprawl up on those hills to the left is Nazareth, although the old town sits down in a bowl. The gumdrop shape straight on is Mt. Tabor. Just out of sight, you have the Jordan Valley to the right and the Sea of Galilee—Lake Kinneret, if you prefer—to the left. The line of mountains in the distance is Gilead. Where I am told there is no balm."

Morris looked at him with narrowed eyes. "You've been here before?"

"We all have," Harris said.

FOUR

· · · · ■ · · · · · · · · ■ · · · · ·

NARAZETH

Lost souls, they stumbled from the buses. In the distance, the sounds of war throbbed, an irregular heartbeat. The men, most of middle age, appeared bewildered, gripping suitcases or dabbing the sweat from their foreheads with fouled handkerchiefs. Their women struggled down the steps behind them, clinging to possessions gathered in haste. A few of the women led children into the chaos, but most had long since passed the fertile years. Those children who had been dragged along wept or shrank into silence. Young or old, everyone looked soiled and worn. And they stank. The buses did not stop for human needs.

Major Michael Nasr watched the human parasites surge past the guards and swarm the new arrivals. Offering food, drink, or a place to sleep. At prices that would break a rich man in a week. There were no tourists in Nazareth now, and none had come for years, but the touts hadn't lost their persistence. They set upon the refugees like fleas.

Refugees? What could you really call them? Nasr wondered. Men and women forced from their homes by their own kind, driven toward a war rather than away from it. He tried to piece the logic of it together. Obviously, there was a purpose to the actions of the Jihadis. But the purpose wasn't obvious to him.

Lifting his robe as he stepped through filth, Nasr noticed the old man again. Not a refugee, but a local. The shriveled character with the goat's beard had popped up repeatedly to scrutinize him, then disappear again. Nasr didn't know what that might be about, but it worried him. His Arabic had been learned at home, in a Christian émigré family in Sacramento, and his father's Lebanese accent came as easily to him as his mother's born-in-Nazareth dialect. He understood the dress, the body language, the insider rules. He'd fooled the officials and the mullahs, and the only problem with his Arabic was that it was too grammatical for the identity he'd chosen.

Had something given him away? A word? A gesture?

If so, the cavalry wasn't going to ride to the rescue. A U.S. Army Special Forces major detailed to a black program, Nasr was on his own. In Indian country.

He smiled at the utterly American phrase. He never felt more American than when he was thrust into the world that had forced his parents to flee. For the crime of being Christians. And yet, the Muslim role came to him easily. As if you inherited knowledge of your enemies.

Well, he was just glad that his parents had found the get-up-and-go to get up and go. Anyone who criticized the United States of America needed to get a good whiff of the Middle East.

The old man was up to something. But then, everybody between Casablanca and Karachi was up to something. Everybody had an angle. Every seven-year-old worked a grift.

Nasr caught himself before he shrugged. He had almost moved his shoulders like a Westerner. Instead, he waved the world away with a dismissive hand. And he entered the crowd, slipping past a policeman who wore his beret straight up from his scalp, like a mushroom cap.

An unshaven man in an old tweed jacket grasped Nasr by the arm.

"Please," he said, "please . . . Can *you* help me?"

"What do you need, brother?" Nasr asked him.

"My wife . . . she's . . . we need . . ."

A volley of artillery rounds struck beyond one of the city's ridges. Closer than the other fires had come. The refugee clinging to Nasr's forearm flinched, almost dropping to his knees.

"Why have they brought us here? Why? Do you know?"

"Where are you from, brother?"

"Why do they bring us here? This is *fitna*. Madness. I'm a professor. Of physics. My wife is a teacher. What do we have to do with their war?"

"Where is your home, brother? Where did they take you from?"

A woman in the crowd began to scream.

"From Homs. From the university. Why bring us

such a long way? Why bring us here? We'll all be killed. Can you help us?"

"We must pray to Allah," Nasr said, "and trust in His beneficence."

The professor looked at him scornfully. Letting go of his forearm. "You're one of *them*? You *believe* that nonsense? After all the world has seen? There is no god . . . none . . ."

"There is no god but God," Nasr corrected him. "And Mohammed is his Prophet. *Insh'Allah*, all will be well with you, brother."

"You," the professor said in a spiteful rage, "it's dogs like you who've done this."

Before turning away, Nasr told the professor, "Get away from this place. Or they'll steal what little you have left. Take your wife and go to the farthest neighborhood your feet can find. Nothing is left down here."

But the professor wasn't listening. Fury had blocked his ears.

"Dogs like you have done this," he repeated.

"And hold your tongue, brother," Nasr warned him. "Not all Nazarenes are as patient with blasphemers as I am."

He scanned the shabby crowd but couldn't spot the old man who'd been trailing him. Pushing on toward the buses, Nasr let himself take in a dozen conversations: pleas, complaints, threats, and furious bargaining, all of it reeking with the stench of shit and fear. Some of the refugees had been brought from as far away as Halab, ancient Aleppo, in northern Syria. And Nasr thought he heard Iraqi accents. *Educated* accents, all of them.

Why on earth drive your intelligentsia—or what passed for one—into the path of an invading army?

Did the Jihadis want them to be killed?

Nasr stopped. Just below the derelict patch where the Church of the Annunciation had stood. His body felt sheathed in ice.

Was that it? Did the Jihadis *want* them to be killed?

Nasr had been inserted weeks before the invasion began, but the influx of refugees had begun just two days before a bombardment announced the landings. The Jihadis had known an attack was coming, of course, if not just when and where.

What else had they known?

Major Nasr sat on a broken wall. A half-block from one of Christendom's holy places—now a ruin used as a public latrine. He wasn't a party to the detailed plan of invasion, but he knew this much: Even Flintlock Harris wouldn't have the pull to bypass Nazareth. Whatever else the corps commander's plan of operations might avoid, the early seizure of Nazareth would be non-negotiable. The vice president, the SecDef, and the MOBIC generals back in the Pentagon would make sure of that.

And the Jihadis were smart enough to figure that one out. Every Christian site would be an objective. Nazareth would be high on the list.

Then why dump their brainpower in the path of the infidel?

Were the Jihadis really so intent on turning back the clock by centuries that they wanted their professors and doctors and scientists exterminated? If so, why not do it themselves? Why go to so much trouble? When they had a war to fight?

Of course, Hitler had made time for a similar distraction. When he had a war to fight.

Nasr knew he was on to something big. But he didn't know what it was.

There *had* to be more to it.

He needed to get back to his transmitter. If the damned thing was working. Sometimes the burst transmissions got through, sometimes they didn't. But he was anxious to send off another report and hand off what he'd seen and heard. Let the brainiacs on the staff figure out what it meant.

Insh'Allah.

Just as Nasr placed his hands on his knees to lever himself to his feet, he saw the old man again. Pointing at him. A half-dozen Arab policemen accompanied him.

There was no point in running. The only hope was to bluff.

"I tell you, he is a spy, that one!" the old man cried.

Nasr felt his guts churn. But he kept his face under control, letting innocent bafflement spread across his features.

The police surrounded him. Artillery fire landed a valley away, but it wasn't going to help him.

Nasr touched his hand to his robe, just above his heart. "How can I help you, my brothers?"

A policeman wearing a captain's pips struck him with his fist. Nasr staggered. The next blow put him on the ground.

"That man is a Christian," the old bastard said. "He's of the Gemalia. They're all gone from Nazareth now, Allah be praised. But this one has returned. I will always recognize a Gemalia pig. I knew him by his nose."

"We'll take care of his nose," the captain said. And he kicked Nasr in the face.

MT. CARMEL RIDGES

Sergeant Garcia listened to the battle down in the plain. Somebody was serious about busting caps on the Jihadis. Garcia would've liked to be in on it.

Con mucho gusto.

He didn't quite trust the way he felt as he marched down the winding road that led off the heights. He'd had an hour or so of pretend sleep, and he knew he was wasted. But he felt like Superman. No meth involved. Just a buzz he couldn't quite figure out.

Garcia looked behind him to make sure his Marines were maintaining a combat interval as they marched along the shoulders of the road. The Army's tanks and shit were hogging the blacktop as they rushed into the fight. Well, let them take their turn.

A Bradley tore into the pavement as it downshifted, throwing off bits of the surface and groaning like a constipated dinosaur. Up from La Brea, Garcia thought. The Dino Gang.

He replayed the scene in the house again and again: the grenades and the gunfire, the rush, and the dead Jihadis. And he just felt *good*. All that crap about how you were supposed to feel bad after killing people. Who made that shit up? Bigger lies than Maria Escobar told in the confessional. To that priest she was hot for. For the priest and everybody else.

Maybe he'd feel bad about it all later. Maybe all the guilt would kick in, the way they said it did. But for now, he just felt like the *conquistadores* must've felt.

It was like sex, man. You just wanted to do it again.

Did that mean he was all dicked up inside? Because all he wanted to do was kill the fuckers who made L.A. glow like a year-round Christmas decoration? And his family so hot with radioactivity you could've used them to cook enchiladas in Ensenada. Watching them blotch up, go bald, get skinny, and die. And his mother worrying about *him* all the time she was dying.

When the captain had come down to ask if the platoon needed to be pulled off the line for a day or two, Garcia had looked at him in shock, then fear, then suck-on-this annoyance. All in the space of ten seconds.

"Naw, sir. We're, like, just getting into the motion, you know? We're cruising."

"Your Marines okay? You sure?"

His Marines.

"Hey, sir. They're Marines. They're good to go."

"The platoon's at sixty-five percent."

Garcia stared at the other man. At this man who threatened to take away his platoon. Who wouldn't say shit when battalion sent down some hotshot to take over. Staff Sergeant McCullough, maybe. Or some gunny who wanted to play lieutenant for a week.

"They're feeling a hundred percent, sir," Garcia told him. "We just need an ammo drop."

He knew he wasn't speaking for every one of his Marines. Some of them wanted to move out and mix it up, while others would've been glad for any excuse to go below decks and sleep until it was all over. But this was what they'd signed up for. He wasn't going to let anybody just walk. They had *business* to do.

It was screwy, but he felt two ways at once. Since the fight in the village the night before, he felt closer to his Marines than ever before. And he felt apart from them, too. Separate. In a new way.

Down in the valley, some tanks were duking it out. The 155s were dropping closer in now. Garcia couldn't see the fight as he walked, but smoke rose and thinned, veiling the horizon. His back hurt pretty bad. But you just kept on humping. His elbow was half-fucked, too. It didn't matter. He felt like calling cadence, like singing out. *Un poco loco.*

> *Hey, ma, I wanna go,*
> *Right back to Quantico . . .*

Well, the platoon was too spread out to hear him. With the big boys clanking in between them. He called cadence to himself, anyway.

A wave of tiredness hit him, almost stopping him cold. Then the buzz came back. Just like that. But his damned back hurt. Too loaded down. Lugging all your stuff around, like some homeless bum back on the block. He looked, enviously for once, at the Army grunts riding by, sticking up through the hatches like Mexican kids standing behind the cab of a pickup.

Same exhaust stink, too.

Garcia just didn't want to come out of this with any kind of injury that would put him out of the Corps. Instinctively, he lifted his forearm to kiss the

Virgin of Guadalupe tattoo underneath his sleeve. But he caught himself. And just made like he was wiping the sweat from his face and resetting his helmet. Dying would be okay. He could handle that. He had what the skinny redhead instructor bitch at the community college called "Latin fatalism." Like the name of some perfume you paid five bucks for off a street vendor. To give to some *chica* so new to the hood she still thought in pesos and didn't know perfumes were all about serious labels.

Yeah, Latin fatalism. Splash it on me, dude. Just don't let me end up a geek crapping himself in a VA hospital.

He knew now that he didn't ever want to leave the Corps. Since the nukes came down, the Corps was his only home. He sure wasn't going to take off his boots for very long down at his grandmother's. If anybody else wanted to be a full-time Mexican for a living, let them. He was an Angeleno. Even without his city.

And he was a Marine.

He saw the firelit face of the Jihadi he'd shot. Clear as any photograph. Clearer. And he just wanted to pull the trigger again.

Garcia wondered if he was some kind of psycho. Were you *supposed* to get this buzzed?

Hand signals relayed back from the head of the column. Take ten. Garcia passed it on. But he didn't want to stop. He was exhausted. Beat. But he didn't want to stop.

He walked back to check on each of his Marines and told Barrett to change his socks. Barrett got blisters just looking at a combat boot. And Garcia made sure everybody had water.

Dodging back between two Abrams tanks that would've qualified for antique-vehicle plates, Garcia dropped to the ground. And as soon as his ass hit the grass, he knew he'd made a mistake. The weariness came over him like a drug. First, he'd been riding the cosmic meth; now, the downers had him.

He made himself breathe deeply. And got just fumes. The column of vehicles had come to a halt. A tank idled in front of him.

The crew had given the big boy a name, painted down the gun tube: "Compton's Revenge."

Garcia looked up at the turret. The tank commander was a black dude. Couldn't see his rank. But he looked right off the block.

Probably a lieutenant, Garcia figured. The Army didn't have standards like the Marines.

Garcia threw the TC a home-boy sign. Just to check him out.

The TC hesitated. Then he grinned big and threw it back.

Garcia smiled and nodded. They understood each other. Let bygones be bygones. Compton, Watts, they were all gone now.

Garcia gestured toward the fighting below and signed again: *We're going to give them a fucking they'll remember.*

The TC signed back: *Righteous.*

The column of vehicles began to move again. The Marines up ahead rose from their spots by the roadside, rolling to their feet, top-heavy, readjusting packs and straps before gripping their rifles at the ready again.

There was no alarm, no warning. Nobody heard

the drones coming in. Until they shrieked as they plunged into the column. Garcia watched the tank with the TC from Compton get hit and explode.

Two Bradleys got it farther down the slope. A burning soldier leapt from one, then fell. Marines rushed to roll him over. But he was a crisp.

The Army didn't screw around. Say that for them. They pushed the burning vehicles out of the way and kept on moving.

All in all, Garcia decided he'd rather walk.

OFFSHORE

"For God's sake, Avi," Harris said, "you'll get your chance." He snorted to himself. "You're going to get more chances than you want."

"I still protest. As commander of the 10th Israeli Armored Brigade, I had the right to lead the first assault."

Harris had to discipline himself. He needed sleep, and his temper was on a short fuse.

"That's bullshit, and you know it. We needed an infantry-heavy force to get up on the heights. Tanks wouldn't have gotten off the beach. The road wouldn't—"

"And now? My brigade is still in your ships. And the battle has moved into the Jezreel."

"First of all, they're not my goddamned ships. Second, you know you're scheduled to go ashore tonight. There'll be plenty of Jihadis left for you and your men. What's this really about, Avi?"

"I protest." The brigadier from the Israeli Exile

Force pointed at the letter he had laid on Harris's desk. "My brigade had a moral and military right to take precedence. We've been treated with prejudice."

"Jesus Christ," Harris said, instantly wishing he'd chosen different words, "your brigade would've been shot to bits going up that single goddamned road. The operation would've been a disaster. And I would've been accused of using your brigade as cannon fodder. Along with sixteen kinds of anti-Semitism. And you damned well know it. Now, to hell with rank. Man to man, I want you to tell me what this is all about."

"You have my letter."

Harris picked up the letter and crumpled it, then pitched it toward a wastebasket. He missed. The uneven ball meandered across the deck.

"Go back to your ship. Just get your brigade ready to go ashore. You're going to get all the fighting you want. And if you deviate one inch from your written orders, I'll relieve you and distribute your battalions among the 1st ID's brigades. You understand me?"

Avi Dorn saluted, turned, and marched out of the compartment.

When the hatch had closed behind the Israeli exile, Harris dropped into a chair. What in the name of God was *that* all about?

He took a long drink of bottled water, then went to check on his staff's preparations to move operations to a command post ashore.

▪

As he was ferried back toward his transport ship, Brigadier Avi Dorn closed his eyes. Shutting out the day and his personal history and the memory of his ruined nation. He just thought about Harris. With regret.

He liked Harris and respected him. And he knew that every word the general had spoken was true. But if the rebirth of Israel meant sacrificing one American general, it would not be the first sacrifice. Nor, Dorn thought, the last.

A renegade spray of salt water slapped his cheek. He opened his eyes again.

Just let them wait until the fighting's done, Dorn thought. He wanted Harris calling the shots until the shooting stopped.

NAZARETH

All he could taste was blood.

Teeth could be replaced, Major Nasr told himself. He'd lost a canine on the upper left and two teeth below it. A couple of others were loose. But he'd had loose teeth before. He tried to keep his tongue from testing them.

And noses could be fixed. He knew that from experience. Which is why it was bullshit that anyone could recognize him by the nose that ran in his mother's family. Anyway, he'd had his father's nose. Broken twice—once playing football in high school and once in Nigeria, in the most desperate brawl of his life. He still had please-wake-me-up-now dreams about that one.

Ribs, too. Just tape 'em up. As long as your lungs weren't punctured.

Don't think like that, he told himself. Don't start thinking like that.

His balls hurt, too. And they'd beat him until his bowels gave out. Which, he figured, just made him stink like their entire goddamned city.

"Holy Nazareth." Personally, he would've been glad to let the Jihadis have it. Even Jesus had packed up and left as soon as he cleared the back orders at the carpentry shop.

The police team came back in. One of them turned Nasr over with his boot. Shining a heavy flashlight in his face. Nasr had gotten intimately familiar with that flashlight.

What surprised him was how crude they were. He would've expected more sophisticated forms of torture. But his captors were content just to beat the hell out of him.

"Who are you?" the officer with the deeper voice asked. For the hundredth time.

"My name is Gemal. I come from Sidon. I was only looking for work. In the lands Allah has given back to his people."

The boot tip found a soft spot in Nasr's back. And it went in hard. Twice.

Kidneys were not so easy to fix as noses.

"You shit-eating dog. Are you laughing at us? You think we don't know who you are? You piece of filth."

"Allah knows the truth of what I say. I swear—"

The boot went into his ribs. More blood came up. Nasr gagged, choked, finally spit out the clot. Or whatever had come loose.

"You're a Christian spy. We know this. Speak the truth. Maybe we'll let you live."

"Brothers . . . My name is Gemal. I come from Sidon. I—"

A fist rebroke his nose, smashing the back of his head into the concrete. Nasr didn't want to go out. To lose consciousness was to lose control.

He almost laughed. At himself. As if he were in control.

"You understand," the deep-voiced officer said, "that we're only preparing you. The men who will question you seriously are on their way. Better to tell us the truth. What they do to a man isn't decent."

The other laughed. "And what they'll do to a Christian . . . I don't like to think of such things . . ."

"Get him up," Deep Voice commanded.

Through the ringing and hammering inside his skull, Nasr heard a door open. Or thought he did. Then he dreamed that an overhead light went on and several figures stood over him.

"You asses," a new voice said. "Who gave you permission to do this? To an innocent man?"

Deep Voice tried to stutter out an answer. Shocked. Or just confused.

Through one badly swollen eyelid, Nasr thought he saw one man strike another.

"I should do the same thing done to *you*," the new voice said. Then, in a tone of still greater disgust, he told the others, "Bring him out. And bring a doctor."

Nasr was utterly confused. Were they speaking about him? Was there another captive in the room?

Heavy arms lifted him to his feet. But he couldn't stand.

"Hold on to him," the new voice commanded. "Or I'll have the flesh stripped from your bodies and fed to your children."

Out in the corridor, as they dragged him along, Nasr was able to make out a few things. White walls. Daylight through smudged windows. A scarred floor. And the old man who had been his accuser. He was being dragged in the opposite direction.

The old man was slopped with blood, and he whimpered. His nose had been cut off. It made him sound like a cartoon character.

FIVE

. . . . ■ . . . . ■ . . . . . ■ . . . .

OFFSHORE

"Our Air Force brethren claim it's suicide," Harris said. Behind him, soldiers packed up the last odds and ends required to stand up the corps forward command post on solid ground.

"Well," Andretti, the G-3, said, "the Marines are willing to give it a try. They think they can put in one wave of deep air strikes behind EW drones and count on local surprise. Since nobody's flying on either side."

"Except the damned UAVs."

The operations officer shook his head. "I'd trade every missile system we've got for a platoon of those old Vulcans, sir. Or Navy chain guns."

"So which targets does Monk Morris rate as important enough to risk a chunk of his air group?"

"I've got them on a map."

A specialist carrying a display screen bumped the general from behind and excused himself.

"Just talk me through the missions."

Colonel Andretti nodded. "First, he wants to use 2,000-pound bombs and fuel-air explosives on the Umm el Fahm pass. Before the lead Marine battalion gets there—and they're on the way. General Morris believes that, given the no-fly environment, he really can take the Jihadis by surprise."

"Serious defense down there? Or just a blocking position?"

"The latter. Big one, though. General Morris thinks it could get messy. He doesn't want to risk unnecessary blue casualties."

"That pass is heavily built-up. Locals still there?"

"Morris's Two thinks they've headed for the hills."

"Even if most of them bailed, we'll still have some civilians hunkered down in their homes. Human nature."

"Want me to red-light the mission, sir?"

Harris chewed on it. For about fifteen seconds. "No. If Monk thinks it's worth risking his pilots plus noncombatant casualties to get that pass open, I'll defer to his judgment. Next target?"

"Assembly area outside of Jenin. We have imagery and SF HUMINT on that one. Big target. And clean."

"Cluster bombs?"

"Mixed ordnance."

"How many aircraft? Jenin's getting deep."

"Four on Jenin. Two on Umm el Fahm."

"Let's hope they hit. There isn't going to be a second chance. Last mission?"

"That's our request. Since they're determined to fly. Recce over the Afula defenses. One aircraft."

"Downlink working? Can it cut through all the soup?"

"We won't really know until the mission's in the air. Doubt the WSO will go hot until he's on final approach."

"Hate to lose aircrew if we can't even get the feed."

"We can always download the images once they get back to Cyprus."

"*If* they get back to Cyprus. Mike, you realize what's at stake, right?"

"Yes, sir. Fourteen Marine aviators. And seven jets."

Harris folded his arms across his chest. "What's at stake, Mike, is the future use of air in this campaign. If Monk Morris's boys go down in flames, I won't get one damned Air Force mission this side of Iceland."

"And if they make it back to base? You'll have a club to beat the zoomies with, sir."

Harris shook his head. "I don't want to beat up the Air Force. I just want them to help us beat our enemies." He grunted. "All right. We're wasting time. Tell them they've got the green light from corps. For all three missions. And God help them."

THE SKY

Dawg Daniels flew low over the water. Jovial with his subordinates on the ground, the group commander was solemn now. This mission would decide whether he and his men sat out the rest of the war. And Dawg Daniels did not intend to spend his days getting a tan on a beach in Cyprus.

He knew he shouldn't be flying the mission himself. But none of them knew what was waiting for them—how quickly the radars would pick them up, despite the jamming, whether enemy drones would be flying CAP and waiting for them, how thick the air defenses on the ground would be . . . or even if the Jihadis' jammers would screw up their electronics so badly that the patched-with-Band-Aids F/A-18Ds would fall out of the sky.

On the other hand, Daniels was glad to have the F/A-18s, rather than the F-35s that had been taken from them to build out the MOBIC air arm. The F-35s were unable to stay in the air in the hyperemissions environment of the war, where artificial electromagnetic pulses were the least of any digital system's problems.

You didn't look down when you were this low. That was the one guaranteed way to go nose in the water. You just monitored the altitude number on the upper right of your helmet display and watched the horizon. Hoping your electronics maintained their integrity and didn't take you diving for mermaids.

He prayed that all seven aircraft would make it to their targets but figured it was too much to ask that all seven would make it back to Cyprus.

His group's informal motto was "Semper Fly." He'd taken a lot of razzing about it when the Air Force pushed through the order to ground all manned aircraft "until the threat environment clarified." If the blue-suiters didn't want to go downtown, fine. But Dawg Daniels believed that Marines should make decisions for Marines.

Now he was out to prove that manned airpower

was still a player. That pilots were still in the game. And he hoped he wasn't wasting his Marines' lives.

Don't think like that, he told himself. *Just fly.*

And God, he loved to fly.

Despite the presence of his weapons systems officer in the dual cockpit, Dawg felt peculiarly alone. No intercom chatter permitted until they were on the target run. And no radio transmissions at any time. The only exception was if an aircraft was going down. The codeword for that was "Mudpie."

Dawg's initial impulse had been to ask for volunteers. But he decided that was the weak man's way out of the moral dilemma the mission posed. So he just selected the pilots he thought would get the job done. Rank immaterial. If feelings were hurt, so be it. At least those with hurt feelings would be alive for evening chow.

▪

Major Robert "Jinx" Jenks saw the cliffs coming toward him. Fast. Five hundred knots of fast. After glancing at his helmet display, he judged his designation and rolled right, hoping his wingman, a mile back and echelon right, was banking just as hard. Screaming over the sunlit waves, Jenks flew as low as he could without dipping his wings, hugging the radar shadow of the ridges. Punching it as if he intended to slam into the rank of cliffs at a forty-five-degree angle.

A lone aircraft shot north. One gleaming speck. Heading for the Haifa Gap.

Dawg Daniels. Good luck and good hunting.

Hold on, Jenks thought. One hundred percent certain that Shimmy was sweating blood in the back seat.

Jenks pulled the old bird right as hard as he could, feeling every seam in the fuselage complain. In a flash, he registered hundreds of vehicles on the strip of beach below. He was flying sideways, fighting to pull his aircraft away from the cliffs. Which were reaching out to grab him.

As he leveled out, tear-off-the-shingles low and heading south, Jenks gave his wings a quick wag.

Next stop, crispy critters for Allah.

■

The men on the beach nearly opened fire. Wary of yet another drone attack. When they realized—a thousand men at once—that two USMC F/A-18s were shrieking overhead, a cheer went up that shook the Land of the Scriptures.

■

Lieutenant Colonel William "The Willies" Morrison turned his four strikers back out to sea. Just far enough to bank again and go straight in, self-escorted, guiding off the ruins of Hadera and the broken chimneys of his number-one marker, the wrecked power plant on the coast. Ahead and to his left, he saw Jenks and his wingman scream up Highway 65.

This was old-school flying to Morrison, and he simultneously reveled in it and worried that, without all the magic guidance gear, they'd miss the target. Forbidden even to use the intercom until he had visual, he had to hope that he got where he was supposed to go and that Banger would pick up the target and put the ordnance where it belonged.

The mountains of the West Bank came up fast, a perfect match to the briefing imagery. The problem was what waited beyond the ridges.

The formation he had chosen was unorthodox. Any student who proposed it would've flunked out of Yuma, and no O-6 Marine aviator besides Dawg Daniels would've gone for it. But Dawg, bless him, just cared about accomplishing the mission. If a Pickett's Charge of F/A-18s on line was the only hope of putting steel on target and then getting out of Dodge, Dawg was ready to fly top-cover with the chain of command.

Morrison considered himself the least-sentimental commander in the group. But when he thought of Dawg Daniels heading deep in a lone aircraft, his eyes almost teared up.

■

Jenks said a quick prayer and shot toward the pass, hoping his attack run would be a surprise for the other guy, not for him and his wingman. Unable to look down at his knee board and hoping he remembered every detail of the Z diagram for the mission, he switched from air-to-air to air-to-ground mode.

He got his azimuth steering line on the long black snake of the road. Coming in at 300 feet, the earth a rush and a blur.

Time to fly. Four miles out, he popped to just over 4,000 feet, banking to offset 30 degrees and give himself and Shimmy a few seconds to acquire the target.

There it was, right where it was supposed to be. A very busy defensive layout centered on the pass.

"Target captured," Shimmy said over the intercom.

Jenks put the target below his nose and lined up the diamond, waiting to reach his release altitude as he descended. He hoped his Dash-2, "Sticks" McCready, was maintaining his interval and not tempted to go down the same chute in this closed terrain. Plenty of bad guys. There was going to be a nasty frag pattern, too.

Jenks felt the lift as the bombs dropped from the wings. Hoping Shimmy could keep the laser on track. Doing it the old-fashioned way. GPS guidance was the stuff of fairy tales now.

"Chicken's in the pot," Shimmy told him over the intercom. "Take us home, stick monkey."

Forty seconds after his pop, Jenks was out of the target area.

"*Mudpie!*" A single cry, then nothing else. Lowell MacCready's voice.

"Shimmy? Visual?"

There was a pause. It seemed to last for minutes. The reality was less than five seconds.

"Into the mountain. No chutes."

Fuck. *Fuck.* All right. Nothing to be done. Stay calm. Take it home.

But he thought, for one flashing instant, of Lowell MacCready's wife. With whom he'd slept back at Cherry Point.

Now Sticks was dead.

The terrain was broken, and it was difficult to stay down tight on the deck as he pulled north, then headed west again. Had to hug the approved egress route, stay out of the artillery fan.

Jenks realized that he was drenched in sweat. His flight suit felt as if he'd put it on straight from the washing machine. Sweat stung his eyes, as well.

So much for central air, he told himself. Then he saw the glittering sea ahead.

■

Monk Morris wondered if he'd been a fool. Too macho. Too damned pigheaded to be trusted with the lives of United States Marines. Green-lighting those air attacks. Maybe the Air Force knew what it was doing, after all.

He ached for news. He knew that, in the great scheme of the war, seven aircraft didn't amount to much. But two Marines who counted on him flew inside each one of them. And Dawg Daniels would've put his best men in the seats.

Dawg was a can-do Marine. Monk Morris saw himself the same way. Maybe it was a poor combination, he thought. Maybe, at this level, you needed somebody sensible enough to put on the brakes.

He stepped back inside his forward command post and asked, in a voice not quite so firm as he wanted it to be, "Any word on those air missions?"

■

Dawg Daniels left the nuclear ruins of Haifa behind, burning sky through the gap and bursting into the Jezreel Valley. So green it hurt the eyes. With clouds of artillery smoke thinning as they rose and spread into the atmosphere.

Big sky, little bullet. He hoped. He'd insisted that the artillery missions continue during his run, figuring that a cessation would alert the Jihadis that something was up. Only the defenses around Afula would be spared. Long enough for him to get clean imagery.

More rounds impacting at two o'clock. Somebody was getting a serious clobbering. Dawg didn't like the idea of taking shrapnel from a Marine 155.

Well, you pays your money, and you takes your chance, he told himself.

He gave the old aircraft every last bit of juice, popping to 4,800 feet AGL. If the bad guys were going to get him, it was going to be now. While he was riding high enough to get the panoramic imagery that corps wanted.

In planning the mission, he'd rationalized the risk in terms of how many lives good intelligence could save in the coming assault on Afula; he figured an attack on the crossroads town was inevitable. But now he was flying on nerves, not reason, and living second to second. Hoping the pod cameras worked. And that the downlink functioned. And that his WSO wasn't asleep at the wheel.

The aircraft roared over Afula and banked north. That quick. Pulling so many G's that Dawg imagined rivets flying off the fuselage like popcorn. He dropped to 500 feet, as low as he could go in the broken terrain. With hills coming up fast, he pulled the aircraft up to 800, then 900.

Getting too old for this, he told himself. But in truth, he felt magnificently alive.

The plan was to leave the downlink—an uplink,

really—turned on until they'd cleared Nazareth on the way out. Then no more emissions until they were wheels-down.

Mount Tabor on the right. Gotcha. Here we go. Hold on, ladies and gentlemen.

"One more flyboy visits Nazareth," Dawg told an invisible audience.

The city sprawled out of a deep bowl, covering the surrounding hillsides with shabby high-rises and haphazard slums.

Every caution light in the cockpit seemed to go off at once. Dawg punched out the flares and switched on the active countermeasures. Nothing else to be done. They had him. It was going to be all-emissions, all-the-time now. And some wicked metal.

An explosion rocked the aircraft.

They were still flying.

Come on, baby. Gimme some juice. Let's go, sweetheart.

Whoomf.

The aircraft shook as if a furious giant had crunched it in his fist and meant to shake out any loose change.

His helmet display died.

Just fly, he told himself. *Just fly.*

Had to get more altitude. Take that risk. Or he was going to plow a field for Farmer John. Dawg could see the Haifa Gap and, as he climbed, he glimpsed the sea beyond. But he was speeding down a broken road on four flat tires.

The aircraft began to go to bits around him.

Not going to make it, ladies and gents.

He pulled back on the stick until it refused to go any further, altering course to head straight for the

Carmel Ridges. Struggling to hold the aircraft together for just a few more seconds. Through sheer willpower. And praying the ejection mechanism was still in working order.

As Dawg pulled high, he imagined his wings coming off. Or maybe it wasn't his imagination. He tried to level off to eject. But the aircraft was unstable, uncontrollable now, gimp-twitching.

"Eject, eject, eject!" he called over the intercom. Unsure if he was speaking to a living human being.

He punched out. It felt like going through an automobile windshield at a thousand miles an hour. Yank on the neck. His shoulder took a whack.

A reassuring jerk told him his chute had opened.

HEADQUARTERS, THIRD JIHADI CORPS, QUNEITRA

"The Americans are attacking! With aircraft. They're everywhere!"

Lieutenant General Abdul al-Ghazi remained calm. Someone had to remain calm. The excitability of his staff filled him with a cold, white anger. Would Arabs never learn discipline?

"With *manned* aircraft, you mean?"

"Yes, yes! Everywhere at once."

"Then they're fools. Shoot them down."

"We *are* shooting them. Everywhere! Dozens of them. It was only that we were surprised."

"Then we've been surprised twice in three days. When will we stop being surprised?"

The chief of staff calmed down. Slightly. *"Insh'Allah,* we soon will drive them back into the sea."

"But first you will shoot their aircraft from the sky—am I correct?"

"Insh'Allah."

"Allah expects us to help. Go back and learn what is truly happening. Their aircraft are not 'everywhere.' Are they here, then? Why do I not hear their bombs?"

"I mean to say . . . that they are attacking at many places. Not everywhere."

"Find out *exactly* where. And if you are told that any of their aircraft have been shot down, you will confirm it. I want no more panic. Men with weak nerves are no use to me."

"Yes, my brother. I only meant—"

"I am not your brother. I'm your commanding officer. If you cannot do your job, another can."

"Yes, General."

"Now leave me."

When he was alone again, Abdul al-Ghazi, the sector commander, thought of two things. First, he thought that he would have very little time to redeem the general situation before the rage of his own superior, Emir-General al-Mahdi, fell upon him. Second, he wondered if the reports that the Crusaders had already reached the suburbs of Jerusalem were true. If that were so, al-Mahdi's anger might be uncontrollable.

Al-Ghazi prided himself on being a professional soldier, trained in the old Jordanian fashion, as well as being a soldier of jihad. And al-Mahdi worried him. Clearly, Allah had touched al-Mahdi with a kind of genius. But al-Mahdi had been touched with madness, too. He could not escape the thrall of the past, and he saw everything through the lens of history, as if there could never be anything new in war or this war-torn landscape. Al-Mahdi's plan of defense had been built upon bleeding the Americans, on the assumption that they would not bear great casualties. But all the reports from the Jerusalem front told of masses of dead and of relentless attacks over corpses.

Was this to be the end of civilization? With the Crusaders returned to rule with fire and sword?

The incompetence in his own ranks outraged him. And he couldn't fully trust al-Mahdi's judgment. Hadn't any of them learned that the way to fight Westerners wasn't by fighting in the Western way? Despite his formal training, al-Ghazi had little faith in mechanized infantry battalions and tank brigades, in the end. You had to strike the Crusaders where they were weak, not where they were strong.

Still, he was a soldier. He would carry out the mission he had been given. He would make the Crusaders pay a terrible price for staining the soil of the emirate with their boots.

But a part of him asked again: Was this to be the end of civilization? One of the orders given to him bit into his blood like a viper. Would nothing be left for which praise might be offered to Allah? Would the Crusaders destroy everything?

Lieutenant General Abdul al-Ghazi did not mean to let that happen. No matter what strange measures might be required.

He pushed an old-fashioned button on his desk. A moment later, an aide-de-camp appeared.

"Go," al-Ghazi told him, "but go quietly, and learn if my instructions have been carried out regarding the American taken in Nazareth."

ASSEMBLY AREA, 77TH MUJAHEDDIN ARMORED BRIGADE

The explosions in the Jenin assembly area continued for an hour after the last of the Crusader planes had departed. No one had been prepared, too much had been done in haste. Stocks of ammunition rent the earth and tore the sky as they exploded. Vehicles burned, and men burned as well. A blackened man with no arms ran about madly, white teeth gleaming where his lips had been, until he dropped over dead.

"We have been betrayed," Colonel al-Masri told his deputy. It was the only idea that came to him. Saying it aloud made him feel better.

MONTEZUMA FIELD, CYPRUS

A lone F/A-18 landed on the strip at the old British airfield on Cyprus. And then there was nothing.

Major Jenks climbed out of his cockpit, followed by his weapons systems officer. Down on the apron, the two of them just bent over, hands on their knees. As if about to vomit.

One aircraft out of seven. Lieutenant Colonel Randall "Wicked" Wilkes, the group's XO, decided, with galling bitterness, that the blue-suiters had been right. It was impossible to send manned aircraft into that electronic stew.

Wilkes watched as Jenks sat down on the tarmac and buried his face in his hands. The XO decided to give him one more minute, after which he would tell him to get up, grow up, and act like a Marine.

One crew out of seven. Jenks was a lucky bastard. Him and his goddamned buddy on the self-pity express.

Then a miracle occurred. Four dots appeared in the heavens. Moments later, four F/A-18s flew over the airfield in perfect formation, taking a victory lap. They disappeared, reappeared, and came down one after the other, clean as if they were landing at an airshow.

"Get on the link to General Morris," the XO shouted. Then he lowered his voice again. But he couldn't stop smiling. "If we're up secure, tell him we've got five crews back out of seven. We're in business!"

Now if only Dawg Daniels would show his ugly mug.

MT. CARMEL RIDGES

"Welcome to the 1st Battalion, 18th Infantry, Colonel. Glad y'all could drop in."

The young officer's face was streaked with camouflage paint that sweat and wear had smeared. He nonetheless qualified as one of the top five most-beautiful human beings Dawg Daniels had ever seen—and the only male on the list.

"We picked up your buddy, too," the lieutenant continued. "He broke his leg."

"Well, we're not supposed to lose our jets."

"Yes, sir . . . Sir, if you don't mind me saying . . . y'all flying like that . . . I mean, God bless you."

Daniels took a deep, wonderful, glorious, gorgeous breath. "We Marines have never been accused of an excess of intelligence," he said. "I'd be grateful for a drink of water, if the Army has any to spare."

SIX

· · · · ■ · · · · · · · ■ · · · · · ■ · · · ·

NAZARETH

Every living thing got out of his way. Nasr limped
and staggered up the lanes of Nazareth, dried blood
lurid on his clothing. His face was so swollen it limited his field of vision. The people he encountered
stared at him for an alarmed instant, then quickly
looked to the side and veered from his path. Only the
children, silent under the sound of the distant guns,
kept their eyes on him: the bogeyman.

Yet, more than a few of the local children were
little bogeymen, deformed by radiation in the womb.
During the Great Jihad, Nazareth had lain within the
fallout zones of Haifa to the West and Zefat to the
north.

Nasr was in no condition to feel much sympathy.
He kept thinking of the old Army expression, "a world
of hurt," repeating it to himself almost hypnotically.
Although he'd taken a round in the hip in Nigeria,
the only part of his body Nasr had worried about in
the past had been his knees, which had gone a few

hundred jumps beyond their warranty. Now everything seemed to hurt. His testicles ached so badly that he imagined himself walking like a sailor in an old cartoon. His ribs punished him with every breath. Back and front, right and left, everything seemed to be broken. Pains flashed through his abdomen, as regular as warning beacons. His head was the least of it. That was just a matter of weird vagueness, as if a few inches of the air around his skull had become a no-man's-land.

The doctor had pawed his ribs and shrugged. They might as well have called a cleaning woman, because just about all the doc did—if he actually was a doctor—had been to clean up his face a bit, splint two broken fingers together with all the skill of a Cub Scout, then offer him a glass of orange juice. When Nasr tried to drink it, the acid burned his smashed-up lips and the inside of his mouth like liquid fire. He spit up blood.

Another miracle of modern medicine. Avicenna, call home.

"I'm going to make it," Nasr told himself as he climbed a narrow alley that reeked of cooking grease and urine. "I'm going to fucking make it. Been through worse than this."

But that was a lie. He'd never been through worse. And he wasn't going to make it.

They *knew* who he was. That one single thing was clear to him. He'd imagined that he was the Invisible Man, Mr. Cultural Affinity, blending in seamlessly. Pride of Man, he told himself, oh, pride of Man. He'd been a horse's ass. They *all* knew who he was.

As he watched, a bearded man grabbed a falafel

sandwich from a boy—who fought to get it back as the thief danced about to avoid his victim's hands, all the while stuffing the food into his maw.

No one interfered. Everyone was afraid. Weary. Famished. In despair.

Welcome to the club, Nasr thought.

He'd never believed that despair was in him. But he had a full-blown case now. He veered between disgust at himself and troughs of indulgence when he tried to catalog his damaged parts. For the first time in his life, he slipped into self-pity. And he hated himself for it.

Nasr stumbled, but righted himself. A bout of dizziness stopped him for a moment, and then he trudged on. Not certain he was doing the right thing. But unable to think of anything else.

They *knew*. His first impulse had been to avoid returning to the closet of a room he'd rented on the western ridge. But that was stupid. If they knew all the rest, they certainly knew where he was bunking. And the transmitter wasn't there, anyway.

He climbed a few more steps, through a played-out avalanche of garbage, and stopped again. There was no obvious alpha pain. Everything hurt. The doc had given him a small handful of pills. For the pain, he said. But Nasr feared taking them. He had to stay clear. As clear as possible. To think.

It hurt to breathe. But when he tried to fuel himself with shallow breaths, the dizziness threatened to drop him. And he couldn't halt the flashes of remembrance, the vivid recollection of a fist coming down into his face or the precise feel—the instant replay—of a boot going into his ribs.

"You're getting soft, Ranger," he told himself. "Never make it through Dahlonega. Forget that SF tab, sissy-boy. You'd wash out of the Q Course in a week."

Sarcasm didn't give him the boost he needed.

What the hell did you do when you knew—when you *knew*—that they were only waiting for you to make your transmission before they killed you?

They'd never spare him. That was clear. They didn't have it in them to let him off with a beating.

Did they know he knew?

Now *that* was a question requiring a bottle of single malt.

Nasr began to walk again, imagining himself marching, but aware that his every movement was a mockery of his past being. Pride of Man, pride of Man . . .

Who wanted what? That was the thing he needed to figure out. The old man hadn't recognized him on his own. He'd been put up to it. But by whom? Where did one scheme end and another plot begin? The old man had threatened to spoil the game that was going so well for the rival team—the team that wanted Nasr to keep on transmitting as the American forces approached. At least one more time.

Had the security boys who beat him up been in on either deal? Or were they just stupid Arab cops doing what they did best?

When the badge-flashers in clean khakis dragged him out and pushed his parts back together, their head honcho had been all too profuse in his apologies and his insistence that a mistake had been made, that everyone was sorry. Arabs were *never* sorry for violence. Nasr knew that. He was one of them. Christian or not.

"Get over that self-hatred thing, bro," his best friend had warned him years before. Nasr had thought it was a nutty thing to say. But he got the point now.

Didn't listen. Didn't take his vitamins. Bad, bad boy. Had to be the number-one grad in every Army school. Just to prove . . . what, exactly? That a Maronite Christian could do more pushups than Presbyterians?

So they wanted him to transmit. But what did they need him to say? The only news from the Nazareth home team was that educated refugees were being bussed in and dumped. Thousands of them. Bad Guys X wanted him dead right now, but Bad Guys Y wanted him to tell mama first.

He stopped again and shook his head. Instinctively. As if the act would clear his thoughts.

All it did was hurt his neck.

Ain't no lucky lady going to share my Arabian nights for a while, Nasr told himself. No, sirree. Mr. Pulp Face. And check those teeth. *Bad* dentistry.

What was his duty? To transmit. Were they capable of monitoring and breaking the transmissions? The techies said no way. But what were the techies going to say? They believed in technology the way the MOBIC pukes believed that Jesus was God's Little Gangster.

When I get a three-day pass, I'm gonna kick old Jody's ass.

Or maybe not. Not going to kick anybody's ass. Not now. Maybe never again.

Self-pity stinks. Got it, sir. But dying hadn't been

a near-term goal. Even Fayetteville was looking good now. Unlike his enemies, Nasr didn't regard death as a promotion. He'd dutifully attended St. Michael's and St. George's right through high school. For his mother's sake. But he hadn't exactly come to terms with the afterlife. SF studs didn't get killed. They did the killing.

The artillery fire swelled again, landing several clicks away. Echoing through the urban canyons. His team wasn't shelling the city. Just kicking up dirt around it. Because we're the good guys. Nice to everybody. You betcha.

He thought of the struggle his father had endured the year before to prove that, although Arabs, his family had always been Christians. Since time immemorial, sir. Since that dude fell off his horse on the way to Damascus.

Christian Arabs didn't have to go into the Providential Communities in Utah and Nevada that the government had established for Muslims, citizens or not, after the Jihadis popped nukes in L.A. and Las Vegas. But it was up to you to produce the paperwork.

Nasr saw his father, sitting on the goddamned couch, the previously undisputed tyrant of the family, with tears rolling down his cheeks, telling his newly promoted-to-major son, "I tell them, I say to them that my son is an officer in the United States Army, that he is in the specialty forces with the green beret. But they only try to trick me with questions about the Book of Revelation. They are men of tricks, like the devil."

And Nasr had set out, yet again, to prove that he

was not only as good an American as anybody else, but a braver and better one.

Well, not much longer. Fucking Jihadis. They'd gotten what they wanted. The new crowd in Washington just didn't get it. All the Jihadis cared about, when it came to Muslim emigres, was preventing them from assimilating into Western societies: better dead than freely wed. In the post-nuke panic, his government had done the Jihadis' work for them. Weren't going to be any mixed marriages now.

What did it matter? The world was going to shit. Nasr figured it was some old blood instinct telling him that the killing had barely started.

He marched uphill, going like a crippled old man pretending to be a soldier. He intended to allow himself thirty minutes. No more. Thirty mikes. To sit down. And calm down. Then he would go straight to the transmitter. And do his duty.

If he truly was a Christian, Nasr considered, Nazareth wouldn't be such a bad place to die.

He stopped. An emaciated cat took one look at him and scrammed. Nasr laughed out loud. It hurt. Awfully. But he couldn't stop laughing.

A good place to die? Nazareth was a fucking pit. No wonder even Golgotha looked better to Jesus.

He hardly noticed that his laughter had faded into tears. Yeah, a world of hurt.

Just as Nasr moved to put one foot in front of the other, to march, he heard a sudden noise that didn't fit. Followed by answering noises.

Bending his entire torso, Nasr looked up. Just in time to see a lone U.S. jet racing westward. Gunfire, missiles and, doubtless, every djinn in the Middle

East chased after it. Before disappearing over the ridge, the aircraft jerked as if hit. But it kept on going.

They were flying. His guys. Americans. It seemed unreasonably important to him, as if the jet had been on a mission just to do a fly-by for his benefit.

Nasr swelled with pride.

OFFSHORE

"Talk to me," Lieutenant General Harris said.

There were only four officers left in the ship's secure compartment: Harris, his G-2 and G-3, Colonels Val Danczuk and Mike Andretti, and the general's aide, Major John Willing. Beyond the sealed hatch, only three others in the entire corps were cleared for access to STARK YANKEE products, the counterintelligence operation the U.S. Army had opened against the Military Order of the Brothers in Christ.

Even seated, the G-2 was the tallest of the four. Every chair seemed a throne to him.

"Sir, it's just remarkable," Danczuk said. The eagerness in his voice was almost juvenile, utterly at odds with the dignified look of the man. "Even the reports coming through standard channels have MOBIC elements fighting in the outskirts of Jerusalem. Lieutenant General of the Order Montfort's lost most of a division killed or wounded. But they just keep on attacking."

Harris shook his head in disgust. And not just at the sour smell of the compartment. "The Jihadis are getting a taste of what it's like to be on the receiving end of fanaticism. It's plain as day where al-Mahdi called it wrong: He didn't take Sim Montfort's speech-ifying seriously. Just the way we refused to listen to what the Islamists said thirty years ago. And al-Mahdi counted on Americans being stingy with their blood." The general readjusted his posture in his chair, trying to soothe a back getting worse with the years. "I suspect al-Mahdi's in shock at the moment. But he'll recover. And then Sim's going to have a real fight on his hands. What else?"

Danczuk dropped his eyes, and the enthusiasm drained from his voice. "Sir . . . We're getting a lot of reports of atrocities . . . pretty ugly stuff."

"Which side?"

"Both. But mostly the MOBIC forces. A lot of it's unconfirmed . . . but it sounds as though a lot of ci-vilians are being killed."

"Not just collateral damage?"

"No, sir."

Harris moved as if to slam his hand down on the table but restrained himself before he'd gotten a third of the way through the motion.

"Sim Montfort doesn't *want* peace. That's the god-damned thing. Old Sim really is on a crusade. And it isn't going to make any part of this easier." He turned to Andretti. "Mike, I don't want RUMINT taking over. No copycat behavior. You make it damned clear through ops channels that we're here to fight armed enemies, not civilians. I don't want any contagion. There's not going to be any killing for Jesus in this sector."

"Got it, sir."

Harris turned back to the G-2. "And the answer to my standard question, Deuce?"

"You mean nukes, sir?"

"Nukes."

"Sir, we still have no indicators for the presence of nuclear weapons. Nothing. No probable hide sites. No special security. No support vehicles . . ."

Harris smiled. Glancing at the other three men. "I know you all think I'm off the reservation on this one. But I just have a gut feeling that there's a few stray nukes out there. And not just tactical nukes, either. So pander to the old man's obsession."

He looked back toward the G-2. "Keep watching it for me, Val. Take it seriously. Okay? All right, then. Let's talk STARK YANKEE. What hasn't made the evening news?"

Danczuk glanced around as though a spy might've slipped into the room while they were speaking. "Sir . . . General Montfort doesn't seem to worry much about blue casualties, but he's extremely worried about equipment readiness. The breakdown rate is high and—"

"How high?"

"Sir, I don't know. Not exactly."

"Find out."

"Yes, sir. The worst problems are with the MO-BIC's armored systems, the NexGen tanks and infantry fighting vehicles. Basically, everything heavily digitized, anything that came out of the Future Combat Systems initiative over the last twenty years, is next to worthless in this environment. The digital shielding fails. The comms just melt down. And the electronic armor's a joke."

Harris had practiced control of his temper for decades. So he managed to keep his voice level, although its tone wasn't kind. "Well, isn't that grand. Those sonsofbitches pulled every lever in the United States Government to draw all of the latest combat equipment from the Army and Marine inventories. Left us with the shit that should've been retired after we left Iraq, for God's sake. And now who's fucked for breakfast?"

"Sir . . . My point is that, if the breakdown rate's as bad as it sounds . . ."

"They're going to need gear. And it's going to have to come from somewhere. And we're 'somewhere.' Got it, Val. When their new toys break, they're going to want the old ones they tossed our way."

"Yes, sir."

Harris looked toward the G-3 again. "Mike . . . You see my point? As to why it's essential to grab Afula as swiftly as we can? I don't want to throw away lives. But we can't waste time. We've got to keep hitting the Jihadis while they're still reeling. I need the Dragon Brigade to winkle out the last buggers dug in around Megiddo tonight."

"1-18 Infantry has the mission, sir. Good unit. They'll do the job."

"*Tonight,* Mike. Come first light, I don't want one more antitank missile hissing down toward that crossroads."

"Yes, sir."

"Okay," Harris continued. "That imagery the Marines downlinked makes Afula look tough. We'd all rather bypass it and come in from behind. Nobody's crazy about doing a Charge of the Light Brigade down the Jezreel, with the Jihadis up on those heights around Nazareth. But we don't have the time. And the

Afula defense is just mobile systems for the meantime. They haven't had time to prep the ground, to really dig in. They weren't expecting customers that far back in the shop, so we're facing a hasty defense with some pretty good anti-armor equipment. But I don't see any serious revetments or any concrete being poured."

"Sir . . . I understand the mission. But you saw the imagery. It's like they've gathered up every antitank system in their inventory. And then you've got the killer-drone problem."

"Understood, Mike."

"And you saw the Deuce's spreadsheet on the EM spectrum."

The G-2 leapt back in. "Sir, when we plot all the jamming and counterjamming, wideband, pinpoint, you name it, and then layer on the digital predators and spoofers . . . The spreadsheet's almost all black."

"It cuts both ways," Harris said. "If we can't talk or bring precision fires to bear, neither can they."

"They'll be defending. And they've got first-rate loophole technology on their antitank systems. Any gaps in our jamming or spoofing, and that's all she wrote."

"Mike, we've been through it. The mission stands. 1 ID gets all the supporting fire the corps can bring to bear."

"Afula may still have a lot of civilians down in the cellars," the G-2 said. "It looked like the Jihadis are forcing the locals to remain in place in the major population centers."

"Got it. And I'm not looking for a bloodbath. That's

Sim Montfort's line of work. But we can't worry about collateral damage on this one. A quick win will save plenty of lives later. Afula's the key to everything else—I'm not sending anybody through those high-radiation valleys to the north if there's any way to avoid it. And if the Jihadis are going to fight from towns—well, that's a course of action they've forced on us. Just give General Scott everything he wants. But, Mike," Harris said to his operations officer, "before we get off this tub, make double-ass sure your people understand that the FRAGO goes out to the Big Red One by 1700, with the completed operations order to General Scott not later than 2100. Scottie's going to need all the time we can give him to pull this together. To say nothing of the brigade and battalion staffs."

Harris swept his forefinger across his nose, back and forth, once. "They're still trying to get themselves unscrewed after getting ashore. I'd hate to be a battalion S-4 or BMO out there tonight. And Three? Chop Avi Dorn's brigade to the Big Red One for this operation. Avi's bitching about not getting into the fight. Tell General Scott to get Avi's ass in it." He thought for a moment. "But not as the main attack. Supporting attack or just a demonstration to the north. Avi's not going to have a lot of time on the ground to get organized. And we're not going to be accused of using the Israelis as cannon fodder."

"Tempting, though," the G-3 said.

"Mike . . . I don't ever want to hear you say anything like that again."

"Yes, sir."

Harris shook his head. "I *hate* this. Every action

we take . . . we have to weigh the politics of it. Why go to Afula before those battalions even know what continent they're on? Because if we don't, not only do the Jihadis dig in and make it tougher—our MO-BIC friends get on the first open link back to Washington and start wailing, 'We took Jerusalem, and the Army and Marines haven't done a damned thing . . . Give us their equipment now, and we'll do the rest.' I mean, Christ. I was talking to the commander of Quarter Cav yesterday, before he went ashore. He's got M-1 hulls that date back almost fifty years. Past a certain point, all the upgrades just don't help anymore. And the MOBIC boys, having utterly miscalled it by grabbing the hot, new gear only to find out it isn't worth a monkey's nuts, are going to go into gimme mode. The whole business makes me sick." He sat back.

The G-2 looked at him, then looked at each of the others. "Sir . . . You know it's more than that. More than just the equipment, I mean."

Harris waved a paw at the problem. "I know, Val. I know. Look, this is a shitty war. There's nothing between here and the Himalayas that's worth a single American soldier's life to me." It was his turn to inspect the other faces in turn. "But we're not fighting for all this crap about taking back the Holy Land. We're fighting to save the United States Army. And the Marine Corps, for that matter. We're all that stands between God's little fascists and control of our country." He swiveled toward his aide. "John, what's the exact wording of the oath they take?"

The aide, whose purpose it was to sit, listen, and have things ready before the general knew he wanted them, leaned toward the table. "The part about 'allegiance to the Military Order of the Brothers in Christ in service to the United States of America,' sir?"

Harris cocked his fingers like a pistol. "Bingo. You all got that, gentlemen? *We* pledge ourselves 'to support and defend the *Constitution* of the United States.' They pledge to the MOBIC 'in service' to the United States. The dumbest lawyer in Lubbock could drive a herd of longhorns through that one. Call me paranoid, but I believe that Sim Montfort and his crowd see us as every bit as much their enemies as the Jihadis are. They're just taking on their enemies in order."

"Yes, sir. That's why we're working ‚STARK YANKEE."

"And I wish the hell we didn't have to. Disgusts me. Everybody spying on everybody. It just goddamned makes me sick. That we've all come to this."

The G-3 said, "Well, the Jihadis—"

"Mike, that's just an excuse. We've done this to ourselves. And I don't know how we're all going to get through it."

"By supporting and defending the Constitution of the United States," the G-3 said.

"Until they change the Constitution. Which they mean to do. Or maybe they'll just manage to change our oath. Listen up, all of you. The Army and Marines have to come out of this looking pure, efficient, effective, and indispensible. Maybe it's just wishful thinking, but my gut instincts tell me that Sim Montfort's going to make a big mistake at some point. And we're going to save the day when he does. Go Army, and Semper Fi."

The G-3 smiled. "The 'fog of war' might have something to say about that, sir."

"To hell with the fog of war. War's clear. It's peace that's foggy. And one more thing, Mike. Before I get back to Val and we wrap things up: Make sure the MPs understand that their number-one mission is protecting the landlines we lay. We haven't seen a flurry of roadside bombs yet. Largely due to the element of surprise, I suspect. But, frankly, I'm not that worried about their stay-behinds planting shaped charges and the like. Oh, it'll happen. But I want the MPs focused on preserving our communications. The Jihadis are smart enough to realize that our wires and cables are more important to us than a handful of vehicles. And—just by the way—I'd be wary of booby traps if I were an MP inspecting a break in a fiber-optic line. Did they get all their Signal Corps attachments, by the way?"

"Yes, sir. The MPs are fully task-organized."

"Okay, Mike. Val, you're on again. Talk to me. Anything new from your man in Nazareth?"

"No, sir. I would've reported it to you. Nothing since last night. I was expecting an update today, but his channel's been quiet."

"One brave sonofabitch. Not a job I'd want. SF?"

"Yes, sir. And a Foreign Area Officer."

"Well, let's hope we get to pin a medal on him. While he's still breathing. But listen up. If his reporting's accurate . . . if they're pushing refugees *into* Nazareth from the rear area . . . there's obviously a purpose. Only the purpose isn't obvious. What do you think, Two?"

"Sir . . . I can't be sure. It strikes me that they may

be planning to hold on to the city by generating images of suffering refugees . . . getting the world involved. We've got the media ban in effect on our side—except for the MOBIC-approved correspondents—but the Jihadis have been working the media for fifty years. And the world media love them. When L.A. and Vegas went down, a couple million people may have died, but a thousand journalists made their bones off the hysteria. And you saw how quickly they bought into the idea that we'd nuked our own cities."

"It wouldn't have surprised me if Sim Montfort and his crowd *had* nuked Las Vegas. 'Sin City' and all that." Harris smiled. "I didn't say that, of course. All right. So what indicators should we be watching, Val? In addition to anything we hear from your man in the sacred carpentry shop?"

"I'd watch the rations, sir. We should be seeing supply trucks going in with those buses. If they mean to feed those refugees and not just stage-manage a humanitarian disaster."

"Three? Any ideas?"

"Val may be right. Or they may be planning to just kill them—and blame us. Humanitarian disaster, plus. Great images for America-haters everywhere."

Harris turned to his aide, something he found himself doing more often these days. Probably the damned loneliness, he told himself. The only human being he could really talk to was his wife. And she was far away and a low priority on the comms account.

"John, how about you? Any ideas why they'd be packing Nazareth with their brethren from deep in the heart of wherever?"

The aide chose his words carefully. As he always did. "Well, sir . . . while you all were talking . . . I was thinking, 'What if the Jihadis want *us* to kill them? What if they're counting on it?' I mean, Colonel Danczuk's source said he thought they were all from the Arab intelligentsia. What if the Jihadis want us to solve a problem for them?"

Harris's eyebrows tightened toward his nose. Which happened only on the rare occasions when he was truly surprised.

The aide slipped back in his chair, as if retreating. "Just a thought, sir."

TACTICAL COMMAND POST, 1-18 INFANTRY, WESTERN APPROACHES TO THE JEZREEL VALLEY

Lieutenant Colonel Pat Cavanaugh was tired of sitting on his ass trying to make sense of broken transmissions while two of his companies were in the fight, another was getting ready to go in, and a fourth was licking its wounds.

"Give me a yell if anything comes in," he told his operations officer. And he stepped outside his command track. The enlisted men assigned to the battalion's tactical command post had almost finished erecting the ghost netting over the vehicles. Cavanaugh pitched in. It wasn't the kind of work a battalion commander was supposed to do, but he needed to use his muscles. Just for a few minutes.

The Jihadis were recovering from their initial surprise. He could feel it. No matter what the S-2 said. Despite the artillery barrage from Hell, antitank snipers were still popping up around Megiddo, appearing amid the rubble just long enough to launch a vampire ATGM and keep the highway intersection closed. Alpha Company had taken a nasty hit when it went in too fast, and now Jake Walker and Charlie Company had the lead, with Bravo in support. Trying to root out the Jihadi "martyrs," so the corps could move forward.

Jake had been the big surprise of the day. Cavanaugh had worried about him back on the beach, when the captain seemed all nerves. But as soon as they came under fire, Jake Walker had turned into the alpha dog among the company commanders. Now Cavanaugh worried that the captain would employ Charlie Company too aggressively.

And Cavanaugh didn't want any unnecessary losses. The battalion was already down three M-1s, four Bradleys, and a half-dozen support vehicles, just from drone attacks and the Megiddo sniping. And those were just the combat losses. Maintenance problems had caused vehicles to grind to a halt in the middle of an attack. They were just too damned old.

He had to remind himself, yet again, that he was the battalion commander, not a company commander. His instinct was to go forward and take charge of the direct-fire fight. But he wasn't going to let himself do that.

Anyway, he was going to give Charlie and Bravo another hour to clean out the Megiddo rubble. Then maybe . . .

A V-hull carrier pulled off the trail just short of the tac's perimeter. Cavanaugh went on with his work, walking a pole up to a steep angle as a buck sergeant made sure the netting didn't bunch. Cavanaugh was anxious to get the netting plugged into the generator so it could go "full ghost" overhead. They'd already had to jump once, after a Jihadi artillery barrage came danger-close.

Had to clear Megiddo. Before the Jihadis really got their shit together. But there was no easy tactical solution. At least, none that wouldn't be a bloody mess.

From the corner of his eye, Cavanaugh glimpsed two figures walking from the V-hull toward the tac. Behind them, a squad of soldiers dismounted and spread out in a tactical array.

Only when one of the approaching figures took off his helmet did Cavanaugh recognize the brigade chaplain.

The other officer was the brigade engineer.

Odd pair, Cavanaugh thought. He stopped fussing with the camouflage net. He couldn't imagine what Father Powers was up to. But he felt a stab of deep pain the instant he recognized him.

The priest made him think of Mary Margaret. His wife who was no longer his wife. Except in the eyes of the Church. And his own.

He'd gone to the chaplain to talk when, after so many months, Mary Margaret would not leave his thoughts. Her and the kids. And the fuck-stick, double-promotion, live-in boyfriend the law said was her husband now. After crying his eyes out in front of the priest, Cavanaugh had been so embarrassed that he hadn't been back to Mass for three months.

Surely, it wasn't about that? Not now?

When the two men were within conversational

distance, Cavanaugh said, "Put your helmet on, Chaplain."

The chaplain smiled, but did as ordered. "I understand that war's a horrible thing, Colonel Cavanaugh. But I don't know why it has to be so damned uncomfortable. Got a minute?"

Cavanaugh looked at the priest, then at the engineer, and back to the priest. "Sure. What can I do for you, Father?"

They stood in softening light, with the slanted rays of the sun gilding the dust that floated around them.

"Well, actually, sir, the visit's about what Jerry here and I might do for you. I was listening in on the situation reports back at brigade, and as best I could make out, you're having trouble with hunter-killer teams up on Megiddo."

"That's right," Cavanaugh said. Hoping that the chaplain wasn't going to lecture him about violating a holy site. "They're all over the place. We take out one team, and another pops up."

"Do you have a tourist guidebook, sir?"

Cavanaugh always felt a bit odd when the chaplain called him "sir." But the chaplain was only a major. When he wasn't in front of an altar or in a confessional, Father Powers observed all gradations of rank.

"No," Cavanaugh said, baffled. "I didn't bring a guidebook."

"Well, if you had—if you'd brought yourself a good one—you'd know what I saw myself during a pilgrimage I made before the world went mad. There's an ancient tunnel that runs under the tel to a water source.

It's deep. Well, it struck me that any imagery of the rubble might make the entrance appear to be just another shell crater. If a big one. And the lower exit's hidden. You'd have to be looking for it *and* know what you're looking for."

"And you think these antitank teams and the snipers are sneaking in and out of that tunnel?"

"That I do, sir. It's deep enough to withstand quite a bombardment."

Cavanaugh was excited. "Father Powers, I wish to hell you were my S-2."

"Well, perhaps not 'to hell,' sir. As I was saying, then: Major Sparks here has brought you his best sapper team—since none of his fine robots seem to be working—and enough explosives to blow shut any tunnel in the world. He thought his team might—"

"Just hang on. Hang on a minute. Let's look at a map. Nate," he called to his S-3. "Come over here."

When the operations officer didn't hear him, Cavanaugh waved his hand. Frantically. That got the ops officer moving.

"Map!" he yelled. "And the recon photos."

The chaplain looked at Cavanaugh. "And with your permission, sir—given that I'm the only one of us who's actually been to the place—I thought I'd tag along. After all, it's my job to help our soldiers find the way."

Cavanaugh's first impulse was to say "Absolutely not." But it occurred to him that, apart from possibly incurring the brigade commander's wrath, there was no practical reason why the chaplain shouldn't go. Just might save a number of lives to have him along, given that he'd actually been on the ground.

"Well, the Lord works in mysterious ways," Cavanaugh said.

"That He does, Colonel. That He does. Now, I've briefed Jerry here about the ins and outs, literally speaking. He can explain things to Major Gascoigne. And I'd appreciate a private word with you."

Cavanaugh didn't have time for private words. Not now. With so much to do, now that he had an idea what he was doing. But he felt he couldn't deny the chaplain's request. Given the gift the man had delivered.

Grudgingly, Cavanaugh nodded toward a grove that had been designated as a sleeping area. Soldiers were stringing concertina wire just out of grenade range.

"Pat," Father Powers said, changing his tone and even his posture, "I've been thinking about our last conversation."

"I've been meaning to come to Mass, but—"

"This isn't about attending Mass. Now, would you just listen to me?"

"Yes, Father."

"You told me that you'd never marry again."

"I can't. Can I? In the eyes of the Church—"

"Pat, it's in times such as these that a man thinks hard about his beliefs. If he's any kind of man and any kind of believer. Yes, in the eyes of the Church, Mary Margaret's still your wife, will be, and shall be. But you know, I begin to suspect that the eyes of the Church and the eyes of God may not always see identical visions." He gestured toward the sounds of war beyond their little sphere. "In the middle of all this, we have to remember that we serve a loving, forgiving Savior. Christ's mercy is endless. Pat, you've got to let go of her. She's not coming back to you, and not all the cardinals in the Vatican can bring her back. Live your life, be a good man. And if you meet the right lady . . . Well, trust your conscience, and don't hide behind doctrine. Cowards do that. Trust me, I know. And you're no coward. Well, that's all I had to say, then. We'd best go back and serve the God of Battles."

As they walked back toward the command post, Cavanaugh said, "And you really don't mind us blowing up that tunnel? It must be a Biblical site, thousands of—"

"Sir, if I could, I'd destroy every stone that men have ever fought over in His name. He wants us to look Heavenward. And we revel in our shit and call it holy. Speaking of which—have you designated a latrine area yet?"

SEVEN

······■·····■······■····

MEGIDDO

"Shit," First Lieutenant Tom Kosinski said. Then, with a sense that his mother hovered at his shoulder, he added, "Sorry, Chaplain."

The priest didn't seem to hear any of it. He gazed in the direction of the mound. Although he was staring into dirt and couldn't see a damned thing from the shell crater.

Still listening. Hoping. Praying. Expecting a miracle.

But there wasn't going to be one. There had been no explosion. That meant McGinley was dead or shot up too badly to get the job done. And McGinley had carried the last satchel charge the engineers had brought with them.

Suicide mission, anyway. Chances of getting close enough to the hole, dropping off the charge, and getting away were about zero. The engineer major, dead as dogshit after tripping a mine, had made it clear that he'd brought down the good stuff. Which was also the bad stuff.

"We don't talk about it much," the major had briefed, "but these charges were developed for just this kind of target. After the blast itself, they throw off enough gas to kill anything within twenty meters in the open air—or down a hundred-meter tunnel. You don't want to hang around. The existence of CV-11 is classified, by the way."

The combat engineer squad the major had brought along was supposed to do the dirty work. Now the engineers were dead, wounded, or scattered out of Kosinski's control radius. And that radius kept shrinking.

Whatever the hell else the Jihadis had in that tunnel, they had some powerful general-purpose jammers. Strong enough to deflect any precision-guided rounds that might still work. And dumb rounds, which the arty boys had dropped in multitudes, just didn't do the trick. It reminded Kosinski of what he'd read about the Japanese dug in on Pacific islands.

The Jihadis fired a volley of smoke canisters. They were nervous-in-the-service, too. He had to remember that. When the waves of doubt came over him.

The jammers wiped out everything. His headset was worthless. And only five of his soldiers were within visual range—two of them in the same crater as Kosinski and the chaplain. Which made a nice target.

So he couldn't talk. And the smoke meant he couldn't get a clear look at the mound. McGinley was KIA or WIA with the last charge up in the mess of blasted shrubs, twisted chain-link fence, wire, mines, and corpses.

It wasn't like Iwo Jima, Kosinski decided. It was like World War I.

What now, Lieutenant? He mocked himself with the immemorial question. Now that you've got a minefield behind you, the enemy's got clear fields of fire if you go forward or pull out, your chain of command wanted the mission accomplished hours ago, the light's failing, and, although there seemed to be fewer of them now, enough Jihadis remained alive to dump the wrath of Allah on anything that moved.

Artillery rounds shrieked overhead. But the shells were headed elsewhere.

Okay, okay, Kosinski thought. I can't talk. But they can't talk, either. I've got the U.S. Army behind me. These bozos are in for Mohammed's Last Stand, and they know it. The battalion S-2 had briefed them all on suicide units that would never surrender. Roger. But there had to be some damned weakness.

They didn't cover this at Benning.

Okay. They had to work in closer. Try to get to McGinley. Get the satchel charge. Which the engineer had described as almost a mininuke. And get it into the mouth of the damned tunnel.

I choose Course of Action B, sir.

You are a no-go at this station.

The Jihadis launched a pair of rifle grenades in Kosinski's general direction. Maybe to check if any Americans were still alive. The smoke from the grenades immediately began to drift off. But the light was going. And with all the flashes on every side, the night-vision gear wouldn't be worth much.

What *now*, Lieutenant?

Forward, sir.

Kosinski motioned to Staff Sergeant Wasserman. You. And Winchell. Move out. Left. Then he signaled to Sergeant Baker, Martinez, and Liu. Covering fire, then move. Classic fire and maneuver. Bounding overwatch. Except this wasn't an exercise with dummy rounds in the Georgia clay.

Let's go. *Follow me.*

"Father. You stay here. You've done your part."

The priest shook his head. He took off at a run before Kosinski could get over the lip of the crater.

Okay, follow the priest.

The Jihadis didn't open up immediately. The smoke grenades might have obscured the tunnel's defenses, but now the last wisps obscured the Americans.

Were the J's low on ammo?

No. They'd have plenty in there. Stacked up.

Run. *Run.*

Kosinski caught up with the chaplain and yanked him into another crater. Just as interlocking fires from two machine guns swept the ground at thigh level.

Kosinski couldn't see any of his soldiers now. He wondered if any had obeyed his order to move out. Past a certain point, he realized, a lieutenant's authority reached its limit. The platoon—what remained of it—had probably passed it.

Machine-gun rounds ripped overhead. You could feel the air getting out of their way.

Couldn't blame his soldiers much if they were still hunkered down. They'd followed him a damned long way. Maneuvering up to approach this Megiddo lump of dirt from the north, they'd hit the first belt of mines. Screams, and men squirming. Lost the weak ones right there, the newbies. Koskinski had watched the engineer major leap into the air like a super-hero. Except that his legs separated from his torso and flew off in their own eccentric directions. For all the noise of battle, he'd heard the thud when the major came back to earth. Anyway, he thought he'd heard it.

Dark coming. Not good news. Mission unaccomplished.

The machine-gun fire ceased. For the moment.

Kosinski looked around in desperation. And found only the priest.

Okay. Game over. Time to pay up. Time to at least *look* like a leader.

Course of Action C, sir?

It was up to him now. His turn. Go in and find McGinley. And the charge. Give it to the bastards.

Or.

No "or."

Just give it to the bastards.

He already saw himself running forward, saw it all play out. It did not end well.

The priest had read his mind. He laid a staying hand on the lieutenant, forcing Kosinski back down as he began to rise. Father Powers inched close, until their uniforms met and the warmth beneath their sleeves connected. So human it made Kosinski wince. With the noise and stink of war roiling around them. In the loneliest place on earth.

"Listen to me," the priest shouted. Or it seemed like a shout. "I've been there. I know where the tunnel starts."

Their eyes met in the dying light. And Kosinski

saw something in the other man's eyes that he never found a word for. Maybe his mom was right and priests knew secrets.

"Stay here," the chaplain commanded. "I'll handle it."

Kosinski felt as though a spell had been cast, as though the priest's authority superseded that of generals. Later, he sometimes asked himself if he'd just been a coward. But even in his most cynical moments, he knew there was more to it than that.

The priest leapt into the dusk, running forward. Alone.

The machine guns opened up again. Kosinski didn't dare raise his head to look. No screams. But heavy-caliber machine guns didn't leave you much to scream with.

One eternity passed, and another began.

Kosinski readied himself. To follow in the priest's footsteps. Suddenly emboldened, telling himself, "What the hell, I'm a bachelor. What does it matter?"

He refused to think further, to contemplate anything but the mission.

Go.

Just as he was about to climb from the crater, the heavens roared, and the earth shook, and darkness covered the land.

NAZARETH

Nasr waited far longer than the thirty minutes he'd granted himself before moving out to make his transmission. After reaching the tiny hole he'd rented and mortifying the landlord through whose rooms he had to pass, he'd fallen into unconsciousness. As soon as he lowered his body onto the mattress. When he woke again, after scorching dreams, the light was going, and it took him several minutes to master reality.

As the shock of the beating wore off, the pain worsened. Yet, the pain itself had an opiate quality on another level, lulling him into a trance he had to resist with his remaining strength.

He decided to wait until full dark to leave again and retrieve the burst transmitter. In the meantime, he constructed his message. Reaching for effective words and economical formulations he could punch in quickly.

The world seemed about as clear as muddy water. And not just because of the enveloping night.

What could he say that would make sense? When things didn't make sense?

Brevity, he cautioned himself. Short sentences. Keep it simple, stupid. Just the bones.

At last, he thought he had it. He hoped he would remember it all, since he couldn't write it down:

Minimum 23 busloads internally displaced persons today. Syrian, Lebanese and possibly Iraqi or Gulf Arab. Educated. Many middle-aged. Purpose of transfers unclear. City overcrowded. Local food-stocks low. Heavy police presence, but few troops and no visible defenses within city. Believe have been compromised. Apparent Jihadi wish that I transmit possible last message. Assess Jihadis want us to know about refugees. No explanation.

Count to remember. Twelve sentence fragments. How many clauses? Too hard. Twelve fragments. Okay, repeat. And repeat again.

He wanted to put on clean clothes but found it too difficult to get the bloody rags off his body. He worried that the pain was beating him down, defeating him. Now and then, he coughed up more blood. But what did it matter? If they were going to kill him?

He tried to reason against his conclusion. Maybe they wanted him to continue transmitting? Maybe they really hadn't pegged him at all?

No. They knew.

Twelve fragments. What's number four, stud? *Many middle-aged.*

You'll never be middle-aged. And you haven't even been married and divorced once. To qualify for full membership in the Special Forces, you had to have at least two marriages in your past and an estranged wife with papers on you.

None of that was going to happen now. Should've married some allotment-hunter from Fayetteville or Columbus. Just to check the block. While waiting for Daddy's little trust-fund baby. Found wandering the streets of Chapel Hill.

Too late now, tiger. *Jody's got your girl and gone.*

The poetry of it all. He snickered at himself and coughed up more blood.

Ain't no use in lookin' back, Jody's got your Cadillac.

He knew that he shouldn't think about death. You had to focus on the mission. But it was hard.

Nasr dragged himself back through his landlord's

rooms, where no living thing was in evidence. All of them hiding. From him. Nasr figured the old bugger was going to lock the door the minute he made the street.

Dad, I'm sorry. I screwed this up. Keep Mom straight, okay?

"Died doing his duty." What a joke. They would've been just as happy to put *his* family in one of the Providential Communities. Call them whatever they wanted to, they were camps. Concentration camps. In the United States of America.

Well, it wasn't the first time. And his family was still safe in Sacramento. Maudlin for an instant, he imagined his father waving a medal in the face of some Jesus-was-really-a-white-American bureaucrat.

Sorry, Dad.

Nasr lugged his body through the streets. There were no lights now. Blackout conditions. Only the stars and a moon hidden by buildings, and the lightning flashes of shell bursts beyond the ridges. His eyes were swollen almost shut, worse than they'd been before he'd gone unconscious among the bedbugs. An exasperated girlfriend had once told him he was blind. Well, now he just about was.

Tina. Oh, yes. So demure in public.

Tina, Tina. Nicest bad girl I ever met. *Carnivorous*.

He smiled at himself. Until his lips, gums, and teeth ached. Which didn't take long.

He'd actually been worried about bedbugs in his room. The truth, which Nasr hid from his comrades, was that he was a clean-freak. Concerned with getting the bedbugs out of his clothing after he exfiltrated. What a joke. Glad to share many more nights with all the little guests in his bed, if only.

The bedbugs would've loved Tina.

For a long moment, he wasn't even sure he was at the right place. But it smelled right. Even with his nose smashed up. The local piss lane. He limped into the corridor, the ammonia smell searing his nostrils. Doing the best he could to check that he was alone. Aware that he was incapable of judging whether he'd been followed.

Nasr reached down into a crumbling foundation and jimmied out a brick with his good hand. Wondering if he'd be able to work the stylus on the keypad.

He meant to bend over to hide the tiny glow of the device but found himself on his knees. With the dizziness on him again.

Twelve fragmentary sentences. Begin.

In the beginning was the Word . . .

And the word was: *Minimum.*

Minimum 23 busloads . . .

Even though he'd reasoned that they wanted him to transmit, he expected to feel a hand upon him. Or a club. To hear footsteps. Anything. Except being left alone to do his work.

He was left alone. He fired the burst transmission, waited, then sent it again. Hoping it would get through.

He didn't want it all to be a waste.

From sheer discipline, he hid the transmitter again. Because that was how soldiers did things. Right to the end.

And he turned back down the stinking corridor, waiting to die.

Instead of being murdered, Nasr made it back to the house where the lovely bedbugs awaited him. He found the front door open and the landlord trying frantically to find any working channel on an uncooperative television.

Nasr muttered, "Salaam Aleikum," and, still expecting to die, went to sleep.

HEADQUARTERS, III (US) CORPS, MT. CARMEL RIDGES

"The SeaBees say they can do it, sir," Colonel Mc-Coy, the corps logistician said. "As soon as the grungies clear the ridges east of the Haifa Gap. They tell me they can lay double flexi-pipe into the Jezreel in twenty-four hours and start pumping. Service with a smile."

"All right, Real-Deal," Harris said. He'd stepped outside of the deserted houses commandeered as the corps' forward command post. Thirsty for fresh air.

The night stank of war.

Harris watched the silhouettes of ammo carriers pass along the road. "All right. But I don't want any of our soldiers playing chicken with gamma rays. Or sailors, either. No short cuts on the protective gear while they're on the ground in Haifa. And rigid adherence to dwell times."

"Yes, sir."

"And remember what I told you last night. I need you. I don't want you turning into a night-light on two hind legs. Stay out of there."

"Yes, sir."

"And tell the SeaBees good work."

"Yes, sir. I'll tell them. As soon as the POL starts flowing."

"Anything else?"

"Water. The doc and I are tight on this, sir. We'll get the water down to the troops. But you've got to hammer 'em: no drinking the local stuff. I mean, no bottled water from Ahmed's refrigerator. It's going to be tempting, if they run into something halfway cold. But the doc's a hard-ass about this—he's worried about radiation, not the runs."

"Got it. But you've got to get that water out there. It's push, not pull, Real-Deal. I don't want full pallets sitting at division or brigade."

"I'll put the fear of God into all the Fours, sir."

Harris grimaced, although his G-4 couldn't see the expression in the darkness. "We've all had enough 'fear of God,' Sean. Just put the fear of Real-Deal McCoy into them, all right?"

"Yes, sir."

"You getting any sleep?"

Before the logistician could answer, a helmeted figure loomed from the shadows. The parade-ground posture, even under the weight of body armor, was unmistakable.

"Over here, Scottie."

The 1st Infantry Division's commander pivoted as if he were still a cadet captain at West Point.

The G-4 saluted, a dark bird-swoop, and stepped away.

"Evening, sir."

"What's up, Scottie? I thought you'd be down in

your CP harassing your staff and complicating the planning process."

Major General Walter Robert Burns Scott took off his helmet and ran his palm over his hair. By the light of day, it was as red as the field of Bannockburn. Now he was a shadow, paler where flesh caught starlight.

"That's what I need to speak to you about, sir."

"Talk to me."

"Sir . . . The fact is that I don't have the guts to make a decision. Without running it by you."

"Doesn't sound like the leash-snapper we all know and love. Talk to me."

"My deputy electronic-warfare officer came up with something. Sir, I need you to hear me out before you decide I'm crazy."

"I'm on receive, Scottie."

"It's this: Yes, we've got all the corps' fire support tomorrow. Layered obscurants. Smart rounds, dumb rounds. And enough jamming to melt circuits in Japan. But it still feels a little like being on the wrong side at Cold Harbor. We're set to take serious losses."

"I know that, Scottie. But we need Afula. And it isn't going to get easier if we wait."

"No, sir. Understood. But this kid . . . a major, so I guess I shouldn't call him a kid—Christ, they look so young—pointed out the obvious to start: The two killers we face are the drones, which we can try to jam the shit out of, and the seventh-gen ATGMs. Mostly loophole systems, Russian designs. Explorer and Hunter knockoffs built in China before the Rising and bought in bulk. This kid—Major Sanger— pointed out that, given the intensity of the jamming and spoofing, the Jihadis are going to have their anti-tank missiles set to take advantage of any windows in the electronic spectrum, any holes in our jamming. You know the drill—the setting takes the man out of the loop completely, and the missile launches automatically when it senses a clear path through the electronic spectrum."

"Remember you're talking to an Infantryman, Scottie."

"I'm Infantry, too, sir."

"I know that. But at West Point, they actually made you learn things. Go on."

"Well, it's a long ride down the Jezreel."

"Got it. 'Charge of the Light Brigade.' I'm as worried as you are."

"Here's the thing. The max range of the Explorer is eight-point-five clicks, but they usually fail at eight. Propulsion issue. But the auto-lock-on goes out an extra kilometer. It's a flaw in the system. Max for the Hunter is six clicks. Auto lock-on at six-and-a-half clicks, but that's integrated with flight times."

"And?"

"Major Sanger suggested that, exactly when our lead formations hit nine clicks out—we'll use an old-fashioned phase line, call it 'Phase Line Hollywood'—we turn off every jamming system in the division and every corps asset in sector. Air and ground."

Harris got it. "How long would they need to be down?"

"He estimates forty seconds."

"The Jihadis could lock onto a lot of targets in forty seconds. And not just in your division."

"Yes, sir. But they're going to be as focused on the Jezreel as we are. And if it works out . . . They launch three or four hundred antitank missiles down the valley and just splash dirt on our glacis plates."

"*If* it works out."

"Yes, sir. And here's the rest of it: We'll have every target acquisition system we've got tuned in, and we'll activate every artillery spotter and amateur bird watcher in the corps. We'll get tech readings, live imagery, and visuals on all those points of light around Afula when the launchers go hot. And you know their tactics, sir. They always pair up their Explorers and Hunters, long-range and mid-range systems. Hit the Explorers, you kill the Hunters as a bonus. The plan would be to dump every round the corps can shoot right smack on the bad guys."

Harris could feel his subordinate watching him through the darkness. He sensed how badly the man wanted reassurance, approval, a blessing.

"What percentage does your Red Leg figure we could take out?"

"At least thirty. Forty, if we're lucky. We'd get disruption of the others, as well. As soon as the arty hits, we'll go pedal to the metal."

"Hell of a risk, Scottie. Leaving the entire corps buck naked for almost a minute."

"Yes, sir. But I'm looking at the difference between twenty percent blue casualties and maybe getting it down to ten percent."

"Guess this is why I get paid the big bucks. Okay. Let's go inside and work it out with the gun-bunnies and Mike Andretti." As they walked, he drew his forefinger back and forth across his nose a single time. "God help us if it doesn't work. And God help you if you're not in Afula by noon, Scottie."

Harris smiled in the darkness. He liked the boldness of the idea. Major Sanger. Have to remember the name, if it worked. Sometimes, fortune really did favor the bold.

Thinking out loud, Harris said, "You'd damned well better make sure your boys hit that phase line right on the money. Or that valley's going to be a junkyard."

"Sir, I have considered that possibility."

"By the way, tell Pat Cavanaugh he did a good job clearing Megiddo. I understand it got ugly."

"Yes, sir. We're still sorting it out. 1-18 took some hits."

Harris put a hand on the taller man's shoulder but felt only body armor.

"And one more thing, Scottie: It's not going to be Phase Line Hollywood. To be honest, I never felt a great deal of sympathy for those folks. Let's call it Phase Line Watts."

▪

As they were wrapping up the corps-level changes to the next day's plan, Major General Scott took a call from his division on the land-line. When the 1st ID commander came back into the plans cell, Harris said, "Scottie, I thought you'd be on your way back to your division by now. They're probably enjoying your absence much too much."

"Yes, sir. May I have another minute? In private?"

"Let's go."

Instead of putting his body armor back on and

stepping outside again, Harris led his subordinate into his makeshift office, a bedroom that smelled more of sheep than of people.

"Talk to me."

"Sir, I just got a summary of the debriefings on the Megiddo fight. The man who actually got the charge into that tunnel was the 4th Brigade chaplain. Apparently, he'd been there on a pilgrimage a while ago. Back before. The platoon leader said they were pinned down and the chaplain took off at a run. After three previous attempts had failed."

"Hell of a chaplain."

"He was killed. He must've dived right into the tunnel's entrance with the charge."

Harris shook his head. But he said nothing.

"Sir," General Scott continued, "if the other debriefs confirm his actions, I'd like to submit him for the Medal of Honor."

"No."

"Sir?"

"Don't waste your time, Scottie. Put him in for a Distinguished Service Cross. That should get him at least a posthumous Silver Star."

"But—"

"Congress isn't going to award anybody in this corps a Medal of Honor. The MOBIC supporters on the Hill would kill it. Especially since they haven't yet amended the law, and MOBIC troops aren't eligible, by my reading. Oh, they'll change the law, once they figure that one out." The corner of his mouth twisted. "Sorry if I sound cynical, Scottie, but between our new SecDef and this Congress, they'll make sure we're just a footnote to the MOBIC annals of the brave." He sighed. "Now go back to your division and gird your loins for battle."

General Scott made a wry face. " 'Girding loins' always sounded goddamned uncomfortable to me. I'll have Charlie Kievenauer write the chaplain up for a DSC."

EIGHT

....■......■......■....

"With all due respect, sir," Command Sergeant Major Dilworth Bratty told the battalion maintenance officer, "I'd like to see more security out."

"Can't do it, Sergeant Major," Captain Butts said. "Can't spare any more mechanics. Bayonet Six wants these tracks up by zero-dark-thirty."

CSM Bratty understood. But he didn't like it. For all the activity down along the road, 1-18's forward maintenance site seemed exposed. An elephants' graveyard of broken-down tanks, infantry tracks, V-hulls, and recovery vehicles, it flickered with shocks of light as walking-dead mechanics plunged through blackout curtains. The noise was at the demolition-derby level.

Bratty stood in silence before the BMO. Giving the captain his disapproving command-sergeant-major face. Calculated to give any officer through the grade of major an irregular heartbeat. Even when the officer couldn't see it properly.

"Tell you what, Sergeant Major," the BMO said suddenly, "I know you're right. Tell Sergeant MacKinley I said to free up two more men and put them out on perimeter with the others. Any word on the XO?"

"Mr. Culver believes it's dysentery, sir. I blame the Navy food. One of life's great disappointments."

"He's going to be pissed as hell at missing the war. So . . . I guess I'll be seeing more of you, Sergeant Major."

"Yes, sir. Colonel Cavanaugh's asked me to look after the maintenance side of things. Until Major Lincoln's back up and running."

"He holding up okay? Bayonet Six?"

It wasn't a question for a captain to ask a battalion command sergeant major about their commander, but Bratty realized it was meant sincerely.

"Lieutenant Colonel Cavanaugh's just fine, sir. Now, if you'll excuse me, I'll get with Sergeant MacKinley and—"

A volley of rocket-propelled grenades whooshed through the night. In quick succession, three of them found targets. The blast and dazzle shocked.

A rush of air tried to push Bratty over. Automatic weapons fire pursued the explosions.

When the BMO didn't react instantly, Bratty yelled, "Sir! Go back and get folks organized. I'll hold here."

But there was no time. Tracers hunted them like flashlight beams. Muzzle flashes approached at a run.

The captain dropped to one knee and raised his carbine.

Good. That was fine. Fighting was better than floundering. Bratty dashed into the maze of vehicles occupying the level bits of ground. He grabbed a running soldier. Unable to recognize the man in the dark, the sergeant major shouted, "Get *down*. Right here. Shoot any bastard in front of you."

He found two mechanics paying out rounds behind the front of a V-hull. Beyond them, a soldier lay still, glistening with blood in the rips of light.

He heard the voices then, calling on Allah.

"That you, Sergeant Major?"

"Just keep shooting."

Bratty leapt across the dead soldier and nuzzled the wheels of a tank whose track had been stripped. Lifting his carbine and crossing his fire with the bursts from the two soldiers he'd just passed. He thought he downed a Jihadi. The wildness made it impossible to be sure.

The J's hurled grenades. Hollering their hey-look-at-me cries of "Allah!" and "Allah is great!"

More firing. Behind him. Various calibers. The Jihadis had made it deep into the site.

Bratty scrambled back to the two soldiers. One was reloading, the other aiming and shooting single rounds.

"Osterholz?"

"It's me, Sergeant Major."

"Who's with you?"

"Bracey."

New man. But he was fighting.

"Both of you. Fix bayonets. Stay here and hold. One of you cover the rear at all times. But don't shoot to the rear unless you're damned sure of the target. You fixed for ammo?"

A blast in the center of the work site hurled wreckage into the sky. It looked like a volcano erupting.

As soon as the metal thunked back to earth, Bratty ran toward the explosion's ghost. Fixing his own bayonet.

Rounding the front of a Bradley, he nearly collided with two Jihadis trotting ahead of him. He gave each one a burst in the back and kept moving.

"Rally on the high ground," he shouted to any soldiers who might be listening. "Rally back on the high ground."

Face to face with a Jihadi bronzed by firelight, Bratty shot first. The J's finger locked on his trigger, spraying errant rounds.

Correcting his path to avoid being silhouetted by flames, Bratty passed a soldier whose head had been hacked off.

Meeting a pack of J's, he almost fired. Before he realized that two of his soldiers, taken prisoner, were in the center of the group.

Bratty dropped to one knee and fired four perfect shots. As if he'd been the demonstrator on the rifle range at Ft. Bliss.

A hammer blow pitched him forward.

"Look out!" one of the soldiers cried. Late.

Bratty rolled to the side and thrust up the bayonet.

His attacker backed off at the sight of the blade. He'd slammed Bratty with an unloaded grenade launcher.

Bratty pulled the trigger.

Nothing.

The Jihadi swung the launcher at Bratty's carbine, knocking the bayonet from his path.

One of the soldiers who'd just had his ass saved grabbed a dead Jihadi's rifle and shot Bratty's attacker.

"You okay, Sergeant Major?"

"Get the fuck away from me. Get out of the line of fire."

The soldiers moved. But they were unsure where to go. Shaken.

"Police up their ammo. *Do it.* Hurry!" Bratty jacked a new mag into his carbine.

The firing didn't slacken. But there were no more blasts.

"Follow me."

He nearly led them into a crossfire. With rounds pinging off the armored flanks of deadlined vehicles.

"Get back. *Move.*"

The two soldiers trailed him back to the display of Jihadi corpses. Bratty's shoulder seemed to pull him toward the ground, and his arm obeyed orders only sluggishly. The Jihadi had given him a good whack.

Something broken?

Find out later.

"Stay *down*," Bratty said. "Okay. We're going in behind those guys back there. We're going to roll them up. But when I stop, you stop. Nobody runs out into friendly fire, understand? *Understand?*"

"Yes, Sergeant Major."

"You. Hanks. On my left. Burton, on my right."

The soldiers obeyed. Willingly. Glad of clear orders. But Bratty could feel that they were still jittery.

"Let's go."

The general chaos had settled into local patches of disorder. They headed toward the loudest exchange of gunfire.

The light of a burning Bradley helped them out as they maneuvered. This time, the J's were silhouetted. With all their attention fixed on the targets to their front.

"Halt. Fire. Give it to the fucks."

Bratty and one soldier dropped to their knees. The PFC to his left stood as he aimed and fired. Bratty clicked his weapon onto single-shot mode and picked his targets. In the confusion, the Jihadis didn't realize they were being fired on from the rear for what seemed like a very long time. Although it was only seconds.

Voices shrieked in Arabic. Some of the J's were closer than Bratty had realized. A half-dozen rose to charge them.

The PFC went down.

Bratty aimed his rounds as long as he could, but events moved at lightning speed. He rose and led with his bayonet. Still firing.

Weapons swung through the air. Bratty shot one man in the face, then parried another who was using his weapon as a club, out of ammunition. The melee became a hypermotion tangle of killing. Abruptly, Bratty sensed that he was fighting alone. He kept on slashing with his bayonet, while managing to work the weapon's butt plate into an approaching jaw.

Screaming "Allah is great!" a Jihadi raised a sword and brought it down.

Bratty got his weapon up to block the blade. In time. It cost him two fingers.

With magical clarity, he watched the stubs of flesh fly toward the firelight. Time to sell the old Gibson Hummingbird.

Pumping blood, he yanked his weapon around to shoot his attacker. The last of them. But his trigger finger was missing. When he managed to get another finger in place, the magazine was empty.

The Jihadi cut the air with the sword again. Somehow, Bratty managed to cling to the slimed carbine, to slap it up to meet the blade. Then, with all the strength left to him, he jammed the stock into the Jihadi's neck.

The man staggered. Before he could lift the sword again, Bratty plunged his bayonet into the center line below his ribs.

The Jihadi looked at him in astonishment. Openmouthed. Bewildered that life was what it was, and no more.

Bratty had stabbed him so hard that the command sergeant major couldn't extract the bayonet before the Jihadi collapsed. The dead man pulled the weapon and Bratty after him.

Shoving his boot into the dead man's rib cage, Bratty yanked on the carbine. His hand slipped. The weapon was slick with his own blood. Coated with it. Two stumps where his right index finger and middle finger had been leaked blood at an impressive rate.

"Shit, goddamnit," Bratty said.

He managed to free the carbine in time to reload and shoot a restless wounded man in the face. It wasn't a night for random acts of kindness.

Except for sporadic shots, the firefight was over.

The voices calling out spoke English now. His side had won. No. *Prevailed*. The mess around him hardly counted as a win.

Bratty sat down with his back to a shot-up tire. Clumsily, he dropped his bandage pack into the dust. After he got it open, he balled up the cloth and pressed it against the stumps of his fingers.

A sergeant major without a goddamned trigger finger. The stuff barracks jokes were made of. And his guitar-picking days were over. He'd never really hated the Jihadis before. He just did his duty and enjoyed doing it well. But now that they'd taken two of his fingers, and his trigger finger at that, he damned them to Hell.

He could already hear the jokes. "What do you call a sergeant major who has to pull the trigger with his pinkie?" "How does a sergeant major lose his trigger finger?" The possibilities were endless.

Captain Butts walked up to him. The last firing had ceased.

"Taking it easy, Sergeant Major?"

"Just relaxing my ass off, sir. You?"

"Never been better. I enjoy these quiet nights."

"Shit, sir."

"Yeah. Shit."

They looked at the dead Jihadis and the two dead Americans. With burning vehicles as a backdrop.

"I hope you downloaded those suckers," Bratty said.

"You were right about the security, Sergeant Major."

"Nothing to do now, sir, but keep on marching. Any sense of how many—"

"Jesus Christ! Your fingers. Medic!"

But the lone medic still alive was busy. Bleeding from the forehead himself, the BMO knelt down and used his own bandage to tie off Bratty's stumps as best he could.

"That hurt?"

"Naw. It just pisses me off, sir."

"You and me both."

"I was talking about my fingers. But I'm pissed about the rest of it, too. Go and get this clusterfuck organized. I'll be right behind you."

"Roger."

"Sir? You know what this means, don't you?"

"It means Bayonet Six isn't going to have many of his down-for-maintenance ponies back in the race tomorrow."

Bratty nodded. "And it means that the J's are working our weaknesses, sir. They've cracked the code that our repair sites are prime targets, that we're fighting with over-the-hill vehicles that are higher maintenance than a rich man's junkie daughter."

The BMO smiled. Or tried to. "What would you know about rich men's junkie daughters, Sergeant Major?"

"Plenty. I married one." Bratty shrugged. His shoulder hurt as if a steel plate had dropped on it. "That was a couple wives back. Just before the waitress with the broken heart. Pitch 'til you win, Captain."

"You're right, though," Captain Butts said, standing up. "They've figured out our weak spot. Unless they picked us by dumb luck."

"They didn't."

"I suppose I'll have to figure out new security arrangements."

A soldier in mechanic's overalls jogged up to them, paused for a second at the sight of the spread of corpses, then said, "Sir?"

"Just a sec, Hunsicker. Sergeant Major? You know you're going to take some razzing about that trigger finger, don't you?"

HEADQUARTERS, III (US) CORPS, MT. CARMEL RIDGES

Harris had resolved to get five hours of sleep. To keep himself alert. But the night dragged on. No matter how willing he was to delegate authority, there were issues only the commanding general could resolve and others that demanded his emphasis. The 1st Cavalry Division commander wanted to relieve one of his brigade commanders just hours before the division was scheduled to come ashore. A medium-tonnage transport ship loaded with old Bradley infantry fighting vehicles and critical spare parts had been hit by multiple kamikaze drones and sunk. Artillery units were expending 155mm HE rounds at twice the projected rate. He had to review and sign off on the daily summary of events before it could go to Cyprus, to his next-higher headquarters, Holy Land Command, HOLCOM or, as the troops had instantly nicknamed it, "Hokum." With HOLCOM's embellishments—and deletions—it would go to Washington. If comms were up.

Harris had taken the document into the room designated as his office, where the staff had set up a cot for him. Sending his aide to collect any global intelligence summaries that had made it through the jamming, the general sat down, put on his reading glasses, and labored over the document.

The work was painful. He had to bring the text irritatingly close to his face. His eyes burned. The docs said it was a result of the corrosive fumes he'd been exposed to in the Nigeria campaign, and they warned him "not to put undue stress on your eyes." But a general had to read. When he asked about the future, the military doctors sought to avoid telling him what he already knew: Before he reached age sixty, he'd be blind. Sarah's brother, a civilian ophthamalogist, had told him the truth.

Perhaps he should've retired already, Harris thought. But he was vain enough to believe that he was the best man to fight this last campaign, to stand up to the madness rising around them all.

Sarah had taken the verdict on his future better than he had. At least outwardly. He often wondered what she felt inside about the prospect of a blind, aging husband. Anyway, he loved her. And wished he had a better future to offer her.

If he had received one great blessing in his life, it was Sarah. He loved his daughters dearly. But what he felt for his wife soared beyond the emotions he felt for any other living thing.

After the girls, only the Army came close.

He hated to think of the incompetencies that would come with the loss of vision. No more camping in the Tetons or Cascades. He wouldn't even be able to get in a car and drive down for a newspaper. Worst of all, the black wall would keep him from looking at the woman he loved. And he had *always* loved to look at her, from the moment he first saw her: a redhead in a pale-blue blouse, eating strawberry ice cream.

By the light of two field lamps, Harris corrected the draft document. The casualty figures made him pause. Not least because he knew they would be even higher the following day.

Was that priest at Megiddo included in the KIA column? Or had his death come too late to make the count?

Harris initialed the report and gave himself a moment to think about the priest and his sacrifice. His thoughts were such that it would not have done to mention them to anyone aloud. Not now. When everyone played politics for God and spied for Jesus. But he longed to talk to someone—he realized he would have to be careful not to take up too much of Monk Morris's time with bullshitting.

Harris couldn't get the priest out of his head. For all the wrong reasons.

It struck him that, when all was said and done, the priest had been a suicide bomber. On the side of the angels, but, nonetheless, a suicide bomber. Deserving of the Medal of Honor he couldn't receive in the current political climate. Magnificently heroic. Self-sacrificing. Admirable. And a suicide bomber.

What else could you call it? Oh, he'd limited himself to a military target. And his sacrifice had saved many lives. Given. But how different the thing looked when the man with the bomb, rushing to his death, was one of your own.

Harris never succumbed to the notion that all men were alike. The Jihadis were barbarians. But based on the initial reports from the Jerusalem Front, he wasn't sure the MOBIC troops were much better. It had been bad enough when the militant fanatics had been on one side only. Now, the fanatical excesses and threats in which Islamic extremists had indulged over the decades had finally provoked a like response. To Harris, the war in which he was leading the U.S. Army's remnants made no geopolitical sense. It wasn't like the Nigeria Intervention. It was a massive crime of passion.

But his role was to fight his country's war, no matter what he thought of it. And to ensure that America's Army survived, however starved and battered.

No more time for reveries, he told himself abruptly. But he thought, again, about the fate awaiting him in five years. Perhaps sooner. It was already too painful for him to read the history books he loved. He'd never had time for frivolous scribbling, for novels and that sort of thing. But all his life he'd studied his profession, past campaigns, leaders, international affairs, economics, religion . . .

Harris had never been one for golf or tennis or season tickets. Or for extramarital affairs. Or for much of anything beyond the Army, his family, daily five-mile runs, and the ramparts of books that filled "his" room at home.

Now the books were already lost to him. Although he took pains that no one but his aide knew that his sight was failing. And he believed he could trust young Willing, the son of a retired general who had mentored Harris early in his career. The Army was a small tribe, in the end.

Major Willing knocked on the office door. His knock was always recognizable. Respectful, just a bit timid. Young Willing's fault, if he had one, was a lack of self-confidence. General's sons were like that. Either they thought themselves entitled to every deference, or they feared not living up to a father's standards. Or both.

Harris rose from the cot and told the younger man to come in.

"Sir? I've got the global INTSUM from the Two shop."

Harris just wanted to take off his boots and sleep. But he said, "Good. Hold here, John. I want to make a last stop by Plans." He pulled on his body armor and picked up his helmet to walk down to the building where the planners had set up.

The planning-cell officers had not bothered to take down the Druze posters and framed photographs on the walls of the house allotted to them by the headquarters commandant. They were a good team, Harris knew, oblivious to anything but their work.

"We're moving right along, sir," Lieutenant Colonel Marty Rose said, by way of greeting.

"Give me the condensed version, Marty."

"Sir . . . if you'll step over to the map . . . It's easier to see this than it is on the monitor . . ."

"I know the map. Talk to me."

Marty Rose never needed a second invitation to talk. Harris saw his lead planner as brilliant but uneven, the intellectual equivalent of a manic-depressive.

Once, Harris had taken the lieutenant colonel aside to tell him, "Please, Marty . . . a little less Clausewitz and a little more common sense."

The other thing that Harris and his G-3 both recognized was that Marty Rose tended to put more effort into his own vision of future operations. It was a constant struggle to get him to devote equal energy to the potential courses of action raised by others. Even when the "other" was the corps commander.

But the care-and-feeding was worth it. Rose delivered.

Midway through the briefing, Harris said, "Good work, Marty. But I also want you to give me an option where the main effort's a wide swing to the north. Left-flank *Schwerpunkt*. In case we can't get there from here. And I want you to start thinking beyond the Golan Heights. You need to be thinking 'Damascus'."

"Yes, sir," Rose said, disappointed that his cell's efforts hadn't satisfied the boss. Harris realized that the planners were weary and frazzled, running on nerves. But they were going to have to keep producing. Harris needed someone thinking seriously while the rest of the corps was fighting.

"Sir . . . your instructions about avoiding contaminated zones . . . If we shift north, we'll come up against—"

"Work it out. If we have to pass through any of the dead zones—if we have no choice—we'll move fast. My point, Marty, was that I didn't want anybody lingering where there's residual radiation. But we're going to do whatever it takes to win."

"Yes, sir. As for Damascus . . . I understand the mission. But do you really think the MOBIC corps is going to let us make the grand entry?"

"Marty, just draw up the plans. I'll worry about Sim·Montfort and his gang."

"Yes, sir."

"And stay in bed with the Four. And with the Marines. If we *do* swing north, we may have to do more over-the-beach log. And when we get to Damascus, whether it's a week from now or a year from now, I want every subordinate command to know exactly which areas of the city remain habitable and which ones are still glowing. No mistakes."

Rose looked at him. "You know, sir . . . I never figured out why the Israelis didn't just wipe Damascus off the map, why they just went small-yield on the government sites. After they erased just about every city in Iran."

"My guess," Harris said, "is that they planned to come back. And Damascus is a lot closer to Jerusalem than Qom or Tehran. Besides, they'd shot most of their load on the Shias before the Sunni Arabs figured out that a nuked Israel was an invitation to the dance. Speaking of nukes, Marty: I want every plan you concoct to have a nuclear-defense variant." The general knew that every officer in the plans cell had been listening all along, but he raised his voice slightly and peered around the room, giving official notice to them all. "If the Jihadis *do* pop any nukes, I want us to be able to act, not just *re*act. Fast. Everybody got that?"

They nodded and murmured. Harris knew the entire staff thought his concern about a last few nuclear weapons in Jihadi hands was evidence of early-onset senility. And he possessed sufficient self-awareness to recognize that he'd allowed it to become at least a mild personal obsession. But his guts just contradicted the intelligence.

And gut instincts had saved his life more than once. Even if they hadn't saved his eyes.

▪

After Harris cleared their area, Marty Rose said, "All right, back to work."

A major asked, "How far north does he want us to plan?"

Rose shrugged. "Fuck, I don't know. Look at the road networks. Identify a close option and a long-march option. Then do the branches and sequels. You're all SAMS grads, aren't you? Just do it. Reichert, you've got the lead. I'm going out to take a dump."

When Rose, too, had gone, one major said to another, "Guess Big Marty didn't get his daily ration of praise from Flintlock."

"Want to know what I think?" his comrade said. "I think Flintlock Harris is losing it. Nukes on the brain. He wants to worry, he ought to worry about Montfort. That Bible-thumper's going to eat old Flintlock for breakfast."

▪

As Harris dragged himself back toward his room, the deputy G-3 ambushed him, excited. There had been two rear-area attacks. That hardly seemed a surprise to Harris, who'd expected more raids and sabotage by now. Proud of himself, the deputy Three told the general that he'd sent out a message by land line, warning all subordinate units to increase their security posture.

Harris almost told the lieutenant colonel that his message was all well and good, but what about the units still not up on land line? Instead, he just folded his arms over his body armor, pressing it into his sweat-damp uniform. The deputy Three was a talker, and Harris knew he wasn't going to get off lightly.

The poor bugger's just trying to do his best, the general reminded himself.

"And lastly," the deputy Three said, "the division surgeon from the Big Red One reports thirty-seven confirmed cases of amoebic dysentery."

"Navy food," Harris responded. "Good night, Bruce."

He walked off to his office-bedroom. Wondering at the kind of sensibility that would build a mansion-sized home such as this, then furnish it with bare, dangling bulbs.

His aide stood up as Harris entered. He looked the general over and asked, "Want me to hold this stuff until morning, sir?"

"No, John." He dropped onto his cot a little too heavily and immediately began unknotting his left boot. "Sing me to sleep."

The remark, often repeated, was a private joke that Harris never explained to his aide—who simply accepted it as a peculiarity of the general's speech. Harris long since had thought, without satisfaction, that the two of them resembled Saul and young David. And Saul's was not a role Harris wished to play.

Well, better than Abraham and Isaac, Harris told himself. Or blind Tobit.

As the general drew off his boots and socks, the major said, "Sir, the big out-of-area headline is that the Turks demolished St. Sophia's in Istanbul. Blew it to rubble."

Harris looked up. And?

Major Willing continued, reading now: "With the Imperial Russian Expeditionary Force fighting in the Galata District of Istanbul, Turkish army engineers destroyed St. Sophia's, St. Irene's, and at least a dozen other Byzantine-era structures. In Moscow, Czar Grigori and the Orthodox patriarch denounced the Turkish actions as a crime against humanity and vowed that those responsible for the wanton destruction—"

"You know, John," Harris interrupted as he loosened his belt to make his uniform comfortable enough to sleep in, "when I was a lieutenant—back when Turkey started down the path to extremism—there was a bestseller and a follow-up movie in Turkey predicting a U.S. invasion that would ultimately be repelled by Russian intervention on Ankara's side." Harris grimaced. "So much for the ability of the creative consciousness to predict the future."

Recalling many a history text he'd plowed through in years past, he added, "I always wanted to visit Istanbul. And Aya Sofya. The greatest surviving monument of the first thousand years of Christianity. I couldn't go, because of my security clearances." He sighed. "Now it's gone."

"You always say you don't care about buildings and archaeological sites, sir."

"That's not exactly right, John. I just don't think they're more important than living human beings. But I might've made an exception for St. Sofia's. It must've been impressive—you know the history? What happened on the day it fell to the Ottomans?"

"No, sir."

"Well, we'll save that for another time. But Sim Montfort and every legislator behind him is going to have a field day with this one. Anything in the summary about the Russian and Armenian forces in eastern Anatolia?"

"I didn't see anything, sir. Not today."

"Our alliance talks with the Russians?"

"Sir, there might've been something in the MOBIC news releases. Do you want me to check?"

Harris waved the thought away. It all could wait. He lay back on his cot. "Excuse me, John. You see before you a general in decline. What's next?"

"Sir, the only other major item is on China. The Army of the Han Messiah has taken Chongging. And the Beijing government bombed Hong Kong again."

"Well, I suppose we'll be eating General Tso's chicken on the spot if we finish with the Jihadis in time. Onward Christian Soldiers."

Harris saw his aide wince.

"Don't worry, John. I promise I won't say such things in public. Any domestic news get through?"

"Yes, sir. The Nevada National Guard and the Mormon Militia have been sent into the Providential Communities to quell the rioting."

"Rioting over?"

"The USG press release says the riots are being staged in support of the Jihadis we're fighting."

Harris snorted. "More likely over bad food and worse treatment. John, one day we're going to be unspeakably ashamed of ourselves for what we've done to our own citizens. Again."

"Sir, some Muslim-Americans *were* terrorists . . ."

"Less than a hundred, John, less than a hundred. And we put—what, four million people into camps in the desert? Shame on us. What else?"

Harris caught the hesitation in the air.

"Nothing really significant, sir."

"Come on, John. You're my aide, not my censor."

"That law passed. By a better-than-two-thirds majority. Declaring the United States . . . Let me check the final wording, sir . . . 'a Christian, God-fearing nation and Providential Asylum for the Jewish People'."

Harris studied the flies on the ceiling, fighting the thought that the Lord of the Flies was triumphant. After a bit, he said, "I'll miss the First Amendment. And the exiled children of Israel had better look out when we start using the word 'providential' on their behalf. In the dictionary, it comes just before 'provi-.sional'."

"Sir . . . May I ask you something? Kind of personal?"

"Majors don't ask generals personal questions. But I suppose we can make a wartime exception. Shoot."

"You *are* a Christian believer. Right, sir?"

"Hoping Jesus will have me, and trusting in His mercy. What's the question behind the question?"

"Why has this amendment bothered you so much? I mean, I'm just trying to understand . . ."

Closing his eyes, Harris said, "A nation that's Christian in its heart doesn't need to write it into law. Now go get some sleep yourself."

NINE

HEADQUARTERS, III (US) CORPS, MT. CARMEL RIDGES

"We've got a parasite inside the Jihadis' fire-control system," the briefer said. The room with the portable screens bore the smell of weary men, of stale breath, sweat, and burnt circuits. "We were able to penetrate them at the corps level. The bug is programmed to activate at 1 ID's LD time. When the first blue vehicle crosses the line, all Jihadi indirect fire assets netted for autocontrol will reprogram to impact three thousand meters short, with a thirty-degree left deviation." He paused to make eye contact with the G-2 and the deputy G-3, who was sitting in for his sleeping boss. "We estimate it will take them fifteen to max thirty minutes to identify the problem and a minimum of two hours to fix it."

"Morphing parasite?" Val Danczuk, the corps intelligence officer, asked.

"Yes, sir. That's why we're pretty sure we've got two hours."

Danczuk turned to the deputy operations officer, wondering if Mike Andretti hadn't made the right decision by catching some sleep. You could run on empty for only so long. "View from the Three side?"

"Two hours should get 1 ID into the Afula defenses. If they're going to get there at all. What about the drones?"

The briefer shook his head. "Sir, we still haven't been able to penetrate their network."

"So the drones, like the poor, will always be with us?" the deputy G-3 said.

There was a slight pause, a half-moment of held breath, before the briefer responded. Mocking Scripture wasn't safe, even in the Army's inner circles.

"Sir, for now the only option on the drones is to continue working the spoofers against them," the briefer told him.

"Which has not," the deputy Three said, "been a raging success."

"Best we can do, sir. We're trying."

The deputy shook his head and turned to Danczuk. Question mark on his face.

"We're working it, Bruce. We all want to crack that particular code. But two out of three isn't bad—indirect fire down and, if things go the way we think they will, at least a brief window of safety from the antitank defenses."

"I wish we had air, sir. Where's the zoomie?"

"He turned in," one of the staffers said.

"Christ." The deputy G-3 held up his hands in mock surrender.

"Okay," Danczuk said, eager to wrap up the briefing, "anything else?" He scanned the tired faces. Even the night-shift officers looked beat. Not much sleep to be had while the headquarters moved ashore.

"Well, I have one last question," the deputy G-3 said. "Anybody here from commo?"

A major raised his hand.

"We going to be able to talk any better tomorrow?"

The major shook his head. "Sir, we're doing the best we can. We're getting jammed on every microfrequency. It's a miracle we can talk at all. At least they're getting intermittent comms at company and below."

The deputy Three looked at Danczuk, who outranked him by one grade. "Sir, I feel like I'm in Korea with my great-grandfather."

"Well, don't get frostbite," Danczuk said. He was getting tired of the deputy Three's swagger. The man was far more subdued when his boss was present. "All right. A-Shift, get some rack time. B-Shift, back to work." He looked at an officer who'd been sitting quietly against the wall. "Major Kim, if you still need to talk to me, hang back. But no epic poetry tonight."

The younger officer nodded. Val Danczuk regarded him as the brightest analyst and reconnaissance officer on his staff. Even if he wasn't a Steelers fan.

When the room had cleared, the G-2 said, "Watcha got?"

"Mind if I shut the door, sir?"

"Shut it."

The major closed the door. It was ill-set and had to be forced. Like everything else in this rathole, Danczuk thought.

Major Kim spread a half-dozen imagery culls on

the table in front of the G-2. "Sir, I'd like you to take a look at these."

Danczuk glanced at them. Same target in each one, although the angles and shadows were different: a tented complex in a grove. Some hardstand. The main facilities bore the Red Crescent signature.

"Okay, Jim. Help me out. I'm too tired to play Twenty Questions."

The major leaned in close enough for the G-2 to smell the last rations the younger man had eaten. "Sir, this site's in the Upper Galilee. Way up, almost to the old Lebanese border. And if it's really a field hospital, I've got three questions."

"Which are?"

"The Jihadis have been taking serious casualties. But look at the imagery. We've got drone shots and two angles from the DSI-40 satellite. We got those this afternoon, when the downlink punched through for a couple of hours. The other shots are from this morning or yesterday—and there's an infrared from less than three hours ago." The major backed off slightly. "Where's the ambulance traffic? Except for the shadows and the angles, the shots are virtually identical. Hardly any movement. Look at this one: exactly two ground personnel visible. But they've got fully manned guardposts down this road." He pointed with a pen. "There. And over here. And here."

"Second question?"

"If it's a field hospital, why isn't it closer to a main road? Why tuck it off a single-lane side road in the boonies?"

"Third question?"

"If it's a hospital, why is part of the site camouflaged?" He pointed again. "What looks like trees over here is ghost netting."

"Chinese?"

"Made in India, sir. Tech transfer from Dassault. If we're reading the wavelengths right."

Danczuk nodded. "And?"

"Sir, the J's are short of ghost netting. It's a prime commodity. Why use it on a hospital? Which you shouldn't be trying to hide at all? And by the way, there's no sign of air-evac activity in any shot. No sign of any patients at all."

"And Major Jim Kim's analysis would be?" Danczuk asked. Afraid he knew damned well what the answer was.

"Sir, I believe this is a nuke field-storage site. I believe they're prepping nuclear munitions in that main tent complex, although I can't say how many. Just look at those generators. Those aren't for a hospital. And we don't know what's under the ghost netting. Could even be launchers, it could be—"

The G-2 held up his hand. But he didn't speak immediately after cutting off his subordinate. He gave him a pay-attention stare first.

"Jim . . . You're a first-rate officer. Best analyst I've got. You read that on your efficiency report. Your pre-landing estimates could be used as models at Ft. Leavenworth. But I need you to listen to me now. Unless you have proof—*proof*—and more than a hackles-up hunch about this, I don't want to hear another word spoken about it. And that's an order. Not a word. Not to anybody."

"But, sir . . . General Harris—"

"You're not listening. I want you to go on receive now. And this is strictly between us. You've got a great career ahead of you in MI. *If* you don't fall into the trap that's taken down more intel officers than straight-ahead bad calls ever did. Don't get on a hobbyhorse. Don't go into target-lock mode." He gestured toward another man whom they both could envision beyond the room's mottled walls. "We've got to protect General Harris on this one. Nukes are turning into *his* hobbyhorse. And every damned agency in D.C. agrees that the Jihadis have no nukes left. Based on the codeword evidence, I agree with the National Intelligence Estimate on this one."

Exhausted, Danczuk sat back, looking at his subordinate again but not quite seeing him this time. Thinking. About the boss he'd served since he'd been a brigade S-2. Best commander he'd ever seen. Normally.

"General Harris is under a lot of pressure," the G-2 said. "Not because he's been wrong about anything, but because he's been right about so many things. And it's not just the MOBIC crowd we have to protect him against. Even in the Army, there's plenty of jealousy toward Flintlock Harris, the general everybody laughed at because he made his lieutenants read maps without the benefit of GPS. Plenty of folks wouldn't mind seeing him make a fool out of himself now, after he was so damned right." Danczuk scratched a sudden itch on his scalp. "Even if that meant Sim Montfort becoming the hero of the day."

"Yes, sir. But couldn't we just hit the site? It's obvious that it isn't a field hospital."

"Tempting," the G-2 said. "It's tempting. Have you considered that it might be their forward command post, by the way?"

Stubborn, Major Kim shook his head. "Not enough vehicular traffic, sir. It's not a command post."

"Well, find out what it is, then. I don't want you on a nuke treasure hunt, but if we can confirm that it's not a field hospital—and I mean 'confirm'—we can go after it. But I know Flintlock Harris well enough to be as certain as bedbugs in Baghdad that he won't green-light attacking a Red Crescent site unless we have confirmation from multiple sources that it isn't what it claims to be."

"But . . . If it *is* a nuke site—"

"It's not. Didn't you hear one goddamned word I said?"

5TH MARINES, SECTOR EAST

"Sir," Garcia whispered to the new lieutenant, "we're on the wrong side of the ridge."

Garcia could barely see the other man's eyes in the darkness. But he registered their flash.

"You telling me I can't read a map, Sergeant?"

"Lieutenant . . . All I said is that we're on the wrong side of the ridge. Please keep your voice down, sir. The men don't need to hear this. Or the J's."

"Sergeant Garcia, I've been appointed platoon commander. Because somebody at battalion happens to believe this platoon needs one. You don't have to like it. But I expect you to obey orders. You understand me?"

"Yes, sir."

"We're exactly where we're supposed to be. This draw leads straight down to our objective. The only reason you can't see the village is that it's blacked out."

"Yes, sir."

"Get the men ready to move out."

"Yes, sir."

Garcia scuttled back along the trail. He would've preferred bushwhacking to the objective, but the lieutenant said he'd had a complete briefing from the S-2 and the trails were clean in the entire southern sector. The Jihadis had been surprised and hadn't had time to lay mines or booby traps before they pulled back.

Second Lieutenant DeWayne Jefferson. East Coast. Probably D.C. or Philly, Garcia calculated. Whatever the Marines may have taught him at Quantico, they hadn't taught him how to read a map.

Garcia couldn't say why, but maps had always seemed clear to him. They just made sense. Like math. The counselor at Montebello had pushed him to apply for a scholarship, but Garcia wasn't having any of that shit. Enough to get through high school and not be jerking off for a GED when you were thirty. He just wanted to be a Marine. Later, the Anglos at the community college he'd dipped into had given him a similar line: Get an education and dump the Marine Corps. But Garcia just wanted their piece of paper so he could make his ratings.

One thing he didn't need some lecturer with a cheap tie and the whisky shakes to tell him: The lieutenant couldn't connect a compass and map to his brain.

"Okay," Garcia hissed. "Let's go, Devil Dogs. We're moving out."

"Hey, Sergeant. That lieutenant have any idea where the fuck we are?"

"Shut up, Cropsey. You've used up your shit ration for the day. Let's go."

They were all tired. And blistered. An hour of sleep here and there wasn't enough. And when there were no gunshots, there was no adrenaline. Once they'd gotten off that mountain road, they hadn't even heard a drone overhead.

"Maintain combat interval," Garcia told them. They'd been stumbling into one another for the last two hours.

Garcia crept back up behind the lieutenant. Making just enough noise not to spook him. The new platoon commander was bossy and jumpy, a combination platter that was all beans and no tacos, as far as Garcia was concerned.

And this wasn't no training exercise. You didn't get a re-do.

"Ready to move out, sir."

The lieutenant turned toward the long file of Marines, shadows in the night, and asked, too loudly, "Who'll volunteer to take over point? I want somebody who knows he's a Marine."

Nobody responded. Larsen had been walking point, but the lieutenant had bitched him out for being too slow. Garcia hadn't had a problem with Larsen, though. Larsen was country. Garcia didn't want him on point down on the block, but he was the best Marine in the platoon in Mr. No-Shoulders' territory.

"I know you're all tired, men," the lieutenant said.

"But we're Marines. And we've got a mission. If I don't have any volunteers—"

"I'll take the point myself, sir," Garcia said.

"No. The platoon sergeant doesn't walk point. You. What's your name?"

"Private Barrett."

"You've got point. Move out."

Garcia could feel the private's I-am-seriously-unhappy vibes as he brushed past.

"Cropsey, Larsen. Close it up. You're between the lieutenant and me now."

The mood in the platoon needed fixing. And Garcia wasn't sure how to fix it. He didn't like the new lieutenant and realized he was carrying a grudge. He'd hoped to keep the platoon to himself. But the lieutenant was real as *la migra* at the kitchen door. You had to deal with it. Get along. One way or the other.

They moved down the trail, with Garcia certain that the platoon was headed almost ninety degrees off course. He'd done what he could. Now he concentrated on the darkness around him, the queerness of too much space. He was confident that he could work any block anywhere in the world. But operating in the Great Wide-Open still made him edgy.

The land mine that blew Barrett apart was only the start of it. The Marine rode a cushion of flames and came apart before their eyes. The night lit up with tracers: Jihadi stay-behinds.

"Charge!" the lieutenant screamed. *"Charge into the ambush!"*

That was what you're supposed to do. But Garcia

didn't do it. The hillside was too steep to charge up. The manual didn't talk about that. And it had taken him only an instant to realize that the Jihadis were overshooting, that they didn't know how to lay their weapons. The platoon had time to get its shit together, to size things up.

Garcia watched the lieutenant's silhouette stump up the steep grade. With no one following. Suddenly, the tall officer spun backward as heavy-caliber machine-gun slugs tore into him. He went down the slope like a one-man avalanche.

"Cropsey . . . You got a fix on them?"

"Yes, Sergeant."

"Larsen. You with us?"

"Here, Sergeant."

"Go with Cropsey. Cropsey, go back up the line and work them from the top. Take your time. Do it right. We'll keep them happy."

"Mama! Oh, my mama!" It was the lieutenant. *"I can't find my leg, Mama! Mama, I can't find none of my legs . . ."*

"Fuck him," Crospey said.

"Shut up. Move out."

Garcia moved along behind them, checking on the Marines. Who were firing up the hillside. Nobody else down.

"Corporal Gallotti. I want *aimed* fire from your squad. Keep them busy. And spread your men out, for the love of Jesus."

The J's were firing madly, their rounds plunging into the opposite hillside, igniting small brushfires. Garcia made it one crew-served heavy weapon and two men out on security.

"Mama, I can't find my legs, I can't find my legs . . ."

"Sergeant, you want—"

"No. Shit. I'll get him."

Garcia scrambled back down the trail, hoping there were no mines short of where Barrett had taken his last steps. With half a mind to let the lieutenant lie and bleed.

He found Barrett first. Or what was left of him. It was the Night of the Missing Legs. And almost everything else from the waist down. Whatever kind of mine it had been had done its job. The blast had sounded like a heavy mortar round.

"Oh, I'm sorry, Mama . . . Mama, I'm so sorry . . ."

Dude, shut *up*, Garcia thought. Stop begging them to lower their aim.

Behind him, Gallotti's squad was laying down good fire. The machine gun had shifted its aim in their direction, but the tracers were still streaking high over the trail. If the lieutenant had just paused to get his bearings, he would've been okay. Instead of jumping up like the teacher's pet and running right into the line of fire.

Goddamned asshole, Garcia thought.

"Oh, Mama, don't let them take my legs away . . ."

Garcia followed the voice into a notch just below the trail. After being hit and going down, the lieutenant had rolled. Garcia scrambled down beside him. Praying there were no more mines.

"I'm with you, sir," Garcia said.

"You tell my mama, you tell her I'm all right . . ."

"Yes, sir. She knows. Where are you hit?"

"My legs. I can't find my legs. Where are my legs?"

Garcia felt down the torso, trying to figure out the body's posture in the shadows. There was blood. Plenty of it. Sticky. Something stank. But he could feel both the lieutenant's legs still joined to the hip.

Warily, he felt down the limbs. Feeling uphill, with the lieutenant's head pointed down into the draw.

Both legs were perfectly intact. Right down to the combat boots. The bones didn't even feel broken.

"Mama, don't you let them take my legs," the lieutenant moaned. "Tell them they can't take my legs."

"Your legs are just fine, Lieutenant. Your legs are fine. I checked them out."

"I can't find my legs. Who're you? Where's my mama?"

"She had to go out for a minute. She'll be back. Don't move, sir."

Garcia felt along the body. It wasn't the lieutenant's legs that were missing. It was his arms. The machine-gun rounds had caught him perfectly at the shoulders, tearing away both of his arms.

Hands covered in blood, Garcia didn't know what to do. There was so much blood, he was slipping in it. The brush, the dirt, everything streamed with blood.

"Tell my mama . . . I need to tell her something . . . please . . ."

"Yes, sir. I'll tell her."

There was no way tourniquets were going to help. There was nothing to tie them around. For a moment, Garcia listened to the firefight above him on the trail. That was where he belonged, he knew. But he couldn't leave this man he didn't like. Who was bleeding to death. Who should've bled to death already. The wounds were catastrophic, with half of each shoulder torn away.

His fellow Marine.

"I can't find my legs nowhere, Mama . . ."

"Hush up, sir. Please. Just be quiet. It's all right."

Revolted by what he found himself doing, Garcia eased down beside the lieutenant's torso and lifted the man's head into his lap. Blood spurted onto him like a hose filled with hot piss.

"My mama, she . . . she . . ."

"Yes, sir. She's here now. She's listening. She's come to help you."

"Mama . . . I tried to do right. I tried to do right, Mama. I tried to do right . . ."

"You did right. Everything's all right now, sir. You're going to be just fine."

"Mama, I'll do anything you say . . . please . . ."

"She just wants you to be quiet now. Just rest, now. Your legs are fine. Everything's going to be fine."

"I don't feel right." Suddenly, the lieutenant's eyes widened. They looked perfectly clear in the light of the tracers and stars. "Sergeant?"

"Yes, sir. It's me. Sergeant Garcia."

"It was my fault."

"Sir, anybody—"

"It was my fault. I take full responsibility. I—am I bleeding?"

"You're going to be fine, sir. Just take it easy."

"You're lying," he said. "You can be court-martialed for lying to a superior." And he died.

Garcia said the quickest prayer of his life, then clawed his way back up to the trail. Hoping his return trip wouldn't collect any mines he'd missed on the way down.

He felt as though he'd been swimming in luke-warm soup. His wet uniform collected dust. Making mud-puppy fudge all over him.

"Corporal Gallotti?"

"Here, Sergeant."

"Go up the line. Pass the word. As soon as Cropsey and Larsen open up from the flank, we're going straight up that hill. Tell everybody to stay low but keep going. Tell them to keep their fires concentrated on the machine-gun position. Anything to the left is blue. Got that?"

"Yes, sergeant."

"Go."

Gallotti scuttled off. Garcia tried to dry his hands and his weapon so the slime wouldn't screw him up. But the lieutenant's blood had already gone sticky.

How long had the business been going on? Ten minutes? Garcia couldn't judge. More like fifteen, he decided. He just hoped Cropsey had taken his time and worked well to the Jihadis' rear. Larsen would do what Crospey said, Garcia knew.

A grenade exploded up the hillside, followed by another.

"Let's go!" Garcia screamed. "Stay low. Let's go, Marines!"

He scrambled up the steep slope, thighs burning, the muscles long tormented. A stream of tracers flirted above his head. But there was no more machine-gun fire.

Voices began to shout on the high ground. In Mussie-talk. At least two of them. The firing above them stopped.

Garcia heard Cropsey's voice. "Stand the fuck up. Both of you."

More Mussie-babble.

"Cease fire, cease fire," Garcia shouted.

"I said for you to stand the fuck up." Cropsey's voice again. "Raise your hands. Let me see them."

Garcia saw two shadows rise, silhouetted against the sky. Hands high. Two English-speaking *hombres*. Good news for the S-2.

A weapon opened up. Two bursts. The Jihadis crumpled.

"Cease fire! Goddamnit."

Breathing heavily, Garcia stumped the last twenty meters up the slope. Legs on fire.

Cropsey stood over the J's. He watched the shadows where they lay, as if for signs of life. Weapon poised to fire again. He didn't seem to register Garcia's approach.

Garcia grabbed him by the upper arm. "What the fuck?"

"I thought they had weapons."

"Their hands were in the goddamned air. I saw it."

"I thought they had weapons, Sergeant."

"Christ."

"Anyway, they killed Barrett."

"You just shot two men who were surrendering. The S-2—"

"Whose side are you on, Sergeant?" Cropsey demanded. "*They* don't matter. What? We got two squads' worth left out of a platoon? You going to send Corporal Gallotti back with prisoners? And the lieutenant doesn't even know where we are?"

"He's dead. And you listen. Carefully, *hombre*." Garcia leaned close. "You think you're a bad motherfucker? My *sister* would've torn off your head and shit down your throat." Garcia felt the other Marines approaching, and he lowered his voice. Without dropping his intensity. "You're going to follow orders. Or you can go to the rear yourself. Under charges. You understand?"

Something in his tone of voice worked. He could feel Cropsey curling inward. Like a slug you tossed salt on. Maybe surviving Montebello was worth something, after all.

"Yeah, Sergeant," Cropsey said. "I got it."

JERUSALEM

Lieutenant General of the Military Order of the Brothers in Christ Simon Montfort stood on a ridge overlooking the flames as the suburbs of Jerusalem burned through the night. He could tell from the excited expressions exactly what his staff had come to report, but he let them wait a little longer. Illustrating his imperturbability, his destiny to command, his place in history. He understood the impression he made as the distant flames glinted off the three onyx crosses on his helmet. Tall, erect. The model of a Christian soldier.

At last, Montfort turned. Smiling calmly at his chief of staff. "What is it, James?"

"Sir, we've taken the Temple Mount."

Montfort nodded. His smile neither widened nor weakened. The sounds of battle from the middle distance were, indeed, far weaker than they had been even an hour earlier.

Montfort fell to his knees, setting his right fist

over his heart, in the attitude of a MOBIC soldier in prayer. Eyes turned Heavenward. Into the red-tinged darkness.

"Lord God of hosts, we give thanks unto You for the glory of this day. Accept this, Your city, as our humble offering. Amen."

"Amen," his staff echoed.

Montfort rose. Taller than any of his immediate subordinates. All of whom had been carefully chosen. For a number of qualities beyond their zealous faith.

"When the sun rises," he said, "I want no stone, no brick—not one splinter—left standing where the enemies of Christ erected their temple. We will erase the Dome of the Rock from history. Praise the Lord."

"Praise the Lord!" his staff echoed. The Guardians, well-armed, repeated the phrase from the shadows.

"Go now," Montfort said. "Each man to his toil in the vineyards of the Lord."

And after each had gone but one, that man came to Montfort. His eyes asked if he might approach.

"What is it, James?"

"Sir . . . I need a decision about the locals. We've got at least twenty thousand of them on our hands. Maybe as many still hiding in the city. We can't put it off any longer. We need to decide where to move them."

"We're not going to move them," Montfort said.

"But . . . Jerusalem was to be purified . . ."

"It will be. And it shall be. Kill them all."

His chief of staff recoiled. His mouth hung open, robbed of speech. At last, he stammered, "But . . .

there are still some Christians . . . Orthodox, Syriac, Chaldeans . . ."

"Kill them all," Montfort said calmly. "God will know his own."

TEN

· · · · ■ · · · · · · · ■ · · · · · · ■ · · · ·

PHASE LINE DEL REY, JEZREEL VALLEY

"Would you be careful, sir?" the gunner said over the tank's intercom. "You're going to put somebody's eye out with that thing."

Lieutenant Colonel Montgomery Maxwell VI resettled his scabbard around his waist. The commander's weapon station in an M-1A4 tank wasn't the ideal place to wear a saber, but Monty Maxwell wasn't about to break a family tradition. The M-1913 cavalry saber had been given to his great-grandfather by Georgie Patton himself . . . although the family glossed over the circumstances, which involved the suppression of the Bonus Marchers. Maxwells had worn the sword with Abrams in northern France and in Vietnam, under McCaffrey in Desert Storm, and under Wallace on the march to Baghdad. At West Point, Maxwell had been the captain of the fencing team, and later, he'd worn the saber himself during the Abuja campaign.

The sword was an inconvenience, but so was taking a crap during a battle. A man had to do what a man had to do.

As the tank plunged across the fields, buttoned up and attacking east toward Afula, Maxwell wondered if the whole plan wasn't madness. He veered between picturing blue-jacketed ancestors riding with Kill-Cavalry Kilpatrick or leading Buffalo Soldiers against Apaches and wondering what on earth he himself was doing charging up a wide-open valley into the morning sun. With orders to switch off his countermeasures and those on every tank and infantry fighting vehicle in Task Force 2-34. At exactly 0621. For exactly forty seconds.

It occurred to Monty Maxwell that the traditional hatred of staff officers was fully justified.

One click to go. Two brigade combat teams attacking abreast, and still no incoming. Were the J's sleeping in? Or waiting to spring an all-arms ambush when it was too late to make a U-turn? As ordered, he had two armor-heavy companies up, sweeping forward in a skirmish line, with his C Company trailing in a hedgehog column. TF 1-16 to his left and TF 1-34 to his right, with another brigade on the right flank. All of them two up, one back. The Jihadis would be looking at well over a hundred combat vehicles rushing toward them in the front rank alone.

It was the kind of shooting gallery antitank gunners dreamed of.

But nobody was shooting. Yet.

The tank took a hard jolt. Severe enough to make Maxwell worry, for an instant, that a track might have snapped. But the big Abrams, a veteran of more overhauls than the face of an aging actress, kept on grinding forward.

As a battalion commander, Maxwell didn't belong in the front line of vehicles. But when he'd heard the plan laid out at the brigade briefing, he'd decided that he wasn't going to order his soldiers to do such a crazy-ass thing unless he was in the forward rank with them. The XO could follow behind and sort things out. If the Jihadis were shooting straight.

Maxwell had no target in view yet—just a lot of long shadows and dazzling early sunlight. But he wanted to be ready to engage at the longest possible range.

"Loader! Load Lima-Delta."

He imagined Specialist Prizzi going about his work, a sailor manhandling a heavy weight on a rolling deck in a storm. The stabilizers and the suspension did only so much.

A long-distance kinetic-energy round had a greater effective range than any imaging system on the tank. It seemed the obvious weapon of choice.

"Lima-Delta up."

"Prepare to cut countermeasures."

That would bring out a sweat on everybody. At least two brigades' worth of soldiers were thinking the same thing: What's this all about?

As they charged down the valley, into the sun, Maxwell wondered if the Jihadis could feel the ground shake yet. *We're coming*, he told them. *Heavy metal. Just for you.*

He scanned his battle computer—hoping it didn't have a parasite in it—then double-checked the time against his watch. Counting down. Although the J's could see them clear as candy in a dish from the high ground to the north, the attacking units had been ordered to move on radio silence. Until their countermeasures suites were reactivated.

He'd scrutinized the distances on the maps. And he hoped the J's didn't have any extended-range surprises in their arsenal. Crazy-ass staff lunacy. Like going naked in a snake pit.

"Approaching Phase Line Watts," Maxwell said. He was sweating terribly. And he didn't like it. Fear was not a Maxwell tradition.

Oh, bull, he thought. Every one of them was afraid. Of something. At some point.

The landscape rushed toward his viewer. Countdown. Six, five, four . . .

Maxwell flipped three switches with one downward sweep of his hand.

"Countermeasures off."

Sweet Jesus, dear Jesus, don't destroy my battalion . . .

Charging ahead. Jolting over neglected fields. Trying to get the speed exactly right.

In the distance, from ten to three o'clock, Maxwell saw dozens of tiny pops of light.

The ATGMs. Headed straight for them all.

Twenty seconds to go. What was the flight time of one of those sonsofbitches?

Sixteen seconds.

Suddenly, all he wanted to do was to max out his speed, to attack, to get at the enemy who was being given this free shot.

Eleven seconds. Another nasty jounce. The hull scraped something hard. After a second's hesitation, the tank grunted forward.

Eight seconds . . .

More and more pops of light. As if the J's had a division's worth of antitank missiles in the Afula pocket. God only knew what was coming down from the hills at them . . .

Five seconds . . .

Maxwell shifted to his thermal viewer just in time to see a black dot with a flare of flame behind it. Heading straight for his tank.

He almost shouted, "Halt!"

He didn't.

Three seconds . . . two . . .

Before he could flip the switches again, the missile plowed into the earth, less than a football field from his tank's glacis plate. It didn't explode, but threw a spray of earth to either side.

All across his field of vision, missiles were dropping to earth. Digging expensive furrows in the dirt.

As the countermeasures suites kicked back in across the division's front, follow-on volleys of missiles went haywire.

"Well, fuck me dead with a reindeer dick," Maxwell said.

"That an offer, sir?" the gunner said. Relief in his voice.

Now Maxwell was back to being a commander. Wondering if any of his vehicles had been hit. They were off radio silence, but Maxwell figured the jamming would be so heavy that he'd be lucky to reach the tanks to either side of him.

"Hey, sir . . . Watch the sword, okay?"

It had slipped around again. Maxwell settled its position as best he could.

"Stay quiet on the intercom," he said, clicking his headset's control to radio comms.

"This is Stallion Six. Dreadnaughts, unit report. Over."

To Maxwell's astonishment, Captain Brickell's voice came back with perfect clarity.

"This is Alpha. No losses. Continuing mission."

"Bravo, report."

"Bravo here. No combat losses. One Bradley tango-uniform. Broke a track. Continuing mission."

"Charlie, report."

"Two big boys down in an irrigation ditch. Wasn't mapped. No combat losses. Continuing mission."

Hallelujah.

"Gentlemen, draw your sabers." Maxwell wished it wasn't just a figure of speech. "And prepare to close with the enemy."

To the front, splashes of flame and clouds of smoke. Artillery fire dropping on the Jihadi antitank positions. Lots of beautiful artillery. It looked as if every tube in the corps was pumping out rounds.

"A thing of beauty is a fucking joy forever," Maxwell said, back on the intercom. "Anybody know who said that?"

"You, sir?"

"John Keats."

"Sir," the gunner said, "Keats never said—"

"Prepare to repel drones."

Maxwell had seen the dark forms darting out of the veil of artillery smoke. Well, at least they'd gotten through the first wave of ATGMs.

He unlocked his hatch and pushed the heavy cover open, taking a beating about the rib cage as he stood to man the .50 cal. Against drones, it was useless to try to control it while buttoned up. He just hoped the stabilizer wasn't broke-dick again.

A shadow flitted over the tank, then another. Coming from behind. Maxwell looked up. Friendly drones. He watched as they soared toward the approaching enemy UAVs.

Any attempt to employ the machine gun would be as likely to bring down a U.S. Army drone as an enemy airframe. Maxwell pushed the lock release and grabbed the handle to button up again. Gingerly. As a captain, he'd smashed his saber hand on maneuvers by shutting a hatch while rolling through broken terrain.

"Gunner. Targets?"

"Negative, sir," Sergeant Nash told him. "It's not just our smoke. The J's have obscurants up. And they're turning their spectrum jammers on and off."

Where was the Jihadi artillery? Were they limiting it to counterfire? Arty wasn't the best weapon against tanks, especially with the new jammers to divert homing rounds. But it seemed weird that they weren't dumping steel on the attack formation anyway.

A barrage of indirect fire struck three clicks ahead and off to the flank. Surely, the J's couldn't be *that* weak at target acquisition.

"Panama Canal coming up. One hundred meters."

This was the second test. While the overhead imagery confirmed that the derelict Israeli irrigation channels were dry, some were wide and deep enough to trap a tank. Maxwell figured that, in the old days, the Israelis had intended the main channels to do double duty as antitank ditches.

The attack had already blown across a series of minor ditches, but the engineers hadn't been entirely sure about this one.

Even if the antitank missiles weren't back in the

game, his tanks would still be sitting ducks for the drones.

All that Maxwell could see in the sky were occasional black forms. Swooping across his viewer like bats.

The driver slowed the Abrams.

"Sir, what can you see from up there? I can't see the bottom."

"Hold one. I'm going up to look."

Maxwell popped the hatch again, standing on his weapons-station platform. Saber clanking off metal. He could smell the blown-powder stink of the artillery barrage from kilometers away.

"Driver. Slow . . . Move out. Take it straight on. Gunner. Traverse up, max elevation. Everybody hold on."

Maxwell braced himself. The tank tipped into the ditch.

It was shallow. A thing of beauty.

Glancing to the right, then left, Maxwell saw another thing of beauty. Third Brigade, faced with no ditch, was surging forward on the flank. His own vehicle and the rest of the 1st Brigade tracks were climbing out of the ditch. Monsters rising from graves. Dozens and dozens of war machines clawed their way forward.

The front of his tank rose skyward as its rear dropped into the ditch.

Perfect time to hit us. Belly shot, he told himself.

But the friendly artillery continued to dump on Afula, and if the J's were shooting at all, their gun-bunnies were up for the world's-worst prize.

Glancing skyward, Maxwell saw that the drone

count had dwindled, too. Why weren't the J's sending in every drone they had?

"Let's go. Get us out of this ditch, Specialist Vasquez."

"Yes, sir. Trying not to throw a track."

As the tank slammed down on the far bank, Maxwell watched a Bradley tip onto its side. The vehicle commander was crushed against the concrete wall of the ditch.

Maxwell flashed on an old commander, a veteran of Iraq, who'd spoken of war's caprices.

To the right, a missile struck a surging tank and exploded. There was no secondary blast, but the M-1 jerked to a stop. As if someone had yanked an invisible leash.

Maxwell buttoned up again. "All stations, all stations. We're entering their secondary kill zone. Let's punch it. Three clicks, and we're on 'em. Bravo, move into the lead. Alpha, echelon left. Dreadnaughts, acknowledge. Over."

"Alpha, roger."

"Bravo, roger."

"Charlie, roger."

The radio remained beautifully clear. What on earth was going on? No Muslim artillery. A handful of drones. No jamming. Was it some kind of trick? Was it all going to come down on them at once?

They entered the veil of smoke and tuned obscurants. Even the late-model thermal sights revealed only ghosts. It was a fistfight through a curtain now.

The LD-KE had been the wrong round to load. They were moving into HE country. Antitank defenses, but no Jihadi tanks reported in Afula.

Were they holding them back? For a counterattack? Was the blow coming? Maxwell decided he'd just plain called it wrong.

"Loader. Reload HE."

"Safe," Specialist Prizzi shouted into the intercom.

Maxwell heard the breech clank open.

A target registered hot in Maxwell's thermal sight. He punched a button, and the gun slewed around.

"HE loaded. Up!"

"ATGM. Two-two-hundred."

"Identified."

"Fire."

"On the way!"

The gun's recoil, too, was a thing of beauty.

The target bloomed.

Maxwell decided to load sabot. For another click, Jihadi vehicles would register as the principal targets. And sabot would get the attention of any ATGM gunners using buildings, too.

"Up."

The gunner, who had a hunter's high-tuned senses, called, "Identified. PC."

"Fire."

"On the way."

The targets came swiftly after that, nebulous forms and shapes, slowly refining themselves. Twice, another tank's rounds struck the chosen targets just before Maxwell's gunner fired.

"Loader up!" Prizzi shouted. He was already hoarse.

"Stallion Six, this is Charlie. Ammo compartment burning. Passing the stick to my Niner."

"Roger. Stay in the box. Break. Charlie Niner. Keep your victors tight with Rapier Six's. Don't let a seam open up over there."

"Roger. We're grinding sprockets."

"Gunner. Target. Seven hundred."

"On the way."

The target exploded. One secondary blast followed. A third eruption raised a wall of flame.

"Good shootin' this morning, Sergeant Nash," Maxwell told his gunner.

"Sir, would you watch that fucking sword?"

The tank jumped a small berm and shot across the north-south highway.

"Up!"

"Driver, *hard left*."

An invisible fist punched the turret, knocking Maxwell's headgear against steel. "Everybody okay?"

"Roger."

"Clear."

"Yes, sir."

"Driver, hold your right track. Let's get back on course, Specialist Vasquez."

"Stallion Six, this is Bravo. Green. Lead elements Phase Line Pasadena now. Two big boys down. One cat-kill. Minefield vicinity Checkpoint Rosie."

"This is Stallion Six. If you're in it, just keep going. Bull through."

"Wilco."

"Stallion Six, this is Saber Six. Status report."

The brigade commander. Clear as a bell.

"Green. Seven victors down. Lead elements Pasadena. We're closing on the first line of buildings. Continuing mission. *Gunner. ATGM. Fire.* Getting interesting down here. Over."

"Good job, Stallion Six. Give 'em hell. Out."

"Target!" the gunner shouted.

"*Driver.* Punch it. Straight ahead . . ."

The gunner fired into an antitank position. Or what was left of it. Every visible Jihadi emplacement was attracting attention from multiple tanks.

The artillery had lifted, and the Jihadi obscurants were fading. Now it was peekaboo in the patches left behind.

"Load canister."

"Canister up."

"Gunner, clear that street."

"On the way."

The round exploded from the gun tube. A torrent cut down a gaggle of Jihadis—some running toward the fight, others fleeing, some just ambling and stunned.

The tank bit into a low earthen barrier.

Sure enough, a missile thunked against the bottom of the hull as the vehicle climbed over the obstacle. Man-portable, judging by the noise. Too light to penetrate.

As the tank came down again, a heavier missile clanged against the turret.

The vehicle kept moving, but Sergeant Nash shouted, "My sights are gone. You've got it, sir."

"Roger. From my position."

"Prizzi's down."

"Any blood?"

"No, sir. He's crumpled up."

"Take over as loader. *Now*, Sergeant Nash. *Canister.*"

Maxwell fired the round into a vehicle that looked like an armored pickup with a missile launcher and gunner perched in its bed. The truck had been coming straight at them. Brave, if nothing else, Maxwell thought. He watched the vehicle disintegrate as the center of mass of a thousand metal balls tore into it. The gunner in the bed simply disappeared.

Flames. Smoke. Smoldering metal.

"Driver. *Forward.*"

The tank crunched over metal, concrete, and bone, grinding through patches of fire. More light missiles bit into its armor, none penetrating. It sounded like a slow-motion hailstorm.

Approaching an intersection, Maxwell told the driver to slow.

"Crew report."

"Gunner up. Sir, I think Prizzi's got a broken neck. He's—"

"Alive or dead?"

"Sir, I don't know . . . I don't—"

"*Load canister.* Pull yourself together."

"Stallion Six, this is Alpha. We're four streets in. One Bradley down. Not sure anybody made it out."

"Roger. Keep pushing."

At least a dozen Jihadis—more—rushed from an alley and leapt from adjacent doorways. Several carried shoulder-fired missiles.

"Up!" Sergeant Nash shouted. The canister round was loaded.

When Maxwell tried to turn the turret to level the gun on the attackers, it refused to move.

At least one of the missiles had done its job.

"*Driver. Hold the right track. Halt,*" Maxwell screamed. "*On the way!*"

He got lucky. The aim was imperfect, but the canister balls that missed flesh and blood punched into masonry, augmenting their effect with chips and splinters. The result was red and ugly.

Something kicked the tank in the rump. The engine died. A hint of smoke rose from the vehicle's bowels.

"This is Stallion Six. I'm a mobility kill. Anybody have me visual?"

No response.

"This is Stallion Six. Alpha is in command. Alpha, how copy?"

"Lima-Charlie. Cav's on the way, Stallion Six."

The smoke thickened inside the turret. It smelled of circuits, not fuel. Looking through his thermal, Maxwell saw Jihadis dodging forward in twos and threes. That probably meant there were others he couldn't see on his six.

"*Nash*. Get on the loader's machine gun. *Vasquez*. Fight from your hatch. I'm on the fifty. It's happy hour."

Maxwell hit the switch to launch his smoke grenades, but nothing happened. Howling curses, he popped his hatch and thrust up behind the heavy machine gun.

"This one's broke-dick," the gunner called over the intercom. Referring to the loader's machine gun.

The turret was porcupined with small penetrators and smudged with blast effects. The bustle racks were torn away or twisted up like pipe cleaners.

"Fight with your carbine," Maxwell said. Then the intercom died.

With the driver and gunner firing from their hatches, Maxwell opened up with the .50 cal. The bucking bronco. Rounds pinged off the tank, and a missile sizzled by.

"On the roof. Nine o'clock," Maxwell shouted. But the warning was late, and no one heard. The Jihadi shot Vasquez, the driver. Perfect aim, just below the crewman's helmet.

Maxwell traversed the .50 cal. and tore apart the roof pediment shielding the gunman. Then he swept the street behind the tank.

The gunner was still firing. With small-arms rounds flashing off the tank's armor like the sparks from a welding torch. Maxwell put multiple bursts into a window where he glimpsed movement. In what seemed all too short a time, he found himself at the bottom of the ammo box.

Ma Deuce done let me down. *Shit*.

Black smoke wafted from the inside of the tank and rose from the grills and rear deck. Something was getting worse.

Maxwell reached down for his carbine. It wasn't there. With the machine gun silenced, a half-dozen Jihadis charged the tank from the right rear.

He looked to the gunner.

Sergeant Nash had slumped down in his hatch. Unmistakably dead.

A thing of fucking beauty is a fucking joy forever, Maxwell told himself. It's lonely at the top.

It struck him that the Jihadis had stopped firing their weapons. They just swarmed the tank now. Several more appeared behind the first wave.

Why not just shoot me? Maxwell wondered.

In an instant, the light came on. It enraged him to think that any man believed he'd let himself be taken prisoner.

He hauled himself out of the turret and drew his pistol. Firing point-blank into faces and chests. But the numbers were on the Jihadis' side. They clambered onto the smoking tank. Mob rules. Searching for handholds, two Jihadis scorched their paws and leapt away. But the rest kept on coming, screaming at him. Maxwell continued firing, dropping them one after another. Until his pistol clicked empty.

Three Jihadis made it onto the deck on the far side of the turret.

Maxwell hurled the pistol into a man's face. And he drew his great-grandfather's sword.

"Dreadnaughts!" he shouted, and he laid into his enemy with cold steel.

■

Captain Brickell witnessed a remarkable thing. As his tank swung around the corner, he saw another M-1 stopped thirty meters ahead of him. Atop its smoking deck, his battalion commander was slashing away with a saber as a group of Jihadis swarmed around him.

It looked like a scene from an old pirate movie.

Brickell turned his co-ax machine gun on the Jihadis who had not yet managed to board Maxwell's tank. The torrent of rounds swept them off their feet like heavy surf toppling children. One Jihadi bravely tried to kneel and launch an antitank rocket. Brickell cut him in half before he could shoot. Brickell's loader was up in the adjacent hatch and firing too.

The attack on their rear distracted the Jihadis just long enough for the battalion commander to thrust his saber into one man's torso, draw back, and smash the hilt into another's mouth, knocking him headlong from the tank.

Suddenly alone, Maxwell looked about wildly. As if disappointed there was no one left to kill.

Behind the battalion commander, one of his crewmen slumped from the loader's hatch. His posture said "KIA."

Maxwell leapt from the tank, stabbed a writhing Jihadi, and jogged back toward Brickell. With his face blackened by smoke, the battalion commander's grin looked like a madman's.

Still clutching the saber that had been the joke of the battalion, he scrambled aboard the tank that had come to his rescue. Panting, he leaned into his subordinate's face.

"Isn't this the most goddamned fun you've ever had in your life?" Maxwell cried.

ELEVEN

. . . . ■ . . . . ■ . . . . . ■ . . . .

HIGH GROUND, NORTH OF THE JEZREEL VALLEY

Brigadier General Avi Dorn wanted to fight. To slay those who destroyed Israel. But Israel's rebirth was more important than personal revenge.

Speaking on his internal brigade net, he gave the command: "All units, all units. Halt at your present locations. I say again, halt at your present locations."

As Dorn expected, Yakov Greenberg responded immediately.

"Avi, are you crazy? I could walk to Miqdal from here. We're smashing them. They're running like mice. We can be in Nazareth before the Americans reach Afula. It's wide open."

"All units. Halt at your present locations."

Zvika Abramoff was next: "Yakov's right. They're simply running away. A halt now makes no sense. And I'm on exposed ground, I don't want to stop here."

"All of you. Listen to me. I gave an order. You're not in the old IDF anymore; this isn't a debating society. I've been ordered by the Americans to halt. You'll halt, or you'll be relieved."

"This is idiocy," Greenberg responded. "You can tell the Americans I said so. I thought they wanted us to cover their attack."

"Plans change. I don't understand everything the Americans are up to. Just do your duty and obey orders. Out."

Avi Dorn switched off the microphone and sat down. He closed his eyes, finding all of this unbearable. But he had to do what was best for the once and future Israel.

Soon enough, the Americans would be calling. The Americans, from whom he had not heard a word since the attack began.

■

Captain Jason Albaugh of B Troop, Quarter Cav, ordered his driver to pivot and head uphill. He wanted to verify personally what 3rd Platoon's leader had just reported.

The Israeli Exile Brigade had been advancing aggressively since it launched its supporting attack onto the heights. Now, Lieutenant Daly reported that they'd come to an abrupt halt, with no tactical rhyme or reason.

Quarter Cavalry's mission had been to screen to the left of 1-18 Infantry, which was moving forward to cover the flank of the 1st ID attack. Albaugh's troop, on the extreme left, was to maintain contact with the Israeli exile brigade.

Albaugh passed a few smoldering Jihadi trucks, but the fighting—what little there had been of it here—had moved on. In less than ten minutes, he spotted the turret of Daly's tank. The lieutenant had put the vehicle in hull defilade, in a swale below a high meadow.

The lieutenant's head poked up from his hatch. When he saw Albaugh approaching, he climbed out of the turret and jumped to the ground. He waited until Albaugh's M-1 had come up behind, then trotted over and gestured that he wanted to climb aboard.

Albaugh clambered out of his hatch. Ready for a stretch. The lieutenant hauled himself up onto the fender.

"What the fuck? Over." Albaugh said.

"Get up on your turret, sir," the lieutenant told him. "If you stand up, you can see them from here."

Albaugh scrambled over his tank's packed bustle racks and stood up between the hatches. Thinking that he made a lovely target for some stay-behind.

Daly was right. The Israelis had just stopped. Albaugh didn't even need binoculars. Half a kilometer away, he could see a half-dozen IEF tanks and a pair of infantry carriers. No flames, no smoke. They were just plain stopped. Some of the crew members milled about. Others were doing maintenance checks.

"You have their freq?"

"Yes, sir. But they're not responding."

"This some kind of union rule? A siesta break?" Albaugh said. Mostly to himself. He was mad that he hadn't taken the lieutenant's word and called in a report immediately.

"What's going on, sir?"

"I'm stumped, T.J. Try to raise them again. If you get a response, give me a holler. Immediately."

"Roger, sir."

Albaugh dropped back into his turret and reconnected his helmet. "Dragoon Six, this is Bravo."

"Go ahead, Bravo."

"The India-Echo-Foxtrot unit is holding in place two clicks west of Miqdal. There's no opposition up here. They just stopped. And they won't respond on the liaison channel."

"Who reported that?"

"I'm up here myself. Just north of the white-ball in sector. When I get up on my turret, I can see them. They're just smoking and joking. One company of them, anyway."

On the other end, there was a pause that amounted to an unspoken obscenity.

"Good copy, Bravo. Stay tied in with them. Maintain visual contact. And let me know immediately if they go boots and saddles again. The Scotsman isn't going to be happy about this. Out."

HEADQUARTERS, III (US) CORPS, MT. CARMEL RIDGES

Things were going a little too well for Harris's peace of mind. Dropping the countermeasures had worked exactly as Scottie's major had predicted—although an entire company had gotten ahead of the phase line and lost every vehicle it had forward. Otherwise, the losses reported thus far were lighter than the low-end projections. The parasite in the Jihadis' target-acquisition system had worked perfectly. Scottie's 1st Brigade was in control of Afula, with lead elements pushing east.

Yet, the general's expression had hardened almost to grimness. He'd just grilled his G-2 publicly with questions he knew Danczuk couldn't answer off the cuff. It was Harris's way of warning the staff not to pop any invisible champagne corks just yet.

"Where's their armor, Deuce? Where's that brigade they had tucked in below Mt. Tabor, the mixed outfit with the Egyptian M-1s and captured Merkavas? That was a counterattack force. So why aren't they counterattacking? Al-Ghazi's a serious soldier. What's he up to? Why didn't we see more drone activity? Why has the jamming fallen off? So we can all listen to the MOBIC Gospel Hour? Christ, Val, they put up just enough of a defense to play pretend. I'm embarrassed that al-Ghazi thinks I'm stupid enough to buy this. And now you tell me they're pulling back all across the sector? What planet are we on? What's al-Ghazi got up his sleeve?"

Danczuk had been smoking from both ears as he marched off to scour the universe for answers.

The staff members stayed out of Harris's way as best they could, heads down over their work or headsets clamped on. Harris was a calm man in adversity, but success made him nervous.

"Sir," the ops officer sitting on the command net for him said, "General Scott needs to talk to you. ASAP."

Harris grabbed the headset. As if repossessing it from a deadbeat.

"Talk to me, Scottie."

"Has anyone up there ordered the India-Echo-Foxtrots to halt their attack?" The 1 ID commander sounded hot. "I'm getting reports that they're taking the longest piss break in human history."

"Who's reporting that?"

"Quarter Cav. They've got visual. And the India-Echos won't respond to the cav's efforts to contact them. The troop commander down there says they're just kicking back and playing with themselves."

"Hold one, Scottie." Harris turned his head. As if it were on a greased swivel. "Three? You have anything new on Avi Dorn's brigade? General Scott says they've halted in place."

Mike Andretti gave Harris a deer-in-the-headlights look.

"Get on it," Harris told the startled officer. He turned his attention back to the comms rig. "We're looking into it, Scottie. I'll get back to you. How's everything else going."

"Almost too good. I'm not sure I like it."

"That makes two of us. So don't let your guys get victory-is-ours syndrome just yet."

"Roger that, sir."

"Out."

Harris looked at the row of officers and NCOs sitting comms. "Somebody get me General Dorn. *Now.*"

HIGH GROUND, NORTH OF THE JEZREEL VALLEY

"I've got reports of minefields ahead," Avi Dorn told the corps commander on the land line. "I need to send out dismounted probes."

"Come on, Avi. Do it with your blade tanks. Shoot

out some line charges. What's the matter with you? Get moving."

"I can't order my men into minefields."

"Avi, what's up? This isn't like you. Yesterday, you couldn't wait to get at the Jihadis. Now you want to break for tea and sympathy. Level with me—are you going to continue the attack, or not?"

"With all due respect, sir . . . How many soldiers does Israel have left? My brigade and the two brigades with the MOBIC corps . . . a battalion of paratroopers in reserve. That's it. I can't risk nearly a third of what's left to us by charging blindly into minefields."

"Who told you there are minefields? We haven't seen any intel on it."

"Local sources. We still have some contacts."

"Then why not share the information?"

"It just came in."

"Avi, this stinks to high heaven."

"I have my responsibilities."

The silence on the other end of the line was easy to read. Dorn pictured Harris fuming, struggling not to burst into obscenities that could not be recalled. He felt sorry for the general, who was a fighter. It all might have been so different. Dorn wished it had been different. But he would've made a deal with the devil if it resurrected Israel from the dust. Even a shrunken, new-beginning Israel.

He *had* made a deal with the devil, Dorn decided. What else could you call it?

When the general's voice returned, it was measured and cold with harnessed fury: "Avi, I'm giving you a direct order to resume the attack. Now."

"Acknowledged," Dorn said. "My brigade will resume the attack. As soon as we clear any minefields between our current positions and Miqdal."

Harris hung up.

HEADQUARTERS, III (US) CORPS, MT. CARMEL RIDGES

Harris turned to his G-3. "Mike, get a FRAGO out to the 1st Cav. I want their lead brigade moving within two hours to assume Avi Dorn's sector and continue the attack."

"Sir, they're still unloading their—"

"I don't care if they have to move out with two Bradleys, one tank, and a three-legged goat, I want them moving. General Stramara's had it easy up to now. It's time for the 1st Cav to pick up the pace."

Without waiting for a response, he turned to the officer and the two NCOs babysitting the primary command-channel comms. "Get me Major General Stramara. On the land line, if it's up."

A staff sergeant straightened his back and said, "Yes, sir." Without meeting Harris's eyes.

Val Danczuk walked back into the room. His gait struck Harris as odd. Almost as if it wasn't really the G-2, but a robot or a zombie got up as the Deuce. And it was the first time in his life that Harris had literally seen a human being's face go white.

"What is it, Val?"

The G-2 stepped close enough for Harris to see that the man's eyes were lost.

"Talk to me, Deuce."

"Sir . . . We've got . . . I've just got in two reports.

One from Jerusalem. The other's from Nazareth. From our man on the ground."

"Jerusalem can wait. I've got a fight going on right here. What's happening in Nazareth?"

Harris was startled to see tears well in the G-2's eyes.

"Sir . . ." Colonel Danczuk told him, ". . . we need to speak in private."

NAZARETH

Major Nasr wet himself. He couldn't even rise from the bed to stagger to the cabin in the yard. He struggled to rise, at least to a sitting position. But it was a no-go. The effort of the night before had drained him of all the juice he had left.

He had slept. Hard. But the penalty was that his body had locked up. As if it were encased in a hard, jointless shell. The lobster man. Through the slits of his swollen eyes, his smashed hand with its broken finger really did look like a claw.

When he coughed and spit up blood, it hurt his entire torso, his neck, his head. Kidneys, groin, ribs, indefinite organs that had never complained before. The sheet was raw with sweat and lumped with clots of maroon blood.

He could hear, though. With at least one ear. The sounds of battle had come much closer. Not just artillery, either. He believed he could hear the crack of main-gun rounds.

"Pussy," he told himself. "You cunt. Get up. Get *up*. You gonna lay here and piss your pants all day?"

Yes, he was going to lie there and piss his pants all day. And all night. As long as he continued to live.

The owner of the house hadn't dared look in on him. At least, the owner hadn't done so while Nasr was awake.

Was he awake? He wasn't even certain if he was conscious with any consistency.

The bastards who had beaten him were artists, he decided. How else could they have done so much damage without killing him?

He tried to straighten his leg, to free it briefly of the cooling piss-wet and grime. But he couldn't even do that.

I'm not going to cry, he insisted. Yesterday, I was weak. But nothing can make me cry. I'm not afraid. Not anymore.

Lies, lies, lies. A spasm wracked his lungs, and he barked up a clot of dark blood. Bright red blood chased it. Despite all the will he could muster, tears came to his eyes.

Get a new body at Ranger Joe's. Next time I get down to Benning. One size larger, please.

Benning. The all-you-can-eat chicken at Country's Barbecue. Goodbye to all that. Iron Mike was made of flesh and blood, after all.

He tried to think rationally, asking himself if he had left any part of his mission undone that he might still accomplish.

Nasr laughed at himself. Hurting his jaw, his smashed lips, his rib cage again.

You can't even get up to piss. Who're you trying to fool?

Me. Just me. Please help me, Jesus. I'm sorry for

all the wrong things that I've done. I need your help now. Here. In Nazareth. I'm out of juice, and I need your touch to bring me back . . .

He was afraid to pray properly. Afraid that it would be a prelude to death.

With an effort that stole energy from elsewhere in the universe, he cocked himself up from the bed. Halfway. Just far enough to notice that he'd pissed blood.

There were people he would've liked to have seen a last time. Most of them women. It hadn't been a bad ride, after all.

Jesus, I need you now. Holy Mary, Mother of God. Help me.

The door opened. Instead of spirits, Nasr saw a compact man in a perfectly pressed uniform. A colonel. In the Jihadi regulars, the Blessed Army of the Great Jihad. The colonel wrinkled his nose.

Yeah, I stink, Nasr thought. Come and have a lick, you cocksucker.

When the colonel spoke, without advancing from the doorway, his English accent was plummy. Oxbridge, Knightsbridge, and contract bridge.

"Dear me, Major Nasr, you're looking the worse for wear. Would it be a great bother for you to get up now, do you think?"

No bother at all. I was just relaxing.

When Nasr didn't move, the colonel said, "You're really looking rather peaked. We'll see about some assistance, shall we?"

The colonel clapped his hands and made way. Two underlings, also uniformed as regulars, excused their way past him and made for Nasr.

He couldn't put up any resistance. The best he

could do was not to break down in tears when they lifted him. It felt as though his every bone and sinew were coming apart.

The officer spoke in Arabic. Telling his subordinates to go gently, that they would suffer themselves if they did Nasr any further damage.

"I suppose," the colonel told Nasr, "I should have brought a nurse along. Thoughtless of me."

As the men carried Nasr down the corridor, only one of his feet dragged. The other leg curled back, as if in an elbow cast.

Outside, the bright sun shut the slits of his eyes. The enlisted Jihadis really did try to be gentle with him. It didn't help much. When they put him in the back seat of the sedan, he imagined himself imploding, collapsing into a mound of gristle and bone fragments.

"Your forces are doing rather well," the colonel told him, once he had settled himself on the seat beside Nasr. "We Arabs never do seem to get the knack of this sort of warfare. Of course, we have our own repertoire." He tapped the back of the front seat with a swagger stick, and the car proceeded to grind down the broken alley.

"We haven't much time," the colonel told him. "I expect your forces to arrive in Nazareth in a matter of hours. Perhaps sooner. And it would hardly do for me to be here."

Nasr was so crumpled that he barely saw over the ledge of the car door, giving him a child's view. The houses were shut up tight.

"The refugees," Nasr said. He had to repeat it several times before he could make himself understood.

"Oh, they're still here," the colonel told him, once he'd deciphered Nasr's mumbling. "Down in the old city. I'm afraid we've had to shoot a few, to make them understand they're not to leave."

"Why?"

"Just riff-raff, really. The 'intelligentsia' of the Middle East. No feeling for Islam. No sense of faith, of purity. We see them as something of a fifth column. Impossible to reform." The colonel half-turned toward Nasr. "They're our gift to you. Perhaps you can build your new Middle East with them. As your president wished to do, when I was a lad. One must never give up hope—isn't that so?"

As the car threaded its way through the labyrinth of Nazareth, Nasr glimpsed crowds of civilians crammed together in the lower streets.

The noise of war ruled the world beyond.

The car turned south. On the main road.

"I really must apologize to you," the colonel said. "In advance. In wartime, one finds oneself compelled to do things that don't really square with the old conscience. Allah will forgive me, of course. Nonetheless, I find it embarrassing."

Nasr didn't find it embarrassing. Nor did he have another word for what he saw when they pulled up to a stretch of the road where empty lots on either side had become the site of an artificial forest.

"Get him out of the car," the colonel told his subordinates.

They came around and drew Nasr into the warm sunlight.

This? Was this the way it would end? Would there be a special dispensation for this?

They held him up in a mockery of standing. Before him, Nasr saw dozens of crucifixes. Each bore an American soldier or Marine.

"Deplorable, I know," the colonel told him. "But we feel we need to make a point. Not least, given what your MOBIC fellows have gotten up to in Jerusalem." He brought his face close to Nasr's, braving the stench. Nasr saw a youngish man, handsome, with skin the color of coffee with milk.

"The message is that there will be no quarter. From this day forward. This is a war of extermination. Do you think this display sufficient to drive that home?" He backed away. Slightly. "We're not complete barbarians, you understand. Unlike your 'Military Order of the Brothers in Christ.' Is it really Christ's message they carry? I'm surprised, really. But what I wanted to say was only that we're not animals. We killed these men before we nailed them up. No need to gild the lily."

Nasr let his head sink. He could bear the sight no longer. The crows were already at some of the crosses. Crows and flies.

"I suppose I should've mentioned it earlier," the colonel resumed. "Bad form on my part. *You* have nothing to fear. Nothing more, I should say. You're not going to share the fate of your comrades. We need you to do us a last favor. If you don't mind."

The colonel clapped his hands. Nasr heard a car door slam behind his back. A moment later, an NCO stepped up, snapped to, and saluted. After which he handed the colonel Nasr's transmitter.

"It seemed unjust," the colonel said, "to make you climb those streets again. Frankly, you don't quite look up to it." He switched to Arabic and told his men to place Nasr on the far side of the road. They dragged him across the asphalt but sat him down almost tenderly on the curb.

The officer stood over him. The man's shadow dulled his polished brown shoes.

The colonel set the transmitter down in front of Nasr, then dropped to his haunches to look Nasr in the face a last time.

"You're a brave fellow," he told Nasr. "One respects that. Even in an enemy. Now, I think I shall be going. Might get sticky, were I to stay. Peace be unto you, Major."

And he walked off. Car doors slammed. Engines gunned. Nasr closed his eyes and listened as the vehicles turned around and sped off.

When he thought he could bear it again, he took another look at the forest of crosses. And he began to count them. When he was done, he managed to pick up the transmitter with his good hand and cradle it in his lap.

HEADQUARTERS, III (US) CORPS, MT. CARMEL RIDGES

Harris strode back into the command cell. Before he got a good look at the general's face, the ops sergeant working command comms said, "Sir, I've got General Stramara on—"

"Three," Harris snapped. "Take it. Just tell Stramara to get moving." He turned to the comms crew again. "Get me General Scott. *Now.*"

The general hovered. It didn't make things go

faster. But he didn't want anyone to get a dead-on look at his face. It might betray too much.

After a flurry of attempts, a captain told him, "Sir, General Scott's on a latrine break. He'll be—"

"Get him off the can. No. Give me the handset. General Harris here. Listen. I need to speak to General Scott. I don't care if you have to run wire out to the shitter. Get him on the line."

The routine noise of the ops center had faded to hospital-ward-at-night level. They'd all worked together long enough to read the ruling mood.

After a reasonable wait that pushed Harris to the brink of fury, the 1st Infantry Division commander came on the line. Harris cut the other man's apology short.

"Scottie. Fire mission. Which unit of yours is closest to Nazareth, to the road into town from the south?"

"That's in the Fourth BCT sector. I've got 1-18 covering—"

"Pat Cavanaugh's unit. Is he the closest to the road?"

"Yes, sir. I've got Quarter Cav screening and holding on to the India-Echoes, with—"

"Jump the chain. Get on the horn with Cavanaugh yourself. Tell him to get on that road and get into Nazareth. Fast. I have reason to believe the road's not mined. I need him to accept maximum risk." Harris paused to choose his words. "And tell Pat he's absolutely got to keep his men under positive control. Weapons tight."

"The Jihadis may still have—"

"Trust me on this one. I want 1-18 going into town with their weapons on safe. The line doggies are going to be tempted to shoot things up. The officers, too. 1-18's mission is to penetrate the city until . . . until they reach the scene of a reported war crime. They'll know it when they see it. That's all I can say about it for now. Just tell Pat Cavanaugh to secure the scene of any suspected war crime, to push out his perimeter and send patrols into the city. With restrictive rules of engagement."

"But, sir, we're in—"

"Just follow my orders, Scottie. And tell Cavanaugh to report directly to you. Get him on your net, and keep everybody else off it. You'll understand soon enough. And frankly, you'll wish you didn't." Harris took a deep breath. "Maximum risk, weapons tight. Get Cavanaugh moving."

JEZREEL VALLEY, SOUTH OF NAZARETH

1-18 Infantry had spent much of the day taking stray Jihadis prisoner and shooting up vehicles fleeing the main battle. Pat Cavanaugh had lost one Bradley to an antitank missile, with four KIA and the rest of the squad and crew burned and busted up, but breakdowns had been a worse headache than battle damage. He'd been living vicariously by listening in on 1st Brigade's net during the attack on Afula.

Now things were getting surreal. With a tank platoon leading Jake Walker's Charlie Company up the Nazareth highway in a hedgehog formation that straddled the median strip, Cavanaugh had positioned his own track as the ninth vehicle. Standing up in the commander's hatch, he watched the M-1s in the lead traverse their turrets as they scanned for targets. Although they knew—and hated—the order that they weren't to fire unless fired upon.

Had the Jihadis just quit? War crime? What was that about? No details. Just the Scotsman himself on the other end, telling him to move out like the wrath of God was on his ass. Accept maximum risk. Weapons tight. A few hours before, the valley had been a slaughterhouse. Jihadi combat vehicles and supply trucks were still smoldering in the road. The M-1s had to slow and push them aside.

They rolled past an intersection where a ruined rest stop and service station looked like relics of a lost civilization. Which they were, Cavanaugh figured. Ahead, the road rose up through a saddle crowned with once-white buildings.

Nazareth. He wondered if he'd feel anything special, any hint of the sacred, when he actually entered the city. Word was that the place was a pit, an Arab town spared by the Iranians in the great nuke duel because of its Muslim population. And its lack of importance.

He lifted the visor of his vehicle commander's helmet. The brighter world and the rush of air stung his eyes for a moment. But the wind of movement soothed his skin.

Almost as good as a shower. Or maybe not quite.

"This is Bayonet Six," he said into his helmet mike. "Perfect ambush site as we get up into that saddle. Make sure everybody stays alert."

But no rounds challenged them as they growled up the highway.

Crazy war. Last night, they were fighting to the

death. Now it's won't-you-please-come-in. Cavanaugh didn't trust it one bit.

There was no sign of life from the building as they approached. Either deserted, or the locals were down in the basements holding their breath. Cavanaugh's first sight of the city of Christ's youth was of grubby sprawl speckled with litter.

He listened while Jake Walker ordered the lead platoon to slow down as the building density increased. Heads and weapons popped up through the hatches of the Bradleys, scanning upper-story windows and rooflines.

As the column approached a small plateau beyond the crest of the saddle, Jake ordered the tanks to go into overwatch. The infantry tracks would lead into the city. Maximum risk, all right.

Cavanaugh let Walker run his company. The captain was making the right calls. So far. Pedal-to-the-metal was fine out in the great wide-open, but you had to throttle back when the road started turning through a maze of high-rises, shops, and residential compounds.

Cavanaugh's track was the fifth vehicle in column now. The Bradleys nosed down the far slope, torturing their brakes.

The lead track stopped. Lurching heavily. The ramp dropped, and the squad scrambled out. Cavanaugh didn't hear any firing. He could just see a break in the line of buildings. Beyond a row of worse-for-wear apartment houses.

Jake Walker came up on the battalion net. He skipped the call signs. "Sir, you need to get up here. Double-quick."

The company commander's voice trembled.

Cavanaugh got on the intercom. "Ryder. Move us out. Forward. Get around those tracks."

The driver released the brakes, and the Bradley groaned down the road, biting into curbs that looked like they'd been bitten by bigger dogs in the past.

The sight that waited was the worst of his life.

▪

Standing in the road and staring, Cavanaugh knew he needed to get on the net and call in his unit's discovery. But he couldn't quite tear himself away. Beside him, Jake Walker fidgeted. The captain's confidence had deserted him.

When Cavanaugh believed he had his voice under control, he told the company commander, "Push out a security perimeter."

"Shall I start getting them down, sir? The bodies?"

Yes. Get them down. Get them down as fast as you can. And get those goddamned flies off them.

"No," Cavanaugh said. "This has to be documented. Find out if any of your men packed their cameras. Start taking pictures. As many as you can." He turned to go back to his vehicle and make his report. Hoping he could keep his voice steady. "And keep everybody off the net. No comms beyond this company. Tell the cannon-cockers and the medics what I said. And wipe your face. It's all right, Jake. But it doesn't help for the troops to see you like that."

"Yes, sir. Got it."

As Cavanaugh walked back toward his track, he saw an infantryman break loose and stride toward a beggar huddled into a ball on the far side of the road, the only sign of local life in evidence. The pathetic creature in Arab rags hadn't said a word, hadn't looked up.

Rocking himself faintly and trembling, the beggar looked to be just about the filthiest human being Cavanaugh had ever seen.

The soldier raised his weapon as he walked. Cavanaugh saw a thumb click off the safety.

"Freeze, soldier," Cavanaugh said. "You pull that trigger and I'll drop you myself." He found himself holding his pistol out at arm's length.

The soldier stopped. And looked at Cavanaugh. In disgust. His expression warned that he just might shoot anyway.

Cavanaugh understood. But he couldn't tell them that. He would've been glad to go back to the track, get his own carbine, and empty a magazine into the beggar himself.

Just for the satisfaction of hurting something, anything, from *their* world.

But he wasn't going to do it. And the soldier wasn't going to do it.

Cavanaugh remembered the soldier's name. De-Santis.

"PFC DeSantis. Lower that weapon. Put it on safe."

Addressed by his rank and name, the soldier obeyed. But he continued to stare at the battalion commander. As if he hated him as much as he now hated the Jihadis. And every Arab.

The soldier's squad leader walked up, spoke to DeSantis, and shooed him away. Cavanaugh sensed that the NCO had let the scene play out before he intervened.

It was going to be hard to keep them under control. Maybe impossible.

Even with his back turned to the field of crosses, Cavanaugh saw them. And the goddamned flies on their faces.

No. It wouldn't be impossible to control the troops. Because he wasn't going to let it be impossible. That was why he drew his 0-5 pay.

Cavanaugh walked over to the beggar hunched on the curb. Up close, the man looked badly beaten, damaged. Infirm.

The Arab stank. He was bloody. And he reeked of urine.

Then Pat Cavanaugh noticed what looked like a compact transmitter by the man's side. The device looked like military hardware.

Cavanaugh nudged the beggar with the barrel of his pistol. Unwilling to touch cloth or flesh.

"You," he said. "Do you speak any English?"

TWELVE

▪▪▪▪▪▪▪▪▪▪▪▪▪▪

FT. HOOD, TEXAS

She tried to ignore the protesters. At a glimpse of her windshield decal, the gate guards waved her on the post, and she left the shouts and hoisted signs behind. But their words—and their underlying message—gripped her.

U.S. Army Delays, Christian Soldiers Die. Flintlock Harris, Friend of Islam. And the one that stabbed so deeply it drew tears of fury from her eyes: *General Harris: Traitor To Christ And Country.*

Sarah Colmer-Harris drove straight to Quarters One, wiping the wet from her eyes with an index finger. The trip into Killeen had been a mistake. On her arrival at the garage that had serviced her car since her husband took command, a supervisor denied that she'd made an appointment. When she asked to make one, she was told there wouldn't be an opening for months.

Good Christians all, she thought bitterly. Feeling her personal disgust with religion vindicated. It had been one of the few issues on which she and her husband had always disagreed: He still prayed like a child, on his knees. And so many passages in his take-along Bible had been underlined—with a ruler, another child's habit—that it looked like a text belonging to the most conscientious grad student in history.

She snorted as she parked. The noise was animal. If the "Christians" protesting saw that Bible, she decided, they'd probably attack him for defacing a sacred book.

No. They wouldn't. Their masters would. A trial lawyer, once successful, she had sufficient acuity left to realize that those perfectly lettered signs outside the gates had been made well in advance.

Why couldn't Gary see it? Why wouldn't he see any of it? Why was he so blind?

Yes, blind. The thought of the man she loved with all her heart made her so angry that she wanted to lash out at him. Going blind? He'd been blind for years. With his naïve faith that his country was indestructible and that his beloved Army would always remain the institution it once had been.

She knew that, technically speaking, her husband was a killer. He'd killed men in close combat, although he never spoke of it. The citations did. And his friends. His ever-fewer friends. But he was a gentle man at heart. And a gentleman. Blind, willfully blind, to what was going on.

The other blindness, the loss of vision he so dreaded, wouldn't be so bad, she didn't think. He'd make the best of that, too. He'd probably be the first blind Olympic marksman. But his blindness to evil, to the evil that had been growing up around him, was unforgivable.

"The Army will always be there," he'd told her. "After all the rest of them have come and gone."

Would it?

And did it matter, anyway? What good was his cherished Army without the law? When "God's law," as interpreted by a Bible-thumping huckster from the Ozarks, superseded the Constitution? Wasn't that what they'd always accused those Muslim terrorists of doing? Setting themselves up as the voice of God and the arbiter of His laws?

You're thinking like a lawyer, she told herself. And Gary thinks like a soldier. We're both fools. There's no place for either of us anymore.

Why couldn't Gary see it?

The closest he had come to despair had been on the day the new Congress passed a law removing women from the armed forces. Shaking his head, he'd told her, "We're becoming our enemies." But even then, he shrugged it off moments later and repeated, "Well, the Army will always be here. We've been through worse."

She had to watch her tongue with the other wives. More than a few were hedging their bets nowadays. And there were always spies. She wanted to lash out, to demand of them all, "What's Christian about what's happening? Where does it say in the Gospels, 'Kill thy neighbor'?" But enough of her upbringing lingered, of the parochial-school lessons and the catechism, to let her see that Gary's tormentors had nothing to do with Christ—that silly man who believed that the wealthy would share with the poor and that the poor would manifest virtue. Vice President Gui and all his self-righteous hangers-on were about as Christian as al-Mahdi. If not less so. They were creatures of the Book of Revelation, of spectacular stunts of hatred, every one of them afraid of the Whore of Babylon next door, presumably got up as a cheerleader. Christ would've puked.

Oh, what did she know? Maybe they were right, after all. Perhaps God did exist, and His particular genius was revenge. Was she paying, now, for the one error she regretted in her adult life? A brief affair she had lulled herself into while her husband was assigned to the Pentagon and she, a K Street lawyer, felt slighted by his dedication to his work? The affair had been as physically disappointing as it was emotionally repellent. Its end had been an abortion. And her husband, off on one of his TDY trips, had come home and barely noticed she was cranky.

But he was a good man. Perhaps that had driven her into the affair. With a fellow K Street slimeball. Because Gary was just so damned good, so virtuous. All of the goddamned time. A Boy Scout whose sterling qualities would've pissed off the other Boy Scouts. His goodness had humiliated her back then.

Before she surrendered to him. To loving him. To really loving him. A mother was supposed to love her children above all, but she wondered if she did.

Now she just wanted her husband to come home. To take off his uniform. To be done with it. Surely, they'd let him alone then.

Wouldn't they?

She checked the household message center, but there was nothing. She wanted to hear from him, to hear his voice. But he was an ass when it came to playing by the rules. He wouldn't tie up some precious communications line, not even to tell his wife he loved her.

But he *did* love her. She knew that. He loved her, and he loved their daughters. And his damned religion. And his country. And his goddamned Army. How could he have that much love in him? Without taking it away from her?

For all that, she was grateful, and she knew it. And she was proud of him. With the kind of pride you had to learn over years. Over decades. She was proud of all the things about him that made her want to snap at him, to mock him. And now she was afraid for him. He simply didn't understand what men and women were really like.

Had he even understood her? Her selfishness? Venality, even?

Maybe he did. And he still loved her. And that was something else to be furious about. There was something downright degrading in being loved so generously.

She snorted again, her least ladylike habit. The sound always made Gary laugh. That was something none of them understood about him: how he laughed. He loved to laugh, full of jokes in private, when he could drop his mask. She walked past his sprawling leather chair—a monstrosity she'd yearned to get rid of for years. The discolored heap of lumpy cushions made her see him as vividly as any present being could have been. Smiling at her with that crooked, country-boy smile of his and putting on a cracker accent to tell her, "Honeybunch,

I love you like a moonshiner loves a new set of tires."

He loved her more than that. She felt it. She had the love of a good man. Of the *best* man.

Why couldn't they see? What he was really like? Why didn't they appreciate what he stood for?

She found herself on the verge of tears again. Sarah Colmer-Harris, the iron-nerved lawyer, lately of the public defender's office. Until the office, with a backlog of almost seven hundred cases, let her go. "Sarah, there's just not enough work to keep you on . . ." That Baptist swine. Who'd pawed her in the hallway until she punched him—Sarah didn't slap—and threatened to tell his wife. Publicly. In their church on Sunday morning.

Why were they doing this? They were winning anyway. Why did they have to do this to Gary? To all of them? Why couldn't they just shriek their hymns and leave everybody else alone? They had the power now. What more did they want?

To punish people like her. And poor, decent, blind, brave, pigheaded Gary. Because they were all sinners. No forgiveness in the Reverend Jeff Gui's Christianity. Protestants didn't even leave room for penance. Did they?

And Emily. Her eldest daughter. A fighter. Like Gary. "Asked" to leave Johns Hopkins medical school "for her own safety." Of course, she'd refused. But her sister, Miranda, had taken the threats to heart, breaking off her undergraduate studies at Texas A&M and going north to be close to her sister.

Why hadn't she come home instead? *I* need her, too. Who's here for me?

Sarah sat down in her husband's chair and let herself cry. Something she would've been too proud to do in his presence.

Gary, let them have it all. Just let them have it. They'll take it anyway. Come home.

But he wouldn't come home, of course. He'd do his duty. The thought of it made her sick to her stomach and shrieking mad at the same time.

What was happening to their world? And Sim Montfort. Gary didn't know about that one, either. How that sonofabitch had tried to lay her when Gary was off fighting in Saudi Arabia. Well, old Sim hadn't gotten very far. Sim, the pretty boy. She couldn't think of him without summoning the word "motherfucker."

Now Sim had religion. Some said he was America's coming man. Well, he hadn't come in her. That was one thing. Better a scumbag lawyer than Sim Montfort. She'd never trusted him an inch. Even before he showed up at her door and got it slammed in his preening snout.

Ashamed of herself, of her weakness, Sarah stopped crying and got up to wash her face. The telephone stopped her halfway down the hall.

"Hello?" Tentative. Wary of yet another harassing phone call.

It was her younger daughter, Miranda. Hysterical.

"Mom, Mom, it's Emily . . . You've got to come . . . please . . ."

"Miranda, calm down. Stop it. What's—"

"Mom, I'm at the hospital. It's Emily. They beat her up so bad . . . Mom, I can't even recognize her. Mom, you've got to come . . ."

Lieutenant General Gary Harris's wife put some steel in her voice. "You just calm down. Right now, young lady. Do you hear me? We can't let your father know about this."

HEADQUARTERS, 2-34 ARMOR, EASTERN OUTSKIRTS OF AFULA

Less than fifteen minutes after the land lines had been laid to the battalion's tactical operations center, a tank recovery vehicle backed over the wires and cut them again. While waiting for the sergeant from the signal platoon to finish the splices, Lt. Col. Montgomery Maxwell VI sipped from a cup of lukewarm, ass-drizzle coffee and tried to concentrate on the map laid out before him. He had a great deal of lost time to make up.

But his mind kept flapping away from the map and returning to roost on the leaflet his recon platoon leader had brought in. The Jihadis were firing artillery rounds filled with the slips of paper throughout the brigade sector.

The leaflet bore a photograph of crucified soldiers above the printed warning: *This death comes to all infidel Crusaders who profane the Emirate of al-Quds and Damaskus.*

The reproduction quality wasn't first-rate. But you got the message.

Annoyed at his inability to focus on the tactical problem at hand, Maxwell reached out and turned the leaflet face down. But the map before him had become a text in an incomprehensible alphabet.

"Three!" he called. "Any comms yet?"

"No, sir. Jamming's so thick I'm surprised we can hear each other talk out loud."

"Sergeant Escovito say anything about those goddamned land lines?"

"Not yet, sir."

"I need to talk to every company commander the instant we're back up."

"Yes, sir."

"Oh, screw this shit. Sergeant Perkins? Where's my damned driver? Tell him to get my V-hull ready to roll."

"You going forward again, sir?" the S-3 asked.

"They can't hear me from here. And I need to get everybody right with Jesus." He reached for the leaflet, flashed it, then slapped it down again. "We're going to have soldiers wanting to take scalps and collect hides once they see this goddamned stuff."

"Don't you want to go out in a big boy, sir? It's getting nasty out there."

Maxwell shook his head. "Lieutenant MacDonald's going to need his full platoon if we get a shitstorm around the TOC."

But that wasn't the true reason Maxwell didn't want to go forward in a tank. It had more to do with the fact that, for the first time in a war zone, he'd taken off his great-grandfather's saber and stowed it with his personal gear.

He didn't want to be tempted to get back in the fight himself.

Maxwell realized that he'd been an ass. Saber Six should've reached down and relieved him of his command for his shenanigans. Oh, he knew the story was already making the rounds about how he'd taken on the Jihadis with a sword. Chop-chop. The battalion's commander's a real stud. Just hours before, he would've reveled in such admiration, calling it good for morale and letting it feed his ego.

But something had happened to him after the street-fight in Afula. As his battalion pushed through the far side of the town and ran into unexpected resistance that brought the order down from brigade: "Assume a hasty defense and consolidate present gains." After he'd lost six tanks in twenty minutes of stumbling into a serious enemy defense. After the exhilaration of fighting had evaporated and left him exhausted, with countless duties left undone.

In a moment of revelation, he'd seen what a fool he'd made of himself. All that macho b.s. about leading from the front and positioning himself in the first rank of the attack . . . What it really amounted to was that he'd lost control of his battalion as soon as the fight got serious in Afula. He'd waged his own private war in the streets, losing his entire tank crew in the process. He'd had *fun*.

Fun. His men had died so that he could have *fun*.

And yes, it had been fun. For all the combat he'd seen over the years, he'd never felt more alive than in those streets. And then, literally "on the road to Damascus," he'd seen himself with indisputable clarity as a fool. Unfit to be a lieutenant.

He hadn't undergone a conversion to pacifism. Maxwell still got it down in his bones that war exhilarated the right kind of men more powerfully than anything else in their lives would ever do. He'd sensed it before he ever saw combat; it was bred into his bones. At West Point, he'd studied German just so he could read *Stahlgewitter* in the original. Ernst Juenger got it. And, more important, admitted it. To Maxwell, the great sin wasn't enjoying the hell out of war, but pretending all the while that the stay-at-homes were right and it was all boo-hoo terrible. Soldiers didn't re-enlist because war sucked but because they loved it more deeply than they understood themselves. And certainly more than they admitted to the wives they left behind. War was the biggest, most satisfying thing they'd ever touch. And if it wasn't, they weren't meant to be soldiers. No, Maxwell wasn't sorry about killing his country's enemies that day but about his dereliction of duty as a commander.

Now he wanted to make up for it, to be the commander he should've been that morning. But the perfect comms they'd enjoyed during the attack were gone. And only a few kilometers east of their main objective, they seemed to be in a different war, with a much tougher enemy.

His S-2 and the brigade Deuce had done a quick battlefield survey of Afula. Conclusion? 2-34 armor and the rest of 1st Brigade had come up against break-through antiarmor systems—manned by third-rate Jihadi units. Fanatical, yes. And trained about to Cub Scout standards.

That explained a lot about the day's fighting. And raised even more questions. Why had the J's thrown the first half of the day's game? Was there a trap no one could see? Who was really dancing to whose tune? Above all, what were those leaflets all about? Did the Jihadis really think that they'd scare

American soldiers into quitting and running away with threats like that? Did they understand so little about Americans?

It was a day of insights. Unexpectedly, Maxwell found himself wondering how much his own kind really understood about the Jihadis.

"Sir?" It was Specialist Kito, his wheeled-vehicle driver, a young soldier from Guam with a chronic smile and the nickname "Tree Snake." "All ready to go now, sir."

Maxwell nodded and tossed the remnants of his coffee out on the ground. Ready to move out.

But an odd look passed over the driver's face. "Don't you want your big sword, sir?"

The battalion commander shook his head. "It just gets in the way."

HEADQUARTERS, III JIHADI CORPS, QUNEITRA (GOLAN HEIGHTS)

Lieutenant General Abdul al-Ghazi of the Blessed Army of the Great Jihad drank his sweet mint tea with satisfaction. His hour as a soldier had come. The ferocity of the Crusaders who had attacked the forces of Emir-General al-Mahdi in the south, coupled with the audacious dash across the Carmel Ridges by the American mercenary forces, had forced a hasty rearrangement of the defensive plans. But now al-Ghazi had satisfied the special requirements imposed by his superior—including the emir's Nazareth gambit—and al-Ghazi was free to fight as professionally as he could, *Insh'Allah*.

Al-Ghazi was a man of uncompromising faith, yet clear-eyed enough to realize that his enemies considered him a fanatic because of that faith and would underestimate him. He understood the weaknesses— and the strengths—of those under his command. His Arabs and those who fought beside them were not yet fully competent to wield every military technology they possessed. They lacked the phlegmatic temperament, advanced staff skills, and even the basic trust essential to sustain complex offensive operations against opponents like the Americans. But he also knew that his men would fight well from prepared defensive positions, as long as they felt that they were being supported and not abandoned, and that their ability, however imperfect, to wield the newest military systems was greater by far than the skills possessed by their fathers and grandfathers, peace and honor be upon them. Finally, their faith would give them strength.

As for his own superior, the emir-general, al-Ghazi still worried about the extremes of passion he glimpsed in the man, nor did he feel confident that he knew how many games of chess al-Mahdi played at once. But for all that, he smelled the genius Allah had granted the emir-general, his talent for victory. And al-Mahdi shared his vision of the one great matter: The only way to buy time to rebuild the strength of the caliphate was to inflict so shocking a defeat upon the Crusaders that they would leave and lick their wounds for ten or twenty or even thirty years before invading the home of Islam again.

And they would come again. The Crusaders always came again. The defenders of the sacred places had been too weak for too long. Accustomed to centuries of easy victories, the Crusaders and their Jew masters were drawn to the lands of the Prophet's revelation, peace be upon Him, as flies were drawn to sticky dates. Or to blood. The Christians and Jews possessed so much, even now, that no man could count it all, but they would not leave the children of Allah in peace in one poor corner of the world.

How long had they been fighting, Muslim, Christian, and Jew? For fourteen hundred years, the sabers of Allah had dueled with the armies of Shaitan. The fortunes of war had gone back and forth, from the days when the turbaned knights of Grenada hunted Frankish dogs among their hovels at the Atlantic's edge, or the Sultan's janissaries seized the beauties of Lehistan, of Poland, for the slave markets of Asia, then on to the grim centuries when Shaitan had given the power to the Christians and finally to the Jews to heap impurity and shame upon the virtuous, the pious, and the good.

Al-Ghazi grasped full well that Islam's struggle now was merely to survive and only later to reclaim the lost lands of the golden age. But he also believed that a new golden age would come, if only in a future century. Allah could not let it be otherwise, although there would be many tests ahead, much atonement for the corruption of the faith, for waywardness, for error. Fools had expected great results quickly. But Allah would bring victories only when He willed them, not when hotheads demanded them.

Meanwhile, Abdul al-Ghazi relished the chance to match his skills against this great American general, this Flintlock Harris. The man seemed a worthy opponent, and al-Ghazi looked forward to inflicting unexpected pain upon this Harris and those he commanded. But he also realized that al-Mahdi was correct about the greater things that must be done. The emir-general had misjudged his ability to defend al-Quds, but everything after its fall appeared to be going as he had planned it. And it was essential to work together, not to succumb to the selfishness and anarchy that had doomed generations of Arabs and Muslims. This time, let the Christians tear at one another's throats.

"The Crusaders cannot see themselves plainly, nor can they see us clearly," al-Mahdi had told him. "They call us 'mad' because we believe in Allah with all our hearts, yet they believe madly in their own misbegotten faith. We know that this life is but a sport and a pastime, yet they call us 'fanatics.' They imagine that devout Muslims cannot think clearly or be wise in the ways of the world, while they let their own faith cloud their every thought. They call us 'dogs,' but they are the ones who bark at shadows. And believe me, my brother, when I say that we will make this dog Montfort dance at *our* command." Al-Mahdi had smiled as if tasting the figs of Paradise. "We hardly need to defeat him. His own pride will destroy him. *Insh'Allah*."

There remained a great deal to be done to spring the great trap, of course. Much could still go wrong, and al-Ghazi refused to succumb to the fantasies and wishful thinking that had haunted too many failed champions of Islam. But he had regained his self-assurance since the day before, when he had wondered if the Crusaders would manage to destroy all civilization this time, to return the Dar al-Islam to enslavement and barbarism. Based on the recent moves of this "Military Order of the Brothers in Christ," it now seemed clear that al-Mahdi understood his opponent with the insight that Saladin had brought to bear on those proud knights of the Kingdom of Jerusalem.

May these Crusaders perish as miserably, al-Ghazi thought.

And Harris? Did they understand him, too? The American general seemed such a simple man. Dull, even. No man with whom to share a pleasant evening. Yet, he had a reputation as a great soldier. Al-Ghazi didn't intend to underestimate him as the pig Montfort, the Butcher of al-Quds, underestimated the emir-general.

Let them come, al-Ghazi thought, and we will give them their catastrophe, *Insh'Allah.*

He buzzed for his aide. The young officer rushed in, as if afraid of being lashed. He was as pretty as a girl from the mountains above Suleimaniye.

"Is there any word from Nazareth?" al-Ghazi asked. "About the American reaction?"

"No, General. Nothing. Nothing yet."

"Then leave me."

"Excuse me, please, General."

Al-Ghazi raised one thick eyebrow.

"Colonel al-Tikriti has been waiting for you," the aide continued. As nervous as a virgin on her wedding night. "I told him you were not to be disturbed. But he said that it was important, that he would wait."

"For Colonel al-Tikriti, I always have time," al-

Ghazi lied. "Send him to me. In a moment. First, leave me and shut the door."

Al-Ghazi got up and straightened his uniform as he walked to the full-length mirror leaning against the wall. Yes, all was in order. He looked as a soldier should look. As a *general* should look. The emir-general looked like a holy man masquerading as an officer, with his unkempt beard and scholar's rounded shoulders. Yet, al-Mahdi was right about so many things.

There *had* to be hatred. Al-Mahdi understood that. The hatred had to cut so deep that Shaitan would never again be able to insinuate himself with the lie that Muslims could live side by side with those of other faiths. An Islam that did not rule was not Islam. An Islam that was not free of impurities was not Islam. An Islam sick with infidels and their practices was not Islam. Look what "cooperation" and "tolerance" had wrought: nothing but misery and betrayal for the children of Allah.

As for all those who had argued for "building bridges" and "peace through understanding," the falsely educated, the Westernizers, the traitors, al-Ghazi would've been pleased to kill them by his own hand. But the emir was right about that, as well.

Better to let the Americans do it.

His aide knocked. Al-Ghazi posed himself, standing, behind his desk.

"Come in!"

The door opened. Colonel al-Tikriti, his personal intelligence officer and a cousin by marriage, spread his mustache with a great smile, answered by a smile of al-Ghazi's own. The general stepped out from behind the desk, opening his arms in greeting. He knew exactly how many paces it took to make a guest feel welcome according to his station. Al-Tikriti would need to come two-thirds of the way across the room to meet him.

After they embraced and kissed, the colonel's smile disappeared. And when he spoke, it was in a whisper.

"The emir is up to mischief with the Crusaders. He's been in contact with one of them for months."

Al-Ghazi stepped back. As if he had embraced a man covered in plague sores.

"How could you know this?" he demanded.

Colonel al-Tikriti smiled. It was a smaller, harder smile this time. "Cousin, when I was a young man in Iraq . . . when we both were younger men . . . an American officer gave me a long lecture about the uselessness of torture during interrogations." The smile grew slightly larger. "He was wrong."

THIRTEEN

....■.....■.....■....

HEADQUARTERS, III (US) CORPS, MT. CARMEL RIDGES

Flintlock Harris tried to look into each face crowded into the ad-hoc briefing room. All of the assembled staff officers and subordinate commanders were overdue for showers, and the closed space stank like a gym during a janitors' strike. Weary hands brushed away flies. It had been impossible to control the news about the crucifixions in Nazareth. Harris could feel the danger, as palpable as sweat, that the behavior of his soldiers would degenerate into savagery.

Which was, Harris figured, what more than one party involved wanted.

The murmurings had quieted the instant Harris got to his feet. Now the loudest sound in the room was the pop-back of a plastic water bottle squeezed too hard. Beyond the walls of the shabby house, spikes of noise reported the commotion attendant to jumping the command post to a new location. More disruption, at a bad time. But staying in one place too long made the headquarters an easy target.

Harris had stripped his field headquarters by almost two-thirds of its personnel from the old, fat days in Saudi or Nigeria. But moving it still reminded him of a circus leaving town.

Time to speak. He'd wasted enough time already. Harris wished he were better with words.

"All right," he said abruptly. "Listen up. We are *not* going to do anything stupid, and we're not going to do anything immoral. Or illegal under present laws and conventions." He stared fiercely into the faces before him. "And I don't give a damn what anyone else does. The units under the control of this corps inherited two hundred and fifty years of U.S. Army and Marine Corps traditions. We are not going to shit on those traditions." He scanned the room again. Not everyone was a happy camper. "Everybody got that?"

Harris took a deep breath, aware that not every head had nodded enthusiastically. "I'm as revolted and disgusted and angry as anybody by what those sonsofbitches did in Nazareth. But we're dealing with an enemy who wants us to respond in kind. They're praying for it. And we are *not* going to do it. We will not answer crimes against humanity with our own war crimes." A fly nearly the size of an attack drone flirted past his face. "The soldiers and Marines under my command are going to fight ferociously to destroy our enemies. I don't want anyone who takes up arms against us to have a second chance to do so. But once an enemy is our prisoner, he will be treated with decency. With appropriate rigor, but with human decency. And we will not kill or otherwise harm civilians, if it can be helped. We're soldiers and Marines, not a lynch mob."

Harris reared up, making his back as rigid as if standing on a parade ground. "I will *not* accept bogus reports of collateral damage. You know what's legitimate and what's not. And I know it. We aren't going to pull any punches on the battlefield. But when the shooting stops, our soldiers and Marines are going to behave with discipline . . . and decency." He wished he could find another word, a stronger word than "decency." But his mental arsenal was empty. "Questions?"

The 1st Infantry Division commander's liaison officer raised his hand.

"Jim?"

"Sir . . . putting Nazareth off-limits . . . Sir, that makes it tough for us to support the 1st Cav in the Golani Junction push. It leaves a gaping hole in the road network."

Harris nodded at Mike Andretti, his G-3.

The Three stood up and faced the liaison officer. "Orders are coming down on that. Units can conduct movement through Nazareth on the primary road and its northern branches. But no stopping in the city, unless it's a legit breakdown. 1-18 Infantry has been placed directly under corps command, and for now, Pat Cavanaugh's the sheriff of Nazareth. When any other unit's inside the city limits, Pat Cavanaugh's the boss. Rank immaterial." Andretti shifted his eyes back to the corps commander.

"Problem solved, Jim?" Harris asked.

"Yes, sir. Thank you."

Harris shifted his attention to his G-2. The intelligence officer looked as neatly pressed and well-scrubbed as ever. Maybe even taller and handsomer than the day before. Ready for a magazine cover. Except for the dark circles. Harris tried to enforce a sleep regimen, but it never worked.

"Talk to me, Val. Short and sweet, so everybody can get back to work."

Colonel Val Danczuk cleared his throat. As if about to deliver a sermon to a multitude. "Sir, the Third Jihadi Corps has its A-Team in the fight. Resistance has stiffened markedly, with the J's committed to a defense along the line of Highway 65 north of Mount Tabor."

"So they gave us Afula and Nazareth. So to speak," Harris interrupted.

"Yes, sir. General al-Ghazi sacrificed a good twenty percent of his best antitank systems, but the troops in Afula were reservists. Stiffened by one commando battalion."

"And Nazareth was undefended." Harris looked around the room again. "You all get the point. Took me until this afternoon to figure it out for certain, but it's evident that the Jihadis are counting on us to give them an atrocity, to turn Nazareth into a butcher shop. That's why they've crammed it full of professors and engineers and so forth. Figure it out: We slaughter their intelligentsia, getting rid of a noisy problem for the Muslim hardliners. And they then use our action to rally the Arab world against us. Just in case Arabs needed any more rallying, after what's happened in Jerusalem. Okay, go ahead, Val."

Danczuk traced his light-pencil over the map.

"Al-Ghazi only has a division-minus as his corps reserve, dispersed across the Golan and curving around to the Metulla pocket. They're out of artillery range but positioned for a counterattack. Intercept—what there is of it—suggests they've got a looming fuel shortage. They're marshaling their supplies . . . to the extent that only the most gravely wounded are being evacuated beyond Quneitra. By the way, we're increasingly certain Quneitra is their corps headquarters. If we had fixed-wing air support, we—"

"We don't have it," Harris snapped. "And we'll discuss that later. Bring everybody up to date on the MOBIC situation down south."

"Yes, sir." The light-pencil went into action again. "The remnants of the Second Jihadi Corps, directly subordinate to General-Emir al-Mahdi, have abandoned Jericho. Al Mahdi appears to have split the corps, sending his 99th and 156th divisions east across the Jordan. We believe they'll set up hasty blocking positions on the east bank after dropping the fixed and temporary bridges, but their primary mission will be the defense of Amman. Meanwhile . . ." the tiny spot of light traced northward on the wall map, ". . . al-Mahdi's 'September 11th' Armored Division and the 40th Jihadi Commando Brigade have been withdrawing up Highway 90, paralleling the Jordan River, as you see here. Al-Mahdi's reportedly with that force."

"A fighting withdrawal?"

"Only when they have to fight. They seem intent on moving northward fast, with the apparent intent to consolidate forces with the Third Jihadi Corps in our area of operations. And the limited road network in the vicinity of the Sea of Galilee would explain why the Third is now so determined to hold onto Highway 65—or at least keep us off it."

"Treatment of civilians?"

"By which side, sir?"

"Both."

"Bad. The J's have attempted to put refugee streams from Jericho between them and the advancing MOBIC elements. Buying time with lives."

"MOBIC?"

"Sir, they're killing everything in sight. Their engineers have been ordered to level Jericho."

Harris grunted. "More work than it was in Joshua's day." He felt the silent gasps. But Harris was sick of pretending. He was furious and disgusted by the behavior of his fellow Americans and their "God wills it" rampage. To the extent that he had flashes of fantasy about turning his corps against the MOBIC corps, to put a stop to the bloodbath.

What had his country come to?

Harris turned back to his operations officer. "Mike, how's the MOBIC corps responding to al-Mahdi splitting his force?"

"Sir, the Military Order of the Brothers in Christ units are pursuing the Jihadis northward along the Jordan as their primary mission. General of the Order Montfort's positioning one division torn up in the Jerusalem fight and a fresh follow-on division to secure the Jordan crossing sites vicinity Jericho and protect the MOBIC lines of communication."

Harris nodded. "Anybody needs the latest enemy order-of-battle info, get with the Deuce's number two after this meeting. Now . . . Let me just think out loud, gentlemen. The worst-kept secret in the world is that our campaign objective is Damascus. And the best approach to Damascus from Jerusalem just now is via Amman. The obvious choice for al-Mahdi would've been to pull his entire Second Corps back to the east bank of the Jordan. But he didn't. Anybody care to guess why? Go ahead, Monk. Speak up. Your eyes are popping."

The Marine general didn't leave his chair. "The Jihadi withdrawal up the west bank of the Jordan is bait. To draw off the MOBIC forces. Keep them from pushing straight for Amman."

"Okay, Monk. That's the bait. What's the trap? How do they spring it?"

"That one . . . I can't figure out yet."

"Anybody? No? Well, I can't crack the code yet, either. Deuce, watch that one. If ever I smelled a setup, al-Mahdi's putting one together. They're playing chess, while we're playing checkers." He looked around the room. "Three? Anything critical you haven't briefed earlier?"

Mike Andretti rose again. "Sir, the 1st Cavalry Division has one brigade ashore, with its lead elements conducting a forward passage of lines with Avi Dorn's brigade. The IEF is still just sitting there west of Nazareth. Another 1st Cav brigade's about 50 percent ashore, as of 1800. General Stramara believes he'll be in position to execute a divisional attack by 1200 tomorrow. General Morris's Marines—"

"We'll go through that later. Drone problems?"

"Sir, they're still coming hot and heavy. Killer

number one of our armored vehicles. And they're still a bitch on the beachhead."

"Jamming."

"Like a sky full of mud. The J's don't want anybody talking. They're blanketing the spectrum so heavily they can't talk, either. And 1st ID reports that a broadcast e-cancer has penetrated their logistics network."

"Four? You got your firewalls up?"

Colonel McCoy nodded. "Corps is clean so far, sir."

"Anything else for the assembled multitude?"

The G-4 looked tired but didn't sound it. "The Haifa pipeline should be partially operational by tomorrow. Full flow in forty-eight hours. God bless the SeaBees. Other than that, sir, everybody needs to understand that the bottled water's for drinking. No washing in it. Or dehydration's going to be a bigger problem than those drones."

"Thanks, Real-Deal. All right, you all heard him. Make sure you've got good water discipline. And good discipline in every other respect. All right, gentlemen. Boots and saddles. Monk, you hang on here. Deuce, Three. You, too." He looked at the plans officer. "And you, Marty."

The other officers cleared the room. Usually, after a briefing, one or two would approach Harris with a problem they didn't want aired too widely. But each man sensed that this was not a day when the corps commander was feeling charitable.

When the last straphanger was gone, Harris turned to his aide and said, "Close the door, John."

Then he turned to the remaining officers, making no further attempt to hide his anger.

"Now, what the fuck is going on?" he demanded.

▪

"Three," the corps commander snapped. "Have your people laid hands on that goddamned zoomie yet?"

Colonel Andretti looked down at the tabletop. It was never good news when the G-3 did that.

"Sir, he flew up to Cyprus this afternoon. To Holy Land Command. He told my deputy—"

"I hope he took his beach towel and flip-flops. Where's *his* deputy?"

"He went with him to HOLCOM."

Harris shook his head. Then he looked at Monk Morris. "Okay, run the scenario by me one more time."

The Marine said, "Dawg Daniels was locked and cocked to run the full series of missions today. Then the Air Force shut down the field."

"I thought it was a Marine airfield."

"The HOLCOM commander backed the Air Force."

"Same rationale from the zoomies?"

"Yes, sir. 'Too dangerous to fly. High threat environment. Can't risk irreplaceable aircraft.' "

"But the MOBIC air arm can fly down south. And carpet-bomb villages."

"Yes, sir."

"Next thing, they'll ground our rotary-wing assets. This stinks like a baboon's ass."

"Yes, sir."

A pure-vinegar smirk twisted Harris's face. It was an expression he never would've permitted himself beyond this small circle. "The Air Force thinks Sim Montfort's going to leave them unmolested. When this is over. Because they helped screw the Army and Marines."

The Marine two-star shrugged. "Divide and conquer. Montfort's read his Sun-Tzu."

Harris's grimace deepened. He looked around. At his G-3, his G-2. At his plans officer and his aide.

"You know one of the reasons Sim Montfort's taking that bait and chasing the J's up the Jordan Valley? Other than the fact that he wants his MOBIC troops to have credit for liberating every possible Christian site? What do you think, gents? Any takers?"

"Because," Monk Morris said calmly, "once he's up here, he'll argue for 'unity of command.' Under his command."

"Bingo!" Harris said, cocking his fingers to imitate a pistol. "And then he's got what's left of the U.S. Army under his thumb."

"And the Marines. Sir, I figure he's going to try to subordinate us to the MOBIC Corps. Replacement cannon fodder."

"God bless us one and all. Monk, you and I are looking at the same target array." Harris pivoted sharply toward his plans officer. Every officer in the room was marked with sweat up and down his uniform. And yearning for fresh air. "Marty, show General Morris what you've got. Lay it out. Monk, here's what I propose. I've got to get the rest of 1st Cav ashore tonight. But I want you to be prepared to start marching, on order, tomorrow morning. As soon as we can clear the junctions on the north-south roads. Your division, plus all attachments, will pull off line—we'll get a Cav screen down there in front of you. You'll road-march from the south of sector, where you're an obvious grab for the MOBIC corps, and head north. Primarly on Route 70, going fast through the hot zones. You will then position your Marines on the corps' northern flank. Marty, point out the—"

"I can see it, sir. I get it," the Marine said.

"You'll be positioned to attack east, on order, to envelop retreating Jihadi forces. On either or both of those axes. Right through what used to be southern Lebanon. Or, if we see a Jihadi counterattack first, you'll be prepared to attack into its northern flank."

Morris said, "We'll need to space the convoy serials more widely than the tables call for. In case somebody gets bogged down where the radiation count's still high."

"Yes, sir," the plans officer, Lieutenant Colonel Marty Rose, put in. "We've already rejiggered the movement tables."

The Marine looked back to the corps commander. "Radio silence, I take it? Full electronic deception efforts?"

The plans officer answered for Harris again. A bit too eagerly. "We're almost finished with the deception plan. Full spoofer support. We're going to make you disappear."

Monk Morris nodded, keeping his eyes on the corps commander. "Sir, if you can, give me one day to refit and rearm once I'm up there in those valleys. Then we'll be ready to go anywhere you want to point us."

"We'll do what we can down here. Part of it depends on the Jihadis, part on whatever shenanigans Sim Montfort and the MOBIC crowd get up to." Shifting his attention to his operations officer, Harris changed the subject. "Mike, can we provide 1-18 Infantry with an MP company? To beef them up in Nazareth? I'm concerned about things getting messy. *Agents provocateur.* From any number of sources." A pair of flies conducted a dogfight in front of his face.

"Sir, we just can't do that. Not for twenty-four hours, anyway. The Mike-Papas have all they can handle with traffic control, patrolling the LOCs, and handling POWs. They're asking for additional support themselves. We're running them ragged."

Harris punched at the flies pestering him. "All right. Mike, scratch the raid those Rangers had scheduled for tonight. Yeah, I know. Got it. Hate to blow off the target. But Nazareth is going to become a strategic issue. I'd bet my retirement pay on it. And Pat Cavanaugh just won't have enough boots on the ground to cope if it turns into a goat-rope. He's going to need the toughest, most-disciplined hombres we've got. Send him a full Ranger company."

"Yes, sir." The Three, a former Ranger battalion commander, smirked. "They won't much like serving under a mech-head, though."

"They'll suck it up, Mike. Just like you suck it up."

"Yes, sir."

Suddenly, Harris smiled. But there was no trace of joy in it. "When I was a junior officer in Iraq, we talked on and on about how there were no front lines in the war. We didn't have a clue." Then he dropped his dead-man's smile and turned to his aide. "John, I want one of those old Black Hawks with the extended-range tanks ready to go. I'm flying to Cyprus. Immediately."

Except for Monk Morris, each of the other officers alerted. Surprised. Monk never let anything surprise him much, and Harris loved the old Marine for it.

After a few seconds, the G-3 asked, "Sir . . . You really think you'll get us fixed-wing support? I mean, do you believe there's any chance at all? I'd love to whack Quneitra. And those reserve units."

"I'm going to try, Mike. But I'm also going to try to do a pre-emptive strike on the command-relationship issue. To keep Sim Montfort's hands off this corps." The sweat-polished skin on the general's face tightened. "We've already got enough blood on our hands."

NAZARETH

"Maybe I should try drinking the local water, sir," Command Sergeant Major Bratty told his battalion commander, gesturing with his bandaged hand. "I haven't taken a dump in four days."

Pat Cavanaugh couldn't help smiling. Despite standing just down the street from two lines of body bags awaiting transport. After documenting the atrocity, he and his men had taken down their crucified comrades. At one point or another, every man had wept. Except the sergeant major. Who insisted on treating everything as just another day at the war.

The sergeant major may have lost his trigger finger, but he was still rock-solid. Cavanaugh envied the sergeant major's strength.

"Stop eating the cheese in the ration packs," Cavanaugh told the other man. "And stop playing with that bandage, Sergeant Major."

The sergeant major shook his head. "I almost envy the XO. Dysentery sounds pretty good right now."

Cavanaugh grew serious again. The evening air had the weight of wet sand on his shoulders. "What do you think, Sergeant Major? Can we keep them under control?"

"There's a few of them I'd keep an eye on. I'll pull the hard cases in close. But I don't think any of our men are going to start anything. I've given the NCOs the full fire-and-brimstone. I'm just worried about some dumb-fuck Arab doing something stupid." The sergeant major opened his hands as if freeing a bird. Cavanaugh noted a spot of blood on the bandage where one of the finger stumps poked up. "It wouldn't take much."

Cavanaugh looked at the line of body bags. Where were the goddamned trucks? "Christ, Sergeant Major. I'd rather be fighting. Bare knuckles against razor blades."

"Come on, sir. No self-pity at the top. Old Flintlock knew what he was doing when he dumped this shit on your shoulders."

"Roger on the first. We'll see about the second. Any word from the rear on Sergeant Brodsky?"

"Comms are still down, sir. Last I heard, they thought he'd lose the second leg, too."

Cavanaugh shook his head. Staring off toward the body bags again, unable to keep his eyes under his command. But the sergeant major wasn't having any of it.

"Come on, sir. This is what we signed up for. You need to eat some chow. Hell, I'll give you my cheese pack . . ."

A shot. Followed by an echo. It punctured the odd stillness of terrified human beings, hiding behind closed doors in their thousands. Framed by the groans of military vehicles in the far streets and the relentless sounds of war beyond the ridges.

"That was downtown," the sergeant major said. His even tone still managed to communicate that it wasn't good news.

"You stay here, Sergeant Major," Cavanaugh called. Already running for his track. "Let's go, Hotel-1. Boots and saddles."

Bratty barked, "Sergeant Rodriguez. Back up Bayonet Six with your squad. *Move.*"

Two Bradleys snorted down the hill, deeper into the unkempt city. Cavanaugh had already paid a quick visit to the old center, with its Biblical memories, while positioning his companies and refining their sectors. A wretched place, it didn't excite any feelings of piety in him. Only repulsion.

In the dead heart of the old town, Cavanaugh spotted a new-model light armored truck. There were none in his battalion's inventory.

"Specialist Quandt," he told his driver over the intercom. "Butt-fuck that guy. I don't want him going anyplace until I find out who he is."

"Roger, sir." The driver pivoted the big armored vehicle to the left, closing off the narrow street.

Cavanaugh saw two more of the brand-new vehicles. And a V-hull truck.

A pair of soldiers popped out of a doorway, weapons up. Not his men.

Cavanaugh had to get very close—snuggled right up behind the line of vehicles—before he could see the black crosses in the fading light. Black crosses, on the left breast of the uniform tunics.

Sonofabitch, he thought to himself. Then he warned himself to keep his temper. But he jumped down from the Bradley's deck like a paratrooper landing ready to fight.

Both MOBIC troops were junior enlisted men. Cavanaugh had no intention of wasting time on them.

"Where's your commanding officer?"

The two soldiers looked at him sullenly. Insolently. Then the corporal said, "Major Brown's reclaiming the site of the Annunciation. For our Lord, Jesus Christ. And Christians everywhere."

"Post one fire team here," Cavanaugh told Sergeant Rodriguez, who had just come up behind him. "Then cover my six."

"You got it, sir."

Cavanaugh plunged ahead. Striding up the lane. Toward the site where the Church of St. Gabriel once stood. He'd stopped by earlier. Briefly. The rubbled lot had been turned into an open-air latrine, and the below-ground cavity where Mary's well lay hidden was a cesspit.

A short block up the hillside, Cavanaugh found a

squad of MOBIC soldiers unspooling white tape printed with black crosses, cordoning off the area.

None of them paid the least attention to the corpse lying in the center of the plaza. The dark blood on the paving slabs shone fresh. The dead man was an elderly Arab.

Cavanaugh tightened his grip on his carbine.

Two MOBIC troops glanced up at his approach. Then they dropped their spool of tape and rushed toward him, holding up their hands like old-fashioned traffic cops.

"Stay where you are. Don't enter this site."

"Get out of my fucking way."

The scattered MOBIC soldiers alerted. They began to close toward the center of the plaza. Slipping their rifles from their shoulders. An officer hurried toward Cavanaugh.

Cavanaugh heard Sergeant Rodriguez and his men entering the plaza behind him.

As the officer approached in the weakening light, Cavanaugh read his rank: a major.

"What do you think you're doing here, Major? No one's authorized to enter this—"

"*I'm* in charge here, Colonel. This is now a reclaimed Christian Heritage site, praise the Lord. You're violating a sacred area."

"It's a fucking latrine. Who the fuck are you?"

"Major Josiah Makepeace Brown. The commander of CHART 55. And you have no further authority here."

"How'd you get here."

"The Lord showed us the way."

"He tell you to shoot that old man?"

"The heathen?"

"Yeah, the heathen. The old man. Him. Which one of you shot him?"

"I did."

"Why? Jesus Christ, he was probably just coming to take a leak."

"You don't believe that those who profane this holy ground, who sow filth amid the lilies of the field, need to be punished?"

"You shot an old man. And I don't see any god-damned lilies. You have no right to be here."

The MOBIC officer maintained an infuriatingly calm voice. As if speaking to a child. But there was an unmistakable threat in his tone, too.

"Colonel, you and your men will have to leave. Immediately. Or I'll be forced to arrest you. In the name of Jesus Christ, our Lord, and the Military Order of the Brothers in Christ."

Cavanaugh broke the major's jaw. It was an awkward punch, with the fist forming only after it left the handgrip and trigger-well of the carbine. But Cavanaugh was comfortable doing a dozen reps on the bench with 280 pounds. He didn't aim with great precision, but the blow landed perfectly, and the jaw snapped with the sound of a broomstick broken over a thigh.

The MOBIC troops weren't well-trained. When the major fell, a few began to point their weapons, but Cavanaugh's men, outnumbered three to one, quickly disarmed them. So roughly that Cavanaugh had to tell them to ease up. He even began to worry that one of his men would pull a trigger. All of the day's anger, the rage at the sight of the crucified soldiers, had transferred onto the MOBIC troops, who were hated by the rank-and-file for their priviliges and the preference they got in equipment and promotions.

"Hey, sir," Sergeant Rodriguez said. "What do you want us to do with these shitbirds?"

Cavanaugh turned to the next-ranking MOBIC officer, a first lieutenant. "You. Get that body out of the square. Put him over on that bench."

The lieutenant turned to give orders to two of his soldiers.

"I said 'you'," Cavanaugh told him. "Take one man to help you, Lieutenant." He looked down at the major, who lay on the ground moaning. Cavanaugh wondered if he'd screwed up. But it had felt good. Almost as good as decking his wife's new, smite-the-Moabites, bullshit husband might have felt. And his orders covered him.

No. That was bullshit. He wasn't going to hide behind orders. He'd called it, and he'd stand by his call.

Cavanaugh faced the distinctly unhappy group of MOBIC soldiers. He was tempted to have them tied up and to leave them just where they said they wanted to be. In the middle of the mounds of shit that covered the site of the old church.

"Treat that body with respect," Cavanaugh snapped at the lieutenant and the MOBIC soldier helping him. "Then I'm going to give you fifteen minutes to get out of Dodge."

The lieutenant turned his face toward Cavanaugh, features vivid with fear. "Sir . . . Can we wait until daylight? Please, sir? It's getting dark, and we might not be able to find our way back now . . . We could get shot in the dark by mistake."

Cavanaugh extended his wrist and looked at his watch.

"Fourteen minutes," he said. "The Lord will show you the way."

FOURTEEN

...·....■......■......■....

The Arab girl was pretty enough to make Sergeant
Garcia jumpy. Fourteen, maybe fifteen. *Muy cali-
ente.* And walking around like she knew it. So much,
he figured, for all that Muslim modesty stuff.

"You," Garcia told her. "You understand me, right?
You tell your mother that all of you got to stay in that
one room. Understand? Nobody comes out, unless
they ask permission. And it's okay now. We're done
searching in there."

The girl stared at him. Absolutely no emotion on
her face. Like some hard little high-school bitch back
home.

"You tell your mother," Garcia continued, "that
nobody's going to hurt anybody. You're safe. But you
all got to stay in that room until we leave."

He hoped they'd be safe. He understood how his
Marines felt when they looked at the girl. He felt more
than he wanted to feel himself. Skinny, yeah. But the
good kind of skinny. The bend-me-every-which-way

kind. She could've been from some high-class Latino family back home.

And that little mustache. Like a smudge of ashes.

"Go in there now," Garcia said. "Tell your mother what I said."

After an insolent few seconds, the girl turned toward the room where her mother and little brother waited. But first she let Garica and the other Marines watch her expression turn from a blank to sheer snottiness.

Garcia read the air in the hallway. "I don't want anybody hassling her," he said. "Everybody got that? No conversations, nothing. That's jailbait. And I mean it."

"They get married when they're, like, six years old," Cropsey said.

"Yeah, well you want to marry her, you come back when all this is over. All right. Corporal Gallotti, your squad has the roof and the first guard rotation. Make sure you got visual with Third Platoon and no dead space you don't know about. Corporal Banks, your squad's in the shacks out in the courtyard. Suck it up. Everybody else is in here. Max four to a room. In case any shit goes down. And get some sleep. There's orders coming down, and we'll probably be moving out at zero-dark-thirty." He paused. Examining the tired, dirty faces. "And one more thing: No souvenirs. No breaking shit, either. Show some respect."

Some murmurs. But nothing to worry about. For the moment. They were tired. Crashing. Like methheads at the end of a long run. The Marines began to disperse, guided by the surviving NCOs.

"Cropsey, Larsen. Polanski," Garcia called. "You're in here. With me."

He wanted to keep an eye on Cropsey. Garcia still wasn't sure how to handle him. Best fighter in the platoon. Natural-born killer. But he needed to be kept on a tight leash.

Sergeant Ricky Garcia didn't want any more trouble. Just a little sleep. The past twenty-four hours had sucked, from the second the clock started ticking. First the new lieutenant. Next, the new lieutenant getting himself killed. Then two more firefights with stay-behinds and a death march, followed by the company commander reaming him because the dead lieutenant, who Garica had pegged as right off the block, had been the nephew of some general. Even after Garcia explained what happened, backed up by Corporal Gallotti and Corporal Banks, Captain Cunningham had left him with a line that burned his ears like battery acid:

"As platoon sergeant, it was your job to look out for him."

How could you look out for an asshole the size of the Central Valley? Garcia asked himself. But the words still ate at him. Because he wanted to be a good platoon sergeant. The best. To show them all.

And he wasn't sure he could do it.

He dropped his gear on the floor. When he slipped off his body armor, his uniform was sealed against his chest and back with old sweat. He wanted to take off his boots and leave them off but decided it wasn't a good idea. He settled for changing his socks and dusting some powder between his toes.

The room smelled of piss and insecticide. Low

couches lined three walls. Other than that, there was only a crap rug, some Mr. Raghead portraits hanging a few inches from the ceiling, and a table with a tinwork top that reminded him of border-town Mex crap. Could've been some junkie's room, he decided. After he sold off everything anybody would buy.

"Where you going, Polanksi?"

"To the shitter. It's outside, Sergeant."

"Take your weapon. And put your body armor on. You think you're at the swimming pool at Lejeune?"

"Yes, Sergeant."

The lance corporal slung his weapon over his shoulder, then stumbled over a fold in the rug. Clumsiest Marine in the platoon. And maybe the dumbest.

Cropsey flopped down on the cushions in one corner. Cradling his weapon. Larsen had his trousers down to his knees, inspecting the prickly heat on the inside of his thighs. Garcia broke out the chili he'd saved from his last ration pack. It didn't need heating. His pocket had warmed it just fine.

Suck-ass, rat-hole country. Who'd want it? He wondered if he should tell the old lady who owned the house to lock her door. Just in case.

Did the Mussies even have locks on their inside doors?

"Yo, Sergeant Garcia," Larsen said. Messing with a pimple on his thigh. "I ask you something?"

"What?"

"You ever think . . . that maybe those MOBIC guys have it right? That we can't really live with these people? That it's us or them?"

"Those MOBIC fucks don't have anything right." Garcia leaned back and closed his eyes.

"But what if it really *is* us or them?"

"Larsen, you need to get some sleep. You want to talk philosophy, go to college."

"I just meant . . . Maybe they have a point. You know?"

Garcia sat up. Tired and short-fused. "You want to know what I think of those MOBIC shitheads? First, they aren't Marines. That's strike one. Second, they're just *loco* gangbangers. I grew up around fucks like that. 'Hey, you're either in our gang, or you must be in some other gang, and you're the enemy, and we're going to mess you up.' I had enough of that shit back home."

"But there's a difference," Larsen pressed on. "They're defending our Christian faith."

"Who says?" Garica was getting angrier than Larsen, who was fascinated by his own reddened skin, realized. "Just who the fuck says? Where does Jesus say, 'Kill everybody who isn't with the program, who isn't in my gang, who isn't running with the J-Town Disciples?' Those MOBIC pukes are gangbangers. Plain and simple. Except the drug they push doesn't come from some lab in a house trailer in Barstow."

Without opening his eyes, Cropsey put in, "Come on, Sergeant G. You got religion like a bad case of superstition yourself, man. That tattoo of the Virgin Mary on your arm and everything."

"It's the Virgin of Guadalupe."

"Same difference. It's still the Virgin Mary."

"Well, it is, and it isn't."

"No, man. It _is_. The Virgin of Guadalupe _is_ the Virgin Mary. As she appeared to some Indian dude back at the Alamo or something."

"It wasn't at the fucking Alamo."

But Cropsey had taken over the conversation. "At least the MOBIC guys don't take any shit from the rags. You got to give them credit. And you heard what they're saying around battalion. How the J's have been crucifying prisoners." Cropsey sat up, grinning. "You know what I think? I think we ought to interrogate that girl. She speaks English. We could ask her where all the men went. Where her daddy is. You could scare her with the Virgin of Guadalupe. You and me, Sergeant G. Good cop, bad cop."

"Shut up and go to sleep."

"Come on, Sergeant G. You telling me you wouldn't like to fuck that little bitch's brains out?"

Garcia rolled to his feet. "That's it. Outside. _Now_. This is two days in a row you've used up your shit ration. And _you_. Larsen. Either see the corpsman, or stop playing with yourself. Cropsey, _move_. And put your armor back on."

Polanski came back in from the hallway, blocking the doorway just as Garcia was dropping his body armor over his head.

"Stop dawdling, Polanski. Clean your weapon and go to sleep."

"I was cleaning my boots, sergeant. The outhouse has turds all over it."

"Just clean your weapon and go to sleep."

Weapon in hand, Garcia led the way under the dangling lightbulb in the hallway and out through the drapery that served as a front door. He wondered where the electricity was coming from. It was hard to believe that anything still worked in the entire country.

Just outside, in the fading heat, Garcia turned on Cropsey. Keeping his voice low. And making a note that it was time to turn out all the inside lights, to go blackout.

The evening had gone the color of his mother's favorite sweater, a soft purple. What did you call it? Lavender? The blotches on her face had been the same color just before she died.

"What's your major malfunction, Cropsey? What is it, man? You don't like the Marines? You don't like sergeants? You don't like Hispanics, maybe? Or maybe you just don't like me."

"I love you, Sergeant Garcia. It's just that I'm afflicted with moral dilemmas and quandaries. I think I'm being traumatized by war."

Garcia wanted to hit him. But he didn't. Instead, he changed his tone of voice.

"Come on, Cropsey. What's eating you? You afraid of something? If you weren't such an asshole, you could be a great Marine."

Cropsey just stared at him. Pale eyes in a fading face as the dark came down. As insolent as the Arab girl.

"We'll settle this another time," Garcia told him. "Meanwhile, I don't want to hear one more word about that girl. That's an order."

Cropsey shrugged.

"You clean your weapon?" Garcia asked him. He wanted things to be normal. As normal as they could be in war. And he felt that Cropsey was getting the better of him.

"My weapon's always clean, Sergeant."

"Then go in and get some sleep."

Cropsey pivoted and pushed aside the drapery.

Just in time for both of them to see the girl. She was standing at the doorway of their room. With a grenade in her hand.

For an instant, her eyes met Garcia's. Then she tossed the grenade into the room and ran.

Cropsey began to swing up his weapon, but Garcia pulled him to the ground. Just before the explosion.

The blast blew out the light and thickened the air with dust and smoke.

"That little cunt," Cropsey screamed. Then they were both on their feet. Weapons up. Heading for the room into which the girl had fled. Kicking masonry scraps out of the way.

"In first," Cropsey yelled.

"Got your back."

"Grenade!" Crospey screamed. He dived forward.

Garcia hurled himself back out through the doorway.

As he hit the ground, the concussion slammed him. And he realized what had just happened, as if watching an instant replay.

Cropsey had thrown himself on top of the grenade.

Garcia stormed back into the house. There were moans now. A male voice. Not Cropsey. And shouting upstairs. Boots thumping.

"Everybody stay put," Garcia shouted.

He rushed toward the room in which the girl and her family had been promised a refuge. Disregarding everything but the need to spill his rage.

He emptied one magazine blindly into the darkness. Then he pulled another magazine from his vest and shot it dry.

He reloaded. But he didn't pull the trigger immediately. He listened.

When he heard a stuttering groan, he spent the third mag in the direction of the sound.

With the room silenced, Garcia dropped to the ground, cradling his weapon amid the dust and smoke.

▪

When the firing stopped, Corporal Tony Gallotti waited for a voice, a command. But all he heard was a faint moan from below: a Marine.

"Sergeant Garcia?"

No reply.

"Sergeant Garcia?"

Gallotti flipped down the night-vision device on his helmet. Peering through the dust and debris.

A voice from down below called, "Sergeant Garcia?"

That was Corporal Banks. Yelling in from the doorway.

"It's Gallotti. I'm coming down from the second deck. Tyrrell, take my back. Yon, you're overwatch. *Corpsman! Marines down!*"

As Gallotti felt his way down the stairs, adjusting to the spook-light in his reticle, he spotted Sergeant Garcia. Slumped against the wall. Not moving.

"Sergeant G? Yo, Sergeant Garcia?"

Then he saw the body. What was left of it. Through the smoke, he couldn't identify the Marine.

He thought he saw Garcia's chest heave.

"Corpsman!"

Moaning haunted the background. It sounded like it might be Larsen.

Gallotti crossed the hall to where Garcia sat. Breathing all right. No blood-shine. Then the corporal saw that Garcia's hand rested on a helmet containing a severed head.

Gallotti flipped up the night-sight and tore the flashlight off his armored vest. With the red light in his face, Garcia looked up. He was crying, but there was no particular expression on his face. Tears streaked the dust caked on his cheeks.

Garcia dropped his head again.

"Sergeant Garcia? You okay? Hey?"

The sergeant didn't respond.

More boots. A lot more boots. More voices. Murphy, the corpsman, spoke from the corporal's rear.

"Who's down."

"I think it's Larsen. In there. Just check it out, Murph."

The corporal squatted by Garcia. He passed his flashlight in front of the sergeant's face. "You okay, Sergeant Garcia? You hit, man?"

Garcia looked up. So abruptly that the corporal recoiled.

"That's Cropsey's head," he told Gallotti. "We have to put him back together."

Garcia hoisted himself to his feet, sliding up the

wall, thrusting his body armor against the force of gravity. He walked outside.

"Sergeant G? You all right?"

Garcia didn't speak again until they were in the courtyard. With Marines gathering from beyond the compound. Captain Cunningham materialized. The company commander had washed his face and shaved.

The captain rushed up to Garcia and Gallotti.

"What happened?"

Gallotti was about to speak for the sergeant, to cover for him, but Garcia's shoulders relaxed, and he answered for himself.

"We didn't check the women, sir. I mean, we kept our hands off them, didn't frisk them or anything. I was worried about things getting out of hand." Garcia's voice was flat, as if he were reporting on missing tent pegs. "She looked like a kid, sir. Not a little kid. But a kid. She tossed a grenade into the room where Larsen and Polanski were bunking. It was quick, sir. Me and Cropsey went after her. I'd been giving him some counseling outside the doorway. Cropsey went in first. And she flipped out another grenade. He jumped on it." Garcia looked past the captain and into the night. "I think I killed them all, sir. There were three of them, and I think I killed them all."

The captain turned to the gathering Marines. "First Sergeant?"

"He's checking the OPs, sir."

"Gunny Matthews?"

"Sir?"

"I want every Arab in this ville strip-searched."

"The women, sir?"

"Girls, women. Give them what privacy you can, and no nonsense. But everyone gets searched. Down to their underwear. Two Marines present at all times. Pass the word."

"Yes, sir."

"You all right, Sergeant Garcia?"

"Cropsey threw himself on the grenade, sir."

"You told me that."

"I don't know why he did it, sir."

"He was a good Marine."

But Garcia was stubborn. "I just don't know why he did it."

"Make a hole!" The corpsman and another Marine lugged out a stretcher.

It was Larsen. His face had been erased. His eyes were gone. The cavity where his mouth had been bubbled pink over scarlet meat.

"I knew the girl was trouble, sir," Garcia said. "I just didn't know what kind of trouble. How could she do some crazy shit like that? I mean, she was a kid. *Why* would she do that?"

"She's dead now?" the captain asked. As if he hadn't heard all that had been said to him.

"I fucking hope so," Garcia told him.

1091ST COMBAT SUPPORT HOSPITAL, ZIKHRON YA'AKOV

The patient evacuation holding area had gone quiet. Now and then, the sound of a man confused by pain and drugs rose and fell away, but the new calm seemed almost eerie to Major Nasr. Drifting in and out of consciousness, he lay intermittently aware of the battery of clamps, splints, bandages, and tubes controlling his body, only to find himself back in Nazareth again, being beaten for reasons he couldn't remember or imagining that he'd pissed himself bloody again.

Had he pissed himself again? He wasn't sure. He wanted to know but couldn't tell for certain. Then he decided, again, that he didn't care.

He counted the crucified men. Thirty-six. He counted them again. Thirty-seven. Again. Only thirty-six.

Why wouldn't the number come right?

Where was he? The doctor was there. No, that had been earlier. He was sure it had happened, though. In a lucid moment, he'd asked a doctor how bad his injuries were. The doctor, a lieutenant colonel, told him, "We don't know. You need tests that we can't do here. But you're going to live."

To live.

What would they tell his parents? He wished he could speak to his father first, before they got to him. His father, who had always seemed so strong but wasn't.

The pain was so strange. He knew it was there. The way you knew another person was in the room, even though you couldn't see him. Plenty of painkillers racing through his bloodstream. But the pain was still there. Dressed up in a bizarre costume.

Guess who I am?

Pain, in an Arab robe. In a crisp uniform patterned on the British military of a previous century. Only Arabs wore those Sam Browne belts nowadays.

He was an Arab.

Was he? What did *that* mean? Wasn't being a Christian more important? Being an American?

It was all in the blood. It would be there after the painkillers thinned out. You knew things with your blood. Things that others couldn't understand.

An officer in battle dress had tried to ask him questions, overriding the nurse and then the doctor. It was urgent. What was urgent? "I have to ask you a few questions . . . I'm sorry . . . The Corps G-2 needs to know . . ."

Who had a need to know? What could be known, anyway? A hundred transfusions wouldn't change what he knew in his blood.

I know that I am still alive. In a field hospital. I know . . . that I'm going to live.

Nasr wondered if he'd be able to have sex. The boots of Arab policemen gravitated toward testicles. Testicles and kidneys.

He'd always heard that badly wounded men wanted their mothers. But he found his thoughts returning to his father. Who had seemed so shockingly frail, so bewildered. "But my son . . . He is in the specialty forces . . ."

Dad, it's going to be okay. You hear me?

Had he accomplished his mission? In Nazareth? Who had he better served? His own kind, or the enemy? But who were "his own kind?"

Not them, not them. *American.* I'm an American. Dad, we're Americans. They can't change that.

A charley horse in his left leg made him cry out. The leg was immobilized, and he couldn't cock it up to ease the spasm. It seemed worse than the pain he'd felt during his beating. Or after.

Then it subsided. "These things, too, shall pass away."

If he could revisit any old girlfriend, who would it be?

That didn't work. For him, it was always the one he was going to meet. The perfect one. Who was waiting.

The nurse who had come into his field of vision while he was lucid had looked like a pit bull. While he was in ROTC in college, he'd had to read *A Farewell to Arms* for a survey of 20th-century American literature. It struck him now as the most dishonest book he'd ever read.

Dad, it's going to be all right. Don't worry. They're not going to take you and Mom to any camps.

He faded again, swirling in and out of dreams of torture. He was in the snack bar at the bowling alley on Ft. Bragg. He told them they had to stop because there were children watching. Then he was back in the Bradley that had evacuated him from Nazareth. But that was impossible. That had to be a dream, because he was already in the field hospital. He was sure of it.

I did my duty, he wanted to scream. I did all I could do.

It wasn't a bowling alley after all. And *he* was doing the torturing. With kitchen knives.

Nasr woke. To the fitful quiet of the evacuation ward. It took him a moment to get a grip on reality. Then, all at once, everything seemed clear.

He was going to *live*.

Dad, I'm going to live. Everything will be okay.

A man in scrubs loomed over him. The man wore a surgical mask. He held up a syringe.

"Who are you?" Nasr asked, alerting.

"A friend," the man said. He stabbed the needle into Nasr's forearm.

A fierce burn spread up Nasr's arm and over his body. In just under two minutes, he was dead.

FIFTEEN

"It's too dangerous to fly," the Air Force three-star told Harris. The blue-suiter's deputy nodded in agreement, sliding a paper down the conference table to his boss. General Schwach, the HOLCOM commander, an Army four-star Harris had known for fifteen years, said nothing.

Harris wanted to reach across the table and smash his Air Force counterpart in the face. But he controlled himself. A complete waste of time, the face-to-face meeting had already cycled through all of the arguments, only to arrive back at a repetition of Lieutenant General Micah's original position.

"The MOBIC air's flying," Harris said. "Dawg Daniels and his Marines flew."

"The air defense environment is different in the MOBIC area of operations. And the Marine sorties were a fluke. They had the element of surprise."

"*How* is the environment different? The MOBIC ground forces are approaching a linkup with my corps.

The sectors are merging. The air defense envelopes already overlap. And we need air support *now*."

"Our intelligence shows a different threat environment in the Third Corps area of responsiblity."

Harris wiped a finger under his nose. "Come on. MOBIC's flying. The Marines want to fly. And I have it on good authority that even your own Air Force pilots want to fly."

"They don't have the big picture. We can't afford to lose irreplaceable, very expensive aircraft in support of purely tactical missions."

"Why do you think the taxpayers paid for your ground-attack fighters?"

"We have to preserve our air power."

"For what?"

"For threats to our national security."

Harris leaned in over the table and lowered his voice, attempting to lock eyes with the Air Force general—who studiously looked down at the paper his deputy had passed to him.

"General Micah, do you understand that we're at war? Right now? That soldiers and Marines are dying? While the United States Air Force is jerking off?"

"The Air Force is prepared to do its part. As soon as conditions permit."

"But why shouldn't the Marines fly, for God's sake? If they're willing to accept the risk?"

"The Marines don't have the big picture. And I object to your taking the Lord's name in vain."

"Exactly what *is* the big picture? What do you have to 'preserve the force' for? Fucking air shows in Orlando?"

"Our decisions are based on sound intelligence

and cost-benefit analysis. Unlike the Army and Marines, the Air Force is a strategic service. We have to think far into the future."

Harris leaned back in his chair. Disgusted. And tired. They just wore you down.

"That much, I believe," Harris said. "About the cost-benefit analysis. What benefits have the MOBIC bunch promised you? Do you or any of your brethren really believe that the Air Force isn't next? Do you really think that, if the U.S. Army goes away, and then the Marines disappear, you're going to get a special dispensation from the Military Order of the Brothers in Christ?"

General Schwach stiffened as Harris spoke. A decent enough officer, if no lion, the four-star looked as if he'd stacked arms on the matter. And perhaps on other matters, too. He clearly didn't want to get into a pissing contest over the MOBIC.

"That's enough, Gary," his commander told Harris.

"Of course, we *want* to fly," the Air Force general added. "That's what we do for a living. We're just waiting for the threat environment to clarify."

"You're full of shit. You don't want to fly at all."

"Are you calling me a coward, General Harris?"

"No. You're not a coward. Cowardice at least has a certain logic. You're a fool."

"That's *enough*, Gary," the HOLCOM commander said. But his voice barely sounded firm. Just drained.

The Air Force general stood up. His deputy aped his action.

"This meeting has been counterproductive," General Micah declared. His uniform was tailored as neatly as a corporate executive's. "If you'll excuse

me, General Schwach, I have Air Force business to
attend to."

But Harris couldn't let go. Even though he recognized the childishness, the sheer spite, in his final
remark: "Mark my words: You're destroying the U.S.
Air Force. Without firing a shot."

The HOLCOM commander made a steeple of his
fingertips and rested his brow against it until the Air
Force officers had left the room.

"Jesus, Gary. That didn't help anything," General
Schwach said at last. "You're smarter than that.
You're *better* than that."

Harris leaned toward his boss. Schwach looked at
least a decade older, although the age difference between them was only three years. "Sir . . . This is
madness. You know it is. Can't you order them to let
the Marines fly? At least that? My Deuce has a foot-
long list of high-value targets even tactical missiles
can't range. That's what air power's for, for God's
sake."

Schwach waved his face back and forth like a flag
of surrender. "It's not General Micah. He's just a
place-holder. Gary, this order comes directly from
Washington: No fixed-wing sorties."

"But the MOBIC aircraft can fly."

"We both know what's going on."

"Sir, we have to do something."

"What?"

"Fight."

The four-star glanced toward the door of his office. Making sure it was closed. "Gary . . . I don't
even know how much I should tell you anymore.
This is all uncharted territory . . . ethically, profes-

sionally, practically." He fortified himself with a deep breath, then continued. "Right now, I'm fighting to keep your rotary-wing assets flying. And I'm not sure it's a fight I can win. You may even lose your helicopters. And when it comes down to it, we're lucky the Army's still able to fly its drones—we've got the Navy to thank for that, God bless 'em. They dug in their heels on the drone issue. They want you in the sky between their ships and the Jihadis." The elder general summoned a last shred of strength and looked directly into his subordinate's face. "Gary, I'm also fighting to prevent you from being relieved."

That knocked the breath out of Harris's lungs for a long moment.

"Why? What's their excuse?"

"They don't have one. Yet. But putting a couple of tap shots into the forehead of that Air Force flunky didn't help your cause any."

"But *why*?"

The four-star smirked. "Don't be obtuse. You've been doing too well. Sim Montfort's got a bloodbath on his hands—Gary, he's lost nine thousand Americans killed in a matter of days. Maybe three times that number wounded. Montfort may have taken Jerusalem, but he's lost half of the combat power in his corps."

"It's a big corps. The biggest that ever fought under an American flag."

"Not big enough, though. And there you are, fighting smart, pulling off a landing that was just short of another Inchon—"

"That was Monk Morris and his Marines."

Schwach waved off the demurral. "And you've committed the unforgivable sin of not bleeding enough. What's your latest KIA figure?"

"Just over six hundred, sir."

"I rest my case. No matter how the MOBIC publicists try to spin it back home, questions do come up. The press isn't totally housebroken yet. And President Bingham doesn't have the nerves of steel the vice president does. Vice President Gui and his Arkansas Inquisition have to do something fast to make Sim Montfort look like the only competent military commander in this war. The script says Montfort's the hero, Gary."

"Sim is competent. He's just a butcher."

General Schwach sighed. "Well, I want you to listen to me: Don't get in his way. Not any more than you absolutely have to. Don't give him any excuses to cry that he's been betrayed by Judas Harris and the U.S. Army."

"I won't tolerate the massacre of civilians in my sector, if that's what it comes down to."

"I'd relieve you myself, if you did. But we both may have to look the other way at what goes on in the MOBIC AO."

"It disgraces everything our nation stands for."

Schwach nodded. "Gary, we both know what's at stake here."

"Yes, sir. The survival of the U.S. Army. And the United States Marine Corps."

"And the country, Gary. Our country as we know it. As we've served it. The Constitution."

"Sir, I know. Got it."

"And I'd be dishonest if I didn't tell you that I'm not sure we'll win."

"We'll win," Harris said. Reflexively.

Schwach slumped back in his chair. "God willing. Gary, these people make me ashamed to call myself a Christian."

"They're not Christians."

"Yes, they are. They're just a different kind of Christian. The kind that burst out of the locked chest the Jihadis banged on until the lid came off." The HOLCOM commander rested his graying temple on one hand. "I wonder if any of our enemies ever regret unleashing *our* demons. With all those whacky demands for a global caliphate. And the terror . . . Los Angeles, Vegas, the European cities. You think they ever regret starting this?"

"No, sir. Not the ones we're fighting. They want a showdown as badly as the MOBIC bunch do."

"Even if they lose?"

"They don't think they *can* lose. Even if they lose on Earth, they win in Paradise.

"With the hot babes of Heaven. Something to be said for their version of things, I suppose. If I were younger."

"It's not about that, sir. It's about death. The greatest seductress of all. Death. We're not fighting a civilization. Middle Eastern civilization's gone. Finished. *Basta.* We're at war with a culture of death."

"You're going a little too deep for me now. I'd prefer to stick with the lithe houris of Paradise. I can understand my enemy on that level." The older general glanced down at the grain of the wood on his conference table. "How do you think this will end, Gary? Between us?"

"It won't."

"Won't what?"

"End. It won't end. Al-Mahdi's Jihadis and Sim Montfort's Crusaders may think this is the Battle of Armageddon, but there've been a lot of battles of Armageddon. The big-dog religions just take turns winning. We massacre you for Jesus. Next time, you massacre us for Allah. But there's always another round." It struck Harris—hard—that it was time to get back to his own headquarters, that there was nothing left for him here. It also struck him that his boss didn't want him to leave, that his old acquaintance was desperate for someone trustworthy to talk to. "Sir, if we get down to just one of them and one of us left, the last two will go at each other with rocks. Each yelling that God's on his side."

"And if one of them knocks the other down and kills him? Doesn't that undo your theory? Isn't he the winner, the last man standing? Or if they kill each other, what then?"

"In the latter case, the monkeys win. Until they evolve. And start creating new theologies to explain that they were never monkeys at all. That God X created them from sandalwood and spices."

"That's pretty cynical. Coming from you, Gary. I thought you were a devout Christian yourself."

"I'm a Sermon on the Mount Christian. Sim Montfort's a Book of Revelation Christian."

"It's hard to square the Sermon on the Mount with being a soldier."

Harris smiled. "That's where faith comes in. 'I know that my Redeemer liveth.' But I can't claim to know it intellectually. I believe in the mercy of Jesus Christ with all my heart and soul. My head just has to catch up. But I *don't* happen to think He wants human skulls piled up at his feet. Sir, I'd better pull pitch. I've got a war to fight." He rose from his chair. Surprised by the stiffness in his back and legs. Too much sitting. The long helicopter flight. The b.s. session that solved nothing. Age. And another flight to come.

"Gary?"

"Yes, sir."

"I need you to have faith in me. I need you to do something for me."

"Sir?"

"You're going to have to chop a brigade to Montfort as soon as his bunch effect the linkup. He was demanding a full division. I held him to one brigade. For now."

Harris opened his mouth to protest. But the beaten face of his superior stopped him. That, and an idea that made him smile.

"All right, sir. I'll give old Sim some shit about it on principle. But he'll get his brigade. Thanks for the top cover."

The older man looked unmistakably relieved that Harris hadn't put up a fight.

"*Vaya con Dios*, Gary."

Harris paused for a farewell salute. Snapped from the end of his right eyebrow.

"He's busy, sir."

▪

Harris crunched a stale chocolate-chip cookie and regretted not bringing his aide along. Major Willing had remained behind at corps to put the day's paperwork in order for Harris's return. He'd made the flight with a single bodyguard. But Willing was responsible for his care and feeding. His aide would've seen to some chow—Harris had realized belatedly that he was as hungry as a bear at his first springtime wake-up call. So the general had just grabbed a couple of care-package cookies from a box by a coffee urn as he left the HOLCOM headquarters for the flight line.

"Get any chow, Sergeant Corbin?" Harris asked the NCO riding beside him in the back seat of the sedan. First my mission, then my men . . .

"I'll eat when we get back, sir."

"Cookie?"

The NCO seemed to avoid looking at him. "Thanks, sir. I don't eat sweets."

"Well, you're not missing anything. Mom sent last year's leftovers. You feeling all right, Sergeant Corbin?"

The vehicle sped along the dark runway apron, outracing the cast of its blackout lights. As the sedan rounded a wall of blast barriers, the moonlight revealed a brand-new UH-80 just ahead.

Only the MOBIC forces had the new helicopters. Harris's old Black Hawk was nowhere to be seen.

The UH-80 was being fueled by a tanker parked close behind it.

"What's going on here?" Harris tossed the last bite of cookie on the floor.

The officer riding shotgun up front turned around. With a pistol in his hand. Sergeant Corbin grasped Harris by the upper arm. The SF NCO had a mighty grip.

"Sir," the officer twisting over the front seat said,

"you need to do exactly what I tell you to do. You need to trust me."

"I tend not to trust people who point guns at me."

The officer didn't waver. "Then don't trust me. Just do as I say."

The vehicle squealed to a halt. Too near the helicopter. The crew chief stepped back.

His bodyguard kept a tight grip on Harris's arm.

"Listen to me, sir," the officer with the pistol said. "I need you to climb into that helicopter. Then you're going to climb right out the other side. The door will be open. You will then low-crawl to the fuel truck. You will crawl around the front end, then enter the cab of the vehicle. You will crouch down on the floor, out of sight. Sergeant Corbin will be right behind you."

"Who are you?"

"Major Daniel Szymanski, sir. U.S. Army Special Forces. Just do as I say right now. You're welcome to court-martial me later."

"And if I don't follow your orders? What are you going to do? Kill me, Major?"

"No, sir. We're trying to keep you alive. Our MOBIC friends intend to kill you. That helicopter is going to explode twenty minutes into its flight, over open water. Theoretically, with you aboard. Now I need you to move out sharply, sir. Or Sergeant Corbin and I will have to drag you along. And flight control might spot us. Even if they don't kill you, you'll never make it back to your command."

"What about the crew? You don't think they'll notice all these shenanigans? You're asking me to take a lot on faith, Major."

"The MOBIC crew has been . . . incapacitated. It was a volunteer suicide crew, by the way. That's a special-ops crew you're looking at, our guys. They're going to take off, set the autopilot, then bail out once the bird's out of sight of land. They're just going to get a little wet tonight."

"And what am I supposed to do, Major? After I climb into your truck? Assuming you're not full of shit and pulling a MOBIC stunt yourself?"

"We're going to put you aboard an LOH-92 out at our black site. The radar cross section's hardly bigger than a seagull. It'll be just you, the pilot, and a long-range fuel tank strapped on—which will make you look like a particularly fat seagull. We'll get Sergeant Corbin back down to you later. But the first thing, sir, is to get you back to corps. General Montfort's already on his way to take command."

"Even if this isn't complete bullshit, how did you—"

"You need to move out, sir. Right now. As for how we cracked this, let's just say there's at least one former Special Forces officer who wishes he'd never jumped to the dark side. And more than one who's sick at what he sees going down these days."

Harris shifted to get out of the vehicle as ordered. Trusting his instincts. And not seeing much of an alternative.

Sergeant Corbin released his grip on the general's upper arm. "Got to move, sir," the NCO said. "Major Szymanski's telling you the truth."

Harris stopped. Turning back to the major one last time.

"Who else knew? That I was going to be killed?"

After a second's hesitation, the major said, "General Schwach."

NAZARETH

Seconds after he found the bodies in the darkness, Command Sergeant Major Bratty came under fire.

"Action, right!" he shouted. Turning into the ambush. His battle instincts raced far ahead of his conscious thoughts.

Instead of ordering the fire team that had dismounted with him to charge the gunmen, Bratty yelled, "Aimed fire only. Two targets. Three o'clock. Between those high-rises."

He wasn't sure his headset was functioning, given the renewed jamming, but the whirr of the Bradley's turret reassured him. The automatic cannon began pumping out rounds, putting on a fireworks display. Ripping into the building facades adjacent to the gunmen's positions. The dismounted soldiers swelled the volume of fire, streaking the night.

This is pure bullshit, Bratty decided. In less than a minute.

"Cease fire! Cease fire! Now!"

The shooting trailed off, then stopped. Leaving a no man's land of silence beyond which the war hammered on.

Just as Command Sergeant Major Dilworth Bratty expected, there was no more incoming fire. And not, he figured, because the Bradley gunner had found the targets.

"Sergeant Tisza," Bratty said into his headset mike.

"Dismount the rest of your squad. Charlie Eight, close on Charlie Seven and kick out your dismounts. I want a three-sixty perimeter set up. And don't hug the Bradleys. Break, break. Bayonet Six, do you copy?"

Nothing. The jamming was so fierce that Bratty couldn't reach his battalion commander across the narrow bowl that cradled the old city. He tried to relay a situation report through the battalion Three, but that was another no-go. No comms beyond the two Bradleys he'd brought along.

Maybe it wasn't a bad thing, Bratty decided. He needed time to think this one through.

He got to his feet and walked toward the bodies again. "Just checking out the corpses in the moonlight," he sang to himself, "and thinking of the Sheikh of Araby . . ." Now that would be a mighty fine country song, he decided. G-major. Strum it and gum it. Then he remembered his missing fingers and that he wouldn't be picking any guitars in the near future.

He sauntered. Upright. Daring anyone watching to take a shot at him. As he expected, nobody pulled a trigger. The gunmen who'd splashed a few magazines in their direction were long gone. Just howdy, folks, then *adios*.

Sergeant Tisza came up beside him.

"Pretty limp-dick ambush, Sergeant Major," the buck sergeant said.

"That wasn't an ambush. That was a pull-the-trigger-and-scoot, half-assed, hearted-hearted pretense at an ambush. And they get a no-go for authenticity. Fuck it. You take the left side of the road. I've got the right. Count the bodies as you go."

"We haven't checked to see if they're all dead."

"They're all dead," Bratty told the buck sergeant.

And mutilated. Uniforms torn off, sometimes the trousers, sometimes the body armor and blouses. A couple of severed heads. The most popular technique had been to slice off the genitals and shove them into the mouths of the dead—in one case, between the lips of a severed head. Jagged crosses had been carved into pale chests.

"Those sonsofbitches," Sergeant Tisza said from the far side of a shot-up four-wheel-drive. "Even MOBIC shits don't deserve this."

Bratty didn't respond. Too much to think about. He'd realized immediately that they were in deep kimchi when the battalion commander got back to the TOC, already aware that he'd poked the pooch by getting into a pissing contest with the MOBIC CHART. Busting the straw boss's jaw, then telling them to get out of Dodge.

Cavanaugh had still been hot when he got back. But smart enough to know he'd blundered. Bratty's worry meter pegged out immediately. He liked Cavanaugh. Who was one of the most decent and most competent officers with whom he'd served. But Cavanaugh was a man with a temper. A mick to his bones.

"Sir, those bozos will probably end up in Baghdad," Bratty had told him. "Let me go after them. I'll find 'em. We'll corral 'em for the night and send 'em home to mama in the morning."

Cavanaugh had just nodded. With a grateful look on his face. But the bring-'em-back mission had been delayed by the arrival of the trucks to carry the crucified bodies to the rear. Time-sensitive mission, but that didn't lessen the paperwork. And the escort tracks had clogged the narrow street. It had taken Bratty almost an hour to get on the road.

Tracking the CHART vehicles hadn't been hard. Bratty just looked at the map and asked himself which route the dumbest-ass lieutenant he'd ever met would choose. Sure enough, they found the MOBIC vehicles and the bodies in the middle of the road on the western ridge, along a route that headed straight for friendly lines.

Bratty squatted down by a corpse that had been castrated and fed its own meat. The J's were setting a pretty high standard for atrocities. First the crucifixions, then this. Just asking for it. And Dilworth Bratty had no objections to giving it to them. But something about the scene made him want to take a chaw of snuff and scratch his ass for a couple of minutes.

Sergeant Tisza came around the front end of a vehicle and stood before him. Boots in the moonlight.

"This stinks like white-trash pussy on Sunday morning," Bratty said.

"Sergeant Major?"

"I said, 'This stinks.' That fake ambush. Supposed to make us think we'd wandered into the same kill zone, facing the same enemy that did all this. Now, you tell me, young sergeant, why the J's didn't make even a half-assed effort to hit anything when they opened up on us."

"Because they wanted us to find the bodies?"

"Congratulations. You are ready for your E-6 board. This isn't just a massacre. It's a display. Now let's see if you're ready for your Smokey-the-Bear hat. If this is a calculated display, what does that tell you?"

"That it was planned?"

"You are a go at this station, Sergeant Tisza. But if it was planned, what was the one piece of critical information the J's needed to make it happen?"

The buck sergeant thought for a moment. A fly did a touch-and-go landing on the corpse that lay between them.

"That somebody'd be coming this way."

"Proceed directly to the Sergeants Major Academy. Somebody knew these poor sonsofbitches were coming this way. In sufficient time to set up an ambush, execute it, disfigure the bodies, then un-ass the AO. Except for Mutt and Jeff, who stayed behind to fire a couple of clips at us before running away as fast as their little legs could go."

"Okay, I follow you."

"Then let's move on to the Sergeant-Major-of-the-Army test question, young sergeant: What's wrong with this ambush? Not the potshots they took at us. I mean the first one. The one that left these poor buggers with their nuts stuffed down their throats."

The buck sergeant thought it over. This time, he was stumped.

"No blasts," Bratty said at last. "No mine craters. No signs of a roadside bomb. No blown-up vehicles. No evidence of any weaponry heavier than a machine gun used on them. And look at the bodies, for Christ's sake. Look at all the head shots. Head shots. In the dark. And the J's can't shoot for shit. What does that tell you, Sergeant Tisza?"

"They were shot at close range."

"And how do you get shot at close range? With no sign that you've put up a fight? Smell their weapons. Where are the shell casings from the turret MGs? How do you get yourself *executed* at close range?"

A fly settled on a dead eye.

"You surrender," Sergeant Tisza said.

"And from what you know of the MOBIC troops . . . They may have their faults, but how many of them do you think would surrender to the J's without a fight?"

"So they didn't surrender, you mean? I don't get it."

Bratty tested his whiskers with the remaining fingers on his right hand, feeling them bristle around his chin strap and catch on the bandage, which already smelled like old socks.

"I'm just an old country boy," Bratty told his subordinate. "But I can tell you one thing: A moonshiner only stops for someone he trusts."

SIXTEEN

HEADQUARTERS, III (US) CORPS, MT. CARMEL RIDGES

The first thing Flintlock Harris heard when he walked into his headquarters well after midnight was his G-3, Mike Andretti, telling General of the Order Simon Montfort, "That's an unlawful order. This corps will not obey it."

The second thing Harris heard was cheering, followed by applause. It took him a moment to understand that the accolade was for him, not for the defiant operations officer.

The officers in the briefing room stood up. Yelling their heads off. Greeting Harris. Electrified, despite the wretched hour.

The welcome gave him an additional shot of adrenaline, reaching down into the part of his soul that would always be a soldier. Yet, Harris found himself behaving calmly. Unexpectedly so. During the wave-skimming flight in the black-ops helicopter, he'd felt a killing rage, imagining variations of revenge. Now, with his subordinates behaving like children who had just been informed that Christmas wasn't canceled after all, Harris simply wanted to take care of business.

Still, he couldn't resist stepping up beside the MOBIC commander, leaning close as the ruckus began to subside, and saying, quietly, "Call me fucking Lazarus. Right, Sim?"

Montfort was stunned, but he'd always been quick on his feet. He thrust out his hand and babbled a welcome.

Harris ignored him, turning to his G-3. "What's this about an unlawful order, Mike?"

"Sir . . . We'd been told by HOLCOM that your helicopter was down, that it disappeared from the radar screen offshore."

"Reports of my death have been greatly exaggerated," Harris said.

"General Montfort . . ." The G-3 looked at the MOBIC commander with molten hatred. ". . . *happened* to be in the area. He claimed he was in command."

"Temporary command, of course," Montfort told Harris. "Until things got themselves sorted out."

"Remarkable timing, Sim," Harris said. "Amazing luck, you being in the vicinity of my headquarters." Then he turned back to the Three. "What was the order, Mike?"

The room had grown death-watch quiet.

"Sir, General Montfort ordered us to kill the civilian refugees in Nazareth."

Harris glared at Montfort. Unable to mask his disgust. The anger burned back up inside him.

In a voice as controlled as he could make it, Harris said, "You were right. That's an unlawful order. In any case, General Montfort has no authority over this corps. Did he issue any other orders?"

"No, sir. He just got here."

"Anything new on the ground?"

"The J's are fighting for every speck of dirt along the Highway 65 line, but they're taking heavy casualties for it. We're chewing into them. Two reports of EMP mines in General Scott's First Brigade sector. 1st Cav's got elements of two brigades in the fight, and the division staff estimates they'll have their last combat brigade in its forward assembly area by 1400. Tactical comms suck."

Harris surveyed the room. Swiftly. "Anybody got anything urgent for me? No-bullshit urgent?"

Some of the faces just stared at him, calculating the situation's implications. Several heads swiveled back and forth: No. Nothing that urgent. All of them were waiting to see what would happen next between their commander and Montfort.

"General Montfort and I have some matters to discuss in private," Harris told his subordinates. "Excuse us, gentlemen. Sim? Join me in my office? It isn't much, but it's home." Harris turned to his aide, who had just stepped inside the room. "John, make sure we're not disturbed."

The MOBIC commander opened his lips to speak, then thought better of it. Old Sim's still reeling, Harris thought. But he knew the man. Sim Montfort would be back in control of himself before a condemned man could smoke a last cigarette.

Harris herded his old acquaintance out into the central hall of the big house, then led him down a corridor to his combination office, bedroom, and refuge.

"I'll say a special prayer of thanks tonight," Montfort told him. "For your safe return. I'd been told—"

"Fuck you, Sim. Let's leave it at that. I'm unfamiliar with the proper etiquette for dealing with a fellow American who tries to kill me."

"That's preposterous."

"I said, 'Let's leave it at that.'"

"As you wish."

"Sit down, Sim. This is going to be a serious talk."

"Gary, I've got commitments. It's three in the morning. We each have a corps to run. There's a war on, if you haven't noticed."

"You weren't concerned about that fifteen minutes ago."

"I was trying to help. We were monitoring the HOLCOM net, of course. And when I heard the report, I was afraid your staff would be demoralized. We couldn't afford—"

"And you were just in the area. By dumb, fuck-me-dead luck. Christ, Sim . . . Save it for Sunday school."

"If we're going to have a conversation, I'll have to ask you not to take the Lord's name in vain. In any of His incarnations."

Harris smiled. "You sound almost like a Hindu, Sim. And to tell you the truth, I could see you as a devotee of Kali."

"Who might you be, then, Gary? Shiva? I think not. Hanuman, perhaps? The monkey god? The prankster?" He raised a dark eyebrow. "Don't stumble in front of the Juggernaut."

"Sim . . . How can you do it?"

"What?"

"All of it. Specifically, ordering American soldiers to massacre defenseless civilians."

"*Are* they defenseless? Or even civilians?"

"They certainly look that way to me."

"Gary, Gary . . . Why do you refuse to understand? This isn't Iraq. You're not a lieutenant. Multicultural playtime's over. This is total war. Us or them. The end game."

"The End of Days?"

"In a sense. Not in the cheap sense."

"What's going on, Sim? Really? You're not stupid. I'll credit you with a better mind than I possess—not that that's the world's highest accolade. So, I ask myself, why would Sim Montfort do exactly what the Jihadis want us to do, what they've set up?"

"What's that? Exactly?"

"Come on, Sim."

"You'll have to explain it to me." Montfort crossed his legs and sat back. He was and had always been a handsome man, but his looks were the lucky kind that photographed better than they fairly should have, the sort of features that made a comprehensive impression that blinded you to the imperfect details. Had he been an actor, he would have disappointed the fan who finally saw him up close.

It struck Harris that the parts didn't really fit. The jaw was *too* strong, as if drawn by a cartoonist. The eyes that burned so intensely were too close together when viewed straight on. And Montfort's forehead, below the widow's peak of still-black hair, was too low. To Harris, it made the other man look as if his skull were weighted down and sagging into that big

jaw. Sarah had noted it, too. Most women saw Montfort as distinguished, but Sarah had labeled him "the
Cro-Magnon glamour-boy."

The others, women or men, never seemed to see
Montfort in detail. That was part of the man's genius, Harris realized. Montfort had undeniable cha-
risma and bulled through life on the strength of the
total package he delivered—or, more accurately, the
external trappings he constructed and fortified. People reacted to Montfort the way men reacted to
women with cascades of long blond hair, falling un-
critically for a commonplace.

Montfort was, in short, the most brilliant con Harris had ever encountered.

"All right, Sim. I'll explain it to you. But first, I've
changed my mind. I've got to reach closure about
your attempt to assassinate me."

"I *never*—"

"Save it. And with suicide volunteers, too. Good
Lord, Sim—what's to choose between you and our
enemies?"

"Between Christ and Mohammed?"

"Save that, too. We may get to it later. Right now, I
have an intellectual dilemma to resolve: This shabby
little plot to kill me says either that you're afraid you
lack the leverage to have me removed, that your support back in Washington is more tenuous than you
thought—watch those casualty figures, Sim—or that
you just got impatient. Now, that *would* worry me.
Impatience, I mean. Because it would establish a pattern. Impatient to get to Jerusalem, you throw away
so many good Christian lives . . . Impatient to have
your way in every last regard, you arrange a death
for me straight from the handbook on how to get rid

of African presidents-for-life. Just doesn't seem like you, Sim. You've always played a controlled game. Admirably so . . . from the standpoint of tactics, if not objectives. So which was it? Eroding political support? Hard to believe, given your chumminess with our vice president, the Reverend Doctor Gui—by the way, will Air Force One go down with the president aboard? Was tonight just a rehearsal for the big game?"

"That's treasonous."

"Sim . . . I don't think you want to get into a pissing contest with me on the subject of treason."

"If you really intend to make something of these nonsensical allegations, Gary . . . file your charges with General Schwach."

Harris smiled. But said nothing.

"Otherwise," Montfort went on, "let's talk strategy. I'm delighted that the report about your helicopter going down proved unfounded. After all, you and I go back a long way. Differences aside."

"We can't put those differences aside anymore. And the helicopter did go down. I just didn't happen to be on it. Your own people betrayed your plot. They're not all with you at the altar rail, Sim."

"That's nonsense."

"We'll see." Harris drew a finger across his nose, banishing an itch. "Maybe it's both, Sim? Maybe your power base is eroding, *and* you're impatient. That would make sense."

"This is getting us nowhere."

"Where do you want us to go, Sim?"

"You need to get some sleep. We're all tired. You've had a difficult day."

"And you've had a disappointing one. But I'm not

tired at all. Surviving an assassination attempt ups a man's natural caffeine content. But back to Nazareth: What do you want to do, make some sort of grand entrance over a carpet of corpses? Montfort the Conqueror, instead of Mehmet the Conqueror?"

His old acquaintance's crossed legs interested Harris. Montfort would never have sat that way in public. Now, the narrow, broken X of Montfort's lower limbs seemed like a defensive obstacle that the MOBIC commander had emplaced between them. Without realizing how much of his discomfort the posture gave away. Montfort had put so much effort into controlling his facial features that he'd failed to discipline the rest of his body.

"All right. Nazareth," Harris continued. "I'd blame al-Mahdi, not al-Ghazi, for that particular plan. Al-Ghazi's a soldier. Al-Mahdi's an opportunist—oh, a great believer, too. But still, an opportunist underneath it all. Like you, Sim." Harris couldn't resist smiling. "I suspect the two of you would get along famously if you ever met. But back to the plan: bussing in thousands of members of the Arab intelligentsia. Including some from beyond the borders of the Emirate of al-Quds and Damaskus. Shove 'em out front, a gift to the Crusaders, a clever blood sacrifice. We're *supposed* to slaughter them, Sim. And you know it. You're a smart man. Al-Mahdi wants them dead. Because his vision of Islam's future really is a return to the past. The people won't need doctors or professors. Just their mullahs. And, of course, Suleiman al-Mahdi." Harris inched forward. Until his rump was almost at the edge of his chair. "I wonder, Sim, if that doesn't reflect your movement's view of America."

"That's ridiculous. And insulting. It's absurd."

"Well, I'm willing to sound absurd, Sim. Because the world's gotten absurd. Absurd and bloody. So bloody no incense of theirs or ours will ever cover the stench. But stay with me now, Sim: Al-Mahdi wants us to do his dirty work for him, so he can get a two-fer. Surely, you see that. First, those annoying intellectuals are exterminated. No more global community of conscience or anything bothersome like that. Second, he gets to rally his fellow Muslims, in the Arab world and beyond, by blaming us for killing them. It all makes perfect sense, once you crack the code." Harris looked at the broad-shouldered man in the other chair. "But what I *don't* get is why a clever man like you would fall in with his plan—when it only strengthens the enemy. After all, those people in Nazareth are the closest thing we'll ever have to allies in this part of the world."

"We have no allies here. We never had any. And we never will."

"But come on, Sim. You're a genius at using people. Why wouldn't you want to use all those scientists and surgeons al-Mahdi's crammed into Nazareth? You could always dispose of them later."

"Gary, you refuse to understand."

"What?"

"The sooner we get this over with, the better."

"Get what over with?"

"Their destruction."

"Who? Those poor bastards in Nazareth? And their families? Win the war by murdering some dentist's wife?"

"Not just the ones in Nazareth. All of them. Every Muslim."

Harris snorted a one-syllable laugh. "Give me a break, Sim. That's crazy."

"Why?"

"You can't kill over a billion people."

It was Montfort's turn to smile. "Are you sure?"

"Sim . . . for God's sake . . ."

"Exactly that. For *God's* sake. Gary, don't you see it? I wish you could. I'd love to have you as my ally. As a *true* ally, a brother in Christ. Don't you see what this fight's really about, how final it is? You can mock me . . . mock us . . . but this is the great struggle between Christ and the Antichrist. Or, I should say, the climax of that struggle." Montfort uncrossed his legs and edged forward on his chair, aping Harris's earlier gesture. "We've tried peaceful cooperation, we've tried compromise, even indulgence. We made excuses for them, looked the other way when they slaughtered the innocent like sheep for one of their satanic festivals. And what did it bring us? Their rage, their intolerance. The savagery in Europe—you were there, weren't you? At the end of all that? Then the destruction of Israel. By fire, as foretold. And then the nuclear massacres in Los Angeles and Las Vegas . . ."

"Sim, I really do wonder . . . whether the rumors aren't true. About your boys helping the Jihadis pull that off. Las Vegas, at least. 'Sin City.' And, I suppose, Los Angeles had plenty of sins to answer for, too. No more naked breasts on movie screens these days. It's time for Susannah to show a little respect for those elders. Honestly, if the Reverend Doctor Gui, our beloved vice president, had picked two American cities to sacrifice, which two do you think he would've picked? Little Rock and Lynchburg? Or Sodom and Gomorrah?"

"I won't dignify that with a response."

"I didn't expect one. Tell me, though . . . exactly *how* do you kill a billion people? Without getting overly sloppy? That's a big project. Even for you."

"You mock me. As those other soldiers mocked Christ."

"Comparing yourself to Christ, Sim? Already?"

"There's no need for blasphemy."

"Of course, there's nothing blasphemous about the idea of killing a billion people. Over a billion. When Jesus said, 'Suffer the little children,' He didn't mean it quite the way you seem to interpret it."

"They're the hordes of the Antichrist. Beyond redemption. Their religion was born in blood, it was spread in blood, and it will end in blood." Montfort turned his head slightly but kept his eyes locked on Harris. "Gary, you can't think in the old ways any more. This isn't geopolitics in some classroom. The old, secular regime is finished. This is the final struggle . . . for new heavens and a new earth. We've worshipped too long at false altars, fallen for the devil's snares, for the folly of believing that those who have been washed in the blood of Jesus Christ must accommodate themselves to the wickedness of the damned. And what have we gained, Gary? What did our tolerance bring us? What did all our efforts at extending the hand of brotherhood, our ecumenical absurdities, what did all of it gain for us? *Nothing.* Nothing beyond the ever-greater madness, the ever-greater demands, the megalomaniacal vanity of an utterly failed civilization, the sickness unto death of this satanic realm of Islam and the heathen occupation of *our* holy shrines . . . and the massacre, the slaughter, of our own kind. Tell me, Gary: What would you have us do? Please. Give me your solution. After all the devastation . . . the nuclear destruction of two great cities in our homeland . . . do you really believe there's room left for compromise?"

"Absolutes are for God's Kingdom."

"We're going to build God's Kingdom. Here. Now."

"By killing over a billion people?" Harris shook his head. "Even if you could pull that off . . . I wouldn't want any part of a God who thought that was a good day's work well done." Rubbed raw in the spirit, Harris asked, "What about the *love* of Jesus Christ, Sim? Don't the Gospels mean anything to you? Or to your 'Military Order of the Brothers in Christ'? Are you proposing that Christ's lost years were spent in a Roman legion, spearing the local nuisances? That He just forgot to mention that killing was perfectly legit? Or that the editors cut the battle cries from the Sermon on the Mount?"

"The Book of Revelation follows mankind's rejection of Christ's message. We nailed the Son of God to a cross and abused Him, scorned Him. The Book of Revelation is God's response."

"Bullshit. The Book of Revelation is the scribbling of a nutcase in a cave. It's Christianity's Koran. It was only included in the New Testament because the message Jesus left behind made the early church's bureaucrats nervous—not least, the idea of living humbly and sharing with the poor, or the fact that Jesus thought women were human beings. You'd be happier as a Muslim yourself, Sim."

"You're no theologian, Gary. You know not of what you speak."

"Do you? Do *you*, Sim? Do you bear the love of Jesus Christ in your heart? Do *you* truly feel the solace of His mercy? You call yourself a Christian, but you'd just as soon cut out everything in the Bible between the Book of Joshua and the Book of Revelation. You're no Christian, Sim. And your kind aren't Christians. No man who could order the massacre of every human being in Jerusalem—then in Nazareth, for God's sake—could ever claim to be a Christian."

Montfort sat back and crossed his legs again. A cock crowed in the distance.

"And what about the home front?" Harris drove on. "What about the United States of America? What would Jesus have to say about your political antics, Sim? Remember that bit about 'Render unto Caesar what is Caesar's'? Remember that part? Or 'My Kingdom is not of this world'? Did I get that right? Did I miss the footnotes? Isn't it enough that the American people are still overwhelmingly Christian? Do we really have to become an official religious state? Like Iran used to be? Or the Sultanate of Baghdad now? Didn't things work pretty well for us over the past two and a half centuries? What were we denied as Christians?"

"The United States was, is, and shall be a Christian country. We have lived in error for many generations, but now we must accept our role as the New Jerusalem."

"Well, you did a fuck of a job on the old Jerusalem."

"Don't mock, Gary. Don't mock what you don't understand."

"I understand that Jesus Christ brought love and mercy into this world."

"And we crucified Him. We had our chance. We failed Him. Now He returns with a sword."

"Convenient. Show me *that* passage in the Gospels."

"Luke 22, Verse 36, 'he that hath no sword, let him sell his garment and buy one.' But you haven't answered *my* questions, Gary. Tell me, please. Instruct me: After fourteen centuries of warfare between our faith and Islam—begun by a conquering, bloodthirsty faith and continued unto this day by its spawn—after all the Christian suffering, the enslavements, the relentless bloodshed, the hatred, the captivity of our churches . . . haven't we had sufficient proof that we can't coexist? That it's us or them? Would you prefer it to be the Muslims who prevail? Should we just surrender? Would our enemies lay down *their* swords? To put it in secular terms for you, religions are competitors in a great struggle for survival. Religions *can't* cooperate, not really. It's not in their DNA. God tells us all that there can be only one path to salvation, one truth, but we refuse to hear. In our vanity and pride, we think we know better. 'All religions share a universal spirit.' Do they, Gary? *Do* they? You love to cite the Gospels. Well, where does Christ say, 'Choose the faith you find convenient, they're all the same to me'? You know better. As a Christian yourself, if a confused one. Christ tells us, in the clearest words He ever spoke, that those who do not believe in Him cannot be saved. He *damns* them. Or do you think He was just in a bad mood that day?" Montfort swept a hand back over his shining hair. "For fourteen centuries, we tried to find a way to live in peace with the forces of the Antichrist. For fourteen hundred years, we wandered aimlessly in a spiritual desert, bereft of comfort because we denied our purpose. And now, at last, our wanderings are over. We have been touched by the fire of God's Word: There is only one true faith, and there shall be only one true faith, and this land will be purged with fire."

"You sound like Charlton Heston in one of his lesser roles. What are you telling me, Sim? That a billion-plus dead Muslims won't be enough? That the Hindus are next? And after them, the Buddhists? Then the Jews? Before you get started on the Catholics?"

Montfort waved his concerns away. "This is a struggle between God and Satan. Our faith is that of the One True God. Mohammed was the messenger of Satan. Allah *is* Satan. Islam is the faith of Satan, of the Antichrist, and must be expunged for this world to be redeemed."

"And the Jews? How about the Jews, Sim? You've made them a lot of promises. Where do they fit in?"

Montfort fidgeted in his chair. "The Jews aren't a problem."

"You're really going to hand everything back to them? To re-create Israel? With what's left?"

"The Jewish people will receive justice."

"Sim, if I were a Jew and I heard *you* say that, I'd run for the trees."

"Don't try to create further dissension. Please, Gary. I'll get down on my knees if you like. Join us. Before it's too late. We're doing God's work. Men *follow* you. As they follow me. Together, we could do great things." Montfort leaned in closer than he had yet done, close enough for Harris to imagine he smelled scorched breath. "It's not too late for you to see the light."

"I see your light, Sim. It comes from burning heretics at the stake."

"Don't wait too long, Gary."

"I'm still waiting for that cock to crow again. A second time. And a third."

"Rhetorical flourishes don't suit you," Montfort said. "You never had a mind for subtleties. You've always been a practical man. Albeit with some mushy idealism thrown in. It would help you if you behaved practically now. If you can't believe, Gary, just go through the motions. Faith will come."

"Isn't that a Catholic regimen, Sim? Sounds odd, coming from a good old Protestant boy like you. Although I do recall you were a great one for skipping chapel at VMI. I suppose you hadn't yet traveled the road to Damascus."

Montfort sighed. "Speaking of roads, I'll have to get on the road myself. Figuratively speaking."

"Careful of those helicopters, Sim. They fall out of the sky. Unexpectedly."

Montfort stood up. Harris followed. The MOBIC commander was almost a full head taller. Charlton Heston, indeed.

"Oh, I almost forgot," Montfort said. "I've had a report that a CHART disappeared. In or around Nazareth. Could you look into it for me?"

"You're not supposed to have any CHARTs in my area of operations, Sim. You know that. As a matter—"

"Just trying to do my duty as a Christian," Montfort cut him off. "I didn't think you'd mind. But see if you can find them, won't you, Gary? For old times' sake? The officers and men selected for our Christian Heritage Advance Rescue Teams are a little too courageous for their own good. I worry about them."

"Wheels within wheels within wheels. You really are amazing, Sim."

"And one other thing. I've got an order for you from General Schwach. You're to detach one armored brigade and put it under my command to reinforce my corps. And not a depleted brigade, either. One that hasn't been shot up, that hasn't been overcommitted. I've also got authorization to assume the primary responsibility for the advance into northern Galilee and beyond, once my corps elements have reached your sector. Which should be any moment now."

"All right."

Montfort's eyebrows tightened. "Not even one word of protest? You're making progress, Gary."

"You can have your brigade, Sim. And you're getting one that hasn't taken any significant casualties. I'm chopping Avi Dorn's outfit to you. From the Israeli Exile Force."

"But—"

"Come on, Sim. What did you expect? You've been working some scam, some deal, with Avi. I'm not *that* stupid. I figure it'll be easier for the two of you to coordinate things when he falls directly under your chain of command."

"I expected—"

"A U.S. Army brigade? Sim, you're not prejudiced

against the Israelis, are you? After all those speeches you made back home? All those interviews? On your way out, just tell Mike Andretti where and when you want Avi to link up with your people. I'll let Mike know I blessed it."

The confident, studied impassiveness that ruled Montfort's features had disappeared again. For an interval of suspended time, the MOBIC commander looked as if he would fill the room with sulfur simply by breathing.

"Anything else?" Harris asked.

"Goodbye, Gary." Montfort did not extend his hand. Slowly, as if wearing ankle weights, he crossed to the door. But halfway through the portal, he turned back toward Harris.

"Yes. There is something else. I'm told you're going blind. I'm concerned that you might be unfit for command."

"I see *you*, Sim. Clearly."

"And one other thing, Gary," he said. "Did your wife ever tell you I fucked her?"

SEVENTEEN

·····■······■·····

HEADQUARTERS, III (US) CORPS, MT. CARMEL RIDGES

Flintlock Harris sat back down after Montfort left. Drained, he brushed back his hair with his hands, pulling his eyelids open. Trying to think clearly. His body yearned for sleep, but his mind paged from thought to thought, unable to staple them together.

Bored flies drifted past the lamp. The dead air smelled of backed-up drains. One room was much the same as another in Sim Montfort's Holy Land.

At any moment, John Willing would bring in the paperwork that absolutely had to be signed before Harris could go to sleep. The general dreaded the thought of straining to read anything smaller than a billboard. But paperwork was as much a part of soldiering as the rest of it.

Montfort knew. About his eyes. Enough to make that remark. Who else knew? How would Montfort use the information? Had he used it already? Was it already in the "Fire Harris" file back in D.C.?

On the other hand, old Sim was rattled. Badly. If

Harris heard one clock ticking, Montfort heard another. The Christian general who threw away his regiments of believers. How much time did Montfort have? The impatience, the unaccustomed insecurity, was obvious. An assassination really wasn't Montfort's style. It wasted too many resources, left too many debts to others, revealed too much. Sim had overplayed that one—and lost the hand. Badly. Harris was confident that his competitor wouldn't try any similar stunts soon.

The down side was that Montfort, turning hasty on the battlefield, might drag them all down with him. With just one big mistake. Despite Sim's rapid conquest of Jerusalem, Harris wasn't ready to write off al-Mahdi as a military commander. Or al-Ghazi, for that matter. Sim would push as hard as he could now, running against a stopwatch only he could hear. And when a leader did that, it was all too easy to lose sight of the enemy's counterdesigns.

Harris could picture the MOBIC corps charging into a classic Middle Eastern trap, the kind that Muslim armies had used for over a thousand years, first luring the opponent on, and then, when the attacker found himself overextended, sweeping in on his forces from the flanks. He scribbled a note to Van Danczuk to send Montfort the study the G-2 shop had done of historical patterns in Jihadi warfare. And to mark it "urgent." Montfort and his men were Americans, too. Troublesome, even revolting, as their differences were, they were still on the same side.

Harris replayed the MOBIC commander's tirade about the centuries of evidence of Muslim viciousness and all the chances the Jihadis had been given. The damned trouble with Montfort, the brilliance of the grift he worked, was that he always started with an ounce of truth. Then he wrapped it in a ton of bullshit. And it worked. Because old Sim told people what they longed to hear.

He'd been doing that since their days at VMI.

Harris didn't buy Montfort's logic, of course. But he had to admit that Sim forced him to think. What alternatives *did* he have to offer? In place of Montfort's vision of hypergenocide? What strategy could he lay out as a substitute? Just an endless muddling through? More of the same? A succession of wars that only bought time at a terrible cost in blood? Was it true . . . irrefutably true . . . that religions were programmed for violent competition, that accommodation was an illusion for soft-minded dreamers? Was it, in the end, us or them? And not just on the battlefield?

Harris dreaded what the coming days and weeks and months and years would bring.

Old Sim was right about one thing, though: Right now, they had a war to fight.

So what was to be done? Harris asked himself. What could he do to bring victory on the battlefield? Without sacrificing the fundamental humanity he still ascribed to his country? And without delivering that country to his own faith's Jihadis?

Keep it rigorous. By the book. Don't make any big mistakes. Keep the Army clean. Prevent the MOBIC command from grabbing the Marines. Deliver the goods.

Okay. Sim and his boys were about to assume the

leading role in the attack. Given the new determination the Jihadis were showing, that promised to be a bloody mess. Especially given Montfort's evident impatience. Harris hoped that his old acquaintance, the man who'd succeeded at virtually everything he'd ever undertaken, wouldn't fall into the trap of overconfidence now. The combination of overconfidence and impatience had defeated no end of generals in the blood-soaked terrain in which they found themselves.

Harris rose. Stiff. Old. He bent to rummage through the kit bag his aide had placed by the foot of his bunk. His body seemed to him a rusty machine, hammered into action. Fishing out an emergency ration stashed for times like this, the general sat back down and began to eat a foil packet of chicken a la king. Cold. The spoon came up with solid white grease. But Harris didn't care.

Where was Willing? He was usually so prompt. Had he fallen asleep himself? Or was he in the field latrine with the runs? Like half the G-3 shop.

A weary fly scouted the ration pouch. More from an insect's sense of duty than from real interest. Harris's shooing gesture was equally halfhearted.

How much sleep could he allow himself? The window of his room had been blackened and blastproofed by his security detail, but Harris sensed the sky lightening beyond the walls. Three hours? He knew he needed four to keep on functioning on overdrive. But he didn't want to miss his own morning briefing. And rescheduling it just screwed everybody else.

Everything was on track. He could let Mike An-

dretti run the show. They'd come get him if any
critical issues came up.

Or would they just let the old man sleep? He could
hear the G-3 saying, "He's been through a lot."

Harris didn't want anybody's pity. Three hours.
He'd make do with that.

If Willing didn't turn up soon, he wouldn't even
get that.

Killing a billion people. Sim was certainly ambitious. And utterly mad. But history was made by
madmen.

Would his own kind really attempt such a thing?
Or was Sim more interested in the process, in the
ambitions a lengthy struggle might fulfill? How
much did Montfort really mean? Even now? And
how much was sheer calculation?

With the acid clarity at the end of a sleepless night,
Harris realized that Sim Montfort was a great man
and he was not. Montfort certainly wasn't a good
man. He reeked of evil. But Montfort was, undeni-
ably, a great man. And Harris knew that he lacked
greatness himself. He was a competent soldier and a
first-rate commander. As dutiful as anyone could
ask. And honest. Or so he liked to think. But there
was no greatness in him, and he recognized, ruefully, that a part of him was jealous of Sim Montfort.

But it was only a small part of him. The rest of
Lieutenant General Gary "Flintlock" Harris just
wanted to see the mission he'd set himself through to
the end: The preservation of the U.S. Army and the
defense of the Constitution of the United States.

He laughed at himself. With a weary, broken
laugh that ended with a sour burp of grease. Who did

he think he was? To assign himself such grand ambitions? Flintlock Harris, Savior of the Army and the Constitution?

Putting it in those terms made him feel like a fool.

Had he been as vain, in his way, as Sim Montfort?

And yet. Somebody had to do it. Didn't they? Who else would have even tried? Poor old Schwach? Who was left to fight them, on both fronts? Here, in the shooting war. And in dubious battle on the plains of the Washington Mall, if not Heaven.

So many had fallen by the wayside. So many of his comrades had just quit. There was so much darkness now. And not just the shade that was slowly eroding his vision, but the darkness that infected souls and defined entire ages.

Harris scraped out the last lumps and smears of chicken a la king, streaking white grease across his knuckles. Then he stood up, defying his joints again. He dropped the foil envelope into the burn bag meant for all his trash, classified and unclassified, and, a bit cranky, turned toward the door to look for his aide.

Just then, Major Willing knocked at last and came into the room.

"Sorry, sir. I dozed off."

"What have you got for me, John?"

"I pared it down, sir. But these can't wait."

Harris held out his hand for the papers. "Get some sleep. Tell the adjutant—whoever's on duty over there—to have a runner wait outside my door."

"Sir, the document with the blue tab has to go straight to the Three shop."

"Have them send a runner, too. I hate to say it, but

there are times I miss my old computer. Now get some sleep."

"Yes, sir." But the aide didn't leave. He looked at the floor, then looked back up. "Sir . . . I'm glad you—"

"Me, too, John. Now get some sleep."

But as the aide was leaving, Flintlock Harris had a moment of weakness.

"John?"

"Sir?"

"How are we doing on long-range comms?"

"Back to Washington?"

"To the States."

"We had some open channels earlier, sir. I can check."

"Before you turn in, see if they can get my wife on the line."

HEADQUARTERS, 2-34 ARMOR, 600 METERS WEST OF PHASE LINE LONG BEACH

As the world emerged from the darkness, restoring the contrast between solid forms and empty space, Lieutenant Colonel Monty Maxwell felt a relief so intense it was almost joy. The night had been hellish. But they'd made it through. Most of them. Even though the lightening sky to the east promised only another day of combat, Maxwell felt an unreasonable confidence that things would be better now.

He had grown up in a world where armor ruled the night, when magic night-vision devices and perfect communications had made his kind masters of the midnight hour. But this was a different world.

First, the jamming had gone crazy again. Then a tank in Alpha Company and a Bradley in Charlie had each run over an EMP mine, wiping out every electronic system on their company property books.

For almost two hours, Maxwell had remained unaware of the company-level crises. Waiting in his command post and listening to slivers of the war, he'd blamed the jamming for the lack of updates from his subordinate commanders. Meanwhile, his forward companies had been fighting for their lives. Even Bravo Company, with intact comms gear, had been hard up against it, infiltrated by commandos wearing cool-suits that masked the body-heat signatures that should have registered on Bravo's thermal sights. With the noise of battle all around and artillery fire falling like an endless avalanche, Maxwell had lost control of his battalion without realizing it.

Only when he grew restless and went forward on a personal recon—half to keep from dozing off—had he encountered the Alpha Company first sergeant, who'd peeled off from the fight to alert battalion.

Maxwell had turned around just in time to warn his command post to be prepared for a knife fight. Suicide commandos had penetrated the line. The TOC got hit just minutes after he got back.

After that, it hadn't been a question of commanding his battalion but of survival. The Headquarters Company clerks and jerks had gotten their chance to kill or be killed in pitch darkness, guided only by tracer streams and cries. Maxwell would've retrieved his sword, on practical grounds. But there hadn't been time. The Jihadis came out of the darkness in waves. Screaming and hurling grenades. Firing wildly. After breaking his carbine while beating a Jihadi to death, Maxwell had scavenged a weapon from a dead soldier. After that, he fought with short bursts and the bayonet. When he wasn't fighting for his own life, he tried to impose order on the free-for-all.

Where Jihadis had tangled themselves in the wire, they blew themselves up as Maxwell's men approached. After that, his soldiers shot anything that screamed or even rustled.

One of the commandos had gotten inside a tank. That set off a razor fight in a locked closet. Out of ammunition, another soldier fought with his bare hands for the cab of his V-hull truck, finishing the job only by biting through his enemy's neck and thumbing out an eyeball.

Neither side took prisoners.

The first orange crack split the horizon into heaven and earth. As if the night had been slashed open with a saber. Maxwell could see faces. Bodies. Damage.

"Sergeant Major?" he called.

No answer.

"Captain Barnes?"

No answer.

But plenty of his soldiers remained alive. More and more of them emerged, ghostly, from the gray depths between the trees. More had survived than seemed reasonable after those infernal hours. But it was hard to spot one who wasn't smeared with blood.

Black lumps littered the ground. Lot more of them than of us, Maxwell thought. But it was slight consolation. Behind scorched trees, a comms vehicle smoldered.

In the eternal voice of the eternal sergeant, an

NCO asked the world, "Anybody got any fucking coffee? I don't care how cold it is . . ."

What was he supposed to do now? Use semaphore? Messengers? In one of the not-quite lulls between wave attacks, he'd managed to raise brigade and report the EMP mines. At least, he thought they'd copied him. Higher had to know about that particular threat. Before everybody in the corps started running into them.

Call the mental roll: Two companies dead, as far as their electronics went—would they have replacement comms gear somewhere up the chain? Actual casualty figures unknown. A battalion headquarters in shreds. And an enemy who meant business after all.

What was a commander supposed to do under the circumstances?

Maxwell had no trouble answering his own question: *Fight.*

QUARTERS ONE, FT. HOOD, TEXAS

Sarah Colmer-Harris wasn't sure she should answer the phone. The crank calls had reached a level of vitriol that shocked her, despite all that she'd heard in her courtroom years. But there was also a chance it would be her daughter calling again. She dreaded that call, too. She didn't have anything left to give to anyone else just now.

Ready to curse the caller, she picked up the phone. "Hello?"

"Sarah?"

"Oh, God. Gary? Is it you?"

"For better, or worse. Worse, if you were close enough to smell me."

"It's so good to hear your voice. I can't tell you how good." She wanted not to cry. But her strength fled. "Is everything okay? Are you all right?"

"I'm tired. Otherwise unscathed. I wake you, darling?"

"No. I hadn't gone to bed yet." She glanced across the room to the half-packed, ill-packed suitcase. "It's just so wonderful to hear your voice."

"I love you, Sarah."

"And I love *you*. God, I feel like I'm back in high school, and the boy I'd been mooning about for months just called."

"Who is he? I'll kill him."

"Only you." She wiped the wet from her nose with the back of her hand, then rubbed at her tears. "I wish you were here."

"Wouldn't mind being there myself. Better than you being here, under the circumstances. Just had one of the memorable meals of my life."

"*Are* you all right? Really?"

"Yes, Sarah. I'm all right. Are *you* all right?"

"Fine. Better now. Since you called." How much did he know? she wondered.

"Listen, Sarah . . . I can't tie up this line. I'm breaking my own rule. But . . . here it is . . . the reason I called . . ."

She cringed. Beginning to shrivel inside. He *knew*.

"What? Tell me."

"Sarah . . . I just wanted you to know that I love you. I needed to tell you that I love you unconditionally, without reservation, and with all my heart. And I have unlimited faith in you. In all things."

"You're making me cry."

"You've been crying for the last five minutes. You've probably got snot all over the phone."

"Mr. Romantic." But he was, he *was*.

"I love you, Sarah. That's all. How are the girls?"

She hesitated. Then she forced herself to speak. Before he began to suspect something.

"Gary . . . I've got something to tell you. But promise me you won't get upset. You've got to promise me."

"That's hard, Sarah. What's wrong?"

"It's nothing so terrible. I just don't want you hearing rumors and—"

"What's *wrong*, Sarah?"

"It's Emily. She's . . . been in an accident. Nothing terrible, nothing too serious. Miranda's with her."

"She's going to be all right, though?"

"Yes," she lied. "She should be fine."

Dear God, she prayed to the being she didn't believe in, Dear God, just let me get through this. Don't let him know. Please. He doesn't need this now. I can bear it for the two of us. Until he comes home.

"Well, if anything—"

"She's going to be fine."

"Sarah . . . I've got to go."

"I know. I love you."

"And I love you. Give my love to Emily. Tell her she's got terrible timing. And give Miranda a hug for me. A big one."

"I promise. Gary . . . Come home safe."

"*I* promise. I'll be there before you know it. What

did the monkey say when he caught his tail in the meat grinder?"

" 'It won't be long now.' Gary, sweetheart . . . If your men only knew what a little boy you are . . ."

"I'm relying on you not to tell."

"I won't. Girl Scout's honor. I love you. *I love you*."

"I love you, Sarah."

Then he was gone. And Sarah turned back to the labor of packing for the flight to her daughter's funeral.

EIGHTEEN

••••••■•••••••■•••••■••••

AT TAYYIBAH, IRBID VILAYET, EMIRATE OF AL-QUDS AND DAMASKUS

"Salaam Aleikum!" Suleiman al-Mahdi said as he rose from his nest of cushions. Instead of his uniform, the emir-general wore layered white robes trimmed in gold. Crossing the room to greet Montfort properly, he switched to English: "The hours I have waited for you, my friend, allowed me to ponder the distance our journeys have taken us!"

The emir-general approached with open arms, as if to embrace Montfort. But just when al-Mahdi's heels stopped clacking on the tile floor, he shifted to the posture for a handshake. The Arab's grip was firm, distinctly unlike the pudgy Saudi paws Montfort recalled from an earlier war. Al-Mahdi's robes accented, rather than concealed, his slump-shouldered build. He had the eyes of a successful pawnbroker.

"I hope your immediate journey was not too difficult?" the Arab said. He released his grip on Montfort and swept his right hand toward a wall. "This house is very dear to me. It belonged to my grandfather, you know. The Royal Jordanian general. I loved to visit in my youth. The water here is very sweet, the people respectful. But please! Sit down, General Montfort."

Al-Mahdi gestured toward a low table laden with plates of fruit and ceramic carafes. Tea steamed, delivered just as Montfort's helicopter throbbed in for a landing. Montfort faced a choice of a cushioned divan, less plush than al-Mahdi's own, or a chair with gilt arms and a striped satin seat, a knockoff of a reject from Versailles.

Montfort took the chair. The emir-general dropped back onto his throne of cushions. A black grape fell onto the tabletop, an extravaganza of mother-of-pearl inlay. The Sunni Arabs Montfort had encountered over the years presented themselves as Islam's Calvinists, but their appetite for florid interiors hinted at private indiscipline.

Veering east from the Jordan Valley, the flight up the Wadi al Tayyibah had been difficult for the pilots, who had to scrape the neglected fields below the wadi's walls to evade the MOBIC's own radar coverage. But Montfort had felt nothing resembling worry. He had no fear of death, although his dismissal of it had more to do with pride than with his faith.

"You look weary, my friend," al-Mahdi told him. The emir-general leaned toward the table and lifted a bowl of dates. "Please. Let me offer you nourishment. You are my guest, after all. In my grandfather's house, we cannot be enemies. And I had these dates brought in just for your pleasure. They come from the finest grove between the Tigris and

Euphrates, not far from Baghdad. Where, I'm told, you acquired a taste for them, when you were a young warrior."

Montfort shook his head. No, thank you. Al-Mahdi smiled. Amused. After setting down the bowl, he brought a glistening date to his lips, bit into its flesh, and sucked away half of the dense, brown pulp. After swallowing, he said, "You see, General Montfort? They are not poisoned. Neither my duty as a host nor my judgment would permit such a thing. And, truth be told, assassinations have never brought my faith lasting successes. They were our version of what your military used to call 'surgical strikes.' Or 'decapitation strikes,' to be still more precise. Just as such shortcuts did not work for you, they also failed us. Although we quite liked to dance about and celebrate the death of this fellow or that." He smiled again, finished the date, then said, "No, the easy solutions never work. Do they? We must grip our problems in their entirety and act boldly if we want results that endure. But you do look weary—some tea, at least?"

Montfort reached for his cooling glass of tea. "I need to confirm that everything's on track."

"But do try a date. They're wondrous. On track? You rather exceeded our agreement regarding Jerusalem. But I ascribe that to uncontrollable enthusiasm. In the future, however, I will expect our agreement to be honored 'to the letter,' as your diplomats like to say."

"Jerusalem was always to be ours. To administer as we see fit."

"Well, then, you've simplified your task, I suppose. You haven't left a great deal to administer. But done is done."

"Since we're on the subject of things not going quite as planned," Montfort said, "I have to tell you that there'll be a slight delay in Nazareth. In eliminating your target group. General Harris is being obstinate."

"You told me he would not last. That he would be removed."

"Some things take time."

"Do you have the time? Do we?"

Montfort tasted the tea. Too sweet. Like mint syrup. "I'll take care of Nazareth. And General Harris."

Al-Mahdi finished his own remaining tea in a gulp. And he sighed. "I allowed for difficulties in Nazareth, given the tender sentiments of General Harris. We've taken certain measures of our own. To simplify your task. But I wonder about this 'Flintlock' Harris. He seems a clever fellow. Moreso than I was led to expect."

"He's not. Astute, perhaps. But certainly not clever."

"But isn't that a more dangerous quality? To be astute? Doesn't Aristotle tell us that cleverness precludes depth? In *The Poetics*, I think. Although I hope you will not pin me down. A clever man will outwit himself in the end. But an astute fellow?"

"I've never read Aristotle."

"Aristotle is a waste of time. But one remembers what one is forced to learn. My point is that there may be more to General Harris than his portrayal as a 'simple soldier' has led us to believe."

"I've known Gary Harris for over thirty years. Don't worry about him. His sense of duty will be his undoing."

"He sounds like a Jihadi."

"Don't worry about Harris."

"I *don't* worry about him. I merely wonder about him. As I have said. But don't you find it pleasurable to analyze your enemies, General Montfort? To solve the marvelous puzzle of the man who seeks to kill you and your kind?"

"What would I find if I analyzed you? Right now?"

"You would find a man asking himself if you will deliver all that you have promised, after you have received all that *you* have been promised."

"You'll get everything we agreed to. Once we have Damascus."

"And your Air Force will support me? When I march against the sultan in Baghdad? And when I reckon with the Shia heretics to the east? What will you tell your associates in the Pentagon, in Washington?"

"That we're helping Muslims destroy each other."

Al-Mahdi's smile returned, spreading his whiskers. "Exactly right. But you and I understand the importance—the indispensible nature—of purifying our faiths. How many Christians do you think *you* will have to destroy? In the end?"

"Not so many."

"That is how it begins. With 'not so many.' But there is always another apostate, a heretic, a renegade . . . another traitor. Myself, I expect to go on killing for the rest of my life. The struggle is never done. And there is neither tragedy nor dishonor in such a struggle that finds no end. On the contrary: A faith that triumphed completely would go to sleep—that was the tragedy of the Arab world in our days of greatness, you know. We were so successful that we just dozed off. And when we awoke, having slept through the Ottoman centuries, we found that the French and English, and, later, you Americans had crept into our house and stolen everything we expected to have for 'breakfast, lunch, and dinner,' as you put it." He picked up a date but delayed lifting it to his mouth. "One of your great founding fathers has written that your system of government must be refreshed now and then with the blood of patriots. So it is with religion: A healthy faith demands a struggle, an enemy, a *Shaitan*. Our religion—any religion— must be refreshed with the blood of heretics and infidels." He grinned. "Were there no heretics left, we would have to create them. Were we deprived of infidels, we would have to imagine them. And we will, my brother. We *must*. Faith without struggle is the faith of a eunuch."

"*My* faith tells me that neither of us will reach our goals if things go wrong during the next forty-eight hours."

"I apologize for rambling. You're right, of course. This is no time for chat. Tell me, then, where we are at this moment, General Montfort."

Montfort sat wrapped in a blanket of exhaustion. Al-Mahdi's philosophical pretensions had only annoyed him, every word a weight on his eyelids. He wished he had a glass of hot tea now. But he was not about to ask for one.

"At this moment, I need al-Ghazi to hold Harris's

forces as close to their current positions as possible. Whatever it takes."

"Easy enough to say! But my men are suffering, such losses cannot be sustained." The emir-general shifted on his cushions. "I need to preserve my own forces. For the other battles to come."

"Well, I need you to hold Harris. Minimize his gains. Until 1800 hours today. Six p.m."

"I understand '1800 hours.' But your General Harris is a tough fellow, you know. He doesn't make mistakes."

"Everybody makes mistakes. Harris has made his share. He'll make more."

"Perhaps. But not on the battlefield."

"I need you to hold him until 1800. That's less than twelve hours."

"And then?"

"My forces will conduct a forward passage of lines, and I'll assume control of the attack in the north."

"Of Harris's corps, as well?"

"Not yet."

"So . . . After 1800, all of the attacking units will be yours. From the Military Order of the Brothers in Christ. And we will begin to give way."

Montfort nodded. "As we agreed. But they can't just quit. Neither of us wants a bloodbath like we had over Jerusalem. But it has to look like a fight—as though my men have broken through where the Army couldn't. On both axes of advance, with the initial main effort directed east to Tiberias and the supporting attack northeast along Highway 65, then swinging east into the Upper Galilee—at which point it becomes the main effort."

"Militarily, of course, Tiberias is worthless to you. A dead end, except for the road that follows the lake. But your faith, like mine, is a powerful matter. And you will accompany this attack yourself? To stand where your Christ is said to have stood when he delivered his great admonition? Only, this time, with cameras to record the event? My friend, I almost expect you to walk on the waters of the Sea of Galilee. Surely, *that* would impress your audience at home."

"You understand the importance of symbols as well as I do. Baghdad matters more than Damascus, for example."

"I did not mean to be insulting. There are times when my attempts at humor in English have an awkward inflection. Forgive me."

"Your last defensive positions facing my main attack will be on the ridge just west of the Sea of Galilee. That has to look like a serious fight. For the holy sites." Montfort stretched across the table and pulled the bowl of dates within reach. Hoping a sugar high would get him through the rest of the meeting. And back to his headquarters.

"It will be up to your MOBIC forces, as well, to give the appearance of a great battle," al-Mahdi said. "You must make it appear that you have employed overwhelming force. For my part, you will permit me to place some of my poorer units on this Galilee ridge for you to use as targets. I must preserve my elite units and formations. For the future."

"Leave me the expendables. As long as it looks like a fight. To liberate the key Christian sites surrounding the Sea of Galilee. And don't worry about overwhelming force. I'm going to mass so much combat power that you won't have any explaining to do to anyone." The dates *were* delicious. The taste carried him back to his days as a junior officer in Iraq. Montfort took another.

"*Insh'Allah*, it will be exactly as you wish. A great show."

"And the uprising in Baghdad? Is *that* on schedule?"

"If all goes as planned this day and this night on the battlefield, my supporters will rise tomorrow. Then I will be forced to withdraw beyond Damaskus, to march east to save the caliphate from anarchy. And you will help me with this great task."

"Just give us the targets, and the Air Force will turn them into rubble."

"I'm glad you're enjoying the dates. They're the best in the world, you know. But one mustn't eat too many. Your flight back down the wadi might be unsettling. And you must be fit for tomorrow, so you can stand where your 'Savior' stood."

"I have the constitution of a horse."

"Not a purebred Arabian, I suppose. But you know, General Montfort, the notion of your Jesus Christ as your 'Savior' has always confused me, given your doctrine that 'God helps those who help themselves'."

"That isn't doctrine. It's just a saying."

"But isn't it *your* doctrine, General Montfort? Your *personal* doctrine? You suspect me of being an idle philosopher, but I know that I lack the quality of mind to be a theologian. There are so many contradictions, both in our Holy Koran and in your Bible.

It's much easier to be a general." Al-Mahdi smiled with one side of his mouth. "But you are yourself a scholar. I know this. I have read your dissertation from Harvard University: 'Case Studies in Governance Challenges After Successful Coups.' Really, it's full of profound insights. Especially into Muslims and our errors. I learned a great deal from it." Suddenly, his smile, ever close to a sneer, became almost shy. "But I don't suppose you have ever read *my* book? It has been printed in the French language, but not, I regret, in English."

"Sorry. I haven't read it."

Al-Mahdi waved it away as of no concern. "Perhaps, when all this is done, I will provide an English translation for you. I think you would find it of interest."

"What's it about?"

"How Arabs turned defeat into victory in the late twelfth century. Of course, I wrote it as a younger man, and young men fail to appreciate the complexity of Allah's creation."

"We all make mistakes when we're young."

"Did *you*? Really? I find it difficult to imagine you as a young man, to begin with. You possess a gravity a fellow can only envy, General Montfort."

Montfort returned his counterpart's smile. "It's not gravity at the moment. It's exhaustion."

"Then I am doubly in your debt for your willingness to make this journey to accommodate me." The emir-general stood up. "You need to return to your troops. To prepare your offensive. Do you really intend to move into the attack so quickly? After your long advance up the Jordan Valley? Won't you need more time? To refuel, to rearm. To catch your breath, as they say."

"Not if you live up to your part of the bargain."

"If you'll permit me the observation, I'm concerned that you may be impatient. Neither of us can afford problems. We must remain methodical. Perhaps al-Ghazi's units could hold Harris for another night, and your attack could commence tomorrow? I'm willing to make that sacrifice, should you deem it necessary to guarantee against failure."

"We attack at 1800. Today. Just do your part. And I'll do mine."

"And then, *Insh'Allah*, we will see American aircraft over Baghdad again. History repeating itself."

Montfort grunted. "Not if you provide better targeting data."

"You will have no worries on that account. But I wonder, General Montfort, when will we meet again? The ambitions that brought us together will pull us asunder now. Physically, I mean. Anyway, I shall send you a translation of my book, when all of this dust has settled. I'll commission one, just for you. Something for you to remember me by, as they say. But I will walk you out."

As they went, side by side, Montfort said, "We despise each other."

"Of course. But it's a curious matter. We respect each other, as well. Respect for the corresponding abilities, for the other's vision to see beyond the moment. But distaste for the reflection we discover of the self. You and I are condemned, General Montfort, to be men of action. Too much introspection would hardly suit us. It's a frailty I struggle against."

The glare of the morning sun on the barren hills that had once been Jordan stunned their eyes. At the sight of Montfort, his helicopter crew immediately set off the rising whine that would bring the rotors to life.

"By the way," al-Mahdi continued, "you don't really plan to hand your new possessions back to the Jews, do you? Isn't that what you've promised them, that the state of Israel will be reborn? In return for their support?"

"The Jews killed Christ," Montfort said. "We're going to remind them."

NAZARETH, TACTICAL OPERATIONS CENTER, 1-18 INFANTRY

"Sir," Command Sergeant Major Bratty said to his battalion commander, "it's not your fault. That was a setup from the get-go. Those MOBIC pukes were going to get whacked no matter what you did."

Overnight, the heaviest sounds of war had rolled east—except for the friendly artillery batteries firing from forward positions down in the Jezreel.

"It's still my fault. I lost my temper."

"Who wouldn't?"

"The truth is," Lieutenant Colonel Pat Cavanaugh said, "that Flintlock Harris should've booted me out of the Army back in Bremerhaven. I lost my temper with some Germans the same way."

"The Krauts get waxed?"

"No. Harris grabbed me by the stacking swivel."

"Too bad."

Cavanaugh shrugged. "Even if it was a setup, I played right into their hands. Whoever was behind it."

"MOBIC's my bet. Blue on blue. They're working so many scams they've probably started scamming each other."

"Your hand hurting, Sergeant Major?"

"It's the damnedest thing, sir. Sometimes I feel the fingers. Like they're still there."

"Your trigger finger, too. And your joker-poker."

"They're the fingers that hold a guitar pick against your thumb. That's what really pisses me off."

"I hadn't thought of that."

Bratty made a same-old-shit-for-breakfast face. "I'll learn to play with my toes or something. The Jihadis are *not* going to fuck with my front-porch retirement plan."

"I shouldn't have lost my temper like that, though. No matter how I cut it, I sent them out like sheep to the slaughter."

"Sheep are meant to be slaughtered," Bratty said. "The point is not to be a sheep. Look, sir. We're all tired. And we're all pissed. And we've drawn about the shittiest duty in this war so far, babysitting Arabs every soldier in this outfit would like to double-tap. And while we're on the subject, I was amazed you didn't deck that smart-ass Ranger major when he reported in. I'll bet he's a closet fag who drives a Volvo."

"In his position, I would've been pissed off, too. This isn't exactly a Ranger mission."

"Well, he needs to suck it up. And I need you to buck up, sir. Don't do this self-pity riff on me—because that's what it sounds like, to tell you the truth.

We can get right with our consciences later. You get any sleep?"

"Couple of hours."

"How's that coffee?"

"Bad beyond belief."

"Glad to hear it. Wouldn't want to think Sergeant Kiefer was losing his touch."

"I'm going to shave and make the rounds. Want to come along?"

"I'd better stay here, sir. 'At the still center of the turning world'."

"That from one of the songs you wrote?"

The S-1 NCOIC approached the command vehicle.

"What now, Sergeant Yannis?" Bratty asked.

"Morning, sir . . . Sergeant Major. Sergeant Major, did you know the water's still on? In the buildings? No shit. There's still water coming through the pipes. With plenty of pressure."

"I told everybody to stay out of the buildings. Let the rags alone."

"The buildings are empty around here. The rags all took off. Back when they nailed up our guys, I'd bet."

"I still don't want anybody going on souvenir hunts."

"Nobody's stealing anything, Sergeant Major. There's no looting or nothing." The sergeant glanced at the battalion commander, then looked back at Bratty. "I just thought that, since it looks like we're going to be stuck here for a while, maybe we could rotate people through for showers."

"Showers?" Bratty cried, going into one of his favorite routines. "Jesus Christ! You're just starting to smell like soldiers. I hear about any enlisted man in this battalion getting a shower before I personally hand him the soap, and he and his chain of command are going to wish they'd been captured by the J's. Got that? You tell everybody in Hindquarters Company what I said."

"Yes, Sergeant Major." The sergeant glanced at Cavanaugh again, then did an about-face and walked off. Radiating dejection like a disappointed kid.

"Fucking clerks," Bratty said. "This is a god-damned Infantry battalion."

"Why won't you let them take showers? Just curious."

Bratty looked at the battalion commander. "Sir, you're a kick-ass officer. But you'd never make an NCO."

"And why's that?"

"You don't think the right way. Look. All our grungies are going through a cold-turkey withdrawal after being in the fight for a couple of days. After the high comes the crash. They don't know what they want, exactly, but tired as they are, they hear the fighting over that ridge, and it's like laying down a scent in front of a pack of hounds. Makes them want to kill people and bust stuff. And right now, the closest people to hand that might be available for killing are the local yokels. Who, in the soldiers' minds, are responsible for yesterday's crucifixion scene. Under the circumstances, the task of a battalion sergeant major is to redirect the negative energies."

"Which means?"

"I'd rather have our soldiers pissed at me and griping because I won't let them wash their nasty asses than have them eyeing the rags and twitching their trigger fingers. Better for them to bitch about the hard-ass, pigheaded, unreasonable sergeant major."

"Thanks for sharing your trade secrets. You know, Frederick the Great believed that his soldiers needed to fear their officers more than they did the enemy. Wouldn't work in our Army, of course."

"Sir, I don't want them to *fear* me. Not exactly. I just want them to stop fantasizing about double-tapping rags and go back to dreaming about getting out of the Army and landing a job that, one fine day, puts them in a position to employ me in cleaning public toilets for the rest of my life."

The battalion command channel crackled to life. It was the Charlie Company commander, Jake Walker.

"Bayonet Six, we got trouble in River City." He sounded out of breath.

"What's the situation?"

"They're bringing corpses out of the houses. All over the place. You should hear them hollering and screaming."

"What kind of corpses? Military?"

"No. Civilians. Kids. Old men. Everybody."

"How many? How many corpses?"

"I don't know . . . dozens . . . hundreds. They must've died during the night. Can't you hear the screaming?"

"Hold tight," Cavanaugh said. "And don't touch any of the bodies. Get your men under positive control. No physical contact with the corpses. Keep your distance. Shoot anybody who gets too close. I'm on my way. Out."

Cavanaugh turned to the sergeant major. "Get Doc

Culver. Wherever he is. We've got an epidemic on our hands."

As the two men exited the command vehicle and stepped into the cool, bright morning, they saw a soldier stagger out of a house, clutching madly at his stomach, then at his throat, then at his lower abdomen. Before anyone could reach him, he toppled to the ground.

NINETEEN

· · · · ■ · · · · · · ■ · · · · · ■ · · · ·

NAZARETH, TACTICAL OPERATIONS CENTER,
1–18 INFANTRY

"Just stay back," Chief Warrant Officer Culver yelled. Lowering his voice, the physician's assistant said, "You, too, sir. Let me figure this out."

"He's dead, Chief?"

"Yeah, he's dead. *Dead* dead. Y'all get back, in case this is some Black Plague from Outer Space."

Doc Culver began stripping off the soldier's uniform.

"Shouldn't you be wearing gloves?" Pat Cavanaugh asked him.

"Yeah, but I'm not. If DeSantis here has anything that could kill him since I saw him doing pushups a half-hour ago, I'm already dead meat."

He tore off uniform parts and undergarments, ripping them with his Buck knife. When the reinforced cloth resisted, Culver's roughness increased. He didn't want anyone to see that his hands were shaking.

Black flies settled on white flesh, scornful of attempts to shoo them.

"Who saw him last? Who was with him? What was he doing? *Anybody?*"

The dead soldier's skin looked unblemished. Culver yanked down the trousers, looking for spots, glandular swelling, discoloration where it would mean something other than a combat bruise.

All he found was a heat rash, raw pink inside the soldier's thighs.

"What was he doing when he ran out of the house? Tell me again. Anybody who saw him."

"Grabbing at himself. His gut, his throat," Bratty said. The command sergeant major surveyed the gawking soldiers. "It's no-bullshit time. Tell Chief Culver what you know. Who was with him in that house? What was DeSantis doing?"

A specialist looked away. Bratty caught it. "Prusinski. You in there with him? What was he up to?"

Cavanaugh inched closer to the physician's assistant, speaking quietly. "Chief, it sounds like we've got an epidemic in the city."

"You told me that, sir." The physician's assistant turned away from the battalion commander and the corpse to glare at the soldier Bratty had called on. "Prusinski, speak up. Unless you want everybody to know why you came crawling into my office last month."

"We weren't doing anything," the specialist said. "Just washing up a little. He just washed his face and brushed his teeth. And I'm, like, washing my feet with this hose they got in there, and I look up, and he's like somebody's sticking a knife in him."

"*He brushed his teeth?*"

"Yes, sir."

"DeSantis brushed his fucking teeth? In rag water? From the tap?"

Specialist Prusinski nodded.

"Jesus Christ," Chief Culver said. Then he turned to Cavanaugh. "It isn't any kind of plague, sir. It's worse. The water supply's been poisoned."

HEADQUARTERS, III (US) CORPS, MT. CARMEL RIDGES

"Trouble in Nazareth, sir," Mike Andretti told Harris as soon as the general walked in for the morning go-round.

That woke Harris up. Helped by the piercing smell of insecticide recently sprayed.

"What kind of trouble? Talk to me."

"Looks like, before they left, the Jihadis poisoned the water supply. Big-time. The rags have been drinking it. And there's a soldier down in 1-18."

"Jesus."

"General Scott's got his PSYOP folks and the Civil Affairs straphangers running some loudspeakers into Nazareth. To warn the population. Meanwhile, Pat Cavanaugh's using locals as town criers. We're pushing up engineers to turn off the system."

"How bad is it?"

"Still unclear, sir. Hundreds dead, at least. Cavanaugh believes there's more of them in the houses. Corpses, I mean. Probably a lot more to come, before the word gets to everybody."

"They poisoned the water supply. On their own people. They knew we wouldn't drink it. And they did that to their own kind." Harris shook his head in reluctant awe of the level of ferocity that took. Maybe old Sim was right: An enemy who would do that couldn't just be defeated but had to be eradicated. Immediately, Harris crushed the thought. But he understood why Montfort's arguments were so seductive.

"Sir . . . The Jihadis wanted those people dead."

"Yeah, got it, Mike. But they wanted *us* to do it. Guess they were afraid we'd be unreliable, that the MOBIC boys wouldn't get here in time. Pretty good assessment of the situation on their part. So . . . What's the *good* news? Got any this morning?"

"Yes, sir. 1st Cav's got Golani Junction. Raised the flag over the ruins of the old McDonald's."

"Blue casualties?"

"Don't sound bad, sir. General Stramara's fighting smart. And the J's aren't. They're just throwing bodies into the mix now. Tough fighting, but they don't have quite the edge some of their units were showing last night. And we're whacking them. General Stramara's Deuce thinks al-Ghazi's pulling his best units off line. Maybe forming a counterattack force."

"Val?" Harris turned to his G-2.

"We've got some drone imagery. Pretty patchy, but it looks like al-Ghazi's preparing a second line of defense. On the ridge just west of the Sea of Galilee. And running north."

"Doesn't make sense. If we—or the MOBIC forces—pushed them off that high ground above Tiberias, they'd have no line of retreat. Just that one road following the lake. It'd be a shooting gallery."

"Yes, sir. But they're digging in up there anyway."

"Well, file that one under 'What the fuck?' See if your folks can figure out the logic behind it. Al-Ghazi's just not that dumb."

"Yes, sir. But al-Mahdi might have ordered him to do it."

Harris folded his arms. Bucking himself up against the not-enough-sleep hangover. "Al-Mahdi's not that stupid, either. There's got to me more to it, Val."

"We'll stay on it, sir."

"Any more *bad* news?" Harris looked around the briefing room. Tired faces. But plenty of energy, nonetheless.

"Ship got hit last night by stealth drones. Crew got off, but it was a catastrophic loss. Lot of 155 mike-mike ammunition on board. And some haulers."

"Shit. What else?"

"Two electromagnetic-pulse mines confirmed down in General Scott's First Brigade sector."

"So the Jihadis did have some, after all." Harris glanced at his G-2, then returned his attention to the G-3. "Which units got hit?"

"2-34 Armor took both mines."

"How bad?"

"Two combined-arms companies without any working electronics."

"The shielding didn't work at all?"

"Powerful mines, sir."

"I want to know, immediately, if we run into any more of them. It's hard enough to communicate as it is."

"Yes, sir."

"What else?"

"The MOBIC elements pushing up the west bank

of the Jordan linked up with General Scott's forward Cav elements at 0445. They're flowing in behind our front lines now. Preparing for the forward passage of lines and reentry into battle. At which point they assume responsibility for the attack in sector."

"Got it. Any more static from HOLCOM?"

"No, sir."

"The MOBIC outfits have an LD time yet?"

"The forward passage of lines is set to commence at 1800."

"Going to be some tired *hombres*. We refueling them?"

"They've requested it."

Harris pivoted toward his G-4. "Real-Deal? Can we top 'em off?"

"Yes, sir. Although I hate to do it."

"Well, they're on our side. And we all need to remember it. But I suspect some of those boys are going to be falling asleep at the wheel by the time they go into action." He shrugged. "We have enough back-up comms gear to fix those two companies down in 2-34 Armor? Get them back into the net?"

"We're checking it out now, sir. Lot of that stuff still hasn't come over the beach."

"Cannibalize any vehicles deadlined for major components or significant battle damage."

The G-4 raised his eyebrows. "Going to be a property-book nightmare. And the tactical units will fight it. But I'll do what I can, sir."

"Write off any systems you lift as combat losses. Blame me. Just get 2-34 talking again."

"Roger, sir."

"Okay, Real-Deal. Now for the major-league question: How do we keep an entire city that's crowded with refugees and has a poisoned water supply from dying of thirst?"

"Sir, depending on the level and kind of poison, there's a chance we can use water-purification units—"

"Assume the worst. That the water can't be processed."

"Jesus, sir . . . There just isn't enough bottled water. Even if we stopped bringing everything else ashore, there's not enough loaded on the ships."

"How many water-purification sites do we have up and running?"

"I don't have a current number, sir. But we don't have the spare tankers, anyway."

"Solve it, Sean. Make it personal."

Colonel Sean "Real-Deal" McCoy gave Harris the polar-bear salute. "Sir, I honestly don't know—"

"Solve it."

"Yes, sir."

Harris turned back to his operations officer. "Mike, what about General Morris's Marines? When do we get road clearance down to them?"

"Already done, sir. At zero-six. The Marines are road-marching north as we speak, with lead elements putting the pedal down east of Haifa. We're moving them over the lowest-threat roads, and we've got the hot stretches marked to get their attention and keep them moving. Got some potential bottlenecks, though."

"Vehicle decon? The Marines don't have much capacity in-theater."

"Our chem folks have three hasty-decon sites

waiting for them up north. Best we can do. Overall, I'd say Marty Rose's planners did a first-rate job."

"Just keep 'em moving. Double intervals between the serials, as we discussed. Keep the Mike-Papas on them about maintaining distance. His Marines won't like it, but Monk Morris will understand. We don't want units backing up while they're in the hot zones."

"Yes, sir."

A captain slipped into the room and made his way between chairbacks and a parapet of knees to hand a scrap of paper to the G-2.

"Val? Anything hot?" Harris asked his intelligence officer.

Val Danczuk began his answers by saying to himself, in a low but audible tone, "The motherfuckers."

"That covers a wide array of characters these days," Harris said. "Exactly which Mike-Foxtrots are we talking about this time?"

"The Jihadis," Colonel Danczuk said. "They didn't waste any time. This is an intercept from a radio station in Baghdad, a big regional sender. They're telling the world that we're poisoning all of our 'captives' in Nazareth."

Harris whistled. In disgust mixed with admiration. It was the same emotional mix he felt toward Sim Montfort.

REAR HEADQUARTERS, I MOBIC CORPS, COMMANDER'S SANCTUM

General of the Order Simon Montfort focused on the only officer seated at the planning table who didn't wear the black cross of the Military Order of the Brothers in Christ or the red Jerusalem Cross of his Guardians.

"Forty-eight hours," Montfort told the Air Force three-star. "You have forty-eight hours. Then you need to be in complete readiness to smite the Jihadi forces with every manned aircraft and drone you have in this theater or capable of flying into this theater. Do you understand?"

"Yes, sir," Lieutenant General Micah said. "You realize, of course, that there are airspace deconfliction issues, and we need to do our weaponeering based upon specific target parameters to maximize—"

"The targets will be al-Mahdi's forces. Wherever they are when I give you the order. Stationary and on the move. We believe that a wide array of high-value targets will be strung out along the highways and secondary routes leading east to Damascus and beyond to the old Iraqi border. Focus your planning on the road network. Use your intelligence resources to identify possible assembly and staging areas. We'll provide whatever intelligence we develop ourselves. Just be ready to fly. When I tell you to."

"They'll be in retreat, you mean?"

"They'll be marching east. They won't expect you."

"How can you be sure?"

Montfort, who was fighting twinges of nausea, straightened his back and turned a practiced gaze on the Air Force officer. "The Lord granted me a vision. Is that sufficient? Be prepared to fly. To do the Lord's work. Be ready to fly at a moment's notice, forty-eight hours from now."

"I can't keep aircrews on alert indefinitely, you realize. We have crew-rest requirements and—"

"If my men can fight for days without sleep, driven only by their commitment to our faith, surely you can do your part, General Micah." Montfort offered the man a friendly smile that did not quite mask the warning behind it. "After all, I need to return to Washington with strong reasons why the Air Force should maintain its independence. When I testify before God and the United States Congress on the conduct of this war."

"The Air Force will do its part. Of course."

"And your part will consist of destroying al-Mahdi's forces as thoroughly as possible. Your mission is to annihilate them. Their equipment must be destroyed, and no Jihadi should be spared. No target will be off-limits, including their field hospitals— which we believe are being used for military purposes. Read the Book of Joshua, if you have any questions."

"Yes, sir. The Air Force is here to help you. You can count on us."

Montfort subdued a grimace before it could weaken his expression. The belly pang faded into queasiness. "And one other thing. My targeting cell will give you the coordinates of a compound a short flight east of the Jordan River. We've identified it as the personal property of Emir-General al-Mahdi. It's a refuge of his, a hide-out. I want the compound destroyed, with not one trace left of it on this Earth. It will be on your initial target list."

The Air Force officer seemed relieved. "That one's easy."

"Good. Go with God, General Micah."

The Air Force officer rose and saluted. No one returned his salute.

When the outsider had left the room, Montfort hunched over, grimacing. Through much of the meeting, he'd warred against bursting pains that worsened by the minute, unwilling to display any kind of weakness in front of the Air Force general. Now he groaned aloud.

"Get my doctor," he barked. *"Get him. Now."*

▪

"No, sir. You haven't been poisoned. Put your mind at rest on that count. I'll run some stool tests to be one hundred percent certain, but I'll tell you right now you've got viral gastroenteritis."

"Dates. I ate dates."

"Local? That was a mistake."

"The person I was with . . . I have reason to believe . . . that he . . . Lord! Can you give me something for these cramps? And to clear my head?"

"I'll do what I can. But we're just going to have to keep you hydrated and let this run its course. Antibiotics can only do so much."

"Maybe poison . . . be sure . . . the person I was with . . . I don't think he got sick . . ."

"From the dates? Sir, all it takes is one bad one. One microscopic speck on one date. And this is a very septic environment."

"You've got to get . . . I've got to be able to think clearly . . . I keep going dizzy."

"Sir, you're going to have to take it easy."

"I've got to go again. Help me up."

"There's a bedpan under you."

"I've got to get up."

The doctor stiffened. "Do you want to get up, or do you want to get better? Now just use the bedpan. I've got to get an orderly in here, anyway. I've got to start an intravenous bag."

"I've *got* to get up." Montfort tried to raise himself but only unsettled the bedpan before collapsing. Stunned. With the world swirling, stopping long enough to tease him, then swirling again. Cramps yanked his knees up toward his belly. He felt as if barbed wire were being dragged through his intestines. His body poured vile liquid.

Had al-Mahdi done this to him? No matter what the doctor had to say? Yes or no, he was going to pay. Al-Mahdi was going to be ground into the dirt, the dust. Into filth. With his face shoved in a bedpan.

"... *God* ..." Montfort said. But he wasn't praying. When he'd been wounded in Nigeria, the pain had been nothing compared to this. He hated to show weakness, even to his doctor. But his body had betrayed him. And now it refused to follow his commands.

Montfort tried to think clearly. And he spoke, unsure of whether the doctor was there to hear him. "Got to get better ... tomorrow morning. Got to get up there ... Everything's set ... Can't happen without me." Lucid for a moment, he saw the doctor staring down at him. With an inscrutable expression. Was the doctor the enemy, too? There were enemies everywhere. Montfort asked, "Can you fix me up by tomorrow morning?"

"Unlikely. I'll do what I can. Maybe I'm wrong and it's not viral. We'll see what the test results say. If it's just Mohammed's Revenge . . . then maybe."

Montfort grasped the doctor's forearm with a soiled hand. "You've got to get me to where I can fly in a helicopter . . . early tomorrow morning. Do you understand me?"

"I'll do what I can."

"Do you understand me?"

"Yes. Yes, I understand you. But your body may not be listening."

"My body . . . will do what I tell it."

"Well, that will make it easier on both of us."

"I *will* stand where my Savior stood . . . tomorrow . . . all arranged."

The doctor broke free and called in the orderly to clean up the mess.

"Get my chief of staff," Montfort called after him. "I need to know that everything's on schedule."

"Yes, sir. We just need to get you cleaned up first. You don't want him to see you like that."

"Get him now. And doctor? No one can know . . . no one . . ."

"We'll keep it quiet, sir. Now you need to rest."

"Can't rest . . ." He was half-aware of being man-handled, then of being cleansed with a warm, wet rag.

"The waters of the Jordan!" Montfort cried.

And he blacked out.

HEADQUARTERS, III (US) CORPS, MT. CARMEL RIDGES

"The old man's going to go through the roof when he hears this," Mike Andretti told the G-2.

"That's just Sim Montfort making sure Flintlock doesn't get any credit. Him, or the Army."

"It's just damned crazy, though. Nuts. We're hammering them. We stop now and it just gives them . . ." The G-3 looked at his watch. "It gives the Jihadis over six hours to get their act back together. And that's if the MOBIC units cross their line of departure on time."

"We could've punched through, Mike," the G-2 said. "You don't even have to look at the reports we're getting in. You can feel the J's thinning out, weakening. We could've rolled them up. And gotten to the Sea of Galilee ourselves."

Andretti nodded. "I guess that wouldn't have fit in with whatever plans Sim Montfort's got in mind. Praying and slaying, and posing for posterity all the while. Makes me fucking sick. That we've come to this. I'd better go tell the old man."

"Better you than me. You know, though," the corps intelligence officer said, "I swear to God something's going on. Things just don't make sense. The J's are weakening their own front lines, giving up good defensive terrain . . . Yet they're busting ass to throw up a hasty line of defense back where they'll be in for Mohammed Custer's Last Stand, guaranteed. Al-Ghazi has to see it. He's the best field commander al-Mahdi's got. Trying to hang onto the heights on this side of the Sea of Galilee . . . That's an amateur-hour stunt. Any Jihadi unit he leaves up there isn't going to live to fight another day. I just can't get inside the logic of it. It's like they're setting themselves up to lose."

"I'll let you figure it out, Val." Andretti half-crumpled the order he held in his hand. "Christ, the old man just doesn't need this."

But before the G-3 could exit the field operations center, Harris walked in.

"You don't look like a happy camper, Mike," he said.

"Sir . . . We just got another order from HOL-COM. It's not enough that they pulled us back from Golani Junction. Now we're under orders, effective immediately, to disengage. To pull back and just wait for the MOBIC corps to start passing through."

"Know what tomorrow's headline is going to be back home?" Harris said. Confounding Andretti's expectations, the general's voice was calm. Almost mellow. He was even smiling, if only slightly. "It's going to read, 'Army Forced To Retreat, MOBIC Comes To Rescue.' I've got to hand it to Sim Montfort. He's outmaneuvered us all on the PR front." Harris's smile faded into a look of infinite bitterness. "He's probably laughing his head off right about now."

"Are we just going to let him—"

"Issue the order, Mike."

"Sir, if you don't mind me saying—"

"I'm giving in too easily? No, Mike. I'm not. All this sanctimonious bullshit and screw-your-buddy crap brings out my latent serial-killer tendencies. But we're going to concentrate on the battles we can win. And we're not going to let ourselves be distracted by friendly fire. Issue the order. Then get Real-Deal hustling. I want every unit that's been in the fight resupplied with ammo, topped off, fed and ready to go the minute they get the order. Old Sim's not in Damascus just yet."

TWENTY

....■......■......■....

Major General "Monk" Morris stood by the roadside
and watched another convoy serial pass as his Marines headed north. Standing in their hatches, the vehicle commanders looked hard and fierce, as if they
wanted just one slight excuse to start fighting on the
spot.

As the tracked vehicles growled past, Morris saw
the many ghosts that trailed them—not the foul
spooks of this bloody landscape but the spirits of two
and a half centuries' worth of Marines. He wouldn't
let anyone see it, but the vision moistened his eyes.

If he was secretly a sentimental man—as so many
Marines were when the hatches closed—he was also
an angry one. The MOBIC general who had paid him
an unannounced and sneaking visit in the night,
spouting Scripture and trailing slime, had laid it out
for him:

"Our blessed nation can't support two armies," the
brigadier general of the Order had told him. Too

well-groomed for a combat zone and wearing a well-pressed uniform with a black cross on the left breast, the MOBIC officer continued, "The Military Order of the Brothers in Christ clearly obviates the need for the U.S. Army. Which, in any case, has been worrying our elected leaders with its recalcitrance on a great many issues—hardly a thing to be tolerated in a democracy. Please hear me out, General Morris. Hear me out, then judge. Now, the Army, you'll have to admit, hasn't exactly covered itself in glory in this campaign. The weight of the endeavor and the casualties have been borne by our MOBIC forces, by men who know what they're fighting for, who believe in something far greater than themselves."

"You fight smart, casualties are lower," Morris said.

"But you have to *fight*," the MOBIC officer responded. "And *if* you fight, if you *really* fight—well, higher casualties are inevitable."

"Just tell me what you want," Morris said. Although he already knew where things were going.

"You're blunt. One expects that from a Marine. Forthrightness. Our Savior was forthright."

"Jesus Christ spoke in more riddles than an insurance salesman."

The brigadier ignored the remark. "You know, General Morris, our MOBIC high command has no problem with the Marine Corps. The Corps is . . . a national treasure. What patriot would want it to disappear? And the Corps is hardly a competitor with us. It's the Army that continues to drain resources from the soldiers of the Lord. Why should the Marines be tarred with the same brush as the Army? Hasn't the Corps thrived on its rivalry with the Army over the years? Hasn't the Corps always done more with less? Fought harder? And had less thanks? Might it not be . . . wiser . . . for the Marines to rethink their present loyalties?"

"I once overheard one lieutenant tell another that the reason they call us 'generals' is because we only speak in generalities," Morris told his visitor. "Get to the point. What exactly do you want?"

The MOBIC brigadier looked at him as if calculating just what it would take to get him to sign the contract to buy the used car.

"Send a request to Holy Land Command for your Marines to be subordinated to First MOBIC Corps. Justify the request by stating that the Army's Third Corps and General Harris misused your Marines, then restrained you from fighting."

"And what—exactly—do my Marines get in return?"

"I told you. The Military Order of the Brothers in Christ has no quarrel with the Marine Corps. We simply need to put an end to the current duplication and waste of our nation's resources caused by the continued existence of the Army."

"That's still not an answer."

"If you require more specificity, I'm authorized to tell you that the MOBIC high command is prepared to guarantee that it will do everything in its power to ensure the survival of the Marine Corps."

"The same assurance that you gave the Air Force, I take it?"

"I wouldn't know anything about such matters. My focus is on finding a way to preserve the Marine Corps. As I said, the Corps is a national treasure."

"Then why should preserving it be contingent on lining up with you against the Army? Or on anything?"

"We live in a practical world. A world of finite resources. Everyone needs allies. Your help at present would obligate us to help you later." The visitor tried to summon a reassuring smile. "I realize the sort of feelings you must have. Military men are loyal to one another. Even across service lines. I know—I used to wear an Army uniform myself, before I decided to better serve my country by bearing arms for the Lord. I don't expect an immediate answer. I can give you twelve hours. But then we'll need your answer. And, if you'll allow me a personal note, I'd be deeply sorry to see a tragic rift develop between the Order and the Corps. When we're natural allies."

Morris wanted to grab the overgroomed brigadier by his shining hair and hammer his face into the table. And not just once. But Morris recognized that he had a duty to control himself. And to think, hard, about what he was being offered.

He didn't believe the man's elusive promises for an instant. But he also wondered what he *did* owe to the Corps, under the circumstances, and what his responsibility really was, given the current climate back in Washington.

He already knew his answer, or thought he did. He saw that this was just a downright insulting attempt to drive a wedge between the Army and the Corps, then to defeat both in detail. Nor did he think he could live with himself if he betrayed Harris at a juncture like this.

But it was, nonetheless, his duty to think the offer through, to analyze the situation as dispassionately as he could and to burrow into every nuance, to overcome his personal and professional prejudices to judge what truly was best for the country.

"Twelve hours?" he said.

His visitor perked up. "You'll think about it then? Good. Grand. I'd love to see the Marine Corps and the Military Order of the Brothers in Christ embrace each other in loving friendship."

Morris almost asked, "And after the embrace, we get fucked, right? In front, or from behind?"

Instead, he told the brigadier, "You'll have my answer in twelve hours. Now I've got work to do."

But he accomplished little after his visitor disappeared back into the night. As soon as the devil with the black cross evaporated, Morris could say with certainty that he wouldn't do as asked, wouldn't betray the Army or Flintlock Harris. The MOBIC creeps wouldn't honor the bargain, anyway. They'd howl with laughter at his stupidity, the gullibility of a dumb-ass Jarhead.

And yet . . . What did it all mean? Would he go down in the books as the man who destroyed the Marine Corps? Was that how Major General Morton Morris, USMC, would be remembered?

Yes, if the MOBIC crowd wrote the history books. And, increasingly, it looked as if they would.

Monk Morris longed for the days of his youth, when men found their devils in wretched foreign holes, or in their sick imaginations, or in Internet lairs. Now the devils wore uniforms and claimed they served his country. They ran for office and won elections by landslide votes. They appeared in the night with cynical offers that left a man with no good alternatives. Monk Morris had no patience with religion of any kind, but he couldn't help thinking of Gethsemane.

Was this what they were fighting for? This goddamned squalor? One moment, Morris saw Flintlock Harris as a brilliant commander, shining with ethical rigor. A moment later, he saw Harris as a fool who would doom them all.

Morris wondered, yet again, who on his own staff reported secretly to MOBIC's Christian Security Service. Who had already betrayed the Corps? The CSS had agents everywhere. Would one of their stooges take his place if he didn't cooperate?

The situation made him clench his fists. He understood how to fight a battle, a war. But he no longer understood how to fight the men who were taking over his country.

God's plan? This? All this? He didn't understand how any man with eyes in his head could believe in any kind of god. After the things he'd seen in the Nigeria fighting, the horrors in Delta State, he'd abandoned his last, perfunctory religious habits. Men had to take responsibility for their own failings, their own viciousness, their own deeds. That was humanity's one slim hope. Blaming the world's horrors on a punitive deity or on a scheming Satan who wanted to spoil the porridge was the coward's way out. Years back, Morris had read something to the effect that, even if there was no God, men should behave as if He existed. A lifetime of coping with what men wrought had convinced Morris that the aphorist, whoever he'd been, had got it exactly backward: If there *was* a God, men should act as if He didn't exist and couldn't be blamed for the messes they made themselves. Real men took responsibility. Wasn't that at the heart of being a Marine? To shoulder responsibilities of a dreadful order when all the others fled, trailing excuses and pointing fingers toward the sky?

What was his responsibility now?

He dozed off and slept fitfully for a few hours. His aide looked in but refused to let anyone wake the general.

In the brightness of the morning, Harris reached him with a request. That he send one company of Marines into Nazareth. To help with a local crisis created by a poisoned water supply. But, above all, to demonstrate Marine-Army solidarity, in case the MOBIC command tried to force HOLCOM to order the massacre of the Arab civilians in the city.

"You sure one company's all you need, sir?" Morris asked. Without hesitation.

"One company. With strong stomachs."

"On the way," Morris said.

And that was that. He didn't bother trying to contact the MOBIC brigadier with a formal answer. With a little guidance from Jesus, they'd figure it out.

And now he stood proudly by the roadside, sucking down dust and saluting his Marines as they drove past.

Above the roar, he heard a vehicle commander shout, "Semper Fi, sir," in his direction.

"Semper Fi," Morris responded. But his voice was lost in the noise of the war machines.

NAZARETH

Sergeant Ricky Garcia had pulled some crappy duties in his time, but he couldn't remember any as bad as this. First, he'd overheard the battalion XO telling Captain Cunningham that Bravo Company was being sent on a mission that would give it time to recover from the hard-luck fighting of the past few days. No company in the 5th Marines had suffered heavier losses, the XO said. He'd try to funnel them some replacements while they were in Nazareth. To bring the company back up to combat strength.

Garcia knew that he should've known better, but when he heard the magic name, he pictured a whitewashed village with donkey carts and women carrying water jugs like in the Bible pictures. Instead, Bravo Company dismounted at the edge of a grubby plot of apartment buildings, with a litter-strewn field on the other side of the road. An Army lieutenant colonel had been waiting for them. After some gladhanding, Garcia heard him tell the company commander, "Make sure you bury them with their heads facing toward Mecca. Keep the trench properly oriented. It's the least we can do for the sorry sonsofbitches. And it might help calm the families down."

But the rags hadn't calmed down. They were still yelling and wailing after the Army fucksticks bailed, leaving Garcia and what remained of Bravo Company to keep a local with a broke-dick backhoe extending a ditch fast enough to keep up with the loads of bodies arriving. You didn't have to understand ragtalk to know that the people on the other side of the cordon of fixed bayonets were cursing their asses off.

The little kids started throwing rocks at the Marines.

Garcia and the other survivors of his platoon took the first shift of unloading bodies from the Army haulers and the civilian vans that had been put to use. Corporal Banks didn't want to touch the bodies, which were wrapped in bedsheets and blankets. Garcia gave him some personal instruction on how to get the fuck over it.

Then it was just sweat and flies and the smell of the corpses and the sting of the dust that rose from each shovel of lime thrown into the trench.

"Hey, Sergeant Garcia," Tyrrell yelled. "Can't we take off our helmets and body armor? While we're doing this, like?"

"Ask your squad leader."

Tyrrell repeated the question to Corporal Gallotti.

"Sergeant?" Gallotti asked Garcia in turn. "Take 'em off?"

"No fucking way. You know better."

The grumbling that followed was okay. And that stopped when a rock hit Gallotti on the back of the helmet and knocked him into the trench. He climbed out dusted with lime and gasping.

"You okay, Corporal?"

"Yeah. Yeah, fine. I love this shit, Sergeant."

"You should've studied harder in school," Garcia said. "Got a real job."

"Hear that?" Tyrrell said in a fake whisper. "Sergeant Garcia made a joke. I think he's learning English."

Garcia grasped the upper torso of another body. "None of you appreciate," he said, "that the Marine

Corps is teaching you valuable job skills." A small stone bounced off his armored vest. "Hey, Staff Sergeant Thomas! Is 2nd Platoon going to get those kids under control, or what?"

But the Marines working the cordon line were taking more stones and rocks than the body handlers.

After an hour, the first sergeant ordered Garcia's platoon to swap duties with 2nd Platoon. Garcia didn't question the order, although his platoon had a dozen fewer Marines. You executed the mission. Period.

As they fixed bayonets and moved up to relieve 2nd Platoon, Garcia saw the first sergeant's point. 2nd Platoon needed a break. Every single Marine coming off the line was bleeding or limping.

Was that how it was when they stoned people in the Bible? All of them yelling like nuts? Except that they all would've been picking on some lonesome *chica* who'd gotten the wrong gang tattoo.

Right thing to do, rotating platoons, Garcia told himself again. Leave one platoon up front too long, and something bad was going to go down on the block.

Garcia trooped the line. "Hold your ground. I want everybody's weapon on safe. Let 'em yell if they want to. You're Marines."

"I wish I'd joined the Navy," Private Crawford said.

"Crawford! Shit! You *can* talk. That's the first word I heard you say since we got off the boat, Marine."

"First time I had anything to say, Sergeant."

Garcia dodged a good-sized rock. Older, bigger kids were throwing them now. Garcia got that, too.

Street rules. First, see how much the other side will put up with. Then, up the ante.

"I'm going to kill one of those shitbirds," Corporal Banks said.

Just then, an old man stepped forward, breaking free of the crowd. Unshaven and bent at the shoulders, he wore a baggy Goodwill Store suit and a V-neck sweater over his shirt despite the heat. Stepping across the broken ground, he headed for Garcia. As if he sensed where the power lay. The barrage of rocks paused.

"Man, I can't wait to hear this," Banks said. "I guess they want us to surrender or something."

Behind the platoon, another truck delivered more corpses.

Up close, the old man wasn't really so ancient. Just grubby. And jumpy. Scared. Beat-looking. And angry, too. With his stained, bought-from-a-street-vendor tie, he looked like a rummy professor.

"Who is the general?" he demanded. Close enough to Garcia to show his uneven, yellow teeth. "Are you the general?"

"No, sir. I'm a sergeant. There aren't any generals around here."

"Then you will give my message to the general. Tell him why you poison us, I don't know. We are not making jihad. We are educated peoples. Why America will poison us?"

"Maybe somebody's been feeding them our rations," Banks said. "I'd be pissed, too."

"I don't know what you're talking about, sir," Garcia told the old man. "And I don't know anything about any poison."

The old man swept his hand toward the trench, toward the stink, the dust, and the sunlit day beyond. "This is the poison making us dead. The poison you bring us. Why? Why? There are no guilty peoples here. Why? Why?"

"Look, sir. I don't know what you're talking about. I mean, I have no idea. And I don't know anything about any poison. I'm sorry, but you'll have to move out of our way. For your own safety," Garcia said.

"Why? Why America brings us poison in the water? *You have done this!* You are *seen* doing this. We know. We hear. We are told. You put this poison in the water. But we are not Jihadis. There is no need to poison us. We are friends."

"Yeah, you're my fucking best pal," Banks said.

"Shut up, Banks."

"Why does he call me 'fucking'? This is a bad word. What do I do that is fucking? You take my daughter. My little daughter. To this place. Look at this!" Again, he waved his arm toward the trench, the backhoe, the sacks of flesh thudding into the pit. "You take my daughter away, so I cannot bury her! You kill my daughter, now you take her body." He began to weep. Exploding with tears. "You do this to my daughter, put her with strangers, with men she does not know. For all the times. This is a bad thing, you understand?"

Garcia caught the flash of complete misery in the man's eyes. It spooked him for a moment.

"Listen, sir . . . I'm sorry for your troubles. I mean, whatever you're talking about. I'm sorry if anything happened to your daughter, man. But we're just trying to do our job. You can't just leave bodies laying all over. You'd all get sick. Do you understand that? You understand 'sick'?"

Garcia wondered what it had been like when they went through and disposed of all the bodies in Los Angeles. At least his mother had lived long enough to be buried right.

"I know this word, too," the old man said. "I know every word. But why do you do this? For the Jews? You do this for the Jews, I think? We ask only for the good burial . . ."

Garcia was out of things to say. But he decided to keep the man talking, after all. The rocks weren't flying as long as the talking went on. The other rags seemed to respect the guy. Garcia considered sending a man to bring up the first sergeant or Captain Cunningham.

And then Garcia heard the shot. Distinct and enormous, standing out with perfect clarity against the distant, lessened sounds of war.

He turned about in time to see Marines rushing toward a fallen figure.

His own Marines were down on their knees, weapons up, scanning.

"Anybody see where that came from?"

"Negative."

"Negative, Sergeant."

"Corporal Gallotti. Your squad covers those windows. Corporal Banks. Your squad has the crowd."

The sniper's second shot killed Captain Cunningham as he jogged toward Garcia's position. It was fired from the crowd. Then the real killing started.

ASSEMBLY AREA, 2-34 ARMOR, VICINITY AFULA

Lieutenant Colonel Monty Maxwell watched the last MOBIC element leave 2-34's assembly area and head toward the reignited battle. He felt a mixture of relief, jealousy, and fury toward the departing vehicles.

Division or corps had dropped the ball on coordination and terrain deconfliction. 2-34 Armor's assembly area had been invaded first by fuel trucks from the Corps Support Command, then by a succession of MOBIC combined-arms "Martyrs" battalions of the ilk Army regulars had nicknamed "the MOBIC Mujaheddin." The confusion and crowding offered the Jihadis a perfect target, although they never seemed to have identified the site, since no artillery fire landed and no drones swooped in. But the glitch over turf was only the start of the problems.

Several fights had broken out while the MOBIC soldiers loitered about, waiting for their vehicles to be topped off. The MOBIC troops mocked Maxwell's tankers for their lack of progress while they themselves had swept into Jerusalem, on to Jericho, then up the Jordan. The language used by both sides fell short of the Christian ideal.

Maxwell had to sort through complex emotions himself. On one hand, any Armor officer had to admire the power and depth of the MOBIC advance, which seemed to have been one long cavalry charge. On the other hand, nothing Maxwell had heard about MOBIC behavior charmed him. And he had yet to see one thing in this godforsaken landscape worth fighting for.

He also had mixed feelings when he looked at the MOBIC war machines queuing to take on fuel, then ammunition. The unit sucking tanker-tit just then had been reduced to half strength, with its remaining vehicles battered and crusted with dust. From the apparent casualty count and the visible damage, it was clear that the NexGen tanks and infantry fighting vehicles had been a huge disappointment, their electronic armor next to worthless. Maxwell realized full well that his battalion had been lucky by default when it had been condemned to go to war with its ancient M-1 tanks instead of the "wonder weapons" that had devoured the Army budget and enriched defense contractors for the past two decades. Yet, for all that, a part of him couldn't help feeling spiteful at the way the Military Order of the Brothers in Christ had been able to commandeer all of the latest and, in theory, best equipment the Army had held in its inventory.

The MOBIC soldiers were unbearably arrogant, with their black crosses and their taunts. Maxwell had no difficulty understanding why more than a few of his tankers felt compelled to land a punch as the afternoon heat thickened toward evening.

But it wasn't an acceptable situation. Maxwell pulled half his staff from the TOC to troop the line and help keep his Dreadnaughts in order. The MOBIC officers made little effort on their side. Maxwell got splashed by a half-full can of chili that struck his body armor from behind. The MOBIC officers lolling nearby claimed to have seen nothing.

"We're preparing to fight the infidel," a captain told him, "and you're worried about table manners." Without adding "sir."

For Maxwell, the series of confrontations culminated in an exchange with a MOBIC battalion commander, a young-looking lieutenant colonel with a thick black beard and bloodshot eyes.

"I'm trying to keep my men under control, for Christ's sake," Maxwell told the officer after tracking him down. "I need you to get your guys to knock off the bullshit. We're supposed to be fighting the J's, not each other."

The MOBIC officer looked at him dismissively. From head to foot, then back up again. As if a downmarket first wife had walked into a society wedding. "When you address me, you will not blaspheme. And as near as I can tell, you and your men haven't been fighting much of anybody."

Maxwell wanted to deck him. Instead, he said, "I'm not looking for love, brother. I just want your soldiers to stop the heckling."

"They want to fight. That's all it is. And soon they will. Again. We're going to finish the job you couldn't do. Perhaps you should humble yourself and learn." He touched the side of his face, where his beard began. "God has been with us. The evidence is before men's eyes. Who's been with you, Colonel?"

Maxwell walked away. Wondering if there was any difference left between the fanatics on either side.

But there *was* a difference, he realized: the age-old difference of my-kind-against-yours, the closing of ranks against those who prayed differently or had gotten different shades of prehistoric suntans. The thought didn't appall him or even irritate him. That was, he realized, just the way humanity did things. What bothered him was the immediate behavior of the MOBIC Mujjies toward his troops—who he wanted to protect and spank at the same time.

When he and his adjutant broke up another incipient brawl, Maxwell ignored the MOBIC troops involved, turning his back to tell his men, "Knock it off. We're better than that. We're soldiers. Now get back to your own vehicles."

As they walked away, a MOBIC soldier transgressed against his faith long enough to shout after them, "Cunts!"

Now the sounds of war had resumed. The MOBIC forces had, indeed, plunged back into battle. They certainly weren't cowards. Maxwell was willing to credit them with that much. The Muslim fanatics had finally conjured men who were their equal in their distaste for mercy.

As the dust faded and the light turned gold between the olive trees, a great roar of battle rose in the east. As much as Maxwell disdained the MOBIC forces, he couldn't help feeling left behind. And wronged.

TWENTY-ONE

...........■.......■.....

HEADQUARTERS, III (US) CORPS, MT. CARMEL RIDGES

As the twilight darkened, so did the mood in the headquarters. No end of tasks remained to be carried out: Units had to be resupplied, convoy routes deconflicted, communications shortfalls remedied, plans written, and orders issued. Yet, as the MOBIC forces passed through the corps' lines to take over the offensive, the air went out of the balloon. And as the reports of impossibly swift progress by the MOBIC lead elements mounted, officers responsible for directing the actions of divisions sank into their chairs, newly aware of their accumulated weariness. The NCOs who made things happen found they had nothing more pressing to do than make a fresh pot of coffee or take an extended trip to the latrine. Radios still crackled, and field phones rang. Printers sawed, and screens glowed. But the network of commandeered buildings and camouflaged tents breathed in the sourness of mourning, as if an unexpected death had occurred and could not be explained. Taking down another report from the front, a captain summed up the collective mood when he put down his headset and demanded of the universe, "What the fuck is going on?"

Flintlock Harris wanted to know, too. As soon as the briefing room door shut on his inner circle—G-2, G-3, and his aide—he said, "Talk to me. Explain how Montfort's doing this. And let's go reverse order: Blue situation first, then Val can brief what little the J's seem to be doing."

Colonel Mike Andretti swept his pointer up over the wall map, settling the tip just north of the Sea of Galilee, then tracing a jagged line down over the western ridge that protected the body of water.

"Sir, the MOBIC forces are advancing all across the front. It's as if they're just out for a Sunday drive. We've got unconfirmed reports that their advance-guard elements have already seized several points along the crest of the ridge—they're already looking down into the Sea of Galilee."

"And ready to walk on water," Harris grunted. "Mike, the Jihadis were giving it all they had to hold the line against us. Now they're just folding their tents and running at the first sight of the MOBIC. Which is the opposite of what you'd expect—they should be fighting to the death against Sim Montfort's crowd after Jerusalem." He looked at each of the three other men, then asked, half rhetorically, "Are they that scared of the black-cross boys, or what?"

"Sir," the operations officer continued, "all I can tell you is that the MOBIC nets we're monitoring report light resistance. At most. They're practically road-marching into Upper Galilee. Our own forward elements report MOBIC vehicles lined up nose-to-asshole as far as they can see. No tactical intervals, no march discipline. Just piling on."

Harris shook his head. Vehemently. "This just makes no sense. It stinks. But I don't know what the hell I'm smelling."

"Maybe we just wore them out," the Three said. "Maybe Montfort just got lucky on the timing. Could be they were ready to crack just when the lead MOBIC units hit them." The colonel's stance remained aggressive from sheer habit, but his eyes were unsteady and frazzled.

"I don't believe that," Harris said. "Even Sim Montfort isn't that lucky. The J's are up to something. And I wish I knew what it was. Val?" He turned to the G-2. "You're up. Give us the enemy situation. If there still is one."

"Sir, as I briefed earlier, it appears they've transitioned into an operational retreat. If not a strategic one. The intel's far from perfect, but we've got indicators that units that were slugging it out with us at dawn are already on the highway to Damascus. With some elite elements possibly located *east* of Damascus—but that's based on intercepts only. As far as imagery goes, we've got some limited satellite coverage and some drone shots from the Golan and points east that just make no sense at all—the Third Jihadi Corps has units dispersed by individual vehicle, just spread all over the place. No sense of defensive perimeters. It looks like they just blindfolded the drivers and sent them off in different directions. It doesn't match al-Ghazi's command template."

Something quickened in Harris. Something down deep. But he couldn't yet put a name on it."

"And?"

"Well, sir, it's not much of a way to wage a war. Or fight a battle. It really does look as if they've just given up, as if they're quitting. Running." The G-2 glanced at the map, then reached into his pocket. Only to find his pointer gone. Tracing a line on the western Galilee ridge with his index finger, he said, "All those entrenchments they were digging as fast as they could? The defensive positions all along the ridge? We got a burst transmission through from a special-ops recon element up here, on the high ground behind Tiberias. They report a few stray Jihadis just hanging out and playing with their dicks. And all those vehicles in defensive positions? All those tanks? Junk. Shot up stuff. Old crap left over from the end-of-Israel fighting. Stripped for parts. It looks like the Jihadis had planned some kind of ruse before they decided to take their ball and go home."

Harris jumped to his feet before the intelligence officer finished speaking. Rushing around the conference table, he shoved first the G-3, then the G-2, out of his way. He had the map memorized. But he needed to see it, anyway. To *know*.

"Show me where that report originated. *Exactly* where. Show me, Val."

"Yes, sir. The recon team's overwatching this stretch of road and the crest beyond it. By Kefar Hittim."

Harris no longer cared whether anyone knew how badly his vision had deteriorated. He pushed his nose up against the map, as if sniffing the G-2's finger.

Then he shoved the colonel's hand away. Staring at the map. With his soul plummeting into the earth.

"Fuck," he said. Bitterly. Almost quietly. Then he swung himself over the nearest table, running for the door. "Let's go. Everybody. Come on."

"What do—"

"Mike. You get everybody you've got working every comms channel that's up. Issue a STRIKE-WARN. The J's are going nuclear. *Soon.* You, too, Val. Use every channel. Forget the protocols."

He was shouting. And running. Officers loitering in the hall leapt out of the general's way. Too stunned at Harris's tone to decipher his meaning immediately.

As Harris led his war party into the ops center, he barked, "I want every armored vehicle buttoned up. Get 'em in defilade. Every dismount gets into a ditch or takes shelter on the western side of the strongest nearby building. Move, *move.*"

Harris grabbed the liaison officer who'd arrived from the MOBIC corps. Seizing the colonel's upper arm. As if arresting him. *"You.* Get on the horn and tell your people they're about to get nuked. They need to pull back, disperse. Immediately."

Unsettled for an instant, the MOBIC colonel quickly mastered himself. His alarmed expression reorganized itself into a sly smile.

"General Harris . . . Surely, you don't expect us to believe any such nonsense. If the infidel enemy can't stop us, do you think *you* can? With some concocted story? Are you *that* embarrassed by our success?"

"Fuck you," Harris said. "Get General Montfort on the line."

"General of the Order Montfort is incommuni-cado."

"Well, he's going to be deep-fried like fucking falafel if you don't listen to me."

The operations center had come to life around them. It was a rare officer or NCO who recalled the format for a STRIKEWARN off the top of his head and the babble of voices reduced the transmissions to a common message: *Take cover, the J's are going nuke.*

"I can't disturb General Montfort," the liaison officer said.

"Well, who *can* you disturb?"

"I won't be a party to this."

"I'm giving you a direct order."

"You have no authority over me."

"Listen. For Christ's sake, man. We're all on the same side. I'm trying to save your comrades, your buddies . . . your whole goddamned corps."

The MOBIC colonel looked at Harris dismissively. "You can't stop us now, General. Your time is over. I'll file your report in the morning."

Exasperated as he had never been in his entire life, Harris said, "You really think I'm staging this— all this—to get you to retreat for a couple of hours?"

The MOBIC colonel just smiled.

"Even if you think I'm crazy," Harris continued, "will you at least report what I'm telling you right now? And let General Montfort judge? Morning's going to be too late."

"As of 2100, our attacking forces switched to ra-dio silence. I'm not authorized—"

A terrible roar tore the night, overpowering the

common sounds of war, a distant thunder akin to the voice of God.

▪

Harris sat alone in the briefing room, face buried in his hands. Waiting for the first casualty reports. His fire-support officer had already assured him that none of the seven reported nuclear detonations had struck within the corps' lines. But there would be casualties, nonetheless. Harris told himself he could have pushed harder, forced the intelligence system, done more about his hunch about the Jihadis' nuclear reserves. But he hadn't done it. And now the two or three nuclear weapons about which he'd worried had turned out to be at least seven. An unknown number of his fellow Americans, MOBIC members or not, had died because he hadn't done his duty.

He should've seen it coming. He knew that. All of the indicators had been there. Every goddamned one. He couldn't blame it on the G-2 or anybody else. He was the commander. Any failures rested on his shoulders, and his alone.

And this was a great failure, something terrible.

Major John Willing knocked on the door. The aide's knuckles had the familiarity of a personal ring-tone.

"Come in."

"Sir, Colonel Andretti has some more data from the fire-support cell. And a number of land-line reports have come in—the radios are still out, though."

"Send him in, John."

"Sir . . . The G-2's with him. Want me to hold him outside?"

"No. Send them both in. And come back in yourself. I may need you to run some messages."

"Yes, sir."

How the mighty have fallen! Harris thought. Unable to force his mind beyond the cliché.

The G-3 came in twitchy, as if he'd just been transfused with a quart of espresso. The G-2 zombie-walked behind him.

Before the Three could report, Val Danczuk said, "Sir, I'm sorry. I wouldn't listen and now—"

"Forget it, Val. Done is done. We've still got a war to fight."

"Yes, sir," the G-2 said. His voice was dull, almost dead.

Harris decided to deal with the man later. And to sack him, at least temporarily, if he couldn't get a grip on himself.

"Mike?"

"Looks like we got off pretty light, sir."

Harris rapped the table. "Don't jinx it. Just give me the details. Whatever you've got."

"Winds are from the north-northwest. Any fall-out's headed down the Jordan Valley and toward Amman. I guess the Jihadis didn't care about their own—"

"Al-Mahdi did what was smart. He fought to win. And didn't count the costs. Go on."

"We've got some drones up with radar-imagery capability and some backup infrared. Nobody knows what'll work and what won't, but we'll try to assess how badly the MOBIC corps's been hit. No comms out there. Oh, and we've registered four more nukes. All out of sector."

"Where?"

"Colonel Tinsley's gizmos read two down south near the Jordan River crossing sites. East of Jericho. And two in Jerusalem. Strategic chatter between the MOBIC rear CP and Washington suggests the J's hit the Temple Mount with a ground burst, followed by an air burst."

Harris snorted. "If they can't have it, MOBIC won't have it. The Holy of Holies is going to be a hot zone for a long time. What about our guys?"

"Like I said, sir: Things don't look that bad. EMP problems, of course. We'll have to sort all of the comms out—and see what else is still working down in the line units, if any of the electonics survived. Other than commo, our biggest problem right now is with MOBIC survivors stampeding back into our lines. They've lost all sense of organization. They're just terrified. But neither of our lead divisions reports any catastrophic losses. Or *any* losses, for that matter. Although I'm sure some casualty reports will filter in. Comms are really—"

"We'll have radiation casualties. Especially in 1st ID, given the fallout pattern. They'll catch some of it. But the effects won't be immediately evident. Everybody's going to feel fit to fight and ready to go. But they won't be. So listen, Mike. Get with our de-con folks and see how fast they can shift the gear they've been using up north on the Marines down to our forward brigades. And I want an assessment by . . . say, 0600, of which units might've been heavily exposed to fallout. They'll need to stand down. Complete rest. I don't even want them opening their own ration packs. We'll do it for them. And we need to round up those MOBIC survivors. They've got a much bigger radiation problem than we do. The poor buggers are going to be dying for years, slow and ugly. If they overexert themselves now, they'll die in a matter of weeks." Harris looked at his G-3. Sternly. "We're not going to let that happen, if we can help it. They're Americans, too. Get them under positive control. Then I want them to receive the same care our own soldiers do."

"Yes, sir."

"Okay, that's part one. Part two: Mike, I want both the 1st Cav and 1st ID to task-organize down into battle groups with all the combat units that had no radiation exposure. I'll accept maximum risk to our front—if the J's want to counterattack through hot zones and what's left of the MOBIC forces, let 'em. We're going to attack. To the north. We'll adjust Marty Rose's left-hook plan on the march."

"Marines in the lead?"

"You got it. They were the farthest from the nuke impacts, so they should be able to move out without any holdups. As soon as you pass on the other orders, get Monk Morris on the line for me. I want to talk to him myself."

Harris stood up. "Gentlemen, we're going to Damascus. We're going to hit the J's before they can reorganize themselves. And we're going to do it before Washington can go nuclear." He considered the other men, then said, "Everyone from the vice president on down is going to want revenge. Maybe from the president on down. I don't know any more. But I want our lead elements to reach Damascus before it can be targeted."

"Why save Damascus?" Val Danczuk asked. "After this . . ."

"Because it's all we have left of who we are. Once this spins completely out of control, it's going to be the worst bloodbath in human history."

"Their blood, not ours, sir," the G-3 said.

Harris shook his head. "Past a certain point, it's just blood." He shifted his attention to the G-2. "Val, see if our STARK YANKEE assets can figure out what's become of Sim Montfort. Alive? Dead? I need to know."

"Yes, sir." The Two looked as if he were coming back to life. "Sir, I'm sorry I didn't listen on the nukes and—"

"I said, 'Forget it'."

"Sir . . . I've got to ask you one thing, though. How did you know? How did you know they were about to go nuclear?"

Harris decided it was time for complete honesty now. About many things. He rose and made his way back to the map.

"Before my vision began to fail, I read history. All I could. Enough to recognize the attachment my enemies might feel to past events, places, symbols . . . enemies and, for that matter, allies. Sim Montfort, for example, allowed himself to become obsessed with Biblical sites. Gospel sites, above all. For all his reported fanaticism, al-Mahdi has a more conventional sense of history—or so you've been telling me, Val."

"Yes, sir."

"And who did you tell me al-Mahdi tries to emulate?"

"Saladin."

Harris made a pistol out of his fingers and pointed it at the G-2. "Exactly. We knew that. And yet we didn't see this coming." He bent toward the map, straining until he found the small black letters. "Kefar Hittim. Westernize the name for me. Anybody?"

Nobody.

"*Hattin,*" Harris said. "The Horns of Hattin. I don't know exactly how he set it up, but al-Mahdi just repeated Saladin's greatest victory over the Kingdom of Jerusalem, when he lured the greatest army the Crusader states ever fielded to just that battlefield, the Horns of Hattin. Where Saladin surrounded and destroyed the Christian knights, the militant orders, virtually all of them. Utterly destroyed." Harris looked at the G-2. "You're not the one who should've seen this coming Val. *I* should've figured it out."

"What happened after the battle?" his aide asked.

Harris smiled. Sadly. "Jerusalem fell." Then he bucked back up. "But the King of Jerusalem didn't have us backstopping him. It's time to get back in the fight, gentlemen."

"But why didn't he use nukes to stop *us*? If he had so many in his pocket?" the G-3 asked.

Harris summoned his smile back from its grave. "Because we're only the Lesser Satan, Mike. The Military Order of the Brothers in Christ is the Great Satan. Destroying the MOBIC corps was more important to al-Mahdi than winning this war. Both Sim Montfort and al-Mahdi see this as a final battle of faiths. We're just a sideshow, a distraction. To both of them."

"And now?"

"Find out if Sim Montfort's alive or dead."

REAR HEADQUARTERS, I MOBIC CORPS, COMMANDER'S SANCTUM

Simon Montfort woke in slime. He had soiled himself again. Yet, it wasn't a burst of filth that had ruptured his sleep. The mess beneath him was already cold. Nor was it the troubling, already vague dreams that had come to him. Something beyond the walls, beyond the afflicted self, had summoned him back to reality. Something great and terrible. As if the world had fractured. As if a trumpet had called the dead from their graves.

A small light glowed in the corner of his room. Steady. Unlike his bowels. Yet, he felt a difference in himself now, as if the sickness were only fighting a vicious rear-guard action. As he lay unmoving in his slops, he felt his mind sharpening. Beyond the closed door, a distant hubbub rose and fell. It was too much noise for the depths of the night.

What was wrong? Something was wrong. What was it?

Still weak of limb, he reached for the buzzer rigged to the cast-iron headboard. But his fingers no sooner located the little cyst of plastic than he drew them away again. Determined to rise on his own. To cleanse himself. Unwilling to let his body's weakness shame him.

As he rose from the bed, caked with shit and dripping, the door opened. The light clicked on.

His chief of staff stared at Montfort for an instant, then looked away.

"What is it?" Montfort asked. "What's wrong?"

The chief of staff could not bring out the words.

"What is it, man?"

"Sir . . . the Jihadis . . . nukes . . . They've used nuclear weapons on us . . . They used nuclear weapons . . ."

Montfort sank back onto the fouled mattress. But he refused to do more than sit. He had to be strong now. To clutch back the pieces of his soul that seemed to be exploding beyond his grasp. He understood that one clear thing: He had to remain strong.

"How bad?"

The chief of staff seemed to shrink as Montfort watched him. "Bad. We don't know. Communications . . . We can't talk . . ."

"How bad?"

"Sir, they must've had ten or a dozen nukes hidden . . . They hit us . . . they hit us everywhere . . ."

"Where? Where's 'everywhere,' man? Be precise."

"Across the front . . . all across the front . . . and the crossing sites . . . Jerusalem . . ."

Al-Mahdi had betrayed him. He'd been a fool. An ass. A dupe. But instead of worsening his condition, the chief of staff's news jolted Montfort back into command of himself. He already saw the first things that would need to be done.

"I see a betrayal in this," he said, his voice a perfect combination of self-righteous anger and confidence in his own judgment. "Don't you see it yourself, man? General Harris is behind this. He's been conspiring with al-Mahdi, with the Jihadis, the infidels. To stop us. It's obvious."

"Yes, sir." But the chief of staff seemed unsure, weak.

"This could never have happened without Harris's complicity. That much is plain as can be. Why didn't al-Mahdi use his nuclear weapons on Harris and his Philistine Army? Why save them for use against us? General Harris has made a deal with the devil. And we needn't keep it a secret." Montfort straightened his back, overruling the cramps in his abdomen. "Listen to me: I want you to do everything in your power to find out how bad the situation is, the condition of our units. They must keep fighting. We can't stop."

"Sir . . . The only reports we have . . . The attacking units appear to be combat ineffective . . . the level of destruction . . ."

"Initial reports are always exaggerated. We'll reorganize. The Jihadis will pay. This is the work of the Antichrist, a sign that we truly are in the final battle. The Lord will not abandon us."

"Yes, sir."

"Go and do as I say. And send in my doctor. Wake him if he's asleep."

But when the chief of staff had gone, shutting the door behind him, Montfort slumped. Unsure if the nausea he felt arose from his sickness or from the shock of the news.

How could God let this happen? Hadn't he been doing the Lord's work? Why had God blinded him to this treachery? Why had He permitted His armies to be shattered?

Why had he let himself be fooled? Imagining that his own schemes must prevail? Putting his trust in an infidel. Was he being punished for his pride?

Montfort forced himself across the floor to the portable sickroom toilet positioned just beyond the foot of the bed. Unsure whether to kneel and vomit, or sit down on it. The energy he had summoned in front of the chief of staff was all gone now, replaced by an unreasoning terror. Had all of his exertions, his sacrifices, come to no more than this?

He settled himself on the flimsy apparatus, sulfuring the room with his waste. And then, when he was sick and empty and broken in spirit, he *saw*.

Simon Montfort had a revelation. He understood, with wrenching power, that God had chosen *him*, even as the Lord had seen fit to warn him that he must rise above all weakness of the spirit. *God*, not al-Mahdi, had sent this sickness to him. Had the mortal flesh not kept him here, he would've been forward with his Christian soldiers, consumed by the Hellfire of Satan, slain in a nuclear inferno.

But God had kept him here. Because the *Lord* had chosen him, and because he was chosen of the Lord. He had been saved in body as in soul so that he could continue to labor in the bloody vineyards of Midian.

But the Lord had warned him as well. Punishing him with the destruction of his army. For bartering with al-Mahdi, consorting with an agent of Satan. The Lord was telling him that he'd been too meek, a creature of too little faith to put his trust in the Lord. Instead, he had put his faith in men and allowed himself to be soft.

Had Joshua's Israelites spared the inhabitants of Ai after the Lord commanded their destruction? Joshua had obeyed his Lord, but Simon Montfort had let Harris protect the infidels in Nazareth.

"For Joshua drew not his hand back, wherewith he stretched out his spear," Montfort quoted to himself, "until he had utterly destroyed *all* the inhabitants of Ai . . . and Joshua burnt Ai, and made it an heap forever, even a desolation until this day."

The enemies of the Lord God had to be exterminated from the Earth to purify it. Harris had embraced abomination. And this abomination was repugnant to the Lord.

Nazareth would only be the beginning. Now was come the Day of Reckoning, the final battle at the End of Days.

His doctor came in, followed by two orderlies. Montfort looked up from the corruption of his body and said, "I need to speak to Vice President Gui."

TWENTY-TWO

······■······■·····

ASSEMBLY AREA, 2-34 ARMOR, VICINITY AFULA

They arrived all through the night. Some still crewed their vehicles, but most stumbled in on foot. Shocked, panicked. A few maintained a fragile haughtiness, outraged by what had been done to them. But the surprise of their defeat, of their catastrophe, left the MOBIC troops undone. Howling Scripture, a captain stood in the middle of a trail, threatening to shoot the enlisted men passing him by if they refused to fall in and resist imaginary pursuers. The soldiers sensed he was talking to himself, stunned by God's unpredictability, and they kept walking. The captain did not shoot, and his arm grew weary. At last, he stopped waving his pistol at Heaven and slumped into the general retreat. Men who had bragged the day before of their invincibility begged water or food from Maxwell's soldiers. Not all responses were courteous, even when rations were shared. And in the terror that had gripped them, the MOBIC troops had forgotten how to pray, but not how to curse.

Lieutenant Colonel Monty Maxwell had stayed busy through another sleepless night. The first problem had been blue-on-blue shootings. His own men had quick trigger fingers after the infiltrations and close combat of the previous night. Even withdrawn to a tactical assembly area well behind the battle, the bleary-eyed tankers of 2-34 alerted at every unexpected sound. Grudges influenced decisions.

For his part, Maxwell did what he could to support the MOBIC officers attempting to impose order on the situation. Not only didn't he want the fleeing MOBIC troops to spread the contagion of panic, he also remembered his training from bygone years: Troops exposed to significant doses of radiation, as the front-line fighters had been, had to limit their exertions drastically, to let their systems concentrate on fighting the intrusion on their bodies. Those wild men running down roads and trails in search of impossible safety were killing themselves. As little as he liked anybody or anything affiliated with the Military Order of the Brothers in Christ, Maxwell didn't want them dead of radiation sickness. He hated what they stood for, but they still were his own kind.

Craving sleep, Maxwell had clamored over the land line for dosimeters to measure the exposure of his own soldiers. But his voice had been only one among dozens of commanders, and most of the division's slight nuclear-defense resources had been sent north in support of the Marines road-marching through dead zones.

In the early morning hours, an order had come down from brigade to organize a demi-battalion from

2-34 Armor's functional vehicles—those that still had working electronics.

"Be prepared to move, on order, not later than 0700."

Maxwell yearned for a few hours of sleep. And his men were as tired as he was. Or wearier. But as soon as his operations officer tracked him down and relayed the order, Maxwell rallied to the task, enlivened by the prospect of getting back in the fight. He gave up trying to persuade stray MOBIC troops to halt where they were and rest and started ruthlessly sorting through his battalion's companies, culling the systems and soldiers he judged capable of fighting on. No one wanted to be left behind, but Maxwell understood the order on a visceral, warrior's level: There wouldn't be time to communicate from tank to tank with hand signals and handkerchiefs. The task force that rolled out of the assembly area had to be lean, mean, and ready.

Where would they be heading? The FRAGO hadn't included routes or objectives or other control measures: just "Be prepared to move." Maxwell couldn't believe they'd be ordered up through the nuked dirt the MOBIC survivors had fled. So that meant roadmarching north, or maybe south, for a wide flanking attack.

What was happening in the great world beyond the range of his thermal sights? And where was the fuel going to come from? The reduced battalion could get through one good fight with the ammo on board, but Maxwell worried about water and chow resupply, given that his tankers had been handing out their rations, however reluctantly, to the MOBIC survivors.

A pair of his mechanics opened fire on MOBIC troops attempting to steal a vehicle, killing one man and wounding three. Then word came up that the Bravo Company first sergeant had died of an apparent heart attack. The Bravo Company and Charlie Company commanders got into a pissing contest over four replacement radios that had been delivered and dumped by a signals team from division. The spat had grown so acrimonious by the time Maxwell arrived that he threatened to relieve both men—and gave all four of the radios to Alpha Company.

It occurred to him that he should be grateful that the situation wasn't worse. Worn down as they were, his soldiers just needed an enemy to fight. He wouldn't have wanted to be the Jihadi outfit that got in their way.

As the first skirmish line of light attacked the horizon, Maxwell wondered where he and his men would be at sunset.

HEADQUARTERS, III (US) CORPS, MT. CARMEL RIDGES

"We're rolling," Monk Morris said over the land line. "We look like the raggle-taggle gypsies, but we're driving east with everything we've got."

"Good work, Monk. Just don't stop. Bypass resistance whenever possible. We'll clean up behind you. I need your Marines to get deep into the J's before al-Ghazi can pull his units back together and put up another real fight. We need to keep them off balance now."

"Got it, sir. How much time do you think we've got?"

Harris paused, then said, "I honestly don't know. But we're running against two clocks. As you know. As far as the J's go, my hunch is that al-Ghazi—and, for that matter, al-Mahdi—will expect us to respond in kind. With nukes, not a ground offensive. And don't discount the psychological effect of their own nuke use on the Jihadi forces. The prospect of a nuclear battlefield focuses any man's attention. Even the guy who was first to yank the lanyard. They'll all be nervous-in-the-service, expecting retaliatory strikes. I don't think al-Ghazi will rescind his dispersal order until he's got solid confirmation that we're all over them. Nukes are his big worry now. And even after he gives the order to establish defensive positions, they won't just snap to attention. Given the age and condition of some of their gear, I'd bet those nukes did more damage to their comms than to ours."

"Guesstimate, though? On how much time we've got, sir?"

"I'd say you've got all day today. Into the early-morning hours. Before even their best units can transition to a coherent defense. I don't expect to see much more than local efforts for the next twenty-four hours. If your recon elements push hard, you should be able to drive right through the gaps. Beat them piecemeal."

Morris laughed. "Now you're telling me how to suck eggs, sir. When do you expect to have 1st Cav falling in behind me?"

"One brigade's already moving. Should be a

divison-minus on your six by 1500. Everything the road net can support. We'll lay down a division boundary once we get east of the Golan—my planners are working it right now. Which follow-on mission do you want, Monk? Turn south to block and envelop? Or keep pushing straight for Damascus?"

"Might as well keep pushing. I'll have the momentum. If you don't mind 1st Cav doing the cleanup duty. Anybody else behind me, after 1st Cav turns?"

"I'm building a reinforced brigade out of 1st ID to follow on as a corps reserve. If you need them, I'll chop them to you as soon as you say the word."

"God bless you. But I gotta ask you, sir. Between the two of us and God."

"I thought you didn't believe in God, Monk."

"I don't, as a rule. But under the present circumstances, I can see where He might come in handy. And I'd say there's pretty potent evidence that the Big Guy ain't happy with your old pal Montfort. So I'm taking a more positive attitude toward Christianity this morning."

"What's your question?"

Harris listened to the Marine two-star breathing on the other end of the line. Then Morris said, "You really think we'll get to Damascus? Before that other time line kicks in?"

"Got to try, Monk. The MOBIC chain of command all the way back to Washington has to be struggling right now. They didn't see this one coming. And the president's going to need some serious convincing before he green-lights nuking cities. Which is what the vice president's going to push for, I guarantee you. Gui won't settle for a simple tit-for-tat after this.

The MOBIC's his private army. And al-Mahdi just broke it, at least temporarily. I'm praying we'll have enough time—and I do mean 'praying.' Not a good enough answer, but there it is."

"Montfort dead? By any lovely chance?"

Harris paused again. "I've got an unconfirmed report that he's alive. Supposedly he was still in the rear area when they popped the nukes."

"Achilles sulking in his tent? Not polite to say it, but I wish that sonofabitch had been on the lead tank and fried like a potato chip. And I don't care if the MOBIC Gestapo is tapping this line and listening. *He'll* push for immediate and general nuke-release."

"Yup," Harris agreed. "Sim Montfort's going to turn this around and use it as an excuse to kill every living thing from here to Baghdad. For a start."

"And our mission is to prove that we can still win without an all-out nuclear response. Before the first red-white-and-blue mushroom cloud."

"Roger. At least, without nuking cities full of civilians."

"Folks back home are going to be a heap of angry, sir. Especially after the MOBIC spin doctors get to work. Not sure mom and pop would mind, say, twenty or thirty million dead Muslims along with their super-saver seniors' breakfast tomorrow morning."

"Would *you* mind, Monk?"

"Contrary to the Hollywood myths of my youth, Marines don't much care for slaughtering old men, women, and children. But to tell you the truth, Gary—Christ, that sounds funny, but I guess we're in this one together now—to tell you the truth, I'd say the odds are against us getting to Damascus before Sim

Montfort gets his finger on a whole row of nuclear triggers. I am determined, but not entirely confident."

"But those odds don't bother you. Right?"

Morris chuckled. "Old Marines like me have trouble with sophisticated math. And I regard it as my personal duty to the Corps to get to Damascus before the U.S. Army shows up. Not that we Devil Dogs are glory hounds, of course."

"Thank you, Monk. See you in Damascus."

"Semper Fi, sir."

NAZARETH

"Well, how does it feel to be mayor of Nazareth?" the colonel from corps asked.

Lieutenant Colonel Pat Cavanaugh would have rolled his eyes, if his eyes hadn't been too damned tired.

"It's cured me of any latent ambitions I might've had to run for public office," Cavanaugh said. Glancing past the full bird with the "McCoy" name patch to the last pallets of bottled water being unloaded, he got back to business. "Sir, I hate to be a whiner, but that isn't going to be enough for this whole city. Not by a long shot."

"I know that," the colonel said. He carried himself like a former athlete who had gone into sales. "We're doing the best we can. First priority has to be keeping the troops hydrated."

"I've got somewhere between fifty and eighty thousand people who need water."

"And I've got a war to support. And the old man's got every vehicle that's still banging on at least two cylinders joining the biggest road rally in history. I don't have enough trucks, I don't have enough fuel, I don't have enough water, and I should've fixed it all to a state of immaculate perfection half an hour ago. Look, I'm told you and the old man go back a long way." The bird colonel nodded toward the heart of the now-quiet city. "Not that he seems to have done you any favors lately. Anyway, if you know him half as well as I do, you know he expects miracles. And gets them. But I'm just about out of tricks. I can't turn water into wine, and I can't turn thin air into water. Or diesel, for that matter. I'll push all the water I can down to you. The old man trusts you to handle this mess down here, and that obligates me to you, and you'll just have to trust me." The colonel lowered his eyes for a moment. "Colonel Cavanaugh, I'm not crazy about infants dying of thirst on my watch, either." He looked back up, suddenly fierce. "But don't get too soft. That won't help. Cut back too far on the water rations for your troops, and it ain't going to help anybody over the long run. Now, can you give my guys an escort back out of this little plot of Paradise? We took some sniper fire coming in."

"I've got a Ranger platoon combing that section right now. We've weeded out a lot of the stay-behinds, but there's still some unfinished business."

"I heard it got ugly yesterday."

Cavanaugh swept a fat black fly off his forearm. "Snipers seeded in a crowd opened up on some Marines I've got OPCON. The Marines let them have it.

All I can say is that the marksmanship training at Lejeune's pretty good."

"That's when it got out of hand?"

"It was already out of hand. That just made it worse."

"You've got things back under control, looks like."

Cavanaugh shrugged, tired of the work, tired of the stench, just plain tired. He wanted a shower, and he wished he could turn himself inside out to get at that dirt, too.

"The nukes did it. I'm not sure how they knew what was going on, but they figured it out fast enough. Jungle telegraph. I've still got some sullen types squatting down in the town square and giving us the hairy eyeball, but most of the rags are staying behind closed doors."

"Figuring we'll be out for revenge?"

"Won't we be?" Cavanaugh asked.

"Not if old Flintlock can help it. Not revenge against civilians." The colonel met Cavanaugh's eyes dead-on. "God knows, I love the old man. But sometimes I wonder if he's trying to piss up a rope."

"We can't just kill them."

"Or let them be killed? By our little MOBIC brothers? I figure Montfort's prayer-book posse still has the wherewithal to execute that particular mission. And they'll be angry enough." The colonel pulled off his helmet and scratched his brushcut. "Speaking for myself, I just don't know anymore. I'm not sure it's not a losing battle. After the J's popped those nukes."

"I can't let myself think like that, sir."

"No, I suppose not. Mission first. Sorry. We're all tired."

"Yes, sir."

"Tired and sick of the shit sandwich we're in. Between the J's and the MOBIC, and not sure who's worse." He reset his helmet and sniffed the air. "Christ, this place stinks."

"When we cut the water supply, it killed the sewage system. Not that it smelled great before, sir."

The colonel twisted his mouth. "I'll never understand what we wanted in this pit. All right. Looks like my boys are empty and itching to go. I'd appreciate that escort."

"Yes, sir. And any more water you can send . . ."

The colonel held up his hand: Cease. "You don't even have to say it."

"Sir? How's General Harris doing? With everything that's happened?"

The colonel from corps grinned, as if too tired to laugh out loud. "He doesn't know how *not* to do the right goddamned thing. And he doesn't know how to stop fighting." The grin disappeared. "It's a shitty combination these days."

After the colonel and his trucks had gone, Cavanaugh rounded up his command sergeant major. They walked downtown, with a dismounted fire team out front and a Bradley infantry fighting vehicle moving behind them in overwatch. Except for the grind of the tracks and the engine whine, the near world remained so quiet you could hear the rustle of scrap paper in the street when the hot day breathed. Even in the distance, the sounds of war had been reduced to the distant throb of vehicles and intermittent shots.

The big guns were silent, and the sky was clear. But Cavanaugh didn't trust any of it.

He knew the war would go on. He wished he were going with it. He couldn't beat down the forebodings he felt about the city cowering and waiting on every side of him: Nothing good was going to happen here. He knew it in his bones.

Maybe, he told himself, his wife had been right to bail out on him. He was a walking bad-luck charm.

"You can just feel them in there," Command Sergeant Major Bratty said, gesturing with his carbine toward the shut-up houses. "Wondering when we're going to lower the boom."

"Well, it's better than it was yesterday. For what it's worth."

"Not much, if you ask my opinion, sir." As if reading his battalion commander's mind, he added, "I can't see any happy ending to this story."

They walked on in silence, entering the valley where a child bride had been startled by the Angel of the Lord, where Jesus played childhood games—did the bully next door beat him up?—and where generations of souvenir vendors fed their families off the insatiable faithful.

"I figure," Cavanaugh said, "that the next riot won't need a sniper to start it. I'm thinking about handing the Rangers the water-distribution mission."

"Don't do it, sir. We need those bad boys with rifles in their hands. Maybe break 'em out by platoon to provide security for our people? While we work the distro?"

"Sounds like a plan, Sergeant Major. I wasn't thinking. How's the hand, by the way?"

"Still pissing me off. I just bought me a sixty-year-old Gibson Hummingbird in mint condition. You drinking enough water, sir?"

"Plenty," Cavanaugh said. But he reached back for his canteen.

Ahead of them, the rumps of two Bradleys framed a crowd. Most of its members were males who had decided to sit down and scratch their beards. They filled the concrete-and-asphalt amphitheater where the web of roads converged in the center of town. The sit-in had the feel of a protest waiting for something specific to bitch about.

"I'm thinking," Cavanaugh said, "that maybe we should only hand over the water rations to the women."

The sergeant major pondered the idea, then said, "The men would only take it away from them, anyway. And probably beat the shit out of them, on principle."

"You're right. Again."

"Let them figure it out, sir. I wouldn't be surprised if they push the women forward on their own. Playing the sympathy card. They just wouldn't like it if we did it."

"I wonder what became of that poor sonofabitch we found sitting by the crosses."

"The guy we almost shot? The SF type? Or FAO, or whatever he was?"

"Yeah, him. The guy who looked like Mr. Shit."

Bratty sighed. "I don't think you have to worry about him, sir. Bunch of docs drawing pro-pay are going to have fun patching him up. At least *his* ass is out of here. Unlike some other posteriors I know."

MONTEZUMA FIELD, CYPRUS

As Dawg Daniels rolled his F-18 from the apron onto the runway, flight control in Akrotiri came back up on the net.

"Flight Leader, this is Base Alpha . . . You are not cleared for take-off. I say again, you are *not* cleared for takeoff . . . Any combat aircraft leaving your location will be regarded as hostile and will not be allowed to return to base . . . I say again, any Marine combat aircraft taking off will be regarded as hostile . . . You will not be permitted to land upon your return. Acknowledge, Flight Leader."

Dawg Daniels glanced over his shoulder at the line of fighter-bombers moving in a conga line behind him, curling back along the apron, each carrying a maximum load of ordnance. Monk Morris hadn't ordered him to fly, but had laid out the situation and let Daniels make his own decision.

For the first time in his life, Daniels had asked for volunteers—reversing the presentation and giving his aviators the option of staying behind. Only two crews had refused to fly in support of the drive on Damascus. Daniels had the four men locked up. Until the mission was over water. He didn't need tattletales running to the Air Force cell up at HOLCOM.

Word had gotten out nonetheless. Now there was no time to delay. Given another ten minutes, HOLCOM could scramble enough Air Force fighters to hold them on the ground. Maybe even bomb the runway.

And Dawg Daniels intended to fly. He was not going to let Monk Morris, or one single ground-pounder Marine, down. Come what may.

"Flight Leader, acknowledge . . . Upon takeoff, you will be regarded as hostile . . . Do you read my transmission, Flight Leader?"

After making sure he was on the right comms channel, Daniels answered:

"Fuck you."

His plane shot down the runway.

TWENTY-THREE

. . . . ■ . . . . . . ■ . . . . . ■ . . . .

HEADQUARTERS, III (US) CORPS, MT. CARMEL RIDGES

"Stop them," Montfort said.

An unexpected tremor in his hand startled Harris, but he kept the earpiece locked against his head. "Sim, we can do this with conventional means. Al-Ghazi and al-Mahdi have their forces scattered between the Golan and Damascus. I can roll them up. We need to give this a chance."

"Stop them," Montfort said. "That's an order."

"You can't give me orders, Sim."

The distant voice had been waiting for that response, setting him up. "Oh, but I can, Gary. I've been given command of your corps. As of one hour ago. I'm only going through you as a courtesy, to save you embarrassment. You've been relieved. But we both want to avoid a spectacle, a needless humiliation . . ."

"I don't believe you. By whose authority?"

"By order of the president."

"The president wouldn't do that. I would've heard something."

"President Gui?"

"Gui's not president. He's the vice president."

The distant voice tut-tutted him. "Gary, your staff isn't keeping you abreast of things. Didn't they tell you about the tragedy? While you're impeding my efforts to win this war, our nation's in mourning. And not just for those brave souls sacrificed to Muslim bloodthirst."

"What are you talking about?"

"The president's helicopter malfunctioned. On the way to Camp David. He'll be greatly missed."

"You bastards."

"Don't say anything you'll regret, Gary. You need to join the team now."

"You bastards."

"President Gui has already been sworn in. And he's decided to make some urgent changes. You can either obey the orders of your president, or not."

"Don't do this, Sim."

"We have to avenge what they did to us. To teach them a lesson Islam will never forget."

"Give me a day. Just one day."

"And how would that benefit the Lord's work? An eye for an eye . . ."

"We don't have to go nuclear. Not against cities."

"Nuclear release has already been granted. Theater-wide. And delegated. To me."

"Don't do this, Sim. I beg you."

"We have to finish this, Gary. You must see that. Or will you continue defending Lucifer's legions to the bitter end?"

"I'm not defending them."

"Oh, really? What about Nazareth?"

"There are no legions in Nazareth. Lucifer's, or anybody else's. Just scared, pathetic civilians shoved into the line of fire. They don't even have enough water to drink, for God's sake. They're not guilty of anything but being alive. *They* didn't nuke your troops, Sim."

"Didn't they? Gary, you simply refuse to understand. I've been praying for you to see the light, but you still talk to me as if I'm a fool. Of course they're guilty. This is the great battle foretold in Revelation. All the signs are there."

"You can't believe that nonsense."

"All the signs are there." Montfort hesitated, but Harris sensed that his old acquaintance hadn't finished speaking. Then Montfort said, "I've been chosen. To finish this. By the Lord, my God. I don't expect you to understand. Any more than the infidels and devil-worshippers in Nazareth could understand."

"Sim, you sound like a madman."

"To a man of no faith. But be that as it may. I've given you my order. To halt the movement of all forces subordinate to Third Corps headquarters. Immediately. If any of those Marines have crossed the old Syrian border to the north, they're to disengage and withdraw immediately. Or they'll be regarded as traitors. And I will not be responsible for what happens to them. You will."

"You mean you'll use nuclear weapons . . . even if our own troops are killed?"

"Your choice. Not mine."

"Don't do this."

Montfort paused again. Then he said, "You have adequate time to warn the Marines. And anyone else in the proximity of our enemies. Of *God's* enemies. You know the drill, Gary. Warheads have to be armed, flight times aren't instantaneous. You have a few hours."

"When? When do you intend to finish destroying your godforsaken Holy Land?"

"The first strikes should hit at 1600," General of the Order Simon Montfort said calmly. "I'll be at your headquarters before then. To assume command."

▪

Lieutenant General Gary "Flintlock" Harris summoned his key officers to his briefing room. He told them what Montfort had said.

"I don't believe him," Mike Andretti, the G-3, snorted. "It's all bluff. More of Montfort's holy-roller bullshit."

But Val Danczuk, the G-2, had come in with a stoned-by-something look even before Harris laid things out.

"It's true, Mike," Danczuk said. "About the president, anyway. We just got the word. I was going to tell General Harris first, then let him—"

"Fuck, goddamnit," the G-3 said. "I *won't* work for that phony, sanctimonious, cocksucking sonofabitch. I just won't do it."

"Easy, pardner," Harris told him. "When I'm gone, it's going to be up to you and the rest of the old team to do whatever damage control you can. To maintain the Army's honor. And keep it alive. As long as there's an Army and they don't change our oath, the country we grew up in is still there, just taking a little nap."

"Where are you going, sir?" Harris's aide, Major John Willing, asked.

"To Nazareth."

"I'll go with you," the aide said. Then the others began to speak.

Harris cut them off. "I'm going alone. It's better. All of you are going to be needed here. *All* of you."

"Stay with us, sir," the G-3 said. "We'll all stand together. He won't be able to command the corps."

"A mutiny won't help," Harris said. "We'd just play into old Sim's hands. I need you to stay here and obey his orders. The legal ones."

"Then at least don't go to Nazareth, sir. There's nothing you can do down there. And you know it. He's just going to rub your face in it."

"No, Mike. You're wrong. I *don't* know that there's nothing I can do. On the contrary, I'm going to do everything I can. To see that the United States Army isn't stained with the blood of tens of thousands of innocent men, women, and children. If Sim wants his massacre, it'll be over my dead body."

After an embarrassed silence, Val Danczuk said, "I hope that's just a figure of speech, sir."

Harris smiled. "Me, too." Then he turned to his aide. "John, have them get my helicopter ready." Addressing all of them again, he said, "Thank you. For everything. Now leave me alone for a few minutes."

▪

When his subordinates had gone, Harris got down on his knees and prayed. For the mercy of Christ. For strength. For forgiveness of his sins. Then he asked the Lord to protect his wife and daughters. And his country.

After that, he wrote his wife a letter. It was shorter than he would have liked. There was so much to say. But there was little time now. And words were inadequate messengers.

He packed some essentials into a rucksack, leaving his kit bag behind. Just before he stepped through the door to head for his helicopter, he paused and said, "Forgive me."

He wasn't sure for whom the words were meant.

▪

When Sarah Colmer-Harris saw the banner headline on the day of her daughter's funeral, she vomited on her bathrobe:

CHRISTIAN SOLDIERS SLAIN BY NUKES
General Harris Betrays MOBIC to Muslims

OFFICE OF THE EMIR OF AL-QUDS AND DAMASKUS, FORMER PRESIDENTIAL PALACE, DAMASCUS

General Abdul al-Ghazi led his officers down the ornamented hallway, shoving aside the functionaries hastily packing files for evacuation. After disarming the final set of guards, he and his trusted subordinates burst into the ceremonial office of the emir.

"In the name of the caliph and sultan, I place you, Suleiman al-Mahdi, under arrest."

To al-Ghazi's surprise, the emir-general displayed

little concern. He merely looked up from the document on his desk and asked, "What are the charges?"

"Unauthorized use of the sultanate's final reserve of nuclear weapons. And consorting with the enemy."

Al-Ghazi thought he saw a smile alight on the emir-general's lips. Then it flew away again.

"Those sound like contradictory charges, General. Let's begin with the second. What do you mean by 'consorting with the enemy'?"

Beyond the filigreed windows and their treasures of stained glass, a bright sun cooked the world. The huge room was cool and shadowed. It made al-Ghazi feel awkward. And unexpectedly small.

"You've communicated and even met personally with General of the Order Montfort, the chief of the Crusaders, the man responsible for the massacre of the Faithful at Jerusalem."

"But I'd hardly deny that! Really, General al-Ghazi, I should be praised, don't you think? I met with that infidel dog only to trick him. And see how it worked! The Crusaders have been shattered. Montfort himself is dead somewhere on the battlefield to which I lured him. Burned, as if by the fires of Hell." This time, al-Mahdi smiled unmistakably. "If I led the infidels into false negotiations that brought them to their destruction, shouldn't that count as the highest art of generalship?"

Unsure of himself, al-Ghazi raised his voice. "You had no right to use nuclear weapons, no authority. Only the caliph and sultan can give that permission. You've handed the Crusaders the excuse they wanted to destroy our cities. Their arsenal is huge, and ours is empty now. Millions of the Faithful will die."

"General al-Ghazi, is your faith so weak? Do you really believe the Christian god is stronger than Allah? Or worse, that He is the same? Do *you* believe that old heresy, that we're all 'People of the Book,' that the Revelation of the Prophet Mohammed, peace be upon him, counts for nothing? Allah is the *only* god. And He has turned from the Christians, given them up to Shaitan. Look at them! They worship hollow statues and crosses! What kind of worshipper drinks the blood of his Lord?"

"You didn't answer the charge. They'll destroy our cities. This city."

"And what are a few cities, or a hundred cities, if the True Faith triumphs in the end? You know the verse from the Holy Koran: 'This world is but a sport and a pasttime.' The weak must be purged, by fire. And then the faithful will rise up, from Dakar to Djakarta, and the sword of Islam shall rise with them."

"You betrayed the sultan."

Al-Mahdi sat back in his great leather chair. "You weary me. How could I betray myself?"

"What?"

"You haven't heard? Oh, my dear General al-Ghazi! Our beloved caliph and sultan, Hamid III, was called to Paradise and his eternal reward. During the night. An unexpected, but, I am told, a peaceful, merciful death, Allah be praised! Humble creature that I am—the least of Allah's creations—I've been acclaimed his replacement."

"By who?"

"By the army."

"That's nonsense."

"Really? Perhaps you should ask these loyal officers who brought you to me!"

Unsettled—alarmed now—al-Ghazi looked around the room. His deputy had a pistol trained on him. The other officers, *his* officers, did nothing.

"It's always an error," al-Mahdi said, "for soldiers to mix themselves up in politics. And when they do, there must be consequences." He reached for a buzzer on his desk and pressed it. "I want you to hear something."

The room fell silent, opening its ears to the uproar of the terrified city beyond the compound's walls. Panic was contagious.

Then the scream began. Resounding from another room, somewhere along the hallway. It was a scream of unearthly power, pausing only to gasp for air. It was a muezzin's call from Hell.

Al-Ghazi swallowed hard.

"Your cousin," the emir-general said, "Colonel al-Tikriti, has been a poor secret policeman. And in wartime, failure must be punished. I'm having him flayed alive." Al-Mahdi looked al-Ghazi in the eyes. "Of course, worse things can happen to a man."

Al-Ghazi reached for his holster and snapped it open. Before he could extract his pistol, his deputy shot him. Other bullets punched his flesh as he toppled, and he struck the marble with an astounded smile: He hadn't intended to shoot al-Mahdi. It was too late for that. He had hoped to kill himself.

Fallen and bleeding and unable to move, he could only hope that he had been mortally wounded.

ASSAULT COMMAND POST, SHQIF ARNUN (BEAUFORT CASTLE), IN THE FORMER LEBANON

For the first time in his career, Major General Monk Morris felt he had lost irretrievably. He even caught himself gnawing his fingernails, a child's habit broken at the Naval Academy.

He stepped back into the communications shelter.

"Have you reached them?"

The captain on the radio set shook his head. "No, sir. We're trying, but the jamming's back full blast."

"Keep trying. No Marine gets left behind. We have confirmed receipt of the withdrawal order from everybody else?"

"Yes, sir. Everybody. They're moving."

"Keep trying to reach Maguire. Those are good Marines."

"Yes, sir."

The deputy operations officer approached Morris. "Sir, we've got to break this thing down and move ourselves."

Morris flicked two fingers at the man, his personal gesture of approval. It looked like the blessing of a lazy priest.

"And sir?"

"Yes, Jack?"

"Sir, Dawg Daniels went down over Quneitra. A drone got him. His wingman called it in."

Morris closed his eyes. But only for a moment. "His exec's got the throttle?"

"Yes, sir. We're bringing all the returning aircraft into the field outside Tyre. The SeaBees patched up the runway. Enough to get them down."

Morris nodded. "All right, Jack. Boots and saddles."

His subordinate looked at the general in astonishment. Then he smiled. Tentatively.

"Sir, you're talking Army."

Morris smiled back. "I know. It's just a phrase I picked up from someone I admire. Think I'll keep it."

"I guess we did have Horse Marines. Back when."

"A little before my time. I'm going to step outside for a few minutes."

The day was hot and clear, with sudden dust devils playing pranks on the stillness. The ruins of the old Crusader fortress rose above the mobile headquarters, dwarfing it. The fanatics were in charge on both sides now. Again.

"It just never fucking ends," Morris said out loud, to no one.

TWENTY-FOUR

......■......■......■.....

NAZARETH

Their faces held him. His vision wasn't too far gone for that. Waiting in the long and nervous line for the last of the water—one plastic two-liter bottle per family—a woman furred with moles hardly looked as if her life had been an endless joy. And yet she held her child in her arms. Some man had found her winning enough for that. The instant her eyes met his, she looked away, down, shuffling a few inches forward, as if to escape his scrutiny, a woman eternally ashamed in the eyes of the world. Behind her, an old, unshaven man stood open-mouthed, spectacles askew on his wet-tipped nose. His eyes wandered over the world, unable to rest, as if misery might come from any direction. A baggy jacket and stained cloth cap didn't speak of a life of triumphs. Next came a man still of fighting age, his expression hard and ready to take umbrage. Harris sensed that the man would have been glad to see him dead.

Was that reason enough to kill him in cold blood?

An almost-pretty girl with gleaming hair held her little brother by the shoulder. Still young enough to imagine that all troubles were temporary, she appeared keen for life and full of expectations. Wide as a sofa, another woman pawed the sweat off her forehead, unsettling her black scarf as she quarreled with a bald man who would have run away had he not been her husband. The next segment in the human caterpillar read a book as he bumped forward, riveted by some useless idea, a caricature of the eternal intellectual as he swept unkempt gray hair out of his face. Children scooted up and down the line, too young for patience or to take thirst seriously, ignoring the calls of worried elders afraid to step out of line and lose their place. After shouting at a boy who marched up and down in a goose step, a mother eyed Harris as if he might draw a gun and shoot the child.

Was that really what they expected now? Or just what they were used to?

Harris was unequipped to romanticize them. He wasn't able to assign them virtues that no random assortment of humans ever possessed. He didn't need to ponder eternal verities to understand, viscerally, that every innocent heart in the crowd was outnumbered by those given to common selfishness.

They were human. Just that.

"Remind you of anything, Pat?" Harris asked the lieutenant colonel beside him.

"Germany, sir?"

"Yes. The Turks in that dockyard. Oh, the skins are a little browner now. And the weather's hotter. We could use a little German rain. But I see the same faces . . . people who woke up utterly screwed. Wondering why all this is happening to them."

At the head of the line, where the last pallet of water bottles shrank with alarming speed, two soldiers dragged an obstreperous man from the crowd and spread-eagled him against a wall.

"I'll check that out, sir," Pat Cavanaugh said.

Harris smiled. "Sorry for the half-assed philosophizing."

"It wasn't that, sir," the younger man said quickly. "It's just . . . The troops are a little prickly. Everybody's fuse is short. I don't want anything getting out of hand."

As he watched the battalion commander march off, Harris turned back to the succession of faces. There was, in the end, a quality of disbelief about the crowd. For all their fears, their worried stares at the dwindling supply of water and their caution around the foreign men with guns, the human collective believed that, somehow, everything would work out: There would be enough water and, no matter what became of the others, the breathing, feeling, sweating "I" would be spared. It was the oddest thing, how the tribulations of the group reassured the individual.

It had to be biological, Harris decided. Long before his own experience in Germany—that inexplicable country—when Jews and Gypsies and queers and stubborn priests had waited in line for the gas chamber, tidily divided by gender, they must have felt the same narcotic hope, the identical mad conviction that "*I* will be saved."

Harris didn't know what to do anymore. He had

briefly contemplated leaving the city, since he saw that he was only giving Montfort and his ilk more ammunition to use against the Army—the wicked general who cared more about protecting Muslim fanatics than about his own countrymen.

Yes, that was how Sim would present it.

But the faces captivated him. Doubtless, there were fanatics among them. Killers who needed to be shot for the common good. Pat Cavanaugh had been nervous about more stay-behind snipers seeded in the crowd. But the faces parading in front of Harris just looked thirsty and scared.

"This can't happen," he told himself. "We can't do this. Sim can't do this."

And then he realized that, in his own rejection of what the future held, he had joined the line of optimists at Auschwitz.

Yes, Sim Montfort would do it. Wasn't a people person, old Sim wasn't.

Harris knew the arguments, beginning with: They'd do it to us if they had the chance. But the problem always unraveled when you got down to who "they" were. Would that woman whose face bore a constellation of black moles pull the trigger? The adolescent girl with the hopeful eyes? The dreamy joker with his nose in his book?

These weren't the people who pulled any major triggers. Or precious few minor ones. It was the people like Montfort . . . or Harris himself . . . or Gui or al-Mahdi . . . who gave the orders to the flunkies who pressed the fatal button.

Harris had no moral qualms about killing his country's enemies. He still believed that Washington's impossibly legalistic treatment of terrorists back when had played into the hands not only of the terrorists themselves but also of men like Gui and Montfort. In the real world, far from the cloistered study, some men and even women *were* your mortal enemies, and you *had* to kill them first.

But you couldn't just "kill them all and let God sort them out." Because you weren't God. And no God worth believing in would want you to do it.

Sometimes, in one of his funks, Harris pictured God as a slumped, disappointed old man, propping up His gray head with one hand, eyes downcast.

Anthropomorphism. Harris understood the silliness of it. God was unimaginable to any human being. But what if that lay at the heart of the problem? The need men felt to imagine a comprehensible God, to measure Him. But God was unimaginable and immeasurable. So they did what men did: They cut the problem down to size and painted a stern old man on the church's ceiling.

Standing in the shabby heart of Nazareth, Harris wondered if Jesus—when he was the age of that young girl waiting in line—had foreseen what would take place on *this* day in His boyhood home. Had He seen anything beyond the cross but Heaven? Was every man and woman in that fetid line lulled by his or her own vision of paradise? Of a Heaven above the clouds, or a happy marriage, or an answer to all of life's questions hidden in a book?

Harris could have wept. At his helplessness in the face of all before him. But he didn't weep. Instead, he pivoted on his right heel and set off after Pat Cavanaugh. To be with his own kind.

He was going to stay in Nazareth. That was a given. He wondered if it might be useful to talk to the crowd, to get up on a vehicle and say something, anything.

He couldn't very well reassure them.

Tell them to flee? To get out of Dodge? That was the best practical advice he could offer. Even though they had nowhere to go.

He longed for the conveniences of his youth, the easy communications, even the scrutiny of the media. Where were the cameras now? His nation's enemies, when they shot down every satellite they could and corrupted the rest, had only assured that their deaths would go unrecorded. They had robbed his kind of the ability to talk freely across oceans but had failed to understand the resilience and ingenuity the West applied to warfare when it sensed its back was against the wall.

When the people of Nazareth died, their epitaph would be written by their killers.

How would Sim have it done? By death squads? *Einsatzkommandos*, the way the Nazis did it? Another blood-orgy like Jerusalem? Or just order out the remaining American troops and start shelling and bombing? Then send in the cleanup crews to root out the woman with the moles from her hiding place in the cellar?

Harris felt a childish impulse to step up to the nearest figure in line and tell him or her, "*You* are not my enemy." But he knew it would only bewilder the already frightened.

As Harris approached the head of the line, he saw that only the bottom layer of the pallet remained.

And the sweat-drenched soldiers on distribution duty were breaking into that. Behind them, Pat Cavanaugh stood erect in his body armor. As if attempting to inspire a confidence he didn't feel himself.

Yet, as Harris edged up to him, the younger man grinned. "Pardon me for saying so, sir," he told the general, "but this is one assignment I'm not going to thank you for."

The attempt at banter fell flat. Cavanaugh's smile was one of despair.

"We just have to focus on the immediate problem," Harris told him. "Do what's doable. Right now, we need to do everything we can to prevent any further outbreaks of violence, anything that certain senior officers might be able to describe as 'an armed rebellion'."

Cavanaugh nodded. He was about to say something when his battalion command sergeant major marched up.

"Sir?" he said to Cavanaugh. "Division wants you. On the land line."

Cavanaugh glanced at Harris. The general nodded: Go see what they have to say.

The sergeant major didn't leave with his commander. Tired and mentally sluggish, Harris had to eye the man's uniform to remind himself of his name.

"Fun, travel, and adventure. Right, Sergeant Major Bratty?"

"All I can stand, sir." He looked at the general, sizing him up, man to man. Then he added, "Don't this suck shit, though?"

"That's a pretty good summation."

Bratty drew off his helmet, wiped his forehead

and scalp with a rag drawn from his battle-rattle, patted the excess sweat from the helmet's interior padding, then set it back down on his skull and snapped the chin-strap together again. He didn't have to fuss with the headgear to resettle it: He had the drill sergeant's gift of getting it right the first time.

Harris noticed, again, that the NCO had a bandaged hand. But he sensed that asking about it would be the wrong kind of small talk with the man standing next to him.

"I expect you'll be getting an order to withdraw from the city," Harris said instead.

Bratty shrugged. It was the old, standard-issue NCO shrug that attempted to deflect any suspicion of emotion. But it didn't work this time.

"Yesterday, I would've been ready to go, sir. To tell you the truth, I'd just about had it. But just look at these poor buggers. A man hates to just walk away . . ."

"Yes," Harris said. "A man does."

"Well, I'm going to make the rounds, sir. Got some Marines up in those buildings across the square, watching the crowd. Don't want 'em to feel the Army's neglecting them."

"Mind if I accompany you, Sergeant Major?"

"You're the corps commander, sir."

Harris began to tell the man, "No, I'm not. Not anymore." But there was no point. There'd be too much else to say. He'd made the situation clear to Pat Cavanaugh, but the battalion commander had either forgotten to tell his sergeant major or just hadn't had the opportunity. Or, Harris realized, had chosen not to tell him. Or anyone. Yet.

He was sorry that he'd gotten Cavanaugh into this. But somebody had needed to do it. And Cavanaugh had been a logical choice. You didn't become a soldier just for the good missions.

"After you, Sergeant Major. I'll try not to get underfoot."

And they walked up the line, the endless line, of faces. A young woman with an infant, sensing that the water would run out before her turn, glittered with tears.

At the sight of Harris and the sergeant major, a fat man waved his arms, complaining noisily in Arabic. His neighbors in the line had been cowed, though. Instead of adding their voices to back him up, they shied away.

The fat man shouted after Harris's back. The words were incomprehensible, but his meaning was clear: How can you do this to us? *Why?*

Harris stiffened his posture as he walked away. As if on a parade ground for a change of command.

When the general was halfway through the crowd, a young man with a beatific expression stepped from the line and rushed up to embrace him.

■

Sergeant Ricky Garcia slept four hours, deep and hard. He dreamed of his mother. She was alive and healthy and smiling like always in the old days, so full of love the supply never ran out. Garcia was a grown man in the dream, but still a boy, too, and the sun shone on a perfect L.A. day, on a city just the way it was when he was a kid, long before the bombs, when a trip across town to the beach at Santa Monica had been a journey to the other side of the world, and his old man, who hadn't left yet, had to lay out so much cash to park they couldn't afford to eat. But that wasn't in the dream. The dream was just all good, only a little disconnected. The kitchen was at the front of the house, where the room with the TV should've been. He tried to explain, but his mother didn't care. She just hugged him. And hugged him.

When he awoke, kicked in the sole of his boot by Lieutenant Niedrig, who was the acting company commander now and babbling about nukes, Garcia felt as if something had been stolen from him—something that he would never be able to get back. It was as if his mother had been right there, alive, happy. Just fat enough for her kids to tease her. And now she was dead again, and the way he had to remember her was lying in a crummy bed in one of those old motels they turned into what they called hospices for all those sick with radiation. And her so thin and frail he was afraid to touch her and hurt her.

After the lieutenant moved on to bother somebody else, Garcia shuffled off to take a dump. But really to be alone for a few minutes. To get a grip. To remember. To stop remembering.

After that, the day wasn't so bad. They weren't ordered back to the burial detail. Instead, they were trucked down to the center of town—which was crummier than Rampart on Sunday morning—and the lieutenant told Garcia to distribute his platoon around the back of the plaza, to get up on the second or third deck of the buildings and keep an eye on the fiesta. Not that the rags were celebrating. At first, it was all men sitting down there, miserable as gangbangers caught in another gang's hood. Garcia was down to two light squads, and he put Corporal Gallotti across the street above a couple of busted-out shops, while he put his own squad in buildings that faced north so the sun would never be in their eyes.

The day before had been ugly, with the company losing six men, including the captain. A bunch more had been sent to the rear, badly injured. The platoon's mood toward the locals had been ugly enough after that village girl did her thing with the grenades, but the crazy-ass bust-up with the demonstrators and snipers by the mass grave had pushed everybody to the edge. Maybe beyond it. His Marines regarded all the rags as the enemy now, and Garcia had to fight the feeling himself. Especially when he thought of Cropsey jumping on that grenade. He still couldn't fit all the pieces of that together, and to keep himself under control he came down all the harder on any why-don't-we-just-whack-'em-and-leave bullshit.

He prayed that the day would be quiet. They needed time to get themselves back together.

As always, he prayed to the Virgin of Guadalupe, a last connection to his mother. But the Virgin was giving him a bad time. The tattoo on his forearm itched like crazy. By noon, when the water drop came around and the rags all popped out of the woodwork, with Army Rangers forcing them to line up and behave, Garcia had scratched the first bloody stripe above his wrist, across the Virgin's feet. He started to worry that he'd picked up scabies or some shit like that while mixing it up with the rags.

The thought of it creeped him out.

Then Lieutenant Niedrig came by again, doing his

checks but really just killing time. Garcia didn't think much of the lieutenant, who didn't seem crisp enough to be a Marine. He wasn't sure that Niedrig would be able to control what remained of the company if things got bad again. Garcia figured he was on his own.

"There's a GO in town," Lieutenant Niedrig told him. "I heard it's the corps commander. God only knows what he's doing here. You need to get your Marines looking sharp, Sergeant Garcia."

Yeah, with what? With all their rucks missing in the back of some truck that took off when the shooting started up on the hill. Probably gone forever. And every man left in the platoon filthy and bloody and stinking like a Guatemalan's asshole.

"Yes, sir. I'll take care of it."

"We don't want the general to think Marines can't keep themselves looking as sharp as those Army Rangers out there."

"No, sir. Sir, you were saying something about nuke use this morning. Any more details?"

"The Jihadis hit the MOBIC attack pretty hard. So I'm told. I did see a couple of them headed through town the wrong way. No question about the nukes, though. I can't believe you slept through it. They weren't just firecrackers. The buildings were shaking."

"I guess I was pretty tired, sir."

"Well, don't worry. I don't think the Jihadis will nuke Nazareth, their own people."

"I wasn't worried, sir."

The lieutenant went off to bother somebody else. When he was gone, one of the Marines mimicked him, but Garcia told him to knock it off.

"Hey, you think there's any chance of us getting out of this shithole anytime soon, Sergeant Garcia?"

"You hear the lieutenant say anything about that? You heard everything I heard. Now, keep your eyes out that window like I told you. Scan for snipers. Anybody suspicious."

"They all look suspicious."

"You clean that rifle this morning?"

"Yes, Sergeant Garcia."

"Well, clean it again when Pacheco gets back."

Garcia moved on to the adjoining building, passing through a hot, still slice of the day and fending off two kids, lazy as dying flies, begging for candy like they really didn't give a shit.

The next building's construction was better, the walls thicker, and it was nice and cool up on the second deck.

"You don't know how lucky you are," he told the members of the fire team. "It sucks out there. This is the lap of luxury."

"Heard anything about chow, Sergeant Garcia?"

"Probably later. After the Army gets the rags squared away."

"I bet *they're* eating right now. The Army takes care of its own."

"Yeah? Look out that window. Like you're supposed to. And tell me how many of those grunts you see chowing down. They're sucking it up. And you can suck it up. And I'll be sure to let you know when the burrito special of the day's posted. You clean that weapon this morning?"

The building had a good diagonal view across the plaza, better than the one next door. Before moving on to inspect Gallotti's squad, Garcia sidled up to a window that hadn't been claimed and looked out over the crowd. The rags looked pathetic. Dirty and whipped. He could get angry enough to kill them, but he'd found, to his surprise, that he couldn't keep up a steady hatred toward them. They were born losers. And you could waste only so much wattage on losers.

As he watched the crowd, a break in the long, curving line showed him that the pallets of water dropped off that morning were gone. The Army grunts on distro were pulling the last bottles from nowhere.

Garcia wondered if the scene was going to get ugly when the rags figured out that there wasn't no more where that came from.

He thought he spotted the general the lieutenant had warned him about. Across the plaza, up past the head of the line, talking to a soldier with the posture of a drill instructor. As Garcia watched, the soldier who was not a general took off his helmet, wiped down his face and the webbing inside the headgear, then put the helmet back on. Crisp as a saltine cracker. Yeah, the guy had been a hat. Officers never got it that perfect. Garcia wanted, badly, to be a DI. Next tour, if possible.

Right now, though, he pictured little bugs drilling into his arm and roaming around. You're imagining shit, man, he told himself. But he pushed up his left sleeve and started scratching at the tattoo again. Once he started, it was hard to stop. He decided that, after checking up on Gallotti's squad, he'd walk over and talk to the company's last surviving corpsman. See if he had some lotion or something.

Suddenly furious at himself, Garcia stopped scratching. He looked up from the inflamed Virgin and yanked his sleeve back down. Then he picked up his carbine and scanned the scene down in the plaza. To make sure he was good to go to the next location, that everything was straight.

He spotted the general and the had-to-be-an NCO making their way along the line of rags waiting for water. As he watched, a man stepped from the crowd and threw himself at the general.

The explosion that chased the flash seemed huge, its noise trapped between the buildings crowding the plaza. Next came the screams. And burning freaks running out of the smoke. Followed by shots. Not the sound of friendly weapons.

Another bomb exploded on the other side of the road, near the water point. His own kind were shooting back now. In the next room, a machine gun opened up, sweeping the crowd.

"Cease fire!" Garcia yelled. "Cease fire!" He ran into the room, yelling, "What the fuck are you shooting at? Cease fire!"

He had to wrench the weapon, its barrel already hot, from the private wielding it. His buddy watched. With murder in his eyes.

"What do you think you're doing? Who told you to open fire?"

"They started it."

"You ever heard of fire discipline, Keogh? You see any clear targets out there? They're fucking civilians, man."

"Like that bitch who got Larsen and Cropsey?"

Garcia shook his head. Furious at the insolence.

On the verge of throwing a punch. Holding himself back only by using the kind of discipline that had saved his ass on the streets of East L.A.

Firing erupted from another room.

"You," he told the private. He shifted his attention briefly to the man's buddy. "And you. Just stay here. Stay at your posts. And you don't shoot again unless you have a clear, no-bullshit target with a weapon in his hand. Do you understand me?"

The machine gunner looked at him sullenly and said nothing. The other Marine looked away.

Garcia still wanted to throw a punch. Instead, he ran to the next room and repeated the scene. With a screaming, crying world in the background. Pierced with gunfire.

"We don't shoot women and children," Garcia yelled. "You understand me?"

They stopped firing. But it just felt like a pause. They *didn't* understand anymore. Garcia got it. In his guts. It had all gone too far. Too many Marines had gone down ugly.

No excuse, sir. Leaders didn't quit. Ricky Garcia didn't quit.

He poked his head back into the room where the machine gunner and his buddy stood at the windows. Vigilant. And mean. Just waiting for an excuse. Garcia didn't say anything this time. He just wanted to let them know he was paying attention. And he took off to see if Corporal Gallotti was doing okay. Pounding down the steps, beating his anger into the dirty concrete.

The odd thing was that his mother was with him now, looking out for him. He realized what the dream had been about. His mother didn't want him to kill kids and shit. Or people like her. That wasn't what she wanted at all. She had come to let him know it was all right.

Before Garcia reached the bottom of the stairs, he heard the machine gun open fire again.

EPILOGUE

How could I know these things? I didn't know all of them, of course. Some had to be imagined. But I saw much myself. I am John Willing, former aide-de-camp to Lieutenant General Gary "Flintlock" Harris and the man who betrayed him. I was the one who reported all of his actions, plans, and weaknesses to General of the Order Montfort's agents. I believed that I was a hero, doing the Lord's work. I did my duty as an officer secretly enlisted in the Military Order of the Brothers in Christ.

I have long wondered if General Harris suspected me toward the end.

I was rewarded. For a time. I ended my career as a black-cross colonel. Despite my good services, I had suffered too much contact with General Harris and his acolytes to be trusted with a higher rank. When I took off my uniform, I applied for a teaching position, for the young have always been dear to me. I then learned that I was not to be trusted with the education of our Christian youth. I had been contaminated by association. So I took a secondary degree in accounting, a discipline that offered no chance of my being put down as a heretic. I kept good books. As the years went by, I consoled myself that there would be a great accounting one day.

Of course, I was far luckier than the others who had contact with General Harris. Even before III Corps redeployed to the United States, all of its officers who held the rank of colonel or higher were taken into custody. "For their own protection," the newspapers reported. We were assured that the good Christian people of America wanted to lynch them for their treason. One lieutenant colonel, Patrick Cavanaugh, was also arrested. He was charged with the premeditated murder of a Christian Heritage Advance Rescue Team in Nazareth.

The old U.S. Disciplinary Barracks on Ft. Leavenworth were reopened to receive the III Corps officers. Before any of the detainees could be absolved or reeducated, an accidental fire swept the prison. The system of electronic locks short-circuited. None of the quarantined officers could be saved.

Later, their names were erased from the chronicle of the Holy War, along with any mention of III Corps, the U.S. Army, or the Marines.

General Harris's wife, Sarah, proved to be an unreasonable woman, a menace to herself. She refused to stop making public allegations that her husband had been the victim of a plot. She had to be institutionalized. For her own good. It is said that General Montfort, an old acquaintance, visited her in the asylum out of Christian charity. To their enduring regret, the doctors charged with her rehabiliation made no progress, and she died, still in restraints, a few years ago. So rumor has it.

Rumor also holds that her surviving daughter became an alcoholic and an immoral woman. But no one can testify to the truth of it, nor is she known to be alive and among us.

General of the Order Montfort fared better. The hero of the first stage of the Holy War, he was chosen by President Gui to serve as his vice president and Generalissimo of the Order. Thus began a long and fruitful age, we are assured, with President Montfort succeeding President Gui when the latter's final term ended—although our Great Prophet continued to assist President Montfort with guidance until the prophet's soul soared upward. In a state of grace, our Christian Congress acceded to the public's demand that the Constitution be amended to allow President Montfort to serve an unlimited number of terms in office, with future elections to be held in church, on Sunday, by a show of hands. It was only last April, during his fifteenth year as president in Christ, that the Lord called the Dear Prophet home. We are told that he passed over in perfect peace while reading Scripture. And yet, he did not reach the four score years and ten predicted for him.

Of course, the Army was disbanded, as was the Marine Corps, their missions assumed by the Military Order of the Brothers in Christ. The Air Force went next—believing to the end it would be spared—then the Navy received its new dispensation. By the end of the Holy War, we were a unified people in every respect. We praised God for it.

General Harris was right about one thing: It *was* difficult to kill a billion people. But it wasn't impossible. After their cities had been destroyed, all of their images and records obliterated and the names of those cities removed from every map and book, we still had to launch the seven Great Hunts—one for each of the Seven Seals foretold—to finish the job. Even now, we hear tales of Deobandi and Naqshbandi fanatics praising Allah in the nuclear deserts.

There was, of course, the dispute with the Chinese Messiah over the radioactive fallout from our nuclear offerings. But our Chinese brothers and sisters were exhausted by their civil war. And Christians were not yet ready to fight Christians. The Chinese eventually aided us in the last several Great Hunts.

At home, we enjoyed an age of sacred glory, albeit with a spike in cancer rates. But we must not question God's purposes.

Yet, as the years went by, I *did* begin to question. The soul is not steady, nor is it still. And I do not believe I have been alone in my swelling discontent. Indeed, I *know* I am not alone. There was the Rebellion of the Fallen Angels in the California Reserve five years ago, for one thing. A number of us who had learned to speak in whispers grew excited by the hope of regained freedoms. Then we learned that the rebels sought to bring our New Jerusalem into the fold of the Chinese Messiah, whose Christianity is sterner still than ours.

I do not overlook the good. We live in comfort and safety, and he who does not transgress need have no fear. But there are so many possible transgressions.

What brought about my private change of heart? It

did not come suddenly. I am a cautious man. I believe my slow turnabout began with the Cleansing of the Books, when a Helpful Visit condemned my entire library. There was even a question, briefly, of a trial, until they realized I truly had been ignorant of the additions to the latest Christian Index. It had become difficult to acquire information, even when the information included the latest rules we were to obey.

Anyway, they burned my books. *Moll Flanders* and *The Great Gatsby*, *Hamlet* and *Anna Karenina*, even poor *Clarissa* in her innocence—they all went to the fire as startled martyrs. I miss them still.

Of course, I speak for my waning generation. The Blessed Teachers discourage personal reading by the young. The young do not seem to mind.

But there you have the heart of how it all went wrong, I think. I do not mean that we suddenly found our courage when they burned our books—the intellectual's valor is a fairy tale. I mean something quite the opposite: We who cherished books believed that books could defend themselves. To the final cinder, we *believed* that the pen was mightier than the sword, for so we had been told. We were such fools.

Others among us trusted to the quality of our laws and failed to see that those laws had little power against men who valued only the law of God. Still others believed that their wealth would insulate them, but their wealth was confiscated for Christ. Some trusted their beauty, their talent, or family ties. All, all were mistaken. Only purity of faith mattered, and no one could be certain his faith would be judged pure.

And General Harris? What a hopeless fool the

man was! For all his skill as a soldier, for all he had endured in bitter wars, he still believed in human goodness. He was as blind as Christ entering Jerusalem.

But Harris was no traitor. No matter what the permitted books may say.

I was the traitor. And now I have turned traitor again. To set down *this* book as penance.

I am Judas.

AUTHOR'S NOTE

This is a novel, not a strategic forecast. That said, the plot does engage several of my enduring concerns, most notably the iniquity of fanaticism in the name of any faith; the danger of nuclear proliferation among parties not dependably subject to deterrence; and our military's reliance on electronics that may prove all too fragile in a major war. Warfare's superficial manifestations change mightily, but its essence remains flesh and blood.

Readers with military experience know that I've taken liberties in three areas. First, I drastically limited the use of acronyms to avoid rendering the book opaque even to veterans. A typical staff officer can work a half-dozen acronyms into a simple declarative sentence, but effective storytelling can't emulate a cryptogram. Second, I simplified the structure of a corps staff to concentrate on a few key players. I sought to capture the *feel* of a staff, based on personal experience, instead of bogging the plot down in the infernal complexity of line-and-block charts and niche responsibilities. Third, I accelerated the pace of events to keep things "high and tight." Forgive me.

Finally, I owe great thanks to several friends who helped me avoid embarrassing mistakes. Given the controversial themes of this novel, I won't embarrass them by using their names, but they know who they are: a cherished wine-drinking buddy who commanded a Marine regiment at war; another old friend and veteran U.S. Army Armor officer who went out of his way to prevent me from "throwing a track" on the page; and, not least, the magnificent Marine aviators out at Miramar who let me "crash" an F/A-18. The misfires in this novel are my own, but the steel on target owes much to these generous men.

KEY CHARACTERS

ANDRETTI, Michael "Mike," colonel, G-3/Operations officer, III (US) Corps. The G-3 is responsible for converting the commander's decisions into orders and translating the commander's intentions into plans. The alpha dog among staff officers, the "Three" is responsible for keeping his grip on the battle at all times and alerting the commander to problems that require a decision on his part. A good G-3 makes his commander's life easier, while a poor Three makes life hell for the rest of the staff.

BRATTY, Dilworth "Brats," command sergeant major, 1st Battalion, 18th Infantry. A battalion command sergeant major is the unit's senior enlisted soldier, responsible for looking after the troops and advising the commander on practical matters. A good CSM keeps both his troops and his commander out of trouble while terrorizing junior officers as required. A poor CSM drinks a great deal of coffee while complaining that the Army isn't what it once was. Bratty is a model CSM.

CAVANAUGH, Patrick Xavier "Pat," lieutenant colonel, commander, 1st Battalion, 18th Infantry. First served under Lieutenant General Harris in Bremerhaven,

Germany, during the great Muslim evacuation, when Harris was a newly appointed brigadier general and Cavanaugh was a captain. A battalion commander is responsible for everything his soldiers do or fail to do.

COLMER-HARRIS, Sarah, wife of Lieutenant General Harris. Overcame her training and career as a lawyer to become a decent human being.

DANCZUK, Valentin "Val," colonel, G-2/Intelligence officer, III (US) Corps. The "Two" (or "Deuce") is responsible for monitoring, analyzing, and forecasting the enemy situation for the commander. A good G-2 helps the commander act more swiftly and incisively than the enemy can do. A poor G-2 gives history lessons.

DANIELS, Barry Douglas "Dawg," colonel, Marine air group commander.

DORN, Avi, brigadier general, commander, 10th Armored Brigade, Israeli Exile Force.

GARCIA, Ricardo "Ricky," sergeant and squad leader, Alpha Company, 1st Battalion, Fifth Marines. Becomes acting platoon sergeant after his company is ambushed and decimated by a Jihadi suicide unit fighting a rear-guard action.

AL-GHAZI, Abdul, lieutenant general, commander of the Third Jihadi Corps, Blessed Army of the Great Jihad, and the immediate battlefield counterpart of Lieutenant General Harris and his III (US) Corps.

HARRIS, Gary "Flintlock," lieutenant general, commander, III (US) Corps. The most-decorated general officer still on active duty in the reduced-in-size U.S. Army, with the following awards: Distinguished Service Cross (Nigeria); Silver Star (Iraq); Silver Star, second award (Saudi Arabia); Silver Star, third award (Nigeria); Bronze Star with V device (Iraq); Bronze Star with V device, second award (Pakistan).

AL-MAHDI, Suleiman, emir-general of the Emirate of al-Quds and Damaskus, commander of all Blessed Army of the Great Jihad (Jihadi) forces in the theater of war.

MAXWELL, Montgomery Masterson "Monty" VI, lieutenant colonel, commander, 2nd battalion, 34th Armor (combined arms). His ancestors have served as U.S. Army officers since 1854, with three reaching the general-officer ranks.

MCCOY, Sean "Real-Deal," G-4/Logistics officer, III (US) Corps. The "Four" is responsible for ensuring that the commander's vision and the G-3's ambitious orders are supported with adequate supplies of fuel, ammunition, food, water, spare parts, major components, and other required items, delivered at the right place and time under combat conditions. He is the only member of the G-staff expected to work actual miracles on a routine basis, whether in the Holy Land or elsewhere.

MICAH, Frederick Rockwell "Stoney," lieutenant general, senior Air Force officer in the theater of war.

Career fighter pilot. Assigned to Holy Land Command during the conflict, Micah would go on to receive his fourth star and appointment as (the last) Air Force chief of staff under President Gui.

MONTFORT, Simon "Sim," lieutenant general and General of the Order, Military Order of the Brothers in Christ. Commander of all MOBIC forces in the theater of war, including the largest corps ever deployed by the United States. A rising star in the U.S. Army, Montfort achieved national prominence after being born again under the spiritual guidance of the Reverend Doctor Gui (later vice president, then president), leading to Montfort's transfer of allegiance to the just-forming MOBIC.

MORRIS, Morton Thurgood "Monk," major general, commander, 1st Marine Division (reinforced with Marine Expeditionary Force assets).

ROSE, Martin "Marty," lieutenant colonel, G-3 Plans officer, III (US) Corps (following General Harris's reinstitution of the old, more compact staff system for the campaign).

SCHWACH, Kurt Konrad, four-star general, commander, Holy Land Command (HOLCOM) and immediate superior of Lieutenant General Harris. Headquartered on Cyprus, out of range of all known Jihadi weapons.

SCOTT, Walter Robert Burns "Scottie," major general, commander, 1st Infantry Division (The Big Red One).

STRAMARA, James Jason "J.J.," major general, commander, 1st Cavalry Division (The First Team).

WALKER, James Ryan "Jake," captain, company commander, 1-18 Infantry.

WILLING, John Jude, major, aide-de-camp to Lieutenant General Harris. Collects books, primarily classic fiction, a hobby he conceals from his peers.

GLOSSARY

A

ABRAMS: M-1 series main battle tank, named in honor of General Creighton Abrams. Widely introduced into the U.S. Army in the 1980s, it remains the finest tank in the world.

ATGM: Antitank guided missile.

B

BIG RED ONE: 1st Infantry Division, U.S. Army.

BMNT: Begin Morning Nautical Twilight. The predawn point at which sailors pretend they can see things.

BMO: Battalion Maintenance Officer. Expected to fix what the other officers break.

"BOOTS AND SADDLES": Old Cavalry expression for "Mount up!" or just "Let's get moving."

BRADLEY: Large, tracked Infantry combat vehicle, first widely introduced in the U.S. Army in the 1980s. Named in honor of General Omar Bradley.

BUNDESGRENZSCHUETZEN: German federal border police.

C

CANISTER ROUND: Tank main gun or artillery round containing hundreds or thousands of small steel balls. Used against attacking personnel, "soft-skin" vehicles, or to clear a street.

CAP: Combat Air Patrol; fighter aircraft (manned or UAVs) flying missions to protect other aircraft with specialized roles, such as ground attack or reconnaissance. A mission Air Force pilots love when faced with inferior enemies.

CHART: Christian Heritage Advance Rescue Team. Biblical-archaeology reconaissance element deployed by MOBIC forces.

COMPUTER PLAGUES: Later-generation computer viruses that, after penetrating a system, can overcome all internal defenses.

D

DEUCE: Nickname for the primary staff officer for intelligence at all tactical and operational levels; from the formal nomenclature "G-2."

DRONE: 1.) Nickname for an unmanned aerial vehicle, or UAV. In this war, they aren't passive drones, but, once launched, can think for themselves, swarm "instinctively," locate targets, act singly or as an integrated force, and duel with other UAVs or manned aircraft. 2.) Any Air Force general.

DSI-40 SATELLITE: Multipurpose intelligence-gathering satellite.

E

ELECTROMAGNETIC SPECTRUM: The invisible realm of wavelengths through which systems communicate. Disruptions, such as jamming, can interfere with everything from radio reception to satellite transmissions, depending on the frequencies attacked and the sophistication of the attacker's weapons.

EMP: Electromagnetic Pulse. Destructive wave generated by a nuclear detonation or simulation thereof.

Burns out electronic circuits to a catastrophic, irreparable degree.

EMP MINE: A landmine designed to simulate an EMP wave on a local level.

EXPLORER ATGM: A French-designed, Russian-enhanced antitank missile system with an effective range of eight kilometers maximum, but which detects a target as early as eight and a half to nine kilometers away. Can be programmed to launch itself, taking the human being out of the decision-making process. After lock-on, it ignores all additional commands. Built under license or pirated by various countries, including China, Pakistan, and South Africa.

F

FAO: Foreign Area Officer. A U.S. Army officer trained in foreign languages and culture. A good FAO will go alone into enemy territory to support his commander.

FIFTY CAL.: M-2 .50 caliber machine gun, nicknamed "Ma Deuce." Introduced into U.S. Army service early in the 20th century, it remains the world's most effective and most reliable heavy machine gun.

FRAGO: Fragmentary Order. A brief, swiftly issued outline of a forthcoming order. Intended to give subordinate commanders and staffs additional time to prepare for a mission. Sometimes preceded by a Warning Order. Followed by a full OPORD, or Operations Order, once the controlling headquarters staff has completed it.

G

G-2: Primary staff officer for intelligence at the division and corps levels. Also known as "the Two," or "the Deuce."

G-3: Primary staff officer for operations—combat activities—at the division and corps levels. Also known as "the Three," or "that sonofabitch."

G-4: Primary staff officer for logistics. Has to supply the elaborate schemes concocted by the G-3. Also known as "the Four."

GAB: "Get-Ashore Boats." Hastily designed and built landing craft deployed in five variants, from a small Number One GAB that carries a reinforced platoon to a Number Five GAB that can land multiple armored vehicles or large quantities of supplies. Number Four and Number Five GABs can extend their own tactical docking facilities to cover a to-the-beach distance of up to thirty-five meters. A U.S. Marine Corps initiative, but crewed by U.S. Navy personnel.

GHOST NETTING: Breakthrough-technology camouflage netting that, once connected to its portable power supply, automatically reads and blends in with the local environment.

GPS: Global Positioning System. Before this war, it has been effectively jammed, with numerous key satellites physically destroyed. Weapons systems reliant upon GPS for guidance or locational data no longer work.

GUARDIANS: Personal bodyguards and support personnel devoted to the MOBIC commander they serve.

H

HE ROUND: High-explosive round for a tank, artillery piece, or mortar.

HHC: Headquarters Company in a battalion, to which all the unit's noncombat resources are assigned. Affectionately known to combat troops as "Hindquarters Company."

HOLCOM: Holy Land Command. Nicknamed "Hokum" by the troops.

HUMINT: Human Intelligence. Information gathered by or from human sources. Of uneven reliability and dependent upon the quality of the source or observer, but often more helpful than data collected through technical means.

HUNTER ATGM: Antitank guided missile system, usually deployed along with the longer-range Explorer ATGM. Maximum effective range of six kilometers, with target identification and lock-on at six and half kilometers. After launch, ignores all additional commands. Can operate robotically, without human control. Built internationally from pirated designs.

HYPERJAMMERS: Late-generation jammers that can wipe out all communications in a sector and, in some cases, physically destroy electronic circuits.

I

IDF: Israeli Defense Force, the military forces of the former state of Israel.

IEF: Israeli Exile Force, the successor to the IDF after the Iranian-launched nuclear holocaust and subsequent Arab conquest of Israel.

K

KILLER DRONE: Also known as a "kamikaze drone" by the troops. A small UAV programmed to seek out targets with specific profiles and crash into them, detonating either a penetrating or high-explosive warhead.

Can loiter for hours over the battlefield until a target is detected.

L

LOC: Line of communication. Military parlance for a road, rail link, or sea route, or a complex of such routes.

LONG-DISTANCE KINETIC-ENERGY ROUND: "Lima-Delta," a tank round designed to destroy other armored vehicles or similar targets.

LOOPHOLE AT (ANTITANK) TECHNOLOGY: Sophisticated programs that allow late-generation antitank missiles to immediately identify gaps in the electronic defenses of an enemy. In wide use in this war.

M

MA DEUCE: An M-2 .50 caliber heavy machine gun.

MOBIC: The Military Order of the Brothers in Christ. A crusading American military organization originally founded on the structure of the National Guard in the wake of the nuclear destruction by terrorists of Los Angeles and Las Vegas. Its leaders are determined that the MOBIC will become the sole military service of the United States.

MORPHING PARASITE: A program that can enter an electronic network and simulate any aspect of its control mechanisms to achieve an attacker's desired ends. Cutting-edge versions can be broadcast at an enemy but can penetrate only systems with a gap or weakness in their shielding.

MR. NO-SHOULDERS: A snake.

MUSSIE-BABBLE: Arabic.

N

NEXGEN ARMORED VEHICLES: Later offshoots of the U.S. Army's Future Combat Systems program. Heavily reliant upon electronic defenses, they prove a disappointment in the field, far more vulnerable than older combat vehicles, such as the M-1 tank, with heavier armor.

O

O-5: A lieutenant colonel.

O-6: A full "bird" colonel.

OPCON: Operational Control. A unit that is OPCON to a headquarters is under the headquarters' control only for a specific mission, purpose, or time frame; essentially, it's on loan.

P

PHASE LINE: A military control measure; a line drawn on a map, usually associated with readily identifiable terrain features, that helps a commander regulate a combat action. Similar in purpose to the yard lines on a football field.

POL: Petroleum, Oil, and Lubricants. Military-speak for fuel.

POW: Prisoner of war.

PROVIDENTIAL COMMUNITIES: Camps constructed for Muslim-Americans after the nuclear terror attacks on Los Angeles and Las Vegas.

R

RUMINT: "Rumor intelligence." Slang for military gossip about a current or anticipated situation.

S

S-2: The primary staff intelligence officer at the battalion, regimental, or brigade level.

S-3: The primary staff operations officer at the battalion, regimental, or brigade level.

S-4: The primary staff logistics officer at the battalion, regimental, or brigade level.

SAMS: School of Advanced Military Studies; a one-year "postgraduate" course for select Army officers following their completion of Command and Staff College at Ft. Leavenworth.

SCHWERPUNKT: The main effort in an attack.

SEABEES: Navy construction engineers who deploy on land. Lineage dates to WWII.

SF: U.S. Army Special Forces, known to the public as "Green Berets." Operating in small groups, they accomplish large missions.

SIGNAL LEECHES: Revolutionary technology that allows broadcast signals to intercept and "ride" other signals to nearby destinations to attack, penetrate, or degrade a communications and control system.

STRIKEWARN: A brief, rigidly formatted message to alert military units to an impending nuclear attack.

T

TC: Tank Commander. Now used for the on-board commander of any combat vehicle.

U

UAV: Unmanned aerial vehicle, a pilotless aircraft that, in different configurations, can perform any air mission. Known colloquially, though inaccurately, as a "drone."

USG: United States Government.

V

VAMPIRE ATGM: Generic term for an antitank guided missile that, once launched, can identify and strike its own targets. An evolution of older, primitive fire-and-forget systems.

W

WSO: Weapons systems officer. The "back-seater" in a fighter aircraft with a two-man crew.

X

XO: 1.) The executive officer, usually of a battalion; 2.) pretty good cognac.

Z

Z DIAGRAM: An old-fashioned, formal calculation for a bombing run, projecting the most advantageous altitudes for the attack profile, point of release for bombs, and the post-detonation fragmentation pattern (which the pilot needs to avoid).

NUMBERS:

155: 155mm artillery piece, self-propelled or towed. The backbone of the Field Artillery.

Forge

Award-winning authors
Compelling stories

. . . .

Please join us at the website
below for more information
about this author and other great
Forge selections, and to sign up for
our monthly newsletter!

. . . . www.tor-forge.com . . . .